BURNT TREE JUNCTION
THE ACCLAIMED HISTORICAL FICTION SERIES
- VOLUME 1 -

ROADSIDE STAND & BROTHER PHIL'S ANGEL

JOANN KLUSMEYER

innovo
PUBLISHING

Published by Innovo Publishing, LLC
www.innovopublishing.com
1-888-546-2111

Providing Full-Service Publishing Services for Christian Authors, Artists & Ministries:
Hardbacks, Paperbacks, eBooks, Audiobooks, Music, Screenplays & Curricula

BURNT TREE JUNCTION: HISTORICAL FICTION FOR ADULTS

VOLUME I (ANTHOLOGY)

ROADSIDE STAND
—
BROTHER PHIL'S ANGEL

ISBN: 978-1-61314-677-4

Cover Design & Interior Layout: Innovo Publishing, LLC

Printed in the United States of America
U.S. Printing History
First Edition: 2021

—

Has God called you to create a Christian book, ebook, audiobook, music album,
screenplay, film, or curricula? If so, visit the ChristianPublishingPortal.com to learn
how to accomplish your calling with excellence. Learn to do everything yourself, or
hire trusted Christian Experts from our Marketplace to help.

CONTENTS

Burley Collins was a wanderer—had been all his life. Stopping here, staying a while there, doing this and that, learning more with each adventure. He stopped to rest where the old man used to have a stand where he sold odds and ends. The old man was gone and the stand was falling apart, but the view was as good as ever. He set his things down and looked around again, taking everything in. There was really nothing to keep him there long... except, perhaps, whatever was hanging from that tree limb.

Angels, as we all know, are created messengers from the Boss, and they might find themselves performing a variety of tasks while furthering the Boss' agenda. One particular angel was assigned to a small Indian boy in northern Arkansas. His assignment was to prepare the boy to walk in the good works the Boss had created for the boy to do. The angel had a tough time with the boy. He really didn't know how stubborn some humans can be. But he was patient, and the boy grew in stature and favor with both God and man.

PART I

ROADSIDE STAND

HANGING TREE

Burley Collins trudged along Ridge Road, his eyes peeled for the sight of the huge oak tree and the storm-tumbled roadside stand that he remembered so well. It wasn't much of a place to stop and rest for the day, but it was better than nothing.

Also, it was a designated point and a place to look forward to reaching when the feet were weary. There was a tree for shade.

His first sight of the limb that extended toward the road included the body of a man… gently swinging from the taut rope slung over the limb. Burley rubbed his eyes… blinked… and looked again. What he thought he saw just couldn't be.

But the body still swung, twisting slightly this way and that, and Burley knew there was no need to rush to the victim's defense. That time had passed some minutes or hours ago.

Below the hanging body was the scuffed hoof prints of a horse, having been slapped on the rump to hurry him forward.

Though he knew what he'd find, Burley touched the limp hand hanging from the sleeve of the plaid, flannel shirt. Still slightly warm.

He bent over the hoof prints. Sharp edges. Relatively new shoes on the animal. That knowledge might be important. He looked up to the limb and noted that he could reach it from his saddle. Bringing his chestnut mare under the limb, he loosened the tension and lowered the body gently.

Hepsebah, or Heppie, stood blinking her eyes as any good pack donkey would be trained to do. She blinked slowly and wisely. Who knew the ways of humans?

For her, no day held a surprise. Go… stop… get fed… walk. Graze… sleep… live through this day and wake up tomorrow.

So… there was a human, hanging from a limb just for the thing of it. She did not know or care what the other human did now… or any time in the future. She waited; she moved when told.

So she just stood by. Strapped to her back were the packed bags containing the worldly goods of the human who gave the orders. And furnished the food. She waited, eying a clump of grass and deciding whether the dusty blades were worth the effort of stepping forward.

Nearby, the chestnut animal, generally referred to as 'Brownie,' watched with interest as the man examined the victim of the hanging. Strange, actually. But who knew the way of humans…? Still, one must admit they were interesting. Sometimes.

Burley checked the pockets. Knife, matches, a few coins and a key chain with one key. He put them aside. Something would have to be done with the body, and any person with legal authority to make a decision in this circumstance was a fresh horse and several miles away. And Brownie was as weary as Burley himself. Best the body be buried, if only temporarily.

He looked around. The crumbled roadside stand leaned drunkenly against an oak. A mallow vine had seemingly attempted to hide the miserable pile of splintered boards and rotting shingles. Burley remembered the old codger, Hake Simms, who ran the stand long after he should have gone to St. Peter or wherever it was that decent people went.

The man had spent the last days of his life tending the stand, offering for sale anything the Simms family could spare. Made a few pennies… asked for very little. Burley sighed and nodded… it was a life and a fellow could do worse. A lotta fellows had.

The fallen stand was located on a bluff where the road made a wide turn. Huge rocks overhung the valley and a small stream of water flowed from around the rocks and made a sparkling descent into a small lake a short distance into the valley. He could take the body down the rocky bluff, but that would be laborious and would accomplish nothing. Rather, he could step into the grove of trees and find a spot of soft soil. He made a mental picture of this young man so he could notify… someone…?

The victim's shoes were new… hardly even scratched on the soles, so Burley removed them. Why waste a valuable item when it did the wearer no good? They would fit someone. His neckerchief, wadded as it was within the noose of the rope, was also new and of an unusual pattern. Should be good for identifying him. Maybe.

He wearily dug the best he could among the tree roots and carefully laid the body straight. Standing and staring down at him, Burley shook his head sadly… what a waste! Young, strong… and gone forever.

Hesitated. Sighed long and dismally. Scoop after scoop with the small shovel from Heppie's back, and eventually the unfortunate victim was covered over. Not good, but the best he could do.

Walking back to the animals, he slouched wearily. He hated waste, and this was one of the worst. The sun was slipping down toward the valley and was settling past the bluff when his supper of beans began to bubble and the coffee in his percolator settled down to issuing fragrant steam.

He had loosed the animals and hobbled their feet to keep them close and had spread his sleeping bag inside the crumbled remains of the roadside stand, when a sound attracted his attention. There in the road, in the direction from which he had come, someone was walking. Strange. No one walked on the ridge road this late in the day unless there had been trouble.

He watched and waited. A young woman and a small boy approached, the boy stumbling, but the woman did not pick him up. She couldn't have. She was already carrying the heaviness of her next child under her light weight clothing, and her own feet wearily stumbled almost as much as those of the child.

Bad trouble. Had to be. Burley watched, scooping a few bites into his mouth and washing them down with coffee. It had been a long time since breakfast. The woman and child reached him and she called out to him.

"Mister…? Was you here very long? Would you have seen a fellow on a spotted horse come by?"

9

How should he answer this? Trouble it was... for certain. "Well, ma'am, I just..."

"Please try to remember. My man... he was just goin' down the road to see if there'd be any help for me. We camped back down the road a piece, me knowin' my time was close. We'd wait there and if help was close, it'd be good help for me." She looked into his face, her eyes pleading. "He couldn't been gone long, but I was gettin' worried. Wouldn't'a been like Sonny to leave me too long."

Burley finally found his tongue. "Ma'am, could you come over here and rest a minute. There's bad news, I'm afraid, and in your... condition...? Well, I think...."

She approached, hopefully, but when she saw the pair of new shoes setting on the crooked counter of the stand, with the neckerchief laying across them, she burst upon Burley with the fury of a crazed wild cat. "DID YOU KILL MY MAN! WHY... YOU... YOU...!" In her anger, words failed her. She came at him with pounding fists held out in front of her protruding abdomen. The child, a small boy, screamed in fright and hid behind a tree.

Burley stood and caught the small fists in his large hands and tried to calm her. "Ma'am, it was me that found him. See yonder rope? It was done by someone that took his horse, I'm thinkin'."

"You didn't... ? But he's... ? Where is he? Those are his shoes and his handkerchief. Where is he?"

Amid her sobs and angry screams, he was able to tell her what he knew... which was precious little. He led her to the fresh earth. He did not scoop away the heaps of dried leaves as it would have been cruelty to the little boy to have the mental picture of his dead father. Better for him to wonder than to know and have that certain image in his head for the rest of his life.

Leading her back to the fire, her anger melting down into sniffs and sobs, he began to take charge. Night was fast coming on. Something had to be done for her and the boy, now blinking sleepily in front of the fire.

"You said you had a camp? How far away?"

"Just past them trees is a lane. Our wagon's there, but no horse."

Burley scratched the top of his head and tousled the black curls... hoping he could scratch up an idea or two. "Wagon...? Well,

I got… Ma'am, if I hurry now, I might find it and bring your wagon on up here. You ain't in no shape to make the trip and you'll be needin' your strength, so you'll just have to trust me. Lay the little fella on my bed roll, and hide yourself in there with him. I'll try to hurry."

She sniffed and nodded.

In minutes, Brownie was thundering back down the road where she had just come. There was still enough light to see the almost hidden lane and the beginning of a camp site just beyond. There was the wagon. Burley, working mainly by feel in the dim light, hitched Brownie to the shafts and led her back to the road.

What a wagon it was! It had been built onto and now it looked like a small house riding along on the wagon bed. Windows and a door. Shingled roof. Heavy for one horse to pull, but they had obviously planned on short days and slow travel.

The last rays of sun slid away as Brownie pulled the tiny house into the campsite while Heppie, her mouth working on a wad of grass, watched with vague interest. There was no knowing what humans might do and this clearly did not involve her.

Brownie was unhitched and again hobbled for the night.

The wagon had been pulled behind the wreckage of the stand and Burley trudged wearily back to the young woman, now hunched pathetically over her abdomen. She looked up, her face a strain of agony. "Mister… there's more bad news. I'm wishin' Sonny could'a brought help, but I can do it alone."

She stood on shaky feet, holding to a loose board of the old stand. She paused, grimaced and groaned slightly as another pain passed.

Staring into his eyes, she began, "I gotta ask something else of you… and us bein' such a trouble already." She paused as another of the sharp-edged daggers of contraction attacked her body.

Burley just stared, not knowing what to say or do. She continued.

"If you was to help me into the wagon and stay away with my little boy, I'd consider it a blessin'. I know what to do, and you mustn't mind for my yellin'. Charlie, there, sleeps like a rock, so he'll not hear… him bein' so tired."

Burley swallowed hard. "But you…"

"Mister, ain't nothin' gonna happen as ain't happened before. Just help me up into the wagon, and if you hear a sound," she paused and waited for the passage of a stabbing pain, "If you hear anything, it'll likely be the nightwind in the trees. And that's what you can tell Charlie if he wakes up."

Burley held steadily to her arm as she negotiated the steps, her feet amazingly strong and determined. She stepped over the endgate and through the door. "I'm thankin' you again, Mister. It sure weren't our intention to put this onto a stranger, and you've been more'n kind." Shutting the door firmly behind her, she was gone.

Burley stood staring... wondering... and then a swathe of soft glow appeared from the tiny glass window. Candle. Had to be. Then he turned and retraced his steps to the bed roll and the sleeping child. He took one of his packed bags carried by Heppie, leaned it against the tree and sighed once again.

What else could he have done that he had not...? And he could think of nothing.

As the stars popped out into the inky blackness overhead, he tried to doze and maybe he did, but it seemed a long time until morning. It was an endless, silent time except for the call of a bobcat from down toward the lake, and the screech of an owl across Ridge Road. The boy slept soundly and at last it was morning.

THE MORNING AFTER

The twenty two year old mother of two crept softly through the trees, clutching a flannel wrapped bundle close to her chest. Somehow, she had to say goodbye to the person to whom she had given her heart.

Burley Collins's sharp ears pulled him from his dozing state to a place of total alert. Someone... oh, it was just the young woman. Sadness for her squeezed uncomfortably at his chest restricting his breathing. What was there for her to do now... no man... no horse... and nowhere to go? The sound of her murmur and her sobs carried faintly toward him on the still, mountain air. What... actually... was ahead for her? And he didn't yet even know her name.

Though more importantly, what was it that he... Burley Collins... was to do? What was meant to be an overnight rest-pause under the spreading oak took on the troubles of a lifetime… or so it seemed. He must somehow notify some authority of the death and hasty burial and that would mean at least fifteen miles and two days. He could surely not leave her alone, but what was there to do with her? Did she have sufficient food in the little house, and could she manage an active two year old and a newborn until he brought help? Somehow it had become Burley's problem and he momentarily wished to go back to sleep.

Through slitted eyes he glanced at the boy, still asleep on the bedroll. His own soft comfortable bedroll. Burley had spent a restless night leaning against his pack saddle propped against the oak tree. The hanging limb branched innocently beside him.

A slight movement attracted his attention and there by the boy he saw the wolf, resting on his haunches staring at the sleeping child, clearly silhouetted against the streaks of light in the east. Then a slight wag of the bushy tail. Burley's muscles tensed like knotted ropes. His right hand crept, quiet as a breeze, to the ground by the gnarled root of the tree. His Colt 45 was there, cocked and ready of course, and he could get a clear aim and it would be a sure shot.

But the animal made a slight movement in the dry leaves and the boy's eyes flew open. Like the spring in a jack-in-the-box the boy was up and throwing his arms around the animal.

"Jumper! You found us!" And the boy and the dog spent a joyous moment entangled with their affection. "You brought rabbits! You couldn't find Papa, so you brought them to me!"

The rising sun shoved away the morning gloom and Burley saw the two cottontail rabbits lying stretched out on a rock. The dog, with wise eyes and a wagging tail, began to investigate the camp. Burley had not a moment's doubt that the dog knew exactly where Papa was, and was searching for what he should do about it.

Burley could see the leather collar around the dog's neck, and the short length of leather strap. Tooth marks on the end. In the dimness of the evening, he had missed seeing the dog when he got the wagon.

What a trained dog, indeed! Most dogs would have barked or at least whined at the approach of a strange human, but this one had waited silently to see what to do next. He had likely scouted the camp, then caught the rabbits, assuming his puzzle would be clearer in the daylight. It had to be.

Well, the presence of the two rabbits erased the concern as to what was for breakfast. Burley heaved his more-than-forty-year-old self to his feet and checked Heppie's backpack, also leaning against the tree, for the huge iron skillet and his jar of frying grease.

He pulled together some scrappy dead limbs and a handful of leaves and built a fire where scores… maybe hundreds… of fires had preceded it. The iron grate left by someone was resting on three solid rocks.

A spring of water flowing from under a rock nearby furnished the water for coffee and it perked merrily in his percolator… his one luxury. Perked coffee instead of boiled… it made a big difference in taste.

Aroma of coffee in the air. Things looked better with the fragrance of the coffee bean. Next problem. While he skinned the rabbits and while the boy played with the dog, he scraped his brain for an idea about the authorities. They had to be notified, and now he could tell them the young man's name as soon as he spoke to Constable Ike. What to do for the widow?

And there she came through the trees, stepping carefully among the accumulated dead leaves.

Sound of wheels on the gravel. Burley's spirits lightened. Someone was coming, and possibly he could share some of his sudden load of responsibilities. Maybe a neighbor who could put her up for a while.

But no, it was Frenchie McFey, the route man for the Watkins Products. He was the man everyone wanted to see as his van carried everything from pepper to Pepto-Bismol, and from matches to Macanaw coats. He called on as many stops as he could, but had to tear himself away from most of them. He was better than a newspaper for spreading information, and closer than a gossiping neighbor across the fence.

Today Frenchie… actually Bertrand, but he preferred Frenchie… had left his camp long before daylight to make the trip along Ridge Road where there were few customers. If he could make it to the Big Oak, he'd cook his breakfast on the grill by the crumbled roadside stand. The way so many other travelers did… and be on his journey. But it was not to be.

It was now light enough for Burley to see the red and black letters on the bright yellow van pulled by the matched paint ponies. Good-looking rig… its black wheels shining with fresh paint. Black letters announcing simply FRENCHIE. No one along the Ridge Road needed any further identification.

The route man sniffed his appreciation at the aroma of coffee, and coffee was always shared. Rules of the road. And he saw the boy. Now would be the time to share a bag of cookies, and maybe leave a candy stick. Sweets helped to spread good will. In addition to that was the sack of peanuts roasted in their shell that he planned to have as a major part of his own breakfast. Fried rabbit would be better.

Then he saw Burley. Frenchie knew everyone and that included the wanderer who seemed to find business to be on the road a lot.

"Hey, man!'"

"Hey, yourself. You're the fellow I need to see. Are you headed back to the warehouse?"

"Sure am. Somethin' you need?"

"Sure thing. Have to get a message to Ike over at the station." The station being the log cabin within spitting distance from the Watkins Products warehouse if the wind was right. Frenchie nodded his attention. The law was to be notified.

"Had a hangin' here at this tree yesterday. Young fellow, seems to'a been robbed and hung, and they his horse took." He glanced toward the boy. "His kid over there don't know it yet. I had to bury him outta sight till I got help, and then here you come. Good timing. Camp wagon back there has the kid's ma and a new baby that come in the night. I been needin' to go two directions, and not bein' able to leave her here, with not even a horse."

Frenchie was quick thinking. A few more sentences explained that Burley was set on tracking down the murderers. Shouldn't be too hard if his other problems could be taken care of.

Frenchie nodded. "Tell you what. I'll swap you this sack of cookies for a leg off that rabbit, and then I'll head on out. Got fresh horses and it's downhill a lot of the way. Should be there in an hour and I'll send 'im back. He can take care of the lady, maybe. Then I'll be back up by here later today. If she's still here, I'll take over till you get word back."

Burley nodded. He'd have expected nothing less from Frenchie or most any local farmer. Folks on the ridge looked after each other.

So, with a steaming, browned rabbit haunch, Frenchie clicked to his horses and was gone, raising a small trail of dust behind the wheels.

Zennia had crept up as the men were talking. *Good*, thought Burley. So he wouldn't have to repeat it. Opening the sack of sugar cookies, he set them and the skillet of rabbit pieces on a loose board. He smiled to assure the silent woman… actually almost a girl for looking so young and scared. Still dry-eyed. Tears and agony would come, but she had wisely put it off in view of the circumstance.

"Don't you be worryin', ma'am. I'm gonna busy myself with the boards for a while. I aim be here a short piece then I have an errand. Seems I got ideas about what to do with this here piece of land."

She nodded. Young Charlie knew what to do with the food, and the dog stood ready for the remains.

The first thing Burley did was put the two rabbit skins together and wrap them tightly, circling them with a scrap of paper from a farm sale… or something. Rabbit fur had uses, and being bound together would keep them soft until he had time to do the job right. Cut in four pieces each, he had cleaning rags that were highly washable and dried soft. A body never had too many of them.

He sorted the pieces of old lumber. Not enough, but some of what was there was usable. His pliers pulled the nails and he set them aside. Couldn't risk them being hidden in the dirt and being stepped on. All the while his hands busied themselves, his mind was on its own journey.

There'd be more than one killer. They'd have a hide-out cave, and his mind sorted through the few he knew of. It was going to be a frustrating search to find the right one in this rough country.

Hooves sounded on the road gravel. The boy squealed happily, "Ma! There's Dapple!" Then he noted with disappointment, "But Pa ain't with 'im!"

Zennia caught her breath in an agonized hiccough. "No, son. It's not…" And that moment Jumper's ears cocked and he ran at the horse who reared and turned into the brush. Charlie was puzzled, looking from his ma to the strange man. Why would Jumper be running at Dapple? They liked each other.

Burley looked at Zennia, who sadly shook her head. "Son, the horse looks like Dapple but he isn't. Jumper knows that."

Burley's mind snapped to attention. "He ain't your horse? Then we'll get 'im and hold 'im till the law gets here." And he proceeded to do just that, with Jumper's help as soon as the dog recognized what the man was going to do. Smart dog... that!

Constable Isaac (Ike) Cordell arrived and was quick to size up a situation. Bringing a deputy to stay with the young lady, he headed down the path to the north toward the nearest cave that he knew of.

By now, Burley was hot and thirsty, and surely the lady was the same. He was not accustomed to caring for a lady in distress, but that was no excuse. There was a first time for everything. Taking his water jug from his pack, he headed down the path to where he knew a spring of water jutted over a rock on its way to a lake some distance down the valley. Cool and good-tasting, as he remembered the water. This was a well known camping site for local travelers.

Jumper had cocked his ears and watched Burley, then came trotting after. *Why not*, the man thought. He might be thirsty too... but there was more. He had hardly gone under the overhanging lip of the bluff until he heard a voice. Sounded young. Couldn't make out the words with the echoes bouncing back and forth. The dog, however, thought he could.

Water. He'd get it and take it back to the lady, and then he'd follow the dog. Needed his gun, anyway. It did not occur to Burley that the deputy might be the best one to check out the noise.

JUMPER IN ACTION

The terrain of an Arkansas mountain was not strange to Burley as he climbed over dead trees felled across the paths, huge rocks, twisting vines and sprouting bushes knitting the hillsides together. The dog stayed about 20 feet ahead of him, leading him on with tail-wagging assurance. Burley watched and nodded, plodding onward. Dog like that deserved to be followed.

Then he could hear the words. "HELP," the voice (young?) pled. Jumper dived into the underbrush and disappeared in that direction. It was only a minute before he was barking 'treed' as if he had a coon or a possum up a tree. Snarling and yelping, he circled the foot of a bois d'arc tree. He would have climbed it if he could have. Obviously there was a reason for the animal to be vicious.

Burley raced toward the ruckus as fast as he could plow through the undergrowth. Jumper was snarling and showing a fine set of fangs. Front paws pounded against the trunk of the tree as he lunged at the feet of the human in the limbs. What was wrong with that dog? He had been so friendly…?

Wedged into the limbs was a boy? Young man? Totally frightened out of his wits. Sizing him up quickly, he seemed to be about 16… maybe 17. Could be only 15. Good clothes, solid shoes and a recent haircut. One hand held to a limb above him and the other hand held a gun.

"Son, drop the gun."

"You gotta help me. This dog's gonna eat me up!"

"First you drop the gun."

"I can't. I brung the gun to prove who I am and what I gotta tell someone."

Remaining safely out of range, Burley reasoned, "In that case, I'm the best you're going to get to listen ya'. I can stand here longer than you can stand there, and I may be able to calm the dog if you tell me who you are."

The young man listened. Made sense. "Mister, I stole this here gun to show I'm who I say I am but when they see it's gone, it's me that they'll come after."

"Who is 'they'?"

"My brother and three other fellows. They made me come along so I wouldn't tell where they went, and they stole a horse and hung a fellow from a tree back up on the road. They thought that horse was stole from them, but then they saw it wasn't and they didn't care. I'm scared and I gotta run away somewhere. I can't go home."

The kid had a point. "First thing, drop the gun or I leave you there all night. Then we'll see about the dog."

A slight pause, and the gun slid down though the bushy limbs of the bois d'arc tree. The snarling dog turned from the boy to gun that landed in the grass. He nipped at the weapon, flipping it over with his nose. Then he came toward Burley, lowering his head as though trying to say something.

Burley, no stranger to strange dogs, reached a friendly hand forward to the dog who sniffed and tail-wagged, and looked back at boy in the tree, apparently satisfied. "Good boy, Jumper. You did good." He picked up the gun and extended it toward the gray-brown canine, who sniffed again and snarled, a growl deep in his throat.

Huh, well, they'd see. "Son, start down the tree slowly and be prepared to climb back up if he runs at you."

The boy didn't want to, but what choice was there? The dog watched from beside the man who held the offending gun.

With both feet on the ground, his eyes were wide with fright. "Mister, I gotta get outta here and off the ridge. My brother said he'd kill me if I didn't do what he said and I believed him."

"Good enough. You can come along and tell your story. I'll try to find help." What he had really hadn't needed was another person who needed help, but, at least, now they knew who did the murder.

There wasn't much to the story. The four others had been stealing animals and vandalizing property (well known to everyone on the ridge). James had overheard the plans, and had been forced to come along. Then he sneaked the gun away while they were sleeping, and tried to reach the ridge. Would have made it if it hadn't been for the dog.

Back at the camp, Deputy Darrell Jones attempted to interrogate James, who pursed his lips and held tight. He had handed over the gun to prove his purpose, but he had a more important lever than that. He wanted safety... and he wanted it NOW. He above all others knew what his brother's gang was capable of.

"You take me away now and hide me, and someone go whisper in my ma's ear where I am, and then I'll tell you where their supplies are hid."

That would be an important lever, for certain. The 'gang' had been going up and down the ridge spreading theft, arson and anger. They committed mayhem, though up to this point, had stopped at murder. That was past. It was speculated on who the perpetrators were, but not all of them or where was their headquarters.

The boy demanded to be taken under cover to a hiding place and provided for until he could leave the state... or at least the county. The deputy looked at Burley, who returned his own puzzled stare. Remaining under cover, and speed would be required... then what? These were the catch.

A sound of gravel crunching on the road turned their heads. Frenchie! The answer for certain. Clear as if handed down from heaven. Maybe it was.

James was not a large boy, and a bit of shuffling of Frenchie's wares provided a hiding place behind a lower shelf. Deputy Jones with the gun rode along, just for safety first.

Burley ran the words through his mind to be able to update Ike, who would soon be showing up. The constable had not actually been prepared to go cave hunting. That would take a posse... fanned out in the directions of the most notable hideaways.

While he waited, his head spinning with the activities of the last two days, he set aside the usable boards and rebuilt, within his mind, the old roadside stand, only better. It would eventually be what he would do with his life. He had not known for the last few decades what it would be, but now he had a twinge of excitement and an eagerness to see this through. Clear as a bell, it was, what he would now do.

He had known about this strip of land that had the 'hanging tree,' the stand, and the spring with its waterfall, as well as the roomy cave behind the waterfall. He also knew that the landowners on both sides had opted to carve that strip of land from their tracts as being untillable due to its rough terrain, therefore not deserving of the 25 cents per year taxes. Burley didn't know, however, if someone else had seen the possibilities and purchased it. He also needed nails which meant a trip one way or the other, and Berryville was closer than Eureka Springs.

But then there was the lady, the new mother, who must not be left alone. How was he going to manage that? Actually, it seemed that it should be Ike's problem as well. So he'd just work with this mess of scraps and lumber and watch out for the little Charlie.

The kid was scuffling with the wolf-shaped dog, rolling and tumbling, with the dog nipping at the air beside the boy's chubby arms and legs, making him giggle and crow with laughter. It was obvious this was a much-played game. No one could have guessed the snarl and growl and the exposed long fangs of the animal, or more surprising, how he had seemed to discern that the gun, not the boy in the tree, was the problem. Could he have witnessed the hanging and known not to attack at that moment and be shot? And that a dead dog would be of no value to his family?

Surely not... but... It gave an interesting puzzle to think on while he made future plans. He'd offer honey for sale at first, there being a wealth of it just past the waterfall. There were also apple trees with small green fruit. And nuts. He hadn't had time to investigate, but then, the land had not been his, either. Soon it would be.

Ike trudged into the camp, weary, scratched and bedraggled. No luck. He had decided, though, on the disposition of the victim's unfortunate wife. He'd just take her back to town and turn her over to those better to deal with the problem.

After he supervised the removal of the body, where the lady refused to be in attendance, not wanting to remember her husband that way, he stood on the steps and knocked gently.

"Ma'am, I've made a decision for your safety. I know your horse was taken, but this one'll take its place in pulling your cabin back to Berryville. We still hope to retrieve yours, and money from the sale of it will be passed to you. I tell you this, because a deputy will come early tomorrow to bring you and your... uh, children... in town to where you will get whatever help you need."

Expecting a smile of thanks, he was amazed to hear, "Thank you, sir, for the use of the horse. I have decided to stay here on this spot as long as Mr. Collins is here, and if he leaves, he will help me. I feel safe with Jumper here and my food will last a fair length of time. But I do thank you so much for making plans for me, not knowing I done made up my mind what's best for Sonny's family. I do ask you, though, to write down where you put him and the grave number. Someday the boy may wish to know, but I know that Sonny would not want me to waste time crying over him when he can't help me no more."

Ike, who thought he'd experienced every action possible from females, was struck silent for a long time, then nodded, attentively. "Yes, ma'am. Just remember we'll be around. I'll send my deputy along in a few days to let you change your mind. After you had time to think."

Zennia's hand on the door moved ever so slowly to close the door. Her smile deepened and she bobbed her head in response. "I thank you for that, Sir."

Ike stood, balanced on the step, facing the wooden boards of the door. Well, if Burley had agreed with her, then that was one problem behind him. But he still had to send someone to stay the first night as it would take Burley at least part of two days to visit the land office and pick up a few spike nails to attach his roadside stand firmly to the tree.

By now, Burley reasoned, Ike would have deputized Carl Hammer to help on this unusual case. Burley would be around till tomorrow and the lady might feel different by then. The spotted horse that was not Dapple stood tethered in a grassy spot, contentedly chewing as he watched the deputy ride away.

FRENCHIE LEFAY

The van driver knew, the instant he heard of the boy's problem, what the answer about the boy would be, at least for the immediate future. The Watkins Products warehouse near Berryville always need manual labor help. The pay was low because food was included, and the 'help' could eat whatever they wanted of the variety of available items. In addition to that, the night watchman needed an alternate to fill in if he had to be away.

And Frenchie had, tucked under his lowest shelf and hidden by cans of Lucky Leaf Lard, an answer to both instances. Not only that the young man on this job was almost never exposed to the public, and that was one reason they had difficulty keeping young men who wanted, more than anything, to be seen.

As he rolled along, the van driver waxed philosophical. Some folks give no thought to the direction of their life path, and take each day as it comes. Some are tossed into a particular duty out of obligation and necessity, and others found their place accidentally.

Frenchie was none of these. At age four he became aware of the visit of the man with the van and horse and all the good smelling things who visited the house. The man was welcomed with tea and cookies while his mother shopped inside the van. Then his mother handed him money (and the child certainly knew the value of that!) and drove away.

In addition, the man was dressed in Sunday clothes, and not dirty or sweaty. His horse was sleek and well kept, his harness was of polished leather and held together with silver brads. The boy had watched the man drive away, whistling a tune, and he turned to his mother, "Ma…?"

"What, Bertrand…?"

"When I'm a man, I'm gonna to bring you things just like that man."

Mrs. McFey smiled and nodded. "That's very good, Son. Of course, you have a lot of time to change your mind. There are many things a man can do."

The young Frenchie had nodded agreement. "And I know what I will do." And so he did.

At fifteen he had begun working and saving every cent for a horse. He already knew, by then, that the Watkins Products Company always had used vans for rent, and he would rent one until he could afford what he truly wanted.

By age seventeen, he was given a short route through the town of Berryville. Not the route that he wanted, but he had to serve his apprenticeship under the eye of the company. Not a problem. Only to be expected that they 'try him out.'

But someday he would travel the Ridge Road, dipping down into lanes and dirt trails to the out-lying, and very grateful ladies of the house who ran out of soda or cinnamon… maybe pepper or vinegar… and he'd be there. He'd relax in the shade of a tree while they shopped, and he would fill his thermos with their fresh spring water. Yes, when Frenchie decided on a lifepath he did not vary from it.

It had been when he was just over two that Annie Josephine had come into his life.

Annie's family, what there was of it, occupied a tract of subsistence land on the bluff side of Echo Mountain. Her two grandparents had produced a daughter who was drawn to the wild side, and left home as a young teen. The next her parents heard of her was when she was knocking on the door, pale and bleeding, limping and bleary eyed with dried blood from a gash across her head.

Also, she was heavily pregnant.

Two days later she passed this life leaving behind a preemie daughter whom the grandparents named Annie Josephine. Annie from a great-grandmother, and Josephine from her dead mother.

The old couple could manage a baby and a toddler, but a six year old who was ready for school was more than they could deal with. It was customary, if one had a problem, to let it be known and someone might have an answer.

This time the answer came from the McFeys. Operating a farm was a full time job for a couple, and the McFeys had a toddler who was like quicksilver to keep up with. They'd take Annie by the week and send her to the one-room school nearby, if she would be there in the evenings to keep up with young Bertrand while other things were attended to.

That worked until November when the weather was so bad that Grandpa could not come after her. It seemed best to leave her there so she wouldn't risk missing school, that being of great importance to all the adults involved, but especially to the girl.

So Frenchie knew Annie Jo very well. She was out of the school, which went to grade four, on the year that he started but Annie Jo stayed on with the family. Two years later, when Frenchie was eight and Annie Jo was twelve, his mother passed on while trying to deliver a child. Mother and baby were buried on a sunny slope, and Annie took over the housekeeping.

The McFeys had a very good in-house library… very unusual for the time and place. Sixty books, to be exact, and Mr. McFey knew a lot more than was needed to run a farm. He could have opted to be a teacher, but it was a single pupil that benefited from his education. Annie Jo absorbed his every word.

It was when Annie was eighteen, Mr. McFey caught an infection from a rusted barbed wire and had to lose a leg or his life. He chose life, but it was hard choice.

Live stock was sold down to the point that Annie could almost care for the animals alone, with sporadic help from young Frenchie who was still determined to be a 'Watkins Man.'

Annie continued to absorb Mr. McFey's knowledge, and when the library books had been covered, he began on the King James Bible. That he actually had a whole Bible was, in itself, a mark of his intelligence. In the year 1909 a whole edition of the King James Version of the Holy Bible was mostly out of reach by its cost, and also was beyond the reading ability of many of the first settlers among those marooned from education by mountain ranges.

Circuit riding preachers filled the gap as best they could, but Mr. McFey, by having lost a leg, was restricted in activity. He partly compensated by being expanded in mind. Annie was an avid student and absorbed knowledge like a sponge.

When the elderly grandparents passed on, their hilltop land was sold for $12.50, actually a good price. That money gave Annie Jo a confidence and stability she had needed, and a new zest for life.

She still kept the McFey farm going, as best she could along with caring for a semi-invalid. Frenchie stopped in regularly with supplies and to encourage Annie Jo, who had made his life's choice possible.

ZENNIA GARDNER

The staunch young lady whose covered wagon still occupied the bluff behind the old roadside stand had also traveled a rocky road.

Just over 20 years back, a young vagabond couple traveling Ridge Road, actually only a trail at that time, had stopped overnight in an abandoned and leaning shack just off the road. Not an unusual occurrence at the time.

The neighbors, ever watchful for forest fires that crept through the leaf litter debris and flared up in homesteads, smelled the fire, and their men folks caught their horses, straddled them and headed for wherever the trouble was.

They were too late to save the shack or the couple, but the fire stopped at the screened-in porch containing the basket containing the baby girl, maybe six months old, and her screams of indignation proclaimed her will to live. It was later decided that the man had undoubtedly lit a pipe (evidence remained) and indulged in some kind of deadening liquid before passing out. It was a likely scenario, and had happened before.

News and any stray information had a strange way of covering great spaces and informing residents on remote farms almost as if carried on the wind, or by one of the many variety of birds.

There would, of course, to be someone to step in and care for the baby. Taking her to the next town did not occur to anyone. The residents of Ridge Road cared for their own. Among the most acceptable of the offers was the young Gardner couple with a two-story house and 40 acres of tillable land. They also had two daughters… Rose Ann, age 3 and Violette, age 1 ½. They seemed to be the best choice, and the current law representative took the screaming and hungry baby to her new home.

Mrs. Gardner was ably equipped to nourish the little girl for a few months until she could do with solid food. Wonderful cereal in abundance and mashed vegetables from the garden, and that allowed the generous foster mother to build her strength for the next child. Not knowing what her name, if any, was meant to be, the new parents named her Zennia, partly because of the bright red hair that was sprouting on her well-shaped head, and that curled so tight they could hardly determine which end was attached to her head.

So after that came two more little girls making a set consisting of Rose Ann, Violette, Zennia, Daisy and Marigold. Young Zennia grew up within an attractive set of girls, but it was obvious from the start she was an attractive and hardy weed in the garden of delicate blossoms.

The four Gardner girls born of the parents were delicate and slight of build, skin as fair as the store-bought flour that made the breakfast biscuits. Their fine, blow-away hair was the color of dandelion blossoms, and as straight as the icicles that formed outside the windows. Zennia's tight, red curls remained, and her nose acquired spots like the breakfast cereal the girls adored. She had a solid frame and developed muscles that her pale sisters could never have produced.

As Papa Gardner's family increased, his farm work increased as well, and his best help was Zennia, from about age 6 upward.

She was especially adept at handling the horses, feeding, brushing, harnessing and driving.

It was when she was age ten that Charles Caldwell came into her life.

Charles (Sonny) was fourteen, and he had made a decision for his life. Born in the middle of a family of migrants, he was never in one place long enough to develop a life of his own. So when he was barely fourteen, he packed his extra shirt and overalls in a sack, tossed in a few left over biscuits and walked out of the migrant camp, caring not whether the beans were picked. Or what his parents would say. Or not say.

No effort seemed to have been made to find him, and indeed, possibly no one even missed him. This knowledge led him to believe he owed his family nothing, and if he stayed, he would have a lifetime of what he had already had too much of. Wasn't going to happen to him. Never.

So, he went west toward the Mississippi River and talked his way across. Northern Arkansas stretched out before him, and it was early spring. It was a good time for a sturdy, clean-cut young man who appeared to be older than his 14 years. Most farms were willing to trade a good meal for a couple hours of work, such as chopping kindling. Often, he was sent on his way with enough food (which all farms had in plenty) for the next meal.

Occasionally he stayed several days, being provided with a pillow and quilt, and a soft hayloft. He passed through Berryville and liked the looks of the terrain around him. Hardly a flat place in sight. Maybe he'd think on staying for a while. He heard of the lumber mill down Sawmill Road and surely there was work there, and maybe a place to winter over. There was. And the way information floated on the air, the whole community soon knew of him.

So it was natural that when Mr. Gardner was caught between pressing duties, and he needed more help than could be provided by his middle daughter, he hiked over to the mill, only two miles away through the brush. Yes, the young vagbond could be spared for a day.

That was how Sonny Caldwell came to load 35 perfect melons onto the wagon and have it ready to go to Berryville for sale. For that, he would be paid 25 cents. It was a start.

Not only that, he was provided with a place in the barn and told that he might also load up the sorghum stalks onto the wagon while Zennia drove the team. Then he could ride with her to the sorghum mill and unload them. That would be another 25 cents!

After several of these day jobs Mr. Gardner realized something. This lad needed to stay around… permanently. His own fragile, blond, light-skinned daughters could not stand the sun without becoming raw and bleeding. Mr. Gardner realized that paying Sonny by the day gave him the liberty to take his money and leave… on a whim. But if he paid him with a heifer calf, the boy would be enticed to stay around until it grew big enough to be valuable. Mr. Gardner was no dummy.

Neither was Sonny Caldwell a dummy. He accepted the offer.

Pa Gardner even enclosed a part of the barn to be winter tight, provided a bed and stove and a permanent place at the dinner table. Sonny's first calf from the heifer was a little bull and was taken to market. He pocketed $1.75 from a butcher over in Eureka Springs. Next came a heifer, and his herd grew. It was better than money in the bank… assuming there had been one close enough to be of use.

This strong revelation of Mr. Gardner came the day he took the load of melons to Berryville. He had come home delighted that the heavy sorghum cane had been worked while he was gone. On this occasion, Zennia was 14 and Sonny was 18. He had expected that half or maybe a bit more of the canes would be piled by the mill, but the entire field had been harvested. The girl on the reins moving the animals slowly beside the young harvester saved time that would have been used in carrying the stalks to the wagon. It saved only minutes, but it was also effort transferred to the animals instead of the man.

That was the day he decided that he had a working team and left a number of his duties to the pair of them, allowing them to figure the best way to get it done. Then he was free to do other things without concern.

When Sonny was 20 and Zennia was 16, they married and stayed on the farm, though staunchly maintaining that it was only temporary. In a year, maybe less, he would take his wife move on. The Gardner farm was becoming crowded from the suitors attracted by the beautiful blond sisters.

Sonny bought a sturdy wagon and spent his spare time building a house in it. Windows. Shingled roof. Rug on the floor. It was amazing what could be done with a wagon bed 4 feet wide and 10 feet long. Little Charles Junior was born and another on the way when he hitched his team to the tongue of the wagon and pulled up out of the valley onto Ridge Road.

The weight of the wagon made the journey slow, but no matter. It provided the honeymoon they had never had, and their nights were filled with whispers and dreams. They camped when they wished and moved on when they were ready, and had camped across the road and near the broken down roadside stand when Zennia's labor became insistent and Sonny had gone for help.

Zennia was a no-nonsense kind of girl. Weeping over his grave would be a waste of time. Sonny knew how she felt, and it was the business of no one else. She must immediately make decisions for three survivors, and they must be good ones.

Somehow, the Good Lord had allowed this tragedy to happen near a good, solid man who was not going to leave her stranded. He had already, with the help of Jumper, located her husband's murderers, and had told her she needn't hurry making a move.

She had a roof and a bed and a sock of money under her mattress. She'd rest and get her strength back with the man close by and Jumper on watch, protecting little Charlie as he played.

Some nights ago in the house on the bluff, Zennia had a dream. She was carrying a candle and walking through a dark wood. Looking out ahead into the black nothingness, she trembled with apprehension, but noticed that every step she took, the light in her hand showed where to place her foot.

She awoke and spent the rest of the night in thought, secure that if she did not get in a hurry, the light would show her where she should step next. The folding rocker that rode attached to the outside of the house was opened out under the deep shade of an oak. Humming softly, she held small Lily to her breast and let time pass. It was early spring and she would know what to do when it was time to do it.

The candle would give her light.

THE ROADSIDE STAND

Burley Collins, in the methodical method of his nature, picked up the boards one at a time and examined them. Some, he tossed aside for kindling for the cooking fires. He had cleaned the old metal grate and balanced it on three rocks for a semi-permanent stove. Worked well. Time later to make it solid.

As his hands and eyes studied the weathered boards, his mind calculated the use of each board... the number of additional boards needed... and what items would eventually be for sale. Of course he could only be open for business a short time of each day, 2 or 3 hours hopefully. Other things had to be done and time would be a premium if he was to be ready by winter to stand the weather.

Sometime before cold weather he needed to build a cabin down over the bluff in sight of the waterfall. Until then, he'd camp inside the cave behind the falls.

Items for sale in the stand. There'd be honey, of course. There were several bee trees on the strip of land that was now his.

While in town for the spike nails, he had visited the land office. No, no one had yet taken on ownership of the land. The taxes would amount to $2.25 per year, and it consisted of 18 acres, one fourth of a mile wide and extending from the site of the stand all the way to about fifty feet into the fishing lake that pooled up in the valley.

His land took in the bluff, the waterfall and the hidden cave. At his age of forty, he had never owned a home or even wanted to. Now he did. He marveled at the sudden change in his own life and ambitions in the past months... even before the hanging. Something about the crumbled stand drew him like a magnet, and even if it had still stood, he would have rebuilt it. He had this pleasant urge to put his own fingerprints on something that he could call his own.

In addition to the honey, there could be apple cider. Someone, decades ago, must have camped for lunch under the bluff and tossed away the apple cores. A dozen-plus bearing trees. Small green balls the apples were now, but growing fast, and he had every plan to gather a few and brown them in a skillet, adding honey right at the last. Fried green apples for the next meal! He could taste them already.

Would the lady... Zennia, was it?... like something like that? He loved to share. She seemed to have food in her little house, at least for a while, but fried green apples would be such a treat. Wouldn't they?

He sensed she did not want to be disturbed during her time of mourning. A real rock of a lady. No whining and expectation of help from others. She had staunchly refused to be taken to town or back to her parents, saying she'd stay on this land as long as he'd let her… if it was all right. More than all right, of course.

And he'd sell pecans. Also walnuts. The high water table grew the nut trees practically into the sky. And then there was that staple that had kept the old stand alive. Jerky. The dried strips of seasoned beef and pork. Most homesteaders could make their own, but did not have it all the time. Travelers liked it because it was filling and light in weight. He, Burley, would like to sell it because he knew how to make it, it never spoiled, was easy to store and almost no one didn't like it. Those who didn't found themselves glad to have a strip or two if they got hungry enough.

So, there were four items he could manage the first year, easily before winter. In the spring there would be travelers… certain to be. The mountains were settling quickly. Paths, roads and lanes branched off Ridge Road in every direction. Customers would come.

While he thought and worked with his hands, he was watchful on the road for the deputy who would come and tell him where the gang was hiding. So clever of the kid to assure his protection by withholding information, but it did delay the hunt.

Many things do not go by schedule, and the sudden storm was proof of that. Lightning came when it came.

It came tonight… for this was the night of the fire. Clouds rolled in from the south and by evening jagged arrows of lightning sewed the clouds together, occasionally dropping to the ground. It was down by the lake that it cracked into a massive sycamore tree, splitting it and throwing sparks in every direction. There was just enough dry leaf litter to smolder, creeping along under the trees and climbing toward the Ridge Road to keep the blaze going.

A ground fire always wanted to climb and the flame was soon hot enough to dry out the vegetation before it, speeding it on its upward climb. A strip of fire about a hundred feet wide clawed its way through the rocks, grasses and leaf litter until it reached the hilltop.

Then, following a dry vine, it reached the 'hanging tree' and climbed the Virginia creeper up the trunk. The creeper had reached the upper limbs and threatened to choke back the oak, but now its leaves were sucked of moisture and it burst into flame. A giant Roman candle of flame burst forth with a roar like the engine of the Santa Fe train.

The roar of the fireball woke Burley from his exhausted sleep. He crawled quickly from his bedroll and hurried back to the covered wagon, but it was not in any danger. It seemed that just a ribbon of fire had crawled up the mountain, appearing, for all the world, that it was coming just for the hanging tree and was leaving only red ashes on the way.

The hanging tree burned for two solid hours with Burley watching, and as flames worked down the trunk, they seemed to become discouraged, and put themselves out, leaving a jagged and blackened mass of points about six feet high. Burnt stump. The woodland was filled with specimens of just that very thing. 'Lightnin' stumps,' they were called, and good for bird nests and snakes.

The cold light of dawn revealed the blackened stump with only a spark or two of red and a few tendrils of thin smoke. While Burley stood and stared, he was joined by Zennia. She broke the silence with, "Looks like somethin' was tryin' to tell us somethin'." Burley nodded... but what was it?

It did, for a fact, appear that way. Now the huge limb that had held the rope was gone. No visible sign of the wicked deed. Most of the remaining vestiges of the crime were in the woman's heart, and in the man's head. He firmed his lips and squared his shoulders. Someone would pay. It might take a while, but someone would pay. Full price.

Deputy Jones appeared on the back of a fast stallion. "The kid told us the gang was hid out in Hidden Cave close to your bluff. Never heard'a that one, but I have a map he drawed. He said who they were, too. Just as we thought. His brother, Robert, and the three from over past Berryville were Slim, Spike and Shorty. No real names. Ike wants you to follow on with me to bring 'em in."

Burley soberly studied the deputy. Did Ike think that he and this deputy could bring in four armed murders? Well, they'd see. He strapped on his gun and reluctantly turned away from his boards. First things first. His livelihood could wait.

Following the pencil drawn map was surprisingly easy, and without it they could never have found the cave. A huge elm tree had grown at the mouth of the roomy cave, and sprouts had sprung up around it. There were a few paths showing signs of occupation.

Splitting up, the pair worked their way down the mountain and crept silently until they were both at the mouth of the cave looking in. Echos. Dim silence. Totally empty, but it showed signs of a stay for a fair amount of time. Empty rifle shells and a few pork and bean cans tossed aside. Dead coals. Cold.

The two men stared at each other, sad and dispirited. Deputy Jones broke the painful silence. "Now we ain't never gonna find 'em."

Burley sighed and said nothing. The deputy was wrong. They would be found. His anger built up in his chest, tightening the muscles of his shoulders, grinding into his fists with clenched fingers and narrowing the gaze of his sharp, gray eyes. They would be found. Certain to be.

Back on the bluff, the deputy leaped onto his stallion and left in little puffs of dust rising from the limestone chips of the road bed. There was a time that the road had been dirt and hardly travelable half the year. Then a wagon and blade came and scraped the bed, laying down a layer of flintstone gravel. Said it was paid for by their taxes. Good show.

Burley watched until the deputy was out of sight, then turned to face his lumber pile. Nodding with satisfaction, he agreed with a prior assessment. The new stand should be facing the east with a minor slant to the north. That would line it up with a slight bend in the road… very visible. Hard to miss.

Then, there were those green apples. He'd go and bring them up before he got busy. Maybe bring up a jug of water for the lady. That chore done, he could return to the tree.

Within the hour, a 10 foot 4X4 of solid oak was affixed to the oak tree and the roughness planed away. The small hand-plane loaned by the lumber mill was a clever little gadget. Just rub it the right way and splinters and roughness disappeared. He'd have to pick up one for himself the next time he went to Eureka Springs.

He had dug a hole for the other 4X4 with a borrowed shovel and he bolstered the pier with rocks. Good and solid but not as solid as it would be with the next two piers and the cross bracing.

He stood back and looked at it, his heart pounding in anticipation. It was going to be perfect, and it would make part-time easy employment for him and a source of cash. Also, he would never have to move as long as he could rake up the $2.25 every year for the taxes.

Also at Eureka Springs, he would need to pick up jugs for the cider and pint jars for the honey. He'd take Heppie along to help lug home the plunder. Of course it was a bit early to need the containers, but somehow their presence would solidify his dreams into a reality. A gift to his anticipation, so to speak.

And speaking of gifts, Jumper brought in a large, fat coon. Zennia seemed to know what to do with it and shared with him. Not his favorite taste, but it was food that he did not have to stop and fix for himself. One can get tired of canned pork and beans.

Frenchie happened by and stopped to watch. "Really gonna sell food and drink, huh? You set regular hours and you'll get folks that'll count on that. It'll be like an outdoor diner."

About that time Charlie and Jumper showed up. "Uncle Burley? Whatcha makin'?"

As Burley searched for a reply to a three year old, Frenchie came to the rescue. "He's makin' somethin' to make little boys ask questions. It worked, didn't it?" Charlie favored him with a little-boy giggle.

Frenchie continued, "I've got a job for you. I need to take somethin' to your ma, and I need help." Arming the little boy with two cans of tomatoes, and putting a stick of candy in his own shirt pocket, he hoisted a full box canned staples into his well-muscled arms. Rather heavy. Eight cans of beans, six cans of peaches, three cans of sardines and topped off with a sack of onions and potatoes.

FRENCHIE AND THE GIFT

He tapped on the door and told the puzzled face that answered. "Just brung along a bit'a stuff sent to you from someone down the road. They hoped you could use it."

Zennia looked from the box to Frenchie and back to the box. She was not born yesterday, and it would have taken a fool not to know who the 'someone' was, and she was no fool. She knew who, and Frenchie knew she knew. She knew that Frenchie knew she knew, but it made a cover for Frenchie, and she knew he was saying that so she would have no burden of needing to repay a favor.

"I'd be pleased to accept. Will you thank the person when you see him?"

With his famous grin that set ladies from eight to eighty at ease, he assured her he would. Not mentioning that he'd be sure to do it the very next time he looked in the mirror to shave.

With a farewell salute, he fished the candy stick from his pocket and presented it to the boy with a bow and a flourish, leaving him in a fit of giggles.

A second salute to Burley and he boarded his van. The wheels crunched their way across the gravel as he departed. What he had just done was not an unusual act for him… he would have done it for anyone he thought might have a need.

What was different here was her face as she accepted the gift. Small nod of appreciation, bobbing the row of red curls that had escaped her ruffled dust-cap. Hint of dimples beside the smile of her face, her skin the color of rosebuds in the spring… pale creme with a tinge of pink.

But most of all was her eyes. Pale blue gray, clear as a spring morning while exhibiting a resolve like a steel trap. Strong… but held in abeyance until needed. Her enemy might be life in general but she would be ready. Like a mama bobcat, she would take on whatever life tossed in her way, and Charlie and Lily would grow up as their papa had intended.

A small shiver of admiration passed from Frenchie's neck down his arms. What a girl… or so she seemed. For a young man who had 'courted' a horse and van, and 'married' a job he loved, this was a new sensation. At age 26 he was decidedly behind the curve in certain parts of his life.

He should have, long ago, picked a girl, courted her and pleased her enough for her to marry him. He and this invisible girl should be on their third child by now. What a late bloomer he was! How could he have neglected so important a part of the rest of his life?

And now, his lame father had taken to his bed, and was preparing to leave this life. He had told his son that when he left, he must be generous to Annie Jo and treat her like the loved sister that she was.

Absolutely, Pa. He didn't have to be told that. It had been Annie Jo who had freed him to follow his own dream.

Meanwhile Annie Jo went about her duties without a murmur, pleased when Frenchie could stop by, but occupied when he didn't. She read and re-read favorite books to the old man. Pa had put aside the money from the animals he was forced to sell and had handed it to Annie. Good old Pa.

In addition, she was to get the Bible that the English King James had commissioned, and to select her choice of twelve additional books.

So what was the problem with him, a fellow so otherwise normal? The homesteads were full of able, beautiful girls he might have convinced to take a chance on him. So, why had he reached this age... like a spiraling buzzard, hungrily circling the carcass and dreading to light and take his chances with the other animals?

So, maybe that was a bad analogy. It was more like he was hovering outside the house where his own birthday party was going on inside. Or maybe... Oh, well.

He reached the bank of the King's River and saw the midmorning sun glistening on the water... the exact same color of Zennia's eyes. Hardened steel. Hers had been a face that could have been carved from marble.

A remembered array of young women and girls passed in a parade before him, all as beautiful as a field of flowers, but how long can a flower last? They bend before the wind and wither below the winter ice. Then what is left in the field but the cactus, green and bristly, and still standing after trial by ice. Now what made him think of a stupid thing like that?

The set of her shoulders, the smile... she had just come through about the worst trial that could fall on a young woman of the mountains. There were offers to take her to town where there were those who would help her, circle her and make decisions for her… or she could certainly return to the Gardners who had raised her. Either choice would give her a chance to recover her balance. One would think.

But no. She seemed to have seen the strength and determination of Burley who only agreed to let her park her covered wagon on his property. Other than that, he was leading his own life, while hoping to find a way to trap the murderers.

For her? No, it was something he would have done for anyone. So now, nothing that would have entailed money, time or effort was turned her way, thereby leaving the girl her pride while she grieved and made decisions.

Frenchie rumbled across the river and on up Ridge Road.

Now why did he think of a cactus when he thought of Zennia? Maybe because animals didn't ordinarily mess with a cactus… unless they were a small rodent looking for protection, or a honeybee seeking cactus honey for the hive, or a starving deer or cow when all other food was under ice. When the need arose, there was the cactus, juicy, green and sustaining, thorny and protective of its identity.

All right, Frenchie. Just admit that you are smitten with admiration for the beautiful girl. With two children. So… what does it mean to you…?

THE GANG

As fleeting as a whiff of smoke from a lightning strike they were, the gang of four young men. They had to be somewhere in the area, but there were just too many places to be, and too many ways to get from one to the other without detection.

Young James, the whistle blower, indeed told where the gang had hid out, but of course, they were not there now. A few spent cartridges from, maybe, an old Enfield, and shells from a 9mm something or other. So the gang had two guns, likely in addition to the one returned by James. Probably more.

Hidden in Frenchie's van, the whistle blower had made a safe trip to the local Watkins Products warehouse and was industriously working for his keep. Other actions were planned for his safety. While the local warehouse would love to keep him, it would be just a matter of time until it was known, and the gang could cause a lot of damage, to the boy and likely to the store as well.

First off, a note had been delivered by Ben Farmer, the delivery person for the fledgling rural mail delivery. Every week a trip was made down Ridge Road, and anyone with a mailbox by the road could receive mail. Ben saw the note pinned to the box belonging to the Wilsons that instructed him to deliver the note to Burley.

That was not the duty of the postal carrier, but he could do it. He went right by the old roadside stand, anyway, and was looking forward to it being back in business.

The note simply said, "Get that gun that was took from us and go to Hidden Cave or something bad will happen to you. We know where you live."

Burley, who didn't have the gun, pocketed the note and handed it to Frenchie to deliver to Ike. Deputy Jones appeared forthwith and took Burley with him to hidden cave. Burley had not been particularly pleased with the timing… he had other things to do, but he went.

Both men, armed, went into the cave which was, of course, empty. So now Burley had returned to work, while the deputy had stayed overnight. Two days later, another note came. It had been pinned with a clothes peg to the Collins's box.

"You didn't do it. You are lucky that we didn't shoot that deputy. Don't do that again."

Burley sent the second note on to Ike, and took more care of his livestock… the two horses and the donkey. He nailed together the boards of his new place of business, scraping his weary brain for hiding places where the gang could be. That was the night two suckling pigs disappeared from a farmer to the east. The gang members were getting meat-hungry but they knew what to do about that.

Constable Ike had six deputies that he could quickly put a badge on, and he had all six scraping the rugged terrain. Among them, they discovered about a dozen new caves to add to their known list of hiding places, and there would certainly have been at least twice that many that they missed. Face it… how much ground could be covered by a single individual climbing up and down hill, crawling over fallen trees and untangling from vines?

And if he found the gang, he could do nothing. He would be only one of four, so he would have to report it and where would the others be by then? But something had to be done... the community was getting restless.

One of the farmers just across from Burley's stand thought he saw someone climbing over one of his rail fences, and centered him in the sights of his own old Enfield. He thought he connected, but on inspection found only scuffed grass and a short trail through the dry leaves. Escaped unhurt, they did.

After that, he saw a wolf sniff the rails and trot after them. Good enough. Maybe the wolf could take care of the job.

For a while there was no report of vandalism or theft, so the community relaxed. Maybe they had left the county and were someone else's problem. Only Jumper knew what happened. One of the persons had lost a small but painful chunk of flesh in the region of his hip pocket. The wolf-colored canine tried to follow and get another bite, but he well recognized the shape of a rifle, and knew the damage it could do. Best go home and fight another day.

He sniffed out a fresh rabbit hole and a few flying clods of dirt revealed four babies, about three days old. He ate one of them, and packed the other three within his sizeable fangs and trotted home. Just another hunting trip.

The gang fled, half carrying the wounded Slim, and holed up by the river until he was healed enough to travel. They weren't through with this community. Getting the gun back, in itself, was not particularly important. Guns could be found. But THIS gun had been 'earned,' was part of the spoils due them. And, by crackies, they were going to get it back.

Was that too much to ask?

Yes, it was. Burley soberly attached board to board and scratched his mop of sweaty black curls. Where were they? There was that brave lady living back on the bluff. Never complaining. No whining or begging for sympathy. She even insisted on bottling the bucket of honey and honeycomb for him. Eight shiny pints of it ready to display. Another board was nailed in place and more head scratching occurred.

He'd really like to get a pig and start him fattening on acorns, but first he needed a fence. Hogs were hard to fence in. Better wait, and buy one already to butcher when he got the stand finished.

Frenchie had stopped by. James was going to be moved from the warehouse to his pa's farm for a few days, and then on to Eureka. Annie'd take care of him there, just in case, and then, hidden in the van, Frenchie would send him on to the Watkins Warehouse in Fayetteville. They could put him on the train when it was possible to tuck him into a family.

Fayetteville was eager to get him, and he was likely set up for life with a good job if he wanted it. His mama wept, but was glad for him.

Burley had put the last board in place… an oak slab fifteen inches by four feet. Perfect counter, and he had drilled through it to spike it to the supporting 2X10 slabs that would be the display shelves. He was now wielding the tiny hand-planer he had borrowed, and every stroke made the counter smoother and the grain glisten more beautifully. Maybe he could do the whole stand that way, and oil the boards rather than painting them. If he had time.

Miss Zennia approached shyly and said she had fed and put the baby to sleep. If Lily should wake, she could be let to cry a bit, and she and Charlie would go under the bluff to bring up some pecans. Maybe he'd help her bring the nuts to the house when she had the bag full…?

Certainly he would. And he'd listen for the baby.

Frenchie came by and pulled the van up to the stand. Without a word, he reached into the van and brought out a board about the size of Burley's counter. It was an oak slab with some of the bark still attached, and printed in large letters was the notice, UNCLE BURLEY'S BISTRO. The letters had been burned out with a torch making the words unmistakable and un-eraseable.

Without further ado, he hatcheted off a section of bark from a nearby tree and attached the sign to the side. He positioned it so when someone came around the jog in the road from the west, they couldn't possibly miss it.

Burley stood back, removed his hat, scratched his head and returned it. What was Frenchie up to? "Uncle," he asked, but

Frenchie shrugged and answered, "That's what the little fellow called you. I thought it was a good idea. It makes you sound friendly."

Burley thought it over. Not a bad idea, really. But, "What in the tarnation is a 'BISTRO'?"

Frenchie grinned widely. "Aw! I thought you'd never ask. It is a word used in France that means something like a diner. A place that specializes in certain foods that are popular and that the diner prepares well."

Burley snapped off a twig and chewed the sap end. "Hate to tell you this, friend, but there ain't to be no eatin' here. Just buyin' and walkin' away."

Frenchie nodded. "I know that, but you will be selling food that could be eaten here. For that, of course, you'll have to make yourself a little picnic table that seats four. Better make two tables because you'll need 'em."

Burley's weathered forehead frowned. "You're talkin' outta your head, man. Ain't gonna be servin' food and havin' it ate here. I got things to do. I'll just be open for a couple'a hours a day, figurin' out what hour's'll be best."

Frenchie nodded. "Course it won't be you doin' the actual servin'. You'll be busy with the preparin' of the jerky, figurin' how many cans of sardines you want to buy from me, and squeezin' the juice outta them apples. You'll have a purty lady back'a that counter. You don't think your ugly mug'd attract customers, to you?"

Burley chewed and thought. Frenchie was good with words, and totally out of Burley's own category for verbal combat. This was going to need some thought.

Frenchie helped himself to the cold, stale coffee in the kettle over the metal-grate stove. "Nother thing, you'll need tall cups to serve the garden tea… maybe peppermint and honey… made with that cold water from the falls. Just think how that'd taste right now, and it's not even a steamy August afternoon and a dusty road trip. Could offer a cold drink free, but how about 3 cents for a glass of tea that you got the makins' of not costin' you a penny?"

Burley still had no words. But did he ever have thoughts!

A sound came from the covered wagon and both men alerted. Burley advised, "Ma's gone over the hill for nuts. Said it was fine for the baby to cry a bit, and she'd be back."

Frenchie paid no attention. Long strides took him to the cabin and through the door. Red faced little mite was soaked. Pinning a diaper should be no mystery, if one just noticed how the wet one came off. Minutes later he held the little girl against the shoulder of his white shirt where she promptly deposited the part of her last meal that was giving her distress. She turned her head and looked Frenchie square in the eyes.

Frenchie was a dead duck from that moment on. Of course he had been picked clean before he came, but the crying baby alone was precious gift. Saved him a lot of the fright of making the first move toward that 'cactus' of a mother. Moving the tiny mite to the other shoulder… the clean one… he patted her dry, padded rear and she nestled her head against his starched collar.

The route man had been brought up right, and he knew where every 'good and precious gift' came from so he cast his eyes thankfully upward. Just as Pa had taught him to do. (James 1:17)

Burley stared from the man juggling the dozing baby to the finished stand, then to the sign, 'UNCLE BURLEY'S BISTRO'. The more he looked at the three objects before him, the more he realized something was going to happen, and it would take no effort on his part. Like the clouds brought rain, and the bees made honey, most things happened without him.

He was, however, going to use the little smoothing plane and smooth every board in the stand, and then go get a gallon of oil. Maybe two gallons so it would be protected for many years. That little stand was going to take on meaning. Important meaning. It would be the first grub stake that would tether him to this spot for the rest of his life.

He also realized he would need more lumber from Turner's Sawmill for the little tables he seemed destined to make. He knew exactly what Frenchie meant. Full sized picnic tables with bench attached… meant to seat four instead of a dozen. Hmmmm, well….

Zennia came up the bluff and Frenchie met her, still patting the baby. Burley watched the transfer, and nodded as Frenchie took the boy and went back down the trail. It appeared that he, Burley, would not need to carry up the gathered nuts.

Frenchie returned and climbed into the van. With a wave, he was gone and Burley returned to the job of smoothing the boards. Who would have thought to watch the movement behind the bushes across the road? However, someone should have.

Neither did they note the eyes watching activity below the bluff. It was Spike who noted all persons accounted for, and slipped into the corral with a note which he pinned to the harness of Burley's horse.

"We want that gun. Watch for instructions."

Later, Burley read the note. "Those evil little beasts. They could have killed my horse." And he sent the note on to Ike.

The next day, Frenchie went past and waved. Under his lower shelf was James, headed for the next leg of his journey. Annie Jo was expecting him. She fed him well and took him to the smokehouse where a hidden bed was set up behind the fireplace.

Burley watched the van go by and thought again about his conversation with Frenchie. He needed a small cart for the other things he would need, and he could easily make it. The thing was, time was becoming valuable and scarce, and he needed to open the business. Best he find a cart to buy, and use his time on the tables.

THE BIRTH OF BURNT TREE JUNCTION

It was an easy birth, all things considered, and it was brought on by Frenchie who noted that the spot of Burley's stand was acquiring the name of "Hanging Tree." That couldn't be allowed to continue. Habits once ingrained were hard to break.

He picked up another slab of oak (bark attached) and fired up his torch. He printed the words BURNT TREE JUNCTION with his pencil, and then attached it with the red hot tip of his welding tool.

Smoothing it over and applying a coat of varnish, as he had done to the bistro sign, he loaded it aboard the van for his next trip.

Miss Zennia had watched, with interest, the completion of the stand. Her jars of honey were proudly displayed. Burley had not gone after the tall glasses for the tea, or decided just what else to buy when she began to softly make comments and ask simple questions. Bit by bit she put together what was going on.

With a nod and a smile on her lovely face, she offered, "Mr. Burley? Times you can't be here, I'd be more'n happen to sit and watch it for you."

"Oh, but you'd...."

"Beg pardon, but I'd put Lily's basket here, and I got a cradle board for her times she's awake. Charlie liked the board when I hung it in the tree while I worked. It sort'a turned this way and that so he could see everything, and when the breeze blew, he was rocked to sleep. I made good grades in school and I can count money. I'd really like to do this… if you'd let me?"

Burley pushed back his hat and ran nervous fingers through his hair. Such a right purty girl, and she was freely offering a gift the same as he offered a gift to her. No fault in that.

And the other thing was, with a pretty face like hers, and being so well known as she was because of the tragedy, it would at least be good advertisement for the future. She could mention that other items would be available. Sometime.

Say, she might have an answer to his next question. "Miss Zennia, you knowin' anything about garden tea?"

Her face lit up like a Chinese holiday lantern. "Oh, Mr. Burley! I know all there is to know about garden tea. When I was at home, I took care'a the tea garden… my special job. Spearmint was the best, but there's a dozen kinds that could be growed right on that bluff in this black dirt. Wish it was spring so I could do it for you. All of us girls loved spearmint tea. You think Mr. Frenchie might have some so I could sell it for you?"

All right. He'd go get that cart tomorrow and get glasses. Jugs. Big bowl. Long spoons to stir tea. What else? Towels, of course. But first a cart. Tomorrow for sure. Maybe a small wagon instead of a cart. What was money for, anyway? Just somethin' heavy to haul around.

And here came Frenchie now. He had everything else, why not tea? But he crawled into the van and emerged with another slab cut from an oak tree. With his hatchet, he skinned the charred bark from the road-facing side of the craggy stump of the burned oak tree. With his hammer and screwdriver, he solidly attached the sign to the stump.

Laying down his tools and stepping into the road, he brushed his hands together with the satisfaction of a job well done. Perfect. It was no longer 'Hanging Tree.' And it was fast becoming a true junction with several roads going north and south off Ridge Road. Having a place that had a name made it easier for everyone giving directions or having a meeting place.

Burley joined him. "Took care'a that problem, huh? I was puttin' it in line to be chopped down, quick as I got time. That might'a not stopped what they was beginnin' to call it, but I didn't have no other idea."

While Frenchie admired the finished stand, Burley remembered, "Frenchie, amongst all that plunder you carry, you got any tea?"

"I got tea but you don't want it."

"I don't…?"

"No. It's got no flavor and I don't know why folks buy it. I can get you fresh tea in a dozen flavors. Most folks think'a peppermint when they think'a garden tea, but there's a lot'a kinds."

"Can you get spearmint?"

"Sure thing. I'll bring it tomorrow. You got a way to dry it?"

"Maybe…."

"It'll need to dry about a week for more flavor."

Burley nodded. That was about how long it'd take him to be ready.

That was when Burley's mule began to set it up with her 'Yonk-ee! Yonk-ee! YEEEeee.' He commented, "I can't think what's wrong with her, all that good grass she has and water runnin' right through the pen." Then he thought no more about it.

Later, he knew what was wrong. She was tied to a tree down toward Blue Lake with a rope around her mouth. Attached to the note was:

"I told you. We want that gun."

Burley shook his head, puzzled about what to do. He didn't even have the stolen gun and if he had it, the note said nothing about how to get it to them.

From his camp inside the cave behind the waterfall, he draped the cheesecloth he had purchased over his brimmed hat and into his shirt collar. Made a good cover against bee stings. Such a wonderful wealth of honey.

The nearby trees, actually a total of twenty to his rough count, were loaded with green apples. Needed to be thinned or the limbs would break. What else could be done with green apples…?

That would be tomorrow's problem. Today more honey would be gathered or the bees would begin to slow down their production. They knew exactly how much to make for the coming winter and they likely had it already.

Miss Zennia made attractive jars, thick golden liquid and slices of honeycomb against the outside of the jar so it showed through. Sometimes she seemed a bit bored and wanted something to do. Just yesterday she picked greens down by the waterfall and brought him some after they were cooked. Made a nice change.

Carefully moving among the buzzing insects, he finished with only two stings… both on the back of his left hand. Frenchie told him of a young hog someone had for sale. He'd pick it up when he returned with his wagon.

It was the next day when he returned from Eureka Springs with the wagon and the pig that he found Miss Zennia in a bath of tears. Little Charlie was gone. She'd hardly looked away as he played in the yard, and he was gone. So was Jumper. She had called and called, and if he was within hearing distance, Jumper would have brought him home.

Leaving the pig in the crate under a tree, Burley jumped on the spotted horse that had wandered into camp, the one that was not Dapple. Clicking him into action, he tore out toward Berryville, thinking that would be the best way to seek help on the way.

It was about a mile down the road that he met Frenchie who flagged him down. Out of the van leaped Jumper and ran to Burley, leaping against him. Frenchie handed down the boy, his dusty face tear streaked. Jumper dashed back and forth between Charlie and Burley, wagging his tail furiously.

Burley faced Frenchie. "The boy wandered off…?"

Frenchie shook his head. "Look at the note."

"Put gun in hidden cave and leave it there. Do not bring a deputy. Next time you won't get the boy back."

Burley's heart sunk. What now? He had to notify Ike. If he did, Ike would not let him go alone. He'd do it anyway, but he did not have the gun they demanded. He couldn't get the gun until he told Ike. Ike would not let the gun get back in the hands of a known murderer.

So what would he lose next? The gang could even burn down Miss Zennia's wagon with the family in it. Burley couldn't stay awake all night. Jumper was a wonderful dog to look for the gang, but he really needed a 'trackerin' dog.' He had a note that had the scent of the kidnapper… dare he keep it from Ike? If he did, he was likely breaking some law. If not breaking, at least bending it dangerously.

He sighed deeply and looked into Frenchie's sympathetic eyes. The van driver asked, "Well, what now?"

"I reckon I'll hold onto this note and look for a trackin' dog. Did the boy say where he went?"

"He was too busy cryin'." He knelt by Charlie. "Son, did you take Jumper for a walk and get lost?"

The wide eyes watched as his head waved from side to side. "A man took me and put his hand over my mouth so I couldn't cry. Then there were more men. They hit me so I didn't cry," and the little fellow sniffed and looked from man to man. "They put me by the road and said stand there or they would hit me again. Then he come along," pointing to Frenchie, "and Jumper jumped outta the brush. Then I was here."

All right. So he was kidnapped, and the smart dog had followed. Being part wolf, he could likely be taught to track, only there wasn't time. This would take some thought, but he was not going to let that note get away.

Frenchie nodded. "Get in and I'll take you both home. Miss Zennia is likely about to go outta her mind." And he was right.

OPENING DAY

Burley got little sleep, but life goes on. Another note would help. He wished he'd kept the others. Miss Zennia was so overcome at the sight of her son she hugged both men before clutching her son until he complained he couldn't breathe.

Today she sang as she trimmed the pieces of honeycomb and placed them against the sides of the jars to show them off best. Seven more jars making a total of fifteen. Could she put them on the counter and spend her time in the little stand. Please…?

The tea glasses had been washed until they shone, and they stood upsidedown on a tray with a snowy tea towel over them. She knew exactly what to do with the fresh tea leaves.

Annie Jo had looked at Frenchie as though he had lost his mind. "You need garden tea? Whatever for? Even city folks have peppermint in their garden."

"Not this place, Annie. I got a little scheme goin' that I ain't gonna tell you about for a while. That tea is a part of it, and you hidin' that young man was another part'a it. I ain't tellin' you 'cause if it don't work, I'd never hear the last'a it."

With a playful fist, she touched his nose. "All right, then. But you be careful. I didn't raise you up from a crawlin' baby to get your hide damaged."

Frenchie grinned. "Nuther thing. That dog'a yours… she's a good tracker you think?"

"You mean Joker? Why wouldn't she be? Bloodhound and timberwolf. Couldn't be better. Ain't been trained, though, and I don't know how and don't have time if I did."

The name Joker was given to the poor dog when she was born a pathetically tiny runt. A joke of a dog. It seemed for all the world that there was just not enough doggy dough for her mama to make that thirteenth pup. All the parts were there, but she would never pass for a massive bloodhound pup.

The thing was, there was a very big doggie inside that tiny bit of hide. She had been birthed by Paula Patrick who dealt in part-bloodhound pups to sell mainly to hunters. Good background, the breeder bragged. Mama a pure bloodhound, and Papa a traveling salesman leading his own pack of wolves. Special pedigree. She never bothered to mate her three females. The wolves knew, apparently, the minute they came in heat.

So poor little Joker was pushed out of the large dog's body as a final exhaustive effort. Then mama heaved a sigh of relief. Paula said she looked twice to make sure it was a dog and not a rat. Would her neighbor, Annie Jo, like to have it? Otherwise… well….

Annie Jo didn't think twice. She was experienced with small orphans. Frenchie had watched the dog grow under Annie's care until she possibly outstripped her mama in size and maybe her papa in smarts. Annie had sighed to realize how the dog was wasted on her, but the dog didn't care. Frenchie liked having Joker around because no one came close without the huge mouth issuing forth a rumbling bark that shook the eardrums.

Frenchie winked at Annie and told her, "I may need to borrow her in a week or so. Will you let me?"

"Is this part of your scheme?"

"A very important part."

Miss Zennia was so excited she was jittery. Four of the empty honey jars had crumbled brown leaves in them, and were inscribed with PEPPERMINT, SPEARMINT, CHAMOMILE, and STRAWBERRY LEAF with CONE FLOWER. A measuring spoon was nearby. Zennia would like to have had hibiscus flowers with marigold leaves, but the hibiscus flowers were not in bloom yet. She especially liked the bright red Lord Baltimore blossoms. They would be gathered the day after they were spent when their flavor was most pronounced. Red Zinger tea, she and her sisters called it.

Fresh, cool water from the falls was in a bucket setting inside a thick wooden box to stay as cool as possible. Burley would replace the water later. She had a tiny kerosene stove in the unlikely event that someone wanted their tea hot.

And, of course, there was Burley's black liquid he called coffee that could be heated on request. Little Charlie liked to taste it so he could make a face and shake his head saying 'Pooeeeee!' and then asking for another taste.

Only five jars of honey sat on the counter. It wouldn't be wise to set out her whole stock at once. The price was 5 cents for the honey if they had their own container. If not, they could buy the jar with the honey for 10 cents. The replacement jar would be only 3 cents, but there was the trouble of buying and bringing it over the road, so the cost of labor had to be figured in. Then, of course, if the customer brought a replacement jar of equal value, a tit-for-tat swap was arranged.

Mr. Burley had bought some of the little flat cans of Frenchie's sardines, and she set three of them on a napkin. She had a fork someone could borrow if their pocket knife had no fork.

The pecans she had gathered were cracked and the kernels added to sugar cookie dough. These were baked on her miniature stove in her tiny wagon and added to the menu. She was proud of her cookie baking. The tiny oven had been included to make biscuits for Sonny and cookies for his little boy. Now she took the cut-glass bowl with a matching lid (a wonderful wedding present from her four sisters) and it was enthroned in a noticeable spot. Cookies inside.

Mr. Burley had tossed a rope over a limb so Lily's cradle board would be eye level when her mama sat on the stool. Lily and mom were now officially in business.

It would be anyone's guess how the first day would go. Frenchie's sign that had been in place for a week had attracted a lot of attention, and the bistro's existence was now widely known. About twenty seven persons had stopped to ask what was a 'bistro'? Good advertisement.

It was almost as though information traveled on the wild-grape vines that laced the county together. When two friends/neighbors met, the favorite first words were, 'Have you heard about….."

The first cookie customer was, of course, Frenchie. He helped himself to the coffee (his was free) and a cookie that he insisted on paying for. If he ate it slowly, he could look at Zennia longer without seeming to stare.

Miss Zennia sat on the high stool behind the counter like a queen on her throne. Peace began to seep gently into her broken heart as she now had something to do to occupy her mind. And, importantly, she now had a service to trade for the lovely spot on Burley's bluff where her wagon sat, and also for taking care of the horse they said was hers.

While she worked, she cracked the rest of the pecans. And thought about what else could be put on the counter.

Mr. Burley left it mostly to her. He was busy with the pig he had brought home, and he had promised her a choice cut of meat for her own supper. There was the liver and heart that would not make jerky, and there were would be wonderful soup bones she could simmer on the metal grate over his fire. They could even be sun-dried for use later.

Life might not have the joy she expected, but she at least knew it was possible. She also had a lot of time for thought.

The June afternoon was steamy, and she had several customers for tea. She had steeped small quantities of each flavor and had the flavored liquid ready for the cool water, and the spot of honey for those who wanted it.

Her day's take was 72 cents in pennies and nickels. She proudly handed the jar to Mr. Burley. He counted it and favored her with a pleased smile and a nod.

"Good job," he told her, and she considered herself well-paid.

THE PLAID SHIRT INCIDENT

It was hungry time for the four young men barely out of their teens. They'd been in the western end of Carroll County, and caused enough damage and theft there that it seemed time for a move. Going south into Madison County would likely have been a wise choice, from the position of their own personal welfare, but these four had not enough collected wisdom to make that decision.

Breaking into Wilkinson's Market had been a mistake. The glass was thicker than they expected, and made a lot of noise. They had hardly made their choices, by the light of a flashlight with weak batteries, when the angry Doberman broke into the party.

The canine bared her stiletto teeth and caught Spike by the leg. Fortunately, for Spike, he was wearing calf-high boots, but there was no prying loose the dog's jaws until he was beaten over the head and pummeled by thrown canned beans.

Splintered glass caught Shorty on his ear and neck but there was more blood than concern for his life. Consequently, they had left downtown Eureka Springs wiser than they had arrived.

Following Ridge Road back east, they remembered the McFey Farm. No one guarded it, and it was early in the morning so the cows would not have been milked. Leaving Shorty with the horses, Spike, Slim and Robert crept through the cornfield toward the barn.

Sure enough, the cows had been contained in the corral and they were full for the milking. With their cans, the thieves crouched under the puzzled bovines and the sound of the musical splat in the cans floated out on the air.

Joker was on guard at her mistress' door. The canine knew Annie Jo had her hands full with the sick old man in the bedroom. Her sensitive nose had smelled the sickness, and her piercing eyes noted the tenseness in Annie. Offering her generous body braced against the door with her chin on her capable paws while she waited was something she could do. Death watch. Something would happen and it would be only days away.

The musical splat was a familiar sound to her sensitive ears. She lifted her head and turned, staring into the semi-darkness. How could they have gotten past her to the barn, and Odus Bare Foot who did the milking on shares always spoke to her when he arrived. Intruders out there for sure.

On feather soft paws she lifted her remarkable body, tensing her shoulder muscles and lifting her nose. She moved her head back and forth to make certain the scent was not a familiar one.

Circling the house she paused, piercing eyes making out the figures that should not be in the corral with her other charges, the senseless cows. She continued her soft steps until she was within feet of one of the crouched figures.

Silently she lifted her impressive head, opened her mouth, and sent forth a thunderous rumble that seemed to shake the very earth. She followed the initial burst with a series of short, choppy barks that would have told a seasoned tracker that she was barking 'treed,' meaning she had her quarry pinned down and the humans could safely approach.

Joker, however, had no one who would approach. She was an attack posse of one, and that was all that was needed.

At the first bark of rolling thunder, the three thieves leaped to their feet, cans of milk being tossed skyward. The puzzled bovines felt the moisture rain down on their backs but thought nothing of it. The ways of humans were always puzzling. Dimple, the jersey, did give vent to a low-pitched 'mooo.'

The three humans dashed for the fence. Spike caught a foot, and it desperately shed its boot… the human leaped to the ground and fled. Slim cast himself to the ground amid its moist and aromatic night residue, rolling under the fence like a log.

Robert picked up Spike's boot and when he stood, realized his shirt was caught. Firmly caught in a dental vice. Even in the dim light, Robert knew a bloodhound when he had heard one, and wisely ripped off the buttons and slid his arms from the garment. At the moment, it seemed to be a small sacrifice.

Joker stood with the shirt hanging from her teeth, wondering if she did right or should her teeth have been a bit deeper. Oh, well….

She sauntered toward the back door with the offending garment in her teeth, and dropped down on the step beside it. She was not lazy, but she abhorred the useless expenditure of energy.

Presently, Annie Jo opened the door to take the vessel of night soil to the privy, as usual. She stopped and stared at the plaid shirt, filthy and somewhat worn. "Joker, what is this?"

Joker arose and padded back to the corral and the restless cows. Empty cans lay on the ground, and instead of relaxed cud-chewing, the cows were staring toward the house as if waiting for someone.

"Hmmm. Milk thieves, huh?" Hobos occasionally stole milk but four cans…? And a lot of scuffed footprints…? Hobos usually didn't mind coming to the door. Most farm families were good for a meal or two, not just milk in an unwashed can. Not hobos… then who?

She wouldn't bother the sick old man, but she'd save the shirt for Frenchie to see. Maybe wash it up for whoever it belonged to, but not today. Today was the day to weed the kitchen garden and prune back the overgrowth of mint plants. That girl in the covered wagon had a use for the sprouts … seemed like.

Robert was now shirtless, so that meant looking for a clothesline to rob. Not an easy task as washings were done on Monday unless it rained or there was a funeral.

They headed back to Hidden Cave for a meeting of the minds. They really wanted that gun. It was going to take another note on something or someone's mailbox to get that old man's attention.

Using an old envelope, Robert printed:

"We want that gun. Bring it to the hidden cave ALONE, or you die. Leave the gun and don't look back".

The note was pinned to the new mailbox Burley had just installed, not that he expected any letters, but a mailbox in this rural area validated it as a place of business or residence.

Zennia was first to see the white paper moving in the breeze. She picked it off the box and read it, sniffed gently, squared her shoulders and marched to where Mr. Burley was tending the fire in the tent he was using for a smokehouse.

Handing it to him, she watched as he read it, and whispered, "That's Sonny's gun, ain't it?"

Burley nodded, folded the paper and pocketed it. "That's the gun, but they ain't gonna get it. Now or later."

The strips of ham were looking good as the heat and the summer air drew out the moisture and heightened the flavor. Some of the strips were sharp and fire-hot while others were mild and flavorful. Grinning to himself, he assured himself that if it didn't sell, it would take himself through the winter. The hams had been rubbed with spices and hung from a tripod within the 'smoke tent.' A house will be better, but one used what one had, until....

He had always hated to put himself forward, but he secretly believed his own jerky was the best made. He'd package it in two sizes of sack. Five pieces and 12 pieces. He'd like to sell some cheaply to get people used to it, but his instinct told him that would be wrong. Prices can be lowered, but when raised again, it instinctively turned the people away.

Maybe Frenchie's suggestion was the best. Save out several pieces, cut them in two inch bites and offer free as a sample. Maybe he'd not offer a five piece sack, and just say a dozen generous strips for a nickel. That seemed a bit high, but there was a lot of work involved.

After this one-time purchase of a ready-to-butcher animal, the pork would be very cheap. He would fence in his apple orchard which would be big enough so that the burrowing porker would not be tempted to leave. Except for a shed for winter, and a small amount of mash, the animals would raise themselves.

He closed the tent flaps and brushed his hands together. On to the next job. He'd get a sheet of paper from Frenchie and give the fellows a note. Anything to play for time. While adjusting the meat strips, he saw the whole message before his eyes.

"Fellows, I can't bring the gun right now. Ike has it locked away and I can't ask for it. If he gave it to me, he would follow me and stake out a posse to find you. I have to figure a way. If you have a suggestion, just leave me another note. Burley Collins."

He completed the note as Frenchie munched sugar cookies laced with pecans. With Jumper at his side, Burley tromped through the brush and vines to the hidden cave, totally resenting the time it took away from his homestead.

There was the fence to put around the apples. At Zennia's request, he brought up a bucket of the green apples he needed to pick to thin out the crop. She insisted she needed them because they let her make blackberry juice into jelly. Purely amazing at the smarts in under that crop of red hair.

He saw evidence that the coons were helping themselves to windfall green apples. He needed to get that young sow, maybe a pair of them, and let them run the coons out. Nothing like a Hampshire sow for wanting her own territory. He'd always liked the look of a Hampshire with its black body and white front legs and belt over the shoulders. They looked, for all the world, like a black hog wearing a white jacket.

While waiting for customers, Zennia was lining up a row of acorns and letting Charlie repeat after her. One. Two. Three. Four. Five.

THE END OF THE JOURNEY

Frenchie sat on the foot of the bed where the old man lay with his Bible on his thin chest. Pa seemed more alive today, and wanting to talk. He enjoyed telling of times when he was a little boy and how different things were. The van driver had a route to keep… a long one. But that could wait. Pa came first.

As he listened, he sensed a difference. Not that he could put his finger on anything for a fact, but just a feeling. Maybe it was only that this was such a beautiful day. The songs of the birds drifted into the room through the open window. Annie Jo was a great believer in fresh air.

Pa smiled as he talked. Such a good life he had been given, and his only despair was of losing Frenchie's ma so soon. No matter… he'd see her soon.

Annie Jo came with tea for them both. Frenchie held the cup before the old man's shaking lips. "Good tea that girl makes. She should'a been mine stead'a the way she was born. No, that's be sayin' God didn't know what He was a'doin'. A big sister to you… that's what she was. Still is. I know you'll take care'a her as much as she wants you to."

When the old man's eyes drooped with weariness, Frenchie took his silent leave. "Looks better today, doesn't he…."

A pause. "Comes and goes, he does." Wide smile and she pointed to a platter of deviled eggs. He'd loved them all his life. Still did. "Got you somethin' to take with you to eat on the way."

Then he was on his way to the next stop, munching the delicious eggs with their golden filling. While rolling down Ridge Road he chuckled to himself over the last time he went this way. Tucked under the lower shelf of his van was James, the whistle blower. Frenchie had met the train and waited, bringing the boy forth when a family of seven appeared, going south.

With the boy was enough money for an emergency, a letter to the Watkins Products Home Warehouse addressed to the person who would meet him. He would be kept inside the plant for the near future, and if he worked out like it seemed he would, he had a job for the rest of his life.

His ma would miss him, but she was proud of him. The only thing was, she wanted to tell the world how clever he was, but she was commanded by law to keep her mouth shut. For his safety, it was pointed out. He was "visiting friends" and furthering his education. He was living in "some little town, away off." She would be able to visit him occasionally, but it all had to be hush-hush.

It was the next morning that Annie Jo was canning tomatoes. The old man loved her tomato soup, flavored with cream and thickened by crumbled leftover biscuits. Seemed to help his digestion.

As she heard no stirring from the room, she went about her business, his morning tea ready, and the hot cereal would be fixed in minutes. But when he remained quiet for so long, she became concerned.

Entering his room, she paused. He was peaceful, almost smiling, his gnarled, wrinkled and bony old hands resting comfortably on his Bible. The scene was not unusual, but there was no rise and fall to the Book he loved.

A covering of shivers passed through her and her heart pounded, painfully. Approaching the bed, she crumbled to her knees onto the colorful braided rug and leaned forward, her forehead against the softness of the sleeve of his night shirt.

Tears poured from her eyes like a spring rain as she raised her arms and placed her open hands over his stiff and cold ones as though she could warm them… or perhaps retain him on the earth for a while longer. But it was not to be.

Old Mr. McFey was not there. He was not in the bed and he would not be taken from the room and out the door. In the dark of the night, the brightness of an angel had born the spirit of the man away, leaving only the worn out shell for his earthbound family.

Joker, who had followed Annie into the room, an action unusual for the bloodhound, pushed her head against Annie's shoulder as she sat crumbled on the rug. Then the canine lifted her head toward the ceiling and released a mournful whine that extended for minutes. After that, she nudged her nose under Annie's arm, gently forcing her way to press her jaw to Annie's face, warm fur against wet skin.

Annie turned to the dog, hugging her and weeping into her fur and against her long, rag-like ears. Knowing this was imminent had not made it any less painful. There would be no tomatoes canned today.

From the near pasture she brought in the old mare being allowed to spend her life in green pastures. There was one more job for her. The animal brightened as she was led with a determined hand to the small, 4X4 foot cart commonly called a 'dog cart.'

Going to the house for her bonnet and her handbag, Annie looked at him once more. Of course it was true, but maybe it wasn't.

It was.

Stepping into the cart and signaling Joker beside her, she clicked to the horse who turned her ears forward and stepped along, glad to again be in the harness, whatever the purpose. There was no question as to where she would go. Burley Collins' outdoor diner had been in business for only two months, but was already a destination place. A meeting place. A convenient stop-over. A place to spread information.

Zennia was not well acquainted with the red-eyed Annie, but she recognized trouble when she saw it, and this was clearly some of the worst. Leaving the stand, she led her into the tiny cabin and sat her at a fold-down shelf table, handing her a towel.

"The old man…?"

Throat too tight to speak, Annie nodded.

The younger woman folded her arms around Annie. "I know how it is." And they wept together.

Burley came toward the stand where small Lily swung gently. Alone. Jumper was positioned directly under the baby, every muscle tense. Joker had followed Annie to the cabin, her body now pressed against the door.

Burley had no reason to ask what had happened.

Two days later, the body of the community's oldest resident was laid away and songs were sung. Words were read from his Bible. What more could anyone do, and they returned to their many duties.

Lottie Bare Foot, knowing Annie's feeling for the old man, had slipped quietly over to the farm house while the burial was in progress. Pulling the bedding from the bed, she had sprinkled it with the perfume of local flowers and located the different linens and coverlet.

She had taken the braided rug to the clothesline and applied the beater with a vengeance. She opened the windows to the late June breeze and quietly left carrying the bed linen. Some day… months, maybe… she would return it. Annie was not in need, and she had enough to remind her of her loss.

Lottie felt free to do this little thing because Annie had done the same for her when they lost their first baby. It was a thing she could do.

ANNIE JO IN DECISION

Frenchie and his almost sister, Annie Josephine, who had begun to use the last name McFey, sat across from each other in the silent kitchen. The only sounds were from the birds in the tree and maybe a restless grunt or two from the pig pen by the kitchen garden. What was there to say that had not already been said? Over and over....

Finally Frenchie. "Annie, I know you better than any other living soul and I know that come tomorrow there will not be a square inch of the inside of this house that has not been cleaned. I have no complaint, but I do have a request.

"I want you to treat this house and everything within this fence as belonging to you. What I want most for you is for you to be and do whatever you want most, and if I can be a part of that life, it will be my pleasure. Whoever comes to live here will be coming to YOUR house, and can never displace you. If, though, you want something new, I'll do my best to see that you get it, even if you decide to leave me and go to Fayetteville. I know that you know all of this, but I had to say it again."

Silence reigned once more as Annie studied the face of her almost brother, the one she had chased after as a crawling baby, taught to walk, then to ride, assisted to grow the business of the rolling Watkins Products store. She knew him better than any other living being, and possibly better than he knew himself. She watched his face and listened to his voice.

"You're right, I will clean the house as well as it was when I came here at age six, and then I will make plans. The tie that bound me here is gone. With that gone, I must build new ties. Cleaning the house will give me time to think. I think it is likely that I need to find people. Our pa was enough by himself, but I must go on, and it will take a lot of people to replace him."

Silence, and she took time to warm the tea. Then, "Our pa said the steps of the righteous were ordered by the Lord, (Psa 37:23) and I do not have my orders yet."

What could he say to that? He busied himself unpacking certain supplies and fitting them into the van. It took careful planning to manage the variety he wanted to carry into so small a space. He grinned as he remembered the times he thought he could use a small trailer, especially as he often over-nighted in the van, and a certain amount of bedding was necessary, along with a change of clothing. Everything took space.

Annie Jo went into the front bedroom and looked at the neatly made bed, the freshly washed curtains and rug. She pulled the curtains together, darkening the room, removed the cleaned night soil vessel, sniffed appreciatively at the fragrance of the herbs left by Lottie. She swallowed hard, sighed softly and left the room, firmly and quietly closing the door.

By closing the door of the room, she closed off a chapter of her life. She went to the mud room and began to sort the accumulation of soiled clothing and linens. By so doing, she figuratively put aside the book of her life while she decided on a new chapter. She knew one thing. She would not stay forever in the house where the reason for staying no longer existed.

Every cow in the corral had been born while she was nearby. The peach orchard was planted with saplings ordered from Starks Nursery somewhere off in the north, and she had canned the fruit. She had made the peach butter that her family loved with biscuits.

The kitchen garden was designed by herself with the placement of the tea plants in the richest soil to strengthen their flavor.

It was for her that the family purchased the small 'dog cart' wagon. As a girl she needed it for errands before Frenchie was old enough to help. Her first five years were a blur of non-memory. A nothing period before she had begun what she considered a full life.

Maybe her life had not been as full as it could have been, but it had seemed enough. So now, at age 29, she would be making a change.

During the 23 years of her life on the farm, she had seen Ridge Road become a hard surface of flint gravel instead of the quagmire of clay that happened with every rain shower.

The Turner family set up a sawmill that turned out finished lumber for builders all the way from Eureka Springs to Berryville. She had gone to school with the Turner boys.

The Ridge Road grew into a massive centipede, made by the roads, lanes and trails leading away and down into the valleys. A funeral brought people from everywhere to grieve with the survivors and to catch up on the latest rumors… to compare opinions on everything from seed corn to knitting needles to the new windmills that could be made to draw water from wells.

People. Annie Jo had not been able to focus on the many people in her house as she would have enjoyed doing as she said the last goodbye. Her eyes were too full of tears and her heart was too heavy to lift.

People. Without them, what would be the use of the world? Since she finished the four years of school, she had seen very few people on a continuing basis.

People. Both Berryville and Eureka Springs had people, but Fayetteville had many more. She could go to Fayetteville and there would be so many things for her to do. That's what everyone said.

She doused the soapy suds over the towels and pillowcases and grabbed a handful of the fabric. Up and down, up and down on the rub-board, a restful routine that required no thinking. She scraped the thick suds from her hands and stood. She turned and leaned against the tub while she looked out over the valley and the faintly blue mountain beyond. There past Echo Mountain was the Bald Knob, with its house-sized boulders on top. Come October, the mountain would be a crazy-quilt of colors as the leaves began to turn.

Like the waters of the Dead Sea from Bible times that had no outlet, Annie's thoughts and words became dammed up in behind her eyes and threatened a headache. What... for goodness' sake... was wrong with her? It was June and that was too late for spring restlessness.

People. Tears blurred her vision and streamed down her face. *ANNIE!* she scolded herself. *Get a hold on yourself! This ain't like you.*

But the fact was, it was not only like her, it WAS her, and she knew that fact...with everything within her. She was like a water pitcher that had poured forth for years, and now had nothing more to give. She was empty. Somehow she must find a way to fill up again.

People. Was that the answer? To determine that, she must first know the question. Turning suddenly, she grabbed up a handful of fabric. Up and down, up and down. Flecks of thick soapsuds flew as she tossed clean towels into the rinse water.

What was the question? She would find it. The burst of energy provided by this realization spurred her with such strength, the washing was on the line and swaying to the sunshiny breeze while her thoughts whirled. What, indeed, was the question?

She opened out one of her accumulation of precious folded cardboard boxes brought by Frenchie. Into it she tenderly placed the clean and fresh smelling clothing that had belonged to her earthly father and teacher. On top she placed his hardly worn shoes.

Folding the top flaps, and wrapping securely with a cord, she set it aside. In a whirl of decision, she pushed back the curtains and tied them, letting the June sunshine stream in on the scrubbed boards of the pine floor, boards that had been sawed flat and smooth by the Turner boys' father.

Lifting the lower sash of the window, she stood in the breeze. Yes. The answer was people, but the question was yet to be formed. No matter, it would come. She left the room, propping the door open with the little rock she had brought in from the cow pasture for that purpose. The rock was made of cubes of almost clear hard, glassy substance and glistened in the lamplight. Pa had said he thought it was something called quartz crystal, a living stone.

Living stone. So extraordinary that it would have grown right there in their cow pasture and it even had a name other than 'doorstop.'

People. It was people who determined that it had a name. She had been about eight when she found it, and smiled as she remembered Pa had said that maybe the angels had put it there for her. She had often been told that the angels were the servants and messengers who were made by God to take care of her. (Psa 91:11)

As the washing swayed on the line, Annie scooped up a bucket of the thick suds made from her own lye soap. With wild abandon she poured the whole bucket of water onto the boards of the kitchen floor, flowing it into every corner and crevass. With the new broom brought by her brother, she scrubbed the bristles into the worn grain of the floor boards, routing out every smidgen of dirt.

She opened the door and spoke to Joker. "You'd better move! Water's coming out and I'm going to wash the porch." Joker moved a few feet and watched. There was no understanding humans, but she liked them anyway.

Annie Jo hung the broom on its peg and fired up the stove. In a pan of water she put a half a dozen eggs laid by the hens she had hatched from her own eggs. She grabbed up her garden bonnet and slapped it on her head, catawampus, actually. With her picking basket, she headed for the garden.

Her onions had just rounded out into tender, many-layered bulbs. She yanked six of them for her basket. She rammed the spade fork into the dirt and heaved out new thin-skinned potatoes. Rubbing the dirt from them, she selected the 6 largest ones.

Her spicy, lily-long-nose peppers were just turning from green to red. Perfect. She picked 6 of the reddest. And she sighed as she looked over her garden. She loved this stage of the plants, though it required a lot of weeding.

Potato salad. That's what she would have, and though it was some bit of trouble, she knew she was worth it. The wonderful French mustard her brother left for her would tie the flavors together, and it would be ready for supper. It was her favorite early summer meal.

She did not yet have the question, but her faith was strong. She was young and healthy and her future was just around the corner. She was a kite cut loose and allowed to fly on the wind. She would go as far as the wind would carry her. That's where she would find the answer.

But wait, there was something… though it was not quite an answer. It was something she had set aside when her life became so complicated. In school and later as a teen she had enjoyed having a tablet where she sketched scenes that interested her. They said she had talent, whatever that was. She'd look for that tablet. Maybe it would give her ideas.

Later, she sat alone at the table, and scooped the colorful potato salad into her plate. The tablet and a sharpened pencil were within arm's reach.

Then she looked up and said, "Thanks, God!"

A WILLOW SEED IN THE WIND

Over the centuries, the trees have developed a way of living and spreading themselves over the continents. Nut trees just drop their seeds, depending on animals or the terrain to spread them. Seems to have worked well.

The maple trees artistically create little single-bladed helicopters capable of whirling and carrying themselves only a short distance, but their webbed wing floats on water, and can move a long way with streams. The oak creates the little food packets called acorns that are distributed by birds and fur-bearers in their winter caches.

But some, including the willow, have dreams for going farther. Finding a special place. Their pollen moves in puffs on the wind, and the seeds blow in the storms. Willows do not always come up where they fall. Incredibly long lived, they prefer to move to water, and once there, root so fast they are seldom moved. Looking like grass as young plants, they are safe until they can root heavily.

People are so like seeds. Some choosing to make homes nearby, some moving small distances, and some are moved by circumstances beyond their control, but others are like the willow… they are seemingly carried on the wind, moving just because they are moving.

Burley Collins came from 'willow' stock. His people were here and there, and then they were gone. Children were born and they either stayed or moved on. Some would say it was a wanderlust. Others would say it was itching heels that were only scratched as the boot tramped on new grounds.

What little of the Collins family there was east of the Mississippi was torn apart by the war of the brothers. When the north/south dispute reached the point that it must be settled, homes and communities were destroyed, and the Collins of Greenwood, Mississippi were a textbook example of those. There could be truth, however, that what happened would have happened anyway, regardless of the war of the brothers.

Those who were conscripted into the war often did not return to their families. Where would the families be, anyway, with their homes destroyed? The attraction of the big river drew young Burley Collins, and at the strapping age of almost twelve, he had walked out of the cotton field, literally, and headed for the water.

The river was good for him, and he built the solid base of muscles that would stay with him for life. The good life there made him strong, but the itchiness of his heels took him away at eighteen. Crossing the water, he could have headed south, but the winds of chance took him north. He'd had enough of the steamy lowlands and the mountains of eastern Arkansas seemed attractive.

It was there in the mountains that he worked in lumber, felling trees needed for the building up of the state. He learned a little about a lot of things, and could find employment anywhere. His needs were small, and when he moved, he could carry all his possessions on his back.

He saw the settlements and was not tempted to stay. He liked people but not enough to make permanent attachments. He enjoyed the blue of the distant mountains, the fire-ball promise of a sunrise and the restful purple of evening clouds.

He enjoyed gatherings of mountain folks, but chose not to become part of them. He helped those in trouble until they were safe, and then he moved on. Like the seed of the willow, he would not stop until he reached the right stopping place, and that possibility was far from his mind.

He met no one that he could not leave on a whim, and saw no place where he wished to be permanent. From eastern Arkansas, he traveled mountain to mountain, and then he reached the terrain of ridges and hollows. He traveled the paths and wagon trails that twisted around as it followed the ridges until he reached the blossoming city of Fayetteville.

Continuing on west, he saw the changes in the land, and he turned away. The wind of his mind had changed. Tracking back to the east, he stayed a while in the valley town of Eureka Springs, then moved on. The city had too many people in one place.

Back on Ridge Road, he traveled the curves, stopping here and there for a while, then moving on. His wind still blew. He passed a crumbling roadside stand and bought a strip of jerky. Not as good as he could make, but it was food. He walked on, still moved by the inner wind.

He passed through Berryville, and on east... but one night he rolled out his bedroll and stretched out under the stars. Big Dipper. Little Dipper. North Star. The wind within him whirled and changed again.

He returned to Berryville and worked for a builder putting together cabins made from dimension lumber rather than logs. He freighted boards from the mill to the jobsite. He took his place on the rafters and shingles with his hammer and nails. He sort of enjoyed the no-nonsense quality of wood, and the myriad of useful and important things to be made from it.

His thirty-ninth birthday was spent behind the mules encouraging them to strain in the harness and draw the heavy loads of logs up the mountains. He could not have known that his inner windstorm was about to settle, but he did recognize the strange restlessness that drove him.

He knew he would leave. He bought Heppie, the donkey to carry his expanded possessions, and the strong, young stallion to ride. It was March when he knew he would again head west.

A shred of memory brought up the crumbing shack where he had bought the jerky, and he thought of the bluff behind the stand. It had been late afternoon that day, and the setting sun had glistened off the lake in the valley. The wizened old fellow behind the counter had said it was called Blue Lake because no matter where you stood, you saw a reflection of the blue sky. Burley liked that.

So, today as he rode, he slowed the steps of the animals. They were all three very weary and if he could just make it to the bluff, they would camp there for a few days and rest.

He rounded the last curve and saw the massive oak with the spreading limbs. A bit farther on, he saw the body, twisting slowly in the early April breeze.

The willow seed had found the place where roots could be formed that would hold it in one place. He had never owned property… he had never wanted to. But now… like the willow seed… he knew when he had reached the plateau of his life, though it would take a few days to realize how profound a change it was.

And now, he was busier than a pup with five children to follow, and had become embroiled in a murder, a vandal gang, a damsel in distress and a business to run. A mental and physical merry-go-round it had become, such as was found at a fair for children to ride.

Events happened. He fell asleep at night in the down-wind smoke of the smoldering coals beside his curing jerky. The flavorful smoke went a long way toward discouraging mosquitoes.

His last thought before he sank into exhausted sleep was how… how… how could he round up and catch the gang that eluded Ike and his posse… without causing damage to himself and those around him?

And how could he spare the time?

FRENCHIE HAS A PLAN

Burley's first waking thought was how to stall the gang for time. They had issued an ultimatum and it required action on his part. Something had to be taken to the hidden cave today, and it couldn't be the gun but how about another note?

So after a couple of browned pork chops (about three eggs would have been good) and a half a dozen biscuits made by Zennia, he settled on one of the tiny picnic tables with a pad of paper and a pencil that he had sharpened with his pen knife. He had a half formed message in mind, but had yet to commit it to paper.

Frenchie, who aimed to have whatever his customers wanted and usually hit the mark, had sold him a pad, an eraser and three pencils for five cents. Then Burley had sold Frenchie three cookies, for which the driver returned the nickel to Zennia's money jar.

Frenchie sipped the coffee (still free to him, in return for errands) and munched the sugar cookies. He had something to say to Burley, but knew he must wait for the note to be written in order to have the man's full attention. Burley preferred one thought at a time… when possible.

"Friend. I would really like to get the gun to you but I'm having difficulty with the plan. I hope you can be patient. I might add that if you do anything to harm me or my place, I will be forced to call Ike and his posse, but if you can wait, I will do my best for you. Burley Collins."

Note finished, Burley put down his pencil and picked up his coffee. Chore one for the day… finished.

Frenchie stared out over the bluff and commented. "Winter'll be here before you know it. Where will you put the cabin for your help?"

"My… help…?"

"Yeah. Whoever you get to help you run this place. You know you can't do it alone. Makin' the cider, smokin' the jerky, tendin' to your runnin' around… and the animals. You gotta have someone available for this stand all the time to make it pay. Folks get to countin' on things bein' there when they want 'em."

Burley's weathered forehead wrinkled with puzzlement. "I got Miss Zennia and she's doin' just fine."

"Sure, right now. But think ahead. Her with two little ones, winter bein' here and that covered wagon ain't gonna stand a northern gale in an Arkansas winter. And the driving rain and icicles. There'll be no tendin' the stand for weeks at a time in the winter. She can't spend the winter with two little ones in that tiny cabin, and she'll need someone to help her."

"Are you rememberin' that she had a offer to be taken to town? She wanted to stay here."

"For the summer. She wasn't in no shape to be makin' a long term decision. This here, what you done for her was the savin' of her mind for the summer months, but you know how the winter gets. You better start in on that log cabin for her and plan on takin' care'a her...."

Frenchie heated up his coffee. That was enough words for now. New subject.

"You got a plan hatched up to get that gang?"

"Maybe. Nothin' really firmed up, though. I sure don't like this interruption to what I need to do here. You got me to thinkin'. That girl can't stay here all winter. I couldn't take care'a her even if I wanted to. I'd have to be three people, 'stead'a two."

"Yeah, you got a point there." Short pause, then, "Say, I might have an idea for you. What you really need is a lady maybe a little older that's lookin' for a change. Don't know how it'd work out, but I know for certain she'd have to have a solid cabin for the winter. Wouldn't have to be big to start with, and if things worked out... well... Anyway, it's a thought."

"...Lady with no youngens to worry with?"

"Sure enough. 'Course I'm just talkin'. Could be nothin' to it for all I know. But you know me, finger on the pulse of the community. I hear all kinds of things and I might ask around."

"You'd do that...? But what about Miss Zennia?"

"Oh, now that'd be easy part. These here mountains are full'a bachelors and widowers that'd swap their eye teeth to have a purty little thing like her to tidy up their house and cook their breakfast. Might even like havin' youngens around.

"The thing is, I could find a place for her where she was the boss of the house and could do everything the way she likes. Then if she didn't like that place, I'd find her somethin' else. You done your part takin' her in when she hadn't a mind past grievin'. Now I'm in position to find somethin' permanent."

"You reckon you'd find someone for here, that'd not need takin' care of?"

"Friend, you under-rate me, and also yourself. There's all kind'a ladies out there that are wantin' somethin' they can run themselves, and they'd be more likely to insist on takin' care'a you than you takin' care'a them. That'd be after you was furnishin' a cabin, firewood and maybe a few other little things that'd be easy for you."

Burley scrubbed a work-worn palm across his budding whiskers and nodded, "I like the sound's that. The way dimension lumber is down at Turner's Sawmill, I could have a two room cabin in place by fall. I learned a lot workin' for a builder over to Berryville a few years back. Those logs over 8 feet for cabins start takin' two men to get 'em up, men I ain't got. With them dimension boards, it's easy for one strong man."

Frenchie wisely picked his teeth with a twig. "Say, you need to let me pick up some tooth picks for you. That jerky gets stuck in teeth, leavin' a guy to worry it out with his tongue. Little things like that are remembered, you runnin' a business."

Burley nodded, absently. "The thing to do would be pick out what I'd need and have one of the Turner boys pull it up the mountain. I did plenty'a that myself, but now I ain't got time. I got apples turnin' red, and a cider press ordered over to Eureka Springs. Need more jugs, too."

Frenchie grinned inside. Burley's mind had already moved on. The world needed more Burleys for the way they could zero into one thought and carry it through, even if they have to have help thinking it up in the first place. There are always Frenchies to do the thinking!

Frenchie had one more bomb shell. "And say, Burley, with all the goin's on, I plum forgot to tell you something important. That gang of nothings decided to help themselves to a little milk one morning while back. Seems they wasn't thinking about my sister's dog, Joker.

"That dog is part wolf but she don't show it. All that shows in her is bloodhound and her size is about a dog and a half. She snuck

6 9

up on them youngens and just about scared the be-jabbers out of 'em. Flung milk cans to the wind and stampeded to the fence. Joker grabbed a mouth full'a shirt off the back of one of 'em. Kid must'a ripped the buttons off to get out of it. Shirt showed a bit of damage."

"A shirt...? Off a kid...?"

"Sure enough. And this'll give you the shivers. I rescued it just before Annie Jo tossed it in the suds. Can't stand dirty clothes... that girl! So I got it wrapped up and tucked in a corner in the van. I'll drop it off on you. I know you're a mite tore up right now but it might turn out handy."

"A shirt and a bloodhound. There's bound to be a use for that. I'm workin' on a plan but my plans don't often pan out. I'll let you know."

FRENCHIE MOVES ON WITH HIS PLAN

It had been two months since Pa died.

Frenchie had picked up a box of chocolates, the kind with a cherry inside, and headed for the farm. Annie Jo would rather have those chocolates than a visit from Santa Claus himself.

Smiling warmly, the excited and energetic new Annie greeted him effusively, sat him at the table with tea and ripped open the chocolates.

Frechie took a sip. "Sis, I got an idea while joggin' along back'a that horse. I got to thinkin' on what you've been through for the last few years and it took a toll on you. A burden is a burden, and just because you happen to be carrying something precious that you love, that doesn't mean it ain't heavy, and I was off on the road lettin' you carry the whole load."

"But I...."

Frenchie lifted a hand, palm toward Annie. "Now don't you be tryin' to put my train of thought off on a siding. It's hard enough to get my engine goin'. I know what you need and it isn't a box of chocolates. It's people. You've been stuck in this house for years and years only getting' to see folks here and there. No one has time for visitin', seems like.

"So now you can have a chance to see people and have a total change of scenery. There's a place I know of where someone's got a need, maybe just temporary but that would be all right. You might not want somethin' permanent quite yet.

"Well, this fellow has got himself so busy with this and that it's leavin' no time for what he really wants. Good fellow… lot older'n you and real sensible. All the things you know how to do are the things he needs done. Now, that'd mean you'd need to stay there all the time, but it's not so far that you couldn't be here on the farm when you wanted to."

"But… I'd have to leave?"

The van driver nodded. "Now don't tell me you haven't given thought to that, anyway. Seems I heard about a longing for a peek at the stores sometimes, and you even wondered how it'd be to live in Fayetteville. Now this place I got in mind ain't Fayetteville, but it wouldn't be leanin' over the bed of a dyin' man every minute. You'd have all kinds'a freedom."

Annie reached for another chocolate. "Now be sensible. Where'd I find a place like that, close enough to come and get vegetables from my garden?"

Frenchie grinned within. She'd walked right into his trap. "I'll tell you where. This fellow needs a bit of help for a while that is so many different things and so unique that if I looked from Eureka to Berryville all up and down this ridge I'd not find it. There ain't nobody like you, Annie Jo. And I ain't sayin' that just 'cause you're my sister. There wasn't never a thing throwed at you that you couldn't handle."

She was interested. He stared at her in a way that he seldom had. Her olive completion and coal black, shiny hair. Thick, soft and long, and very few persons had ever seen it as he had… hanging softly over her shoulders, seeming to ripple when she moved suddenly. Beautiful. She had no idea how she looked, even though she polished her mirror along with the other furniture, and used it to twist up her hair and cram it into that floppy bonnet.

Why, if she went down the streets of Fayetteville with her hair down and not wearing a bonnet, she'd have traffic snarled in a minute, horses squealing from twisted wagon wheels, and old fellows running across the street for a look to see if it was real.

There were questions whispered about her pa, and there seemed to be a consensus that he must have come from the native

Ouachita community. Didn't matter. Whoever it was that started her created tough stuff and put it in a beautiful container. Nice smile, too. Perfect teeth, and that was valued very highly. Dentists were a day's train ride away.

He had paused, and turned his gaze to the window. Beautiful day. Beautiful sister... and a beautiful idea of the present he was going to give her.

"Sis, I don't want an answer on what I just said, but I'd like you to ride along when I see old lady Donally. She asked me to pick up a potent for her from over to Eureka, and she really likes to talk. I'm not good at old-woman talk especially when they can't hardly hear, and you can talk with a fence post and get a answer."

Annie had planned to pull the ears of ripe corn, but if he needed a favor, she was the one to give it. Besides, she really liked to ride along in the van when it was handy for him to have her. It'd been a year... more like three or four... since she'd just dropped everything and did something pleasant.

At her nod, he suggested, "Go put on your bonnet and we're ready. Don't take time to twist up your hair. We're just going there and back." And now he was grateful for the old lady's potent, even though it took a couple of hours of his time to drop over and get it. So timely to think of it right now. Come to think of it, so many things in his life worked out that way. Wonder how that happened...?

Feeling bubbly and festive, Annie Jo grabbed up her pink bonnet and tossed off her apron. Kicking off her garden shoes, she pushed her toes into the patent leather pumps he had insisted she must have. She was ready.

"Stay," she told Joker. That meant the bloodhound was now in charge, and the canine had no doubts concerning her ability. Stepping up onto the clean porch, she flopped down with her back protectively against the door. Her way of saying 'goodbye.'

Annie perched on the jump seat, actually just a foot square stool behind the driver. At the signal, the muscular rumps of the stallions rippled with strength, and he pulled the loaded van from the yard and up the short drive to Ridge Road. It was a beautiful day and she saw that the possum grapes on the rail fence were ripening. It was always a fight to get any before the possums, coons and crows got them.

When he reached the curve just before Burley's place, he slowed the stallion to a walk. The sign she had seen him make, UNCLE BURLEY'S BISTRO, blazed forth. And there was the other sign, BURNT TREE JUNCTION, nailed to that cursed old tree stump.

There was the log wagon from Turner's Mill and a spry young fellow was perched on a rafter while Burley drilled a hole through it and the top of the wall, preparing for the 8 inch spike that would tie the roof rafter in place. Even Frenchie was impressed.

For a drifter, old Burley had really learned a lot. A little about a lot of things and apparently a lot about some things. He said that cabin would be ready in three weeks… that is, he meant 'in the dry with shingles on.' The paneled interior would take longer because the boards must be prepared.

Annie's sharp black eyes didn't miss a thing. "Look at that! He's buildin' hisself a house."

Behind his smile, he responded, "Well, fancy that!"

"I'd sure like to see it up close but that would be getting' in his way."

"Maybe we can stop on the way back. He should be off the roof by then."

Oh, Frenchie, he congratulated himself. *You're nothing but good!*

Zennia was on the job with Lily in her cradle board. Little Charlie was irritated that the 'van man' did not stop and have a goodie for him. But then he was back at the counter counting acorns all the way to 25. Then he was told to say the letters.

A deep breath and a hesitant voice, "A. B. C. D. Pitchfork."

"No, Charlie. It's not a pitchfork. It's an 'E'."

"Ma, just look. It's a pitchfork without a handle."

Zennia looked sternly into the eyes of her firstborn. "Charlie, today it's an 'E'."

"All right. Tomorrow it's a pitchfork. Next is the pitchfork that lost one of its fingers."

"No! It's called an 'F'."

Charlie's ma didn't even see Annie Jo wave hello. The hammering on the new cabin kept waking Lily. And what she really wanted to do was pick the possum grapes she saw hanging over the bluff.

She did, however, appreciate that she finally had an actual privy. There were a lot of trees, but a girl always likes privacy. The small house was in plain view from the stand.

She released Charlie from his educational endeavors and took the whining Lily from the tree. While she fed her… again… she hoped this time it would be quiet enough for the restless child to sleep.

Perched on the stool behind the counter, the warm softness of the baby and the gentle tug at her breast played music on the strings of her heart. The words of the van driver drummed themselves over and over in her mind.

A home she could take care of. That's what Sonny wanted to get for her. He had said she would be the queen of his castle and everyone would obey her wishes. She had smiled at that. The center person of five girls hardly had experience with being a queen… whatever that was.

It wouldn't need to be a big house, but it needed to be a fair size larger than her covered wagon. She could only imagine keeping Charlie inside and occupied for days at a time come winter weather.

And what would they eat? Eventually she would run out of money. She remembered the man said everything would be paid for and she would have animals to care for and a garden. She loved a garden.

It was almost as though that strange, helpful man knew the secrets of her heart. He told her to think about it and they would talk again, and she had hardly thought of anything else.

The tugging at her breast stopped and Lily's eyes were tight shut. A drool of milk escaped her mouth. Oh, if Sonny could only see his little girl! The van man said he would find a place where children were welcomed and loved. If only….

Zennia tucked the baby back into the cradle board and propped it against the side of the stand. She wiped away the small accumulation of dust (where did it all come from?) and shined the top of the honey jars.

Someone was stopping at the mailbox and turning off the road. A little girl of about ten came running toward her. She placed two dimes on the counter and picked up four pints of honey, tucking three under her arm against her chest and holding the fourth in her hand.

Looking up at Zennia she grinned. "Ma said to thank you." With a giggle she added, "Ma's gonna let me make cookies." Wheeling around on a heel, she dashed back to the buggy and the buggy driver waved and moved on.

Zennia watched. Red-gold hair in braids tied with green ribbons. She was Lily in ten years. Would there be dimes to let Lily buy honey just to play with? Maybe… if she moved to the house where she was needed.

The man must know the owner of the house very well. Maybe it was a friend of his. And there he was, turning into the short drive way. He wasn't alone. Oh, that was the neighbor who lost her father and needed someone to cry with. Well, she came to the right place because Zennia had a lot of recent practice at producing tears. Annie seemed like a really nice person. Maybe she'd live close to where Zennia was going to be.

Annie Jo left the van with a bouncy little jump. Hmmm, she seemed younger than last time. Why, she was hardly more than a few years older than Zennia, herself.

Annie Jo headed for the stand, reaching out to hug Zennia who had been such a help. She peeked at the sleeping baby and whispered. "I stopped to see what's getting' built. I'm a very nosy person."

Zennia grinned and answered, helpfully. "He's makin' a place for his help to live. Says it'll be in the dry in two weeks, and finished by fall. He's a fast builder."

Annie Jo nodded. "I'll bet it's for you! A nice, new house with room for your children. I'm happy for you."

Zennia shook her head. "Not for me. I'm goin' somewhere else to get a job takin' care of someone's house. I don't have time to keep up with my little boy and wash their clothes and still be here to sell to customers."

Her words whirled around in Annie's clever brain. She was always good at puzzles, knowing which piece went where. She could even work jigsaw puzzles upside-down. Zennia did not have time to meet the people, and she was going to be going somewhere else. Mr. Burley was making a new house for someone… had he already decided who?

Her glance took in the whole of the stand, placing non-existent shelves across the north end. Her agile mind added two more of the stools where Zennia had sat. And all across the lower back would be a box like a window box with a hinged lid that lifted for storage of back stock. She even knew the right words… Frenchie's back stock occupied what was his childhood bedroom.

She'd manage a rag rug like the one in the pantry to cover the dirt floor behind the counter. That would keep the person's shoes clean.

Blinking and shaking her head to clear her thoughts, she headed out to the two room cabin, now just a shell, but fast acquiring the outside walls. She looked up and saw the pitch of the roof that would allow a lot of storage above. A ladder stairway would allow a very cozy winter bed up there if one should want it.

The pine plank boards had been placed on the floor, a solid platform of logs placed in the opposite direction. There'd be no squeak on that floor. No sneaky winter drafts, either.

Sighting the floor from corner to corner, it looked like 16 feet square, each room. North windows were high and narrow. She saw them draped with yellow flowered chintz, and made to easily slide aside for light. A large window toward the road gave a view all the way from the burnt tree to the curve in the road to the south.

The door between the rooms was double wide, and Annie Jo saw it draped with something heavy as a quilt in the winter, with tie-backs on each side. Summer, the opening would be bare for more breeze.

Annie was unaware of her brother's eyes watching her every move, and even Burley who was splitting shingles from a cedar log with a shiny new hatchet. Also watching. All Annie saw was the new house that had never belonged to another woman. An open slate.

A clean sheet of paper, such as she had valued in her teens. A new sheet of paper had limitless possibilities and she alone could determine what appeared. She remember the way the paper had taken away her loneliness and she had filled it with her creations. HER creations.

She stood in the wide doorway between the rooms and felt the skin of her scalp tighten, sending shivers down her neck into her arms. Her heart pounded and her mouth seemed dry. She swallowed and swallowed again.

What was going on? She blinked her eyes tightly, and turned to the facing of the door. Raising her arms, she buried her face in her elbows and sighed a long, long sigh. Forget it. Some other girl had already mentally placed her furniture and laid her rugs. Someone else had already found a nice, flat, gray Arkansas rock for a front door step instead of a piece of wood.

Probably she was already making the curtains for the windows, and they would be the wrong colors for this size of room. She likely wanted the floors to be painted when they should be oiled to bring up the beautiful grain of the planks of white pine. She felt actual pain that this wonderful canvas, a whole sheet of paper, should be ruined.

Frenchie had strolled over to where Burley worked, and Zennia had returned to the stand and Lily. The van driver firmed his lips and stroked a knowing hand over his chin. Positively uncanny it was how things could happen, but often didn't. He knew people. He knew his customers because he studied them, so he could please them with what they wanted.

He had lived with Annie Jo for his whole life, and she had been his sister, mother, companion and advisor for years. He knew Annie Jo and his heart pounded with pleasure that he could give her a gift worth a lot more than a box of chocolates. This was a unique and once-in-a-lifetime situation, and he was lucky enough to have control of it. Pa would have said that every perfect gift came from above, and that it was more blessed to give than to receive. Pa was right. Certain to have been.

In this instance, Frenchie claimed all the credit the Power above would give him. He had put together this entire three way dance, and was now moving the puppets into place.

Sighing deeply, Annie lifted her head from her arms, squared her shoulders and headed toward him. She opened her mouth to speak, but turned instead to Burley.

"Mr. Burley, I suspect you already got help lined up that'll live in this little cabin, but I had to ask. If somethin' happens she don't want it, could you let me try…?"

Somewhat dumbstruck, Burley turned to Frenchie. The smug look on Frenchie's face would have out-done the look of the cat that ate the cream.

"Burley, this here lady is called Annie Jo and she's my sister. She's askin' for the job of running your stand and livin' in this doll house. Ordinarily she makes sense but right now she's purty much dumbstruck." Burley looked from the girl to the house to his friend.

"The thing is, Burley, you could look the world over and not find better help. Right now she's needin' something different to do, and she'd do you a good job until you found someone better."

Burley looked at Annie Jo... really looked. She wasn't no girl... like Miss Zennia. She had a look he loved. Determined. Knowing. He would almost see the wheels of her thoughts whirling. He may not know people as well as Frenchie, but he was no novice in sizing people up. He hadn't spent decades wandering and not learning anything.

Her confidence placed her near thirty, but her beautiful face could be any age. He could see the black, black hair billowing below her ruffle of her pink bonnet. Her cheeks were tinged with the flush of excitement of someone who knew EXACTLY what she wanted. And thought there was a chance that she would get it. Of all the qualities of a co-worker, that was one he valued most. Hem-hawing around wasted a sight of time.

And there she stood, waiting. "Miss... uh.. Annie. I would love to have you run my stand. I have no one else in mind. I hoped your brother knew of someone, but you would be even better than that. The job is yours soon as we get this house together. Two weeks...?"

"I could help. I could start oiling that floor, and... well, curtains... maybe? You got ideas what you want, you tell me and I could help."

Burley just stared, speechless. Frenchie came to the rescue.

"Annie Jo, better you decide what you want and he'll help you. He's got no way of knowin' that you've already made curtains for windows that don't have no glass yet. He don't know you've already put your cook stove by that south window where you can look out over the bluff at the lake."

He turned to Burley, "You don't know that she's remodeled the stand, too. She's put in shelves and a locker, and tidied up the place. She's noticed that the big north window gives a view of anyone approaching so she can be in place to serve them. Before this day is over, she'll have doubled the menu."

Burley just looked at Annie. Frenchie continued.

"I've found a place for Miss Zennia and it'll be ready in a week."

Annie Jo turned wide eyes to her brother. "She could stay at our house til then. That'd be perfect for her youngens. Don't you think?"

Frenchie frowned his thoughts. "I'll swear if that wouldn't be an even better idea. She'd just fit in there till she found somethin' she liked better."

"But I'd need a week to clean everything up for her."

Frenchie nodded, agreeably. "So it'll be ready in about a week, huh?"

Annie nodded, her mind already on curtains, varnished floors and a flat rock for a stepping stone.

THE RESTLESS GANG

A new note had made its way to Burley saying, "Tired of waiting. Do something."

Burley had answered, "I'm trying. Ike is my friend and I don't want him to get suspicious and start looking for your hide-out again."

Zennia had looked with wide eyes at Frenchie and said how would she know what she should do when she moved to the farm. Frenchie insisted that there were no rules. Annie would be gone, and he would use the house only for a storage room and maybe to sleep there sometimes… come winter. He assured her that Odus Bare Foot would do the milking twice a day and give her as much as she wanted each time.

She brightened and almost smiled. Milk for Charlie and later for Lily, and there would even be milk for her, and the meals. She was still apprehensive as it seemed too good.

Annie begged and received permission to put the linseed oil on the floors of the cabin. She hitched a pony to the dog cart and headed out. She borrowed minutes from the cleaning to paint the pine planks with the magic protection. The dull grain of the pine shone forth with burnished gold highlights and the light areas turned to antique ivory. She closed windows and doors tightly to keep away the dust until the oil seeped into the wood.

Two days later she appeared with buckets of thick lye soap suds, a broom and a mop. She sloshed the soapy water onto the treated floors and scrubbed it in with the bristles of her broom. Pushing out the water, she mopped it completely with soft cloths. Then she closed the windows and doors again to let the floor dry before the protective finish would be applied.

On this second trip, Joker came along, trotting beside the pony. Reaching the stand, she was met by the resident canine, Jumper. Joker approached, softly wagging her tail. She extended her sizeable nose toward Jumper who bristled slightly but returned the sniff. Joker was half again larger than Jumper, but she waited for him to make the first move.

Stalking on stiff legs, he circled her and sniffed pointedly, remaining still for her to sniff him. Then by seeming mutual agreement, the two canines settled onto the ground facing each other. Introductions now complete, they lay panting in the early July heat.

The dogs, while maybe not exactly friends, they were at least not competitors. Joker totally ignored young Charlie who played in a sandy spot of ground, and Jumper seemed to have no interest in Annie or her pony. There was no trespassing of territory… therefore, no reason to fight. And besides, the weather was much too hot for that much exercise.

The July heat brought out a restlessness in the gang of four. Their notes seemed to be getting them nowhere, so it was time to create a little excitement.

For instance, there was Old Pete Langley. As a youth, he had fought in the war of the brothers and had served himself proud. He was released with his own Henry Repeating Rifle that loaded multiple shot. The infantry loved the smaller rifle for convenience and the gunners liked the multiple shot. It was chucklingly said that it could be loaded on Sunday, so they could shoot all week.

Slight exaggeration, but it was a huge improvement on whatever came before. It was a great mark of favor to take away the valuable weapon and for those favored persons, it was a precious possession.

The Henry had kept them alive, and it would be treasured by them until they left the earth.

In addition to the gun, Old Pete received a generous pension of $7.00 a month… every month for as long as he lived. The whole community loved the old man, and were happy he was taken care of.

He built a house and farmed until he became too old, then he turned the farm over to his oldest daughter and her family. Olivia Langley Masters moved her family into the house, and at her pa's request, had built him a cabin not far away.

He had picked the spot, and it was close enough to see the house he had built and have meals delivered to him if he felt like it, but far enough away that sound did not disturb his naps.

The gang also knew this. So, what did the old man have to spend all that money on? Who said he deserved it, anyway, and shouldn't it be taken and spent by those who needed it? He was sure to have all that money stashed away, maybe in a sock under his mattress. Maybe in a cookie jar in his cupboard.

The gang of four discussed this situation, and assured each other that they needed and deserved the money more than the old man, so they must make plans to get it. It was not their fault they were still in Carroll County and causing trouble. All they wanted was the gun that was rightfully theirs now that they'd stolen it (fair and square) and killed the owner. If they'd been given the gun when they asked for it, they'd be down south in Madison County by now. They'd been promised, but they still did not have the gun so they couldn't go.

Of course, the farm house was dangerously close, and there were several dogs that slept in the barn, but it would just take care. They would be as silent as a thought as they sneaked in from downwind. They'd pick a night of the new moon with very little light.

They'd raise the window and slip through. No bigger than the cabin was, two of them could hold the feeble old man while the other two searched for the money. There was a chance he would be scared and tell them where it was, but likely not. It was said that he had fought bravely, and maybe he still thought he could outwit four strong, young men.

They made it to the window without being scented or heard by the dogs. The window went up smoothly, and the opening was large enough for them to enter without strain or the possibility of a sound. All was going well.

The old man was at that moment lying comfortably on his pillow, eyes open, looking at the ceiling in the pale reflected light from the window. He told himself that the angel who finally came for him would suddenly appear on that ceiling and he wanted to see that wonderful sight with his human eyes. He had said everything he had wanted to say on this earth, done what he wanted to do, and his emotional bags were packed for his final journey.

He might have heard the slight noise of the window if he had not first felt a change in the air… a faint current of air with the fragrance of the woodland. Turning his head a fraction toward the window, he saw the figures silhouetted as they entered, counting four in all.

Reaching silently with his left hand, he eased the Henry rifle from under the pillow beside him. Moving his bony, arthritic legs over the bed, he pushed himself up with his left hand… his right hand in place for a quick shot. Lowering his feet, he straightened his leg and his age-worn knee issued a resounding crack… as it was often wont to do.

The four moving figures jerked to attention, as did Old Pete. Knowing that the battle had started as surely as if the bugle had sounded, he pulled himself totteringly upright. Not wanting to kill… he'd done enough of that… he aimed low and his bullet sliced through between the upper thighs of both Slim's legs, just inches below his private parts. He screamed, but felt the slap of Robert's hand over his mouth.

Spike picked up the chair beside the bed, sloshing over the glass of water Old Pete always placed there. The glass crashed noisily against the flatiron beside the bed, the one that Pete used to warm his feet in winter. Shards of glass flayed out over the floor. Slim fell into them but was dragged away by Robert.

Spike grasped the back of the chair and swung it, crashing against the old man who fell, limp, back on the bed. Old Pete saw the shape of the chair coming toward him, but was amazed to feel no pain. He fell against the soft stuffed mattress and looked up at the reflected light. It happened!

There was the angel, just as he had been certain it would be. It glowed from a light within and extended its hands. He saw it all with his human eyes... what more was there to be alive for?

It was in the strong and loving arms of the heavenly being that Old Pete's last earthly battle had been won, and he was going home to eternal rest. With him, he carried the trophy of a life lived for his Master, and the trophy would be laid at his Master's feet.

Robert, eyes not adjusted to the darkness, decided they had to get out of there, and take the bony old body with them. Maybe folks'd think the old man lost his senses and walked out in the night. They'd dispose of him somewhere close.

Shorty had hauled Slim, now passed out from pain, to his strong back, and headed for the door that Spike held open. Then, on a sudden impulse, Spike ducked back and fumbled for the Henry... hadn't they needed another gun? Dashing through the door he caught up with the others... Shorty carrying Slim, and Robert with Old Pete's remains over his shoulder.

The Langley's pasture had a lot of huge boulders, most of them the size of an outhouse, and the worn-out body was dumped within the crevasse of two of them. It'd take a while to find him, and they could have Slim patched up and the horses on the road by then. The darkness would shield them until they put some distance behind them and the destruction.

Before they reached their current hideout, Slim began to come around, groaning from the pain. Carrying one of their number slowed them down and it was daylight before they were safely out of sight.

The gunshot merely damaged the inner thighs with torn flesh but no broken bones. The gang, however, did not have bandages, but a towel was torn to make a tourniquet of sorts until the bleeding stopped, though it was doubtful that he would be able to straddle a horse.

Rather, they decided, they'd stay put for the day, and come night they would put him across the horse, dead-man style, and slip away. A dead-man-carry in daylight would attract far too much attention.

Back at the farmhouse, the scuffling and activity had attracted the dogs that tore through the distance from the barn, barking their lungs out.

Douglas Masters jammed heels into his boots and grabbed his gun and his flashlight. Johnny, a well-built fourteen year old, was right behind him, taking the flashlight so Pa could better handle the gun.

They joined the snarling, barking dogs at the cabin, pausing at the still-open door. Johnny stepped in and flashed the light around. "He ain't here, Pa. Speck he could have wandered out, not knowin' where he was."

Douglas sized up the room in the dimming morning light. No, he had not gone. A wandering mind had never been Pa's problem. The Henry was not on the bed and he would not have taken it out, anyway.

His shoes were still by the bed, and glass splinters were everywhere. So was blood, seeping stickingly into the cracks of the flooring. He had been taken, or something, and likely been killed. This could only be the work of the marauding gang and for that, he would need help.

Back at the house he quickly dressed, telling Johnny to grab whatever biscuits were in the warming oven, and get dressed. He'd get the horses.

In a bare twenty minutes, they were headed to the nearest readily available help, in the person of one who had experience with the gang.

Galloping past the roadside stand, he yelled, "BURLEY COLLINS! WHERE ARE YOU?"

Burley, tucked into his bedroll beside the smokehouse tent, pulled himself out and answered.

In a pair of sentences, Burley knew the worse. Nodding, he woke Annie Jo who was asleep on the floor inside her cabin, ready to get an early start on the varnishing.

"Miss Annie, we need your trackin' dog. We got trouble, but we got that shirt your dog pulled off that gang. Can you make your dog know we need her to go with us?"

Annie Jo gouged knuckles into her sleep-filled eyes, and attempted to wrap her mind around the problem. Joker was needed. So, how did she get her to understand?

Burley took the shirt from inside his bedroll, protected in the sack where Frenchie had tucked it. Joker stood beside Annie, as taut and intent as a bow string. Something unusual was afoot and she meant to see what it was. Her canine mind was whetted sharp as a razor.

Burley pulled the plaid shirt from the sack, and Joker's long-hanging ears quivered and shook. Joker waved her nose back and forth to center on the offending scent, and snarled, leaping at Burley.

Burley's reflex jerked him aside as he tossed the shirt. Joker pounced on the shirt, snapping her efficient jaws.

Annie Jo moved toward her dog and hugged her. She took the shirt from the dog and handed it back to Burley, who really didn't want it, but held it gingerly between thumb and finger.

Annie patted the bloodhound and told her, "Go!" To the men, she said, "Be ready to ride. Maybe she'll follow."

Brownie was grazing nearby, and Burley jumped on her, still holding the shirt. "Joker! Here, Joker!" Amazingly, the dog loped after the three horses, her eyes on the shirt, its colors bright in the early morning light.

Annie Jo stared after them. "I don't believe it! I really don't believe it."

The Langleys' lane was near, and the loping dog kept up well all the way to the house. Burley still wasn't confident. The dog had no training or practice… but she was all they had. She was enticed inside the strange house, sniffed at the bed, the chair and the blood. She looked back at the men for further orders.

They called her out of the house, and started to circle in the small yard. The dog trailed along, nose down. Then a soft snort, a woof and a lift of her head. Swinging back and forth, she centered on the scent, and started out loping through the brush.

By now the men could see the tracks, broken sticks and laid-over grass. The dog was going right. In minutes, she found the remains of Old Pete, but was not satisfied.

The Masters' pair groaned and Johnny swallowed hard. They both knew that time was not important to the old man, now, so they turned their attention to the dog who was again casting for a scent.

Burley was speechless. Some things just had to be born into wild creatures. Tracking instinct she would have gotten from both the wolf and bloodhound, and an understanding of humans from the recent ancestors of the bloodhound.

But how can she know so quickly what the humans wanted? Burley just shook his head, happy that she did, and they were still on trail. From here, even he could track, but this was wonderful experience for the dog, and would give her confidence. The four had made no effort the cover their trail.

Obviously, from the trail, they could tell one of them was being carried. So there was a wound and the blood must have been his and not the old man's. The sun was peeping over Echo Mountain when they came onto what had been the hideout. A horse stood tethered near the mouth of the cave under the ledge. The cave was smallish, but showed having been occupied.

Johnny held up a hand, palm outward. He'd sneak closer and see what was going on. Slim was seated, both legs hastily bandaged above the knee, and resting on one knee was his hand with a gun aimed outward. But even Slim knew the score, and read the eventual outcome. Wounded, cornered and being one gun against three, he put it quietly on the ground and looked at his captors.

Within minutes, he was strapped across his horse, stomach on the saddle, feet and head hanging down... the only way he could ride and not break open his wound.

Joker was not satisfied. She nosed in circles and looked at Burley for help. He had no idea what to do for her, but he joined her and widened the circle.

By now with a bit of discussion, it was decided Johnny would go back with the wounded man and his pa to get a fresh horse and Burley's Brownie and catch up to the gang. It shouldn't be hard, now.

Doug Masters had every intent to allow the wounded man a short rest from being head down, then his hands would be tied, he would be put in a buggy and hauled toward Berryville and Ike. He would pick up help on the way to go back and bring in the body of his father-in-law. It was not a job for Olivia.

Johnny caught up to Burley in the valley between the Ridge and the beginning of Echo Mountain. A rushing stream bubbled through the rocks with white water. Joker lost the scent at the water's edge and looked back inquiringly at Burley. Burley advanced to the dog speaking softly and encouraged her to follow him back the way they had come. She didn't want to, but she was young and attuned to humans, so she allowed herself to be led.

The clever gang had walked up the rushing creek, and there was no telling how far. It would be a huge risk of time to cross the stream and try to follow. The gang was not dumb. After all, they'd been able to elude the law for several months.

Johnny was having difficulty managing the day. It seemed that Mr. Burley was stranger enough for him to admit his weakness. "Yeah, old granddad and me, we was buddies. It was me takin' his meals most of the time, or walkin' with him if he wanted to come to the table. He had times of bein' unsteady… like… you know? So times we was talkin' he'd tell me about the war. Same stories a lot of the time, but I loved 'em every time. I loved hearin' 'im talk. He said to me one time, 'John, boy, you bein' the onlyist boy grand youngen I got, seemed like my Henry outta go to you. Your ma and pa know my feelin's.'"

After a few more plodding steps, he added, "I reckon now it won't happen. I was hopin' to have that gun for the times I'd miss havin' his words."

Burley took a few more steps, then stopped and clutched Johnny by the shoulder. "Don't you be thinkin' like that. You're gonna get that gun back and that's a promise."

Johnny yanked a red bandana from his hip pocket and turned away to dab his eyes. "Law, thanks, Mr. Burley! I'd be so obliged…" He gulped away his embarrassment, and crammed the bandana back it his pocket.

Now, however, with yet another murder, the law would be back on the case. Johnny trudged with Burley back to the Langley house. The gang was now down to three, and they were heavily armed. The gun left with Slim was the 22mm. The rifle, Sonny's gun and the

Henry were with the gang, and there were possibly more hidden here and there.

Burley headed Brownie toward the bluff, discouraged and depressed. He really didn't have the time to be doing the law's work. His cider press would be waiting over in the depot in Eureka Springs. It was time to go get it. It would mean getting a bigger wagon… and… well….

Joker trotted along beside Brownie and also seemed discouraged. She did not get to do what she was certain the humans wanted her to do. But one thing was for sure… what she did was right and the humans praised her for it.

Back in his camp behind the waterfall he took out his tablet and wrote: "See what happens when you don't wait? I wanted to see you all safe and able to go on with your life. Now I have to make another plan."

He'd deliver it to Hidden Cave because that seemed to be their idea of a mailbox.

MOVING DAY

Annie Jo had brought a quilt and a pillow, and staked her pony on the grassy bluff. This would be an overnighter. Not so much that there was work ready to do, but she just had to see how it was to sleep there. Good planning, because somewhere around midnight, her mind switched the kitchen to the front so she could see the road, and the bedroom/parlor to the south with a view of the bluff, and changed the parlor curtains to a sky blue, maybe with tiny dots.

Two days ago she had taken time from her farmhouse cleaning (how dirty could it be, anyway?) because Frenchie insisted on taking her to Eureka Springs to pick out her furniture. He didn't often go that far with his route, so this was a good opportunity.

On the way back, she had perched on the stool behind him and rode along silently, bending to the sway of the van on the gravel road. Her brother thought she might just be tired when she declined to step out when he took care of several stops. Eyes closed and leaning against the spice and liniment cabinet, she pictured the iron stove she had just ordered, sized perfect for the north wall.

And there was the table that was perfect for 3 or 4 persons, or could be expanded with one or two inserted expansions to accommodate 7 or 8. Sometime in the winter, she would paint flowers on the expansion boards.

Then, she thought of the settee. If it would only be as lovely as it was in the catalog! Iron work in shiny curves and twists, and the filigree background had vines and flowers intertwined. She might even paint the vines green and flowers yellow or something. That was for later. And the two chairs that matched.

The thing was, with those three pieces there was no room for the bed that matched, so she'd just be sleeping on the settee. It was a nice size and she would make a bedroll that could be wound up in the daytime. The floor had turned out beautifully, and Mr. Burley said she could varnish the wall panels when they were ready.

Mr. Burley sure was good with his hands on wood. Yes… he'd make her wall sconces the way she sketched them. Little triangles held up by a brace that was another triangle. And he'd attach a bookshelf to the wall where she wanted it. It would be braced by the same little triangles.

Come winter, he'd have time to make other little niceties. And a lean-to kitchen if she wanted it.

Well, not a kitchen, maybe, but a place for the beautiful bed and matching stand. And her chest of drawers from the farm.

"Miss Annie Jo, you wantin' another room on the cabin, you got only to say so. 'Course, to do a good job of it, I'd need to wait till after the cider, the butcherin' and the fencin' in for the animals."

"I'll wait! But that means orderin' the bed to make sure they still have it. My brother can store it a few weeks."

Burley nodded, mentally scrounging for a way to say he would pay for her furniture, but it seemed to be a dealing that should be done man to man. Frenchie had told him that she had money, and that she knew what she wanted. This way, if the job didn't work out, she'd still have what she wanted.

….If the job didn't work out…? Where did that come from…? It was a scary thought. Miss Annie Jo had been coming to work with her hair done up on top like woman did it, but before long, her efforts began to slide toward her ears... without the bonnet to keep it in place.

Frenchie did say, though, that his sis required being kept in drawing pads and pencils. "Without them she gets mean and dangerous," he insisted. He grinned his charming grin and added, "Also, she'll demand bones from your jerky for that ugly beast of hers."

Burley glanced over at the 'ugly beast,' and thought she looked pretty good to him. And a drawing pad (whatever that was) and pencils were a cheap price to pay for the sight of her hurried step, and hairpins on the window sill, meaning her hair had slipped down. Again. Could he count on that being a regular occurrence...? One could hope....

Frenchie left in his van, and Burley just stood there. There was so much to think on.

Such as when he kept trying to think of something to ask Annie or tell her so he had a reason go to wherever she was working. Before the hairdo slid too far, it became a nuisance so she yanked out the pins and piled them on the window sill. Hair. He shook his head in disbelief that anything so beautiful could possibly be close enough for him to see it every day. And just imagine the waste of having it tucked inside that cloth cap.

Flowing over her ears and hanging down in front when she bent over... and in a sheath like a cape on her back. Glossy as the wings of a crow, and wavy as a field of spring grass... all the way down below her shoulder blades.

He hired not only a wagon from Turner's Mill, but one of the Turner boys to go pick up his cider press and all the furniture now in the Santa Fe depot in Eureka Springs. It was worth the extra money, so he could hitch Brownie and the stray horse to the log chain and drag up enough logs for a miniature smokehouse. Tents were not weather safe and they let a lot of the fragrant smoke leak out.

While he was at it, Simon Turner would pick up a dozen more gallon jugs. More if he had room in his wagon. The apples were coming on by the bushel, and he needed to get that cider on the market. The sterilized juice, bottled along with a half teaspoon of salt and a whole teaspoon of cinnamon would be saleable in a week from the day of bottling. Good strong cork and it stayed sweet for weeks. Maybe for months… in the back of the cave.

Then the crushed apple leavin's could be fed to the pigs this year, but next year he might turn them into vinegar. Folks always ran out of vinegar for pickle making.

Miss Zennia was all wide eyes and nervous jitters as she gathered a few necessities and climbed in the van with Charlie and Lily. Was this the right thing do to… but what other offer did she have?

At the farmhouse, she gazed in wonder at the size of it, at the number of outbuildings and the garden, fenced in animal-tight. "Mr. uh… what part of this is mine to care for?'

Frenchie turned to her… puzzled. "Why, all of it you want. Annie Jo has moved, and sometimes I sleep here in my storage room, especially in the winter, but that won't need to be a bother for you."

Zennia was a realist. She was determined to learn what was expected of her, and she couldn't afford any mistakes. "You want I should take care of the whole house, garden and see to animals and… everything…?"

Frenchie groaned, inwardly. Oh, what a mistake he'd made. "Oh, no. When you need help, I'll get it for you. I wouldn't expect…."

Squaring her shoulders bravely, she waded in. "What I'm sayin' is, it won't be no trouble to me to take care of all of this. I just wanted to know what you wanted me not to do. And what part belonged to Annie."

Frenchie swallowed his relief. He forced his arms to his side to keep them from hugging her. Maybe someday, but not soon. "Annie will be comin' here with her washin' on times she needs to, and she'll want this and that from the garden, like tea plants, until she has her own. That's all."

Zennia managed a small, weak smile and a nod. "I'll like seein' Annie when she can come."

That just about took care of it, and she removed her bonnet, allowing her bouncy red curls to escape. Picking up Lily, she marched into HER house like a queen to her throne. Frenchie ached to follow her through the doors, but forcibly restrained himself. That was for later. If things went right.

The tiny smokehouse took most of the day, the logs needing to be sawed eight feet long and notched to almost fit together. Some smoke escaping was good… it let more flavor surround the meat.

Annie Jo came along behind the load of furniture, prepared to stay. With her was the beloved Bible that still had the smell of the bedroom, the medication for his cough, and the scent of his hands. It was the fragrance of love, security, knowledge. It was a memory of the only pa she knew, her protector, her friend, her teacher, her companion, and then her patient, her responsibility, her dedication and finally her loss. She hoped that his scent would always overpower that of the old, worn leather, grown soft with use.

Her first responsibility, of course, was the roadside stand. Her job. She attacked it with her broom to move the accumulated road dust. There really wasn't much to sell, but the coming cider would make a big difference.

Watching the dust rise and drift away, she remembered a commandment given to the disciples as their teacher prepared to leave: "Go ye into all the world and preach the gospel to every creature." (Mark 16.15)

When they reached that part, she had asked Pa, "How can I go into all the world…?" And Pa had looked at her and smiled. "Don't worry, little one. Until God tells you how to do it, just let the world come to you."

She had been satisfied with the answer, but of later years wondered how the world was going to find her on the farm in a small state, and not even close to another part of the world. So… now, did she have her answer? Was this her opportunity? If so, God would have to let her know how.

She lifted the worn book onto the shelf (just call me Burley) had made just for it. It looked so good there, and so right that she just sighed and smiled.

Then she picked up the blue fabric with white clouds and colorful butterflies. So perfect for the high, shallow north windows. Then a solid blue for the window that looked out onto the road.

Road! There was someone coming. It was a buggy, and a well dressed man approached the stand just as she reached it. Hurried steps. Flying hair.

"Read your sign. I have a young man of ten who says he's starving. I wouldn't want that to happen so… what do you have?"

The starving young man took a flying leap from the buggy. "Look, Pa! They say they got jerky! I love jerky. And look, Pa, honey still in its little pens. I like to chew the gum they make the pens out of."

'Pa' grinned, indulgently. "We'll have a package of that jerky, and a jar of honey. No, make it two jars." He smiled, put a quarter on the counter and turned to go.

"Sir, your change…"

"Keep it and thanks," and he was halfway to the buggy. Annie Jo looked at him and at the quarter. He was due… what… about a dime back…? Hmmmm.

While she was there, she dusted the counter and the tops of the jars. She checked the cool water in the jug and the dried tea leaves, some already soaked the way Zennia had told her she sold it. Good idea. Leaves didn't steep good in cold water.

While she tidied up, horse hooves sounded on the flint gravel. The rider drew up with a "Whoa, there." He leaped to the ground and strolled over. "I'm so dry, I'm spittin' sandhills. I was even thinkin' on makin' a trip down to the lake. Gimme a glass of tea. Spearmint if you got it. And a cookie."

"Yes, sir. That'll be six cents."

"Wait, I'll take the glass along and another cookie… how much?"

Annie added 6 to the nickel for the glass and three cents for another cookie. "Fourteen cents."

Fishing a dime and a nickel from his pocket, he tossed it to the counter, took giant steps back to the horse, and managed to leap into the saddle still holding the glass upright. "Git up, there. Let's go."

While Annie watched, he waved the hand with the glass of tea, still not spilling any that she could see. Exciting few minutes. She popped the coins into the jar and loved the sound of the jingle, music to the beat of hooves of the road.

She hurried to the house for her pad and pencil. There ought to be other things she could quickly create to produce that wonderful jingle. Candy, for instance, nut-filled fudge and honey-drop suck-on candy being her specialties. Also, caramel popcorn made with honey.

How much honey did he have down there, anyway? Would coffee made fresh be profitable? And those little flat cans of sardines... don't young men like those especially?

Cans. She ran an inventory through her mind of the canned items Frenchie carried. Pork and beans, for sure. She'd need a can opener, and serve them in the can. Fellows who did hard work liked them. Peanuts. Would Burley's land grow them? What about those rice cakes with peanut butter she made for herself and her brother when they were small? Messy, but delicious. That'd mean paper napkins. How much did they cost? That'd need to be figured.

She had gone to sleep thinking of new items for the menu. They must be planned for folks on the move... no one would ever say, "Let's go have a meal at the roadside stand." Her customers would be 'spur of the moment' occasions. She was now awake, having bumped her elbow against the iron flowers on the back of her settee. Granted, the settee was not as comfortable as her old bed, but it more than made up for the minor discomfort in looks. It was stunning, and she could always move her bedroll to the floor.

Leaving the menu temporarily, her thoughts moved to the 'Go ye' part of God's commandment, and Pa saying if God did not prepare a way for her to go, then He must have meant for the world (at least part of it) to come to her.

The man in the buggy read her sign, and it only said 'Uncle Burley's Bistro.' What if there was a sign that said more? Maybe a temporary sign that could be changed to keep the subject fresh. That was something to think on.

On the farm she had highly valued something, ANYTHING, that could provide thought for her under-stimulated mind. Here, it seemed that new ideas crowded each other for space... and time.

"GO YE INTO ALL THE WORLD..."

The gang of three saw the clouds building, and headed for the nearest cave. They were armed with a quart jar of peaches from someone's cellar, two onions and several cucumbers from a garden and a dozen hot rolls that had been cooling on a windowsill. Occasionally, window sills produced pies, but buns were also nice.

They ate well and bedded down until the rain let up. Shorty crawled into his corner, huddled in his own filthy clothes and sighed himself to sleep. There had to be a better way to live but he didn't know how to get from here to there. Maybe he'd hop the Santa Fe and ride down to the next county. He'd heard of those who did it.

He finally dozed and dreamed that he was again carrying Slim and blood was running cold down his back and into his shoes. How did little old Slim have so much blood? He shook himself awake and sat up. A crevasse in the cave room was spilling water on his head and feet, and he decided he'd had enough.

Feeling in the dark for whatever gun he could reach, he eased out of the cave and headed downhill which he knew would take him to the railroad eventually. Maybe he could hitch as far south as Crawford County. He thought he had folks there.

There were things a novice railroad hobo should know, and one of the things was that those bars on the tops of box cars were handholds, and were put there for a purpose. No one had told Shorty.

At the watering tank, the engine huffed to a stop and Shorty climbed the convenient ladder up the back side of the car. Hey… that was simple. He seated himself comfortably and thought he'd take off his shoes and wring the water from his socks. Surely they'd be on the road in minutes.

The whistle sounded and the engine roared, moving in jerks to take the 'play' from the couplings so it could pull forward. Shorty had good balance, and the jerks only served to alert him. He'd soon be on the road and never more would he join a 'gang.' Then, suddenly all cars were in tune so in a mighty huff, the engine pulled away from the water tower.

Shortly sat humped over and tying his second shoe when the car where he sat received the force of the tug. A hefty tug. He threw out his hands for balance, but found himself flying through the air on the uphill side of the track.

Momentum rolled him toward the iron drivers and the glistening rails. What was later found would not have been identifiable if it was not for the remains of the gun in his overall pocket. Needless to say, Shorty never did join another gang.

Robert and Spike were left, and should have taken warning, but they did not often do what they should. Robert wrote another note and attached it to Burley's mailbox.

"When are you going to tell me your plan? I'm about ready to do something myself."

Burley was quick with his answer:

"Don't you think you done enough? Slim hurt, Shorty dead. Which one of you wants to go next? I'm waiting to hear about the Henry."

Burley put the pieces of his cider press together and dumped a bucket of apples in his vat of water. Didn't need bugs in the cider and there would be some to remove. Sure to be.

He tossed in the first bunch and turned the lever. Neat little gadget it was. Juice came pouring out the spout into another vat he would use to sterilize the juice before bottling. Color sort of a rosy gold.

He dipped in a cup and tasted the raw product. Not bad, hey! Coming all the way to the cabin (empty) for a tall glass, he went back to the cave and filled it... then stood wondering. What was happening to him, anyway? A year ago he would not thought of taking a glass of cider to the 'help.' And it wasn't just for a chance to see her hair down. Maybe....

He'd always considered that female women folks were sort of an alien species created to do what they did best... produce babies and food. Both were necessary and deserved respect. A time or two he speculated of how it would be to actually have one of them, but his thoughts ended negatively. Sort of died on the vine. He'd really been pushed into taking Annie, but he'd needed immediate, at least temporarily, assistance. With Zennia gone, he did admire the clever way Frenchie gave his sister something to do, and managed to get Zennia and her babies into his own house.

Come on, Burley told himself. *If she don't like fresh apple juice, I reckon she'll tell me.* He trudged back to the bluff and found her seated on the stool behind the counter writing something. Hair hanging over her shoulders and a sparkling look in her eyes... like she just thought of something that pleased her.

Silently he handed her the glass and she looked, sniffed and sipped. "Say, this is wonderful! How soon do I get to sell some?"

He thought a minute. "Now? Before it's sterilized in the jug?"

"Why not? Why not bring a peck or so of apples. If they don't sell, I'll eat 'em. Maybe make fried apples for supper. You like fried apples? You'd like mine. I'll put your name in the skillet and you can see."

When he returned with a jug of fresh juice and a quantity of the fruit, she had printed on her paper,

FRESH APPLE JUICE.

2 GLASSES 5 CENTS

She tied the notice around the jug and set it prominently on the counter with the apples.

Burley tore his eyes from her hair, the way she tossed it back while she worked. Each toss created glistening ripples all the way to the end. Back at the press, he pushed enough apples through to make four jugs, and had brought them to a boil in the jug. Corking would come when they cooled. Good day's work if they actually sold for a quarter (20 cents if you brought your own jug.) Jugs were so bulky to transport.

Annie looked them over, tapped a finger on her lips and suggested, "I think a quarter, and then ten cents deposit for the jug. That might make some people want to use it up and bring that jug back for more? What'da'you think?"

He thought it was a wonderful idea. A breeze lifted her hair. Also wonderful.

Next person on the road was an older couple in a small buggy generally called a 'courtin' buggy.' They sat close together, seeming to enjoy themselves and each other.

He helped her down from the buggy, and she tripped across the gravel to the stand. Motioning Annie closer, she asked, "I find myself needin' the Necessary Room. May I?"

She pointed delicately toward the log privy located about fifty feet back. She continued. "Honey, you get older, you'll see how it hurts the knees when there ain't no bench for holdin' ya up." With sly grin and a twinkle, she made her way back without waiting for permission. No one ever refused use of a privy.

The little old man watched until she was safely on her way, and then he took a seat at one of the picnic tables. "I saw your sign there, sayin' 'I will give you rest. Matt 28:11.'" With a grin he added, "Thought I'd take you up on it."

Annie Jo's heart pounded. The first person of the world who came to her! Just like Pa had said it might happen. She quickly responded, "Do you know who said it?"

"Sure do. It was Jesus, and because of that, I managed to get to be 67 years old. I rest when I can, and let Him help with my burdens. Say, is that apple juice in the jug? I can't hardly read it from here."

"Yes, sir. Squeezed today. From apples like these. Tall glasses, two for a nickel."

"Just happen to have a nickel. Fill up a couple'a them glasses. That way I'll make a hit with Mamie."

She brought the glasses to the table just as the little lady returned from her errand. "Oh, look, honey, what this darling man has bought for me. Married 50 years and he's been spoilin' me for all that time!"

Annie took the nickel and went back to her stool, elbow on counter and chin in her palm. Imagine! Fifty years and they can still talk like that.

They sipped their juice and talked, commenting on the stand, the huge oak trees that created a good breeze. About the apples and the dog. "Didn't your cousin Calvin have a dog that looked like that?"

They left with a dozen of the apples, and Annie banked another nickel. She watched the small buggy move out of sight, and sighed, happily. What verse could she use tomorrow…? That'd take thought and she just loved to think.

The sun was lowering when she counted the day's take. $1.78. She giggled with excitement. She'd get to do this just about every day that it wasn't raining. Way up into October, maybe. This was just the first full day, and word would get around. It always did… good or bad!

She put on a clean apron and carved a generous portion from the ham being smoked in the new smokehouse. Diced, it would be perfect. Wasn't cured yet, but no matter, it wouldn't last the evening. Steaming a small kettle of brown rice, she dumped it into the browned and sizzling ham dices and stirred the other skillet, turning the apple slices. A dash of salt and a generous sprinkling of cinnamon. Lid back on to steam and mix the flavors.

Burley was washed up and ready when she called. It was such fun to have someone else at the table, like when little brother could manage it. Burley sniffed and eyed the food. It was enough to make his head swim… that and the lady in the white apron… shiny black braid hanging over one shoulder.

Annie's little table was so small that if Burley really stretched out his feet, they would surely bump Annie's. That would be unforgiveable. He knew that much about women, and he tucked them tidily under his chair.

After a comfortably full stomach and a relaxing half hour with a cup of steaming tea, he thanked her and excused himself.

He had a few evening chores before he could retire to the comfort of Zennia's little covered wagon. A tiny bit crowded, but better than the cave. Sonny had done a good job making things that folded down and pushed up. After all, he'd expected to be there with Zennia and Charlie, and maybe the baby for most of the summer while he found a place for them in town.

Zennia. He stared out over the bluff thinking that less than a month back, he had been concerned that she had enough to eat, and what he should do about it, and now he was wondering if he would be invited back to Annie's table… and if so, how often.

Seeping into his brain was the fact that, though women and girls may still seem to be an alien race, they were not to be grouped together as being all alike.

Well, that was food for thought, but right now it seemed to choke him. What if he did the wrong thing? Well, she had mentioned milk. He was not ready for cows yet, but a pair of goats would do a really good job of trimming away the undergrowth and brush.

Heading down the rocky path toward the mouth of the cave, he gave a crooked smile to the sight of a picture in his head. As a ten to fifteen year old, he had done the dirtiest jobs on the river for pennies. Lots of ships, boats and rafts.

He saw a lot of things, but one of the most impressive might have been the large crafts of many sorts that just could not seem to maneuver in close spaces, or take themselves out into the current. They just floundered and raced their engines until a tug boat the size of an outhouse pushed against their stern or maybe pulled their tow rope to straighten their rudder.

And now. Here he was, like a big old efficient workhorse being nudged in the rump by a pony. Unable to see ahead without a push from behind. But what a lovely pusher had come into his life. That was a change!

PREACH THE GOSPEL TO EVERY CREATURE

Today was hot. Of course August in northern Arkansas is usually hot, but this was a heat that sent waves shimmering up from large rocks and hard ground, and the spring grass was withered brown.

Annie Jo put on her coolest dress, a pink dotted-swiss with loose ruffled sleeves. No collar. Sleeves and neckline were trimmed with a narrow white lace like that looked like it had been hand-tatted.

Her tablet was laid out before her ready to accept her verse for the day… the subject of her preaching 'to every creature.' Today she wanted to mention God by name.

Hey, how about 'God is love…'? So simple. (I John 4:8.) For people who belonged to God, He was a member of their family. For those who did not know him, He was love. His love was so huge that He could forgive anything that they did. He could forget it and toss it 'as far is the east is from the west.' (Psa 103:12) Say, that would make a good one for tomorrow!

A lady in a tiny buggy barely made for two people if they were small came by. She was dressed in pink, and wore a straw hat with flowers. As she rode, she fanned herself to make a little breeze.

"Gee, there," her small voice spoke to the animal, which then turned obediently to the right. "Whoa!" and the buggy came to a halt.

A tiny lady eased herself carefully and slowly to the buggy step and then to the ground. Annie wondered if she should rush to help… or would that embarrass the lady? But she made it.

"Honey," she began. "Could I trouble you for a little drink? It's so hot and dry out there and we've been visiting my friend who is sick."

Annie Jo drew in a breath. "We have tea and cider, but then we have plain water, too. What can I get you? You could sit over under the shade if you want, and I'll bring it."

The old lady turned and faced the scrap of paper on the tree. GOD IS LOVE, it said. She paused, raised her hand to her mouth and bowed her head. She shook her head slowly from side to side if saying 'no' and went to the table. "I'll take cider, honey, if you please."

Annie brought the drink and put it before her, seating herself opposite. There were tears following the wrinkles down the side of her face. Her skin looked as thin as tissue paper and layers of wrinkles outlined her eyes.

"Honey, that paper. If God was not love, I think I could not stand another day on this earth. My friend is so ill her family is praying for her to be allowed to go, and I think their prayers are being answered. I am sure I'll never see her again. Her pain and her family's pain is so great, we think we cannot make another day. I held her hand and talked, but she did not hear me. I knew I was talking to myself. I think she was already gone, but her body just didn't know it yet."

Taking a lace hankie from her sleeve, she dabbed at the tears pooled in her eyes.

Annie had no idea what she should do next. She just sat and watched, her hands on the table, palms up. The lady sniffed and looked up. "I used to stop here on occasion for jerky, but there were no notes on the tree. Sometimes folks need encouragement to just cry sad or happy tears. I am so glad God is actually love, and I know where Mamie is. Perhaps her body will release her breath tomorrow."

She picked up the glass of cool cider and sipped. Sniffed again and dabbed her eyes, then sipped again. "Honey, you don't have an idea of how much you helped me. I need to be getting on, now, or my people will be worried."

She pushed against the table and stood, turning toward the buggy. Her pony stood with his head down, breathing into the dust.

"Ma'am, I have some water for your horse. I'll get it while you climb aboard." The thirsty animal slurped and gulped, and drained the bucket. She removed the bucket from his mouth and saw the lady's hand outstretched to her.

She put a coin in Annie's hand and told her animal to 'git up.' Annie watched until she was out of sight, standing and holding the coin. Then she frowned with dismay that she had not told the lady a nickel covered two glasses of cider, but when she dropped the coin in the jar, she saw it was a quarter.

Later, a small boy wanted to know how God could be love and also be God. Annie thought a minute. "Well, you are a boy, but you are also suntanned all over. That makes you brown and also a boy. And I'll bet sometimes you're dirty, and also a boy. Isn't that right?"

The boy giggled.

BROTHER PHILEMON DARKHORSE: PREACHER PHIL

Annie Jo sat in the stand, ready should someone come along. She was using her time with a bucket of greens and a bucket of water. Each leaf of the lamb's quarter, poke sallet, wild lettuce and dandelion was examined thoroughly for any tiny creatures hiding in the crevasses. The high water table under the bluff created a salad of great variety and free for the picking.

The note on the tree had simply said, "...Not one of them shall fall..." and there had been two individuals who stopped to ask what 'one' was she referring to. With sparkling eyed excitement, she explained how important everyone was to God, and no sparrow fell to the ground without His attention.

Also very few of them knew that God had counted all the hairs on their heads. Always an interesting fact.

All the greens cleaned and tossed in a pail to be ready to cook for supper, another passerby turned in. It was a three animal caravan, led by a magnificent black stallion and followed by two donkeys loaded to their limits.

Sitting on the stallion was a tall man in a felt hat, almost clean white shirt and tie. Shiny boots were tucked into the silver stirrups of a tooled leather saddle. One glance would say that he was 'somebody,' and truly he was. Weathered skin, abundant hair black as the inside of a cellar at midnight. Walked straight and proud like he knew who he was.

"Mind if my animals rest in your shade? Pullin' up out'a Devil's Canyon plum wore 'em out. That is one straight up and down hill."

Annie called out, "Please come and rest. There's a table and bench for you if you have time."

The tall man steered his animals to deep shade and advanced to the stand, extending his hand. "Brother Philemon Darkhorse here. Some folks call me Brother Phil and that's all right. I've heard about you and your notes on trees. Seems like everyone knows someone who's stopped to read them. What a glorious idea."

Annie allowed the hand shake. "Wasn't my idea, though. My pa said maybe I didn't have to go away to tell the world about God. Maybe God wanted the world to come to me. A good part of it has!"

A smile and an agreeable nod from the man. "Believe I'll have a package of that jerky and a glass of cider. I wasn't sure if my packed lunch was going to get me all the way to Dead Horse Springs. Besides, I always had a taste for good jerky, and I hear yours is good."

"Mr. Burley makes it. Grows his own meat down in the apple orchard. Makes his own cider, too."

Preacher Phil took the jerky and seated himself while she poured the cider from the jug. Bringing the glass, she sat across from him at the table. It was obvious he wanted to talk, and she was more than willing. So much to say to a preacher. She'd heard of him, but he was always too far away for her to attend his services. Now she had a preacher all to herself. What would he think of what she was doing?

The preacher was impressed. He was taking six month assignments all over Carroll County and some adjoining locations. Who knew the country better than a member from the native Ouachita community?

A bit later Burley came for a pick-me-up at the stand, and was impressed to see the three animals resting in the shade. And who was that at the table with Annie? Advancing, he poured cider and strolled over. Annie scooted down the bench to make room, and it would have been an insult to refuse her offer.

Preacher Phil extended his hand. "I've been enjoying a talk with your lady here." At a pause, he amended, "She IS your lady, I'm sure."

Poor Burley. His mind searched frantically for a response, and some ridiculous moment made him say, "Well... not yet...."

The preacher nodded pleasantly and picked up the conversation. He rested for an hour and said he had to be on the way to the new place before it got too dark to find his way.

Burley walked him to his horse, and heard the preacher's words, "Mr. Burley, Miss Annie IS your lady, of course. Made to order for you."

Quick shake of the head. "Preacher, I was over ten years old and already workin' on the river when she was born. She can do much better'n me."

"Maybe, maybe not. She can't do nothin' else if you don't speak up." Broad smile showing a row of pearly white teeth. "Just a word to the wise, and I know you're wise. I'll say this, when it comes time for the weddin', get me word and I'll tie the knot. I'm experienced and legal for doin' that." With a springy leap, he landed in the beautifully tooled saddle. "Work on it… and God bless you."

Burley stared after him until the rump of the last donkey was out of sight. Turning back to the stand, he saw she was back inside, wiping the dust from the counter and the jars of honey. That preacher couldn't be right… could he…?

The greens appeared on the supper table, along with the crisply browned rabbits that just happened along at the wrong (right) time. Burley carefully folded his ankles and pulled his feet back under his chair. Annie had kicked off her shoes and her toes appeared peeking excitingly from under the ruffle of her skirt.

Among the furniture she had purchased was a tall wooden box, maybe as tall as his chin, where she had set one of her lamps. Sometimes her Bible was there.

He hadn't really wondered what the box was for until she opened it and took her apron from the back of the door. Inside the box was a rod with dress hangers and about a dozen different dresses, all pushed together with ruffles gathered in a wad. Something was totally wrong about that.

He figured in another month, at least before the November rains, he would have the time to put on the room for her new bed. He could make a box a lot better than that one, and it would have enough room for as many dresses as she had and would continue to make.

He'd planned to make a lean-to shed for the animals next but maybe they could stay in the cave a while longer. If he put up a wind wall, they might just make the winter. It was surprisingly warm there.

Rather than a lean-to addition to the cabin, he could tie in at the roof gable and it would look really good. Take a little longer, maybe, but there'd be that extra attic space most women set store by. If he did that, it would turn the building into a real house and not a cabin.

Blackberry dumplings were served for dessert, and Annie commented, "When we have milk, we can put cream on our dumplings."

Just a comment but it set Burley's head into a whirl. "When…" not "If…". "We…" not "I…". That settled it. Not ready for cows, but goats would be quick. There were always goats for sale, they popped up like weeds because they were independent, economical and gave a lot of milk. They were also hard to keep in the pen, but he could handle that. Also, the little billies could be butchered. Made really good sausage, if he could just remember the spices it took.

That settled it. Next duty for him was a pen and then goats. Certain to be.

Frenchie's van came into view with Hobo limping on his off hind leg. Rattlesnake had skittered across the road and Hobo startled. Pulled a hip muscle. No matter, help was near.

He pulled in the driveway and hopped down carrying a bucket, and a strip of onions, their tops braided together. "Hey, sis. Potatoes in the bottom, corn on top and here's the onions. Stopped by for supplies and Zennia had these ready to come to you. She said the sweet potatoes were about 2 weeks away and she couldn't wait. Said she'd send you some."

Annie brightened. The day was looking up. Right now she liked the gift from what was her garden more than money in the jar. A hungry man lived just next door to her and she couldn't cook pennies and nickels.

Frenchie continued, "Got a case'a pork and beans in the van. Want you to take it for sometimes when you can't make a big meal. Burley's workin' hard and ain't got time to make food, and I know you're makin' his meals.

"And Zennia said to tell you she loved the garden you put in, but next year, if she's still there, she wants to switch the tomatoes and corn."

Annie grinned. "What's the chance of her not being there next year?"

Without a hesitation, he answered, "Zero to none. She's got no horse and her wagon's here. She ain't leavin'."

He poured stale coffee. "Another reason I stopped, Hobo shied at a rattler and pulled a crick in his leg. I want to swap out with the stray horse and leave Hobo on Burley's grass for a few days. He seems to be slowin' down." With that, he began to remove the horse from the harness and lead him down the hill while Annie removed the cans of pork and beans.

For the next words on her paper, she had printed, "The Lord is my shepherd."

A single rider galloped by, wheeled around and circled back. "What does that sign say? Shepherd…? I don't see no sheep."

"'Course not. You're not one of the Great Shepherd's flock. But you could be."

"You're nuts, lady. I'm getting outta here."

Annie Jo smiled to herself as she watched him gallop away. Not everyone was a success. What was that verse about the planter who went out to sow seed? "Some fell in the weeds, some fell in the hard soil of the roadway and some fell among thorns. Some fell on the good soil and produced a harvest." (Matt 13:19-23)

Her thoughts continued, remembering that some seeds were eaten by the birds, and that young man on the horse clearly was in a flock of birds. As the day went on, there were several observations that were more promising.

Around supper time, traffic slowed to a halt and she slipped to the house to start a meal. Pork loin… the last of the fresh pork. Oh, well, it was fun while it lasted. How about steaming a dozen ears of corn that Zennia had sent… nodding approval to herself. Maybe raisin fried pies. Didn't take milk or eggs, both being in short supply.

Annie sat across the table buttering the leftover toasted biscuits. "You know, Burley. If you was to be way down by the lake when the meal was ready, it'd be hard to hear me. We need a horn or a bell or something."

Small problem. If a signal was what it took to have a permanent invitation to this table, that would be the next undertaking. "How about a gong made of metal and hooked to the tree? A bar'a iron ought'a make a sound that'd carry that far."

Today had been hot and sultry. The wealth of long black hair had been put into a braid and twisted in a spiral straight up from the top of her head. Maybe not his favorite style, but it did keep her from putting on a bonnet because it wouldn't fit over the point.

One took what one could get.

A COLT AND A HENRY

In late August the spring vegetation that was so bright was beginning to turn yellow, or even tan. The leaves on the sumac bushes that produced the lemon flavored cones of brilliant red had, themselves, began to turn to bright red bushes along the roadsides.

The willows were beginning to turn yellow on their lower limbs, so would not the other trees be close behind? The summer heat had 'broken its back' and the farmers were gathering their second, and sometimes their third cutting of hay in the meadow. The animals must eat during the winter.

It was in Wagonshed Cave that the conversation turned to 'what's next?'. Slim in the pokey and nothing left of Shorty meant only half the gang and one extra horse. The fourth horse had been sold cheaply to a farmer down back of Blue Lake who hadn't actually heard of the original troublemakers. The money they got was used to fill out their wardrobe and buy shoes. They also ate better than they had a right to expect.

So now, they sat down and faced each other, and tried to face their future. Being picked up by the law in Arkansas and even Missouri would land them into jail at the very best. What they needed to do was recruit another partner, or spring Slim from the pokey because three would be the minimum number for survival, what with standing watch and keeping the horses hidden.

Recruitment was not easy to do while running from the law, so the other option would be to somehow spring Slim while he was still in the state infirmary and not sent on to Berryville slammer.

Spike sat on a rock, absently drawing in the dirt floor with a stick. "You ain't thinkin' we both could get him out'a there. You're nuts!"

"Maybe not so much as you think," Robert responded.

Spike jerked up his chin and sneered, "What? You think maybe you know a angel ready to lift him out'a that cell and drop him here with us?"

"Almost."

"All right, how're we gonna get the message to that angel?"

Robert breathed deeply and retorted, "Just watch me. Who I know don't really look like no angel I ever saw a picture of, but he's the one that'll do it."

"What'll it cost us?"

"The Colt and the Henry. That dumb hayseed up on the bluff is wantin' them two fire pieces in the worst way. He hinted that he wanted us to be together, and he'd be willing to help if he had them two guns. I'm thinkin' it's time to write a'nother note."

"Sayin' what?"

"Well, ya see, he's a friend'a old Ike over to the station. Says he'll take care'a seein' Ike ain't there, and he'll do what he can. Ye see, if we get Slim, we got this horse and we got all the guns we need. I just figgered we earned the Colt and I took a shine to the Henry. No matter."

"What then?"

"We head on down to Texas where the winters are better... or maybe Louisiana. Bein' three of us, we should make it by cold weather."

Spike sighed. "You really reckon that'll work out? Some'a your plans fall flat when it comes to puttin' 'em in action."

Robert slumped his shoulders and eased back against the wall of the cave. "You got a better plan...maybe...?"

A very long pause, and then, "Nope."

Robert scrumbled around in his baggage and came up with a piece of paper and a pencil with a broken lead. Knife from his pocket, and a bit of whittling produced a usable shape.

"Burley, we thought it over and want to take you up on your plan. You said you wanted to see us together again if we'd leave the county. We got that in mind, so if we give back the Colt and the Henry, and you tell us how to get around old Ike, we'll go back across the river and never come back. If you trick us, you will be sorry. Leave message in the cave."

They waited until dark and traveled down Ridge Road to the bluff. Spike stayed back with the horses while Robert tied the note to the mailbox.

The answer came quickly. Burley took precious minutes and hours to write the note and deliver it, with Joker at his heels. He wanted the bloodhound to be familiar with the trail. Could make tracking easier later.

"You ain't gonna see no plan until I have those guns in my hand. I can say this, Ike ain't got too many friends, and there ain't another one of them that wants to see you fellows together and gone. So you better deal with me, and I want an answer in one week. I got more things to do than to mess with bums like you."

Robert read the note and handed it to Spike, who read it and turned to Robert with a grin. "Say, we can watch and put a slug in him when he comes after the guns. That'll tend to him permanent."

Robert frowned, and then sneered, "You dumb, stupid idiot! Then how'd we get the plan?"

"Oh. Well, we...."

"We'll do what I said. Go get the guns out'a the pack and put 'em here in the cave in plain sight. I'll write the next note."

"Burley, them guns are laying in Hidden Cave. When you take 'em, tell us exactly what you are going to do."

Annie was the one who picked the note off the mailbox because Burley was not at home. When he came back he smiled with satisfaction, and took out his note paper.

Burley headed out to Hidden Cave for the guns. It seemed safe to go alone because they were antsy and wanted the message. In his pocket was simply:

"Look on my mailbox for the plan."

Sure enough, there was the Colt and the Henry. Joker didn't want to leave the cave. It had too many scents for her to ignore. She did obey certain commands, and one was "HEEL."

Burley had checked with the dog's breeder for the best way to command a dog, and was given the five magic words she used to train puppies. After SIT, STAY, GO, and ATTACK, they were ready to HEEL. Any other training was to be done by the hunter who purchased her pups.

He walked up the hill with Joker at his heels. Back at the bluff, he swung up to Brownie's back and went to the Langleys'. Johnny happened to be at home, and again he was forced to take the red bandana from his pocket to wipe his eyes at the sight of grandpop's Henry.

So far, so good. Then he carefully tied the note to his mailbox. It read:

"I got it fixed up. Ike is going to be at my place, and we'll be in plain sight when you sneak by. He will be looking at the covered wagon at my place, and then he will have supper with me. I'm thinking he'll stay overnight in the wagon to see how it sleeps. He would like to buy it.

"You need to go to the station, and enter by the cellar door at the back. They don't lock it. There'll be a hall and go all the way and then up the stairs to the left. You'll see another hall. Go down to the end and you will see keys hanging on the wall. Slim is in the end cell. Use the key on the door, and the next cell is the evidence room where his gun will be. Just take Slim and the gun and go back the way you came in, and don't trick me up. The deputies are all doing other things, so you should be safe. You need to do this on Thursday, 4 days from now because that is the only day Ike will be at my place."

Robert grinned to himself in his self-satisfaction. That old dummy on the bluff was selling out his friend for a little peace and quiet. Did he really think the gang would be gone forever…? Going south was just for the winter.

On Thursday afternoon, Ike rode in on his Appaloosa mare, a well-shaped and easy riding animal. He and Burley sat for a long time at the picnic table discussing this and that. They actually made several trips out to the covered wagon, not knowing just when the fellows would go by and see them, but it was no problem.

When it was completely dark, the men were treated to a meal created by the two fat geese Burley's gun had brought down as they hovered over Blue Lake on a migration stop south.

They finished up with 'spotted dick,' the English boiled pudding packed with raisins. And coffee made on a stove and not a grill over a flame.

The moon was high when Ike climbed into the miniature house on wheels and flaked out. He tried to think about important things, but instead relaxed and slept the sleep of the just.

Robert and Spike along with the third horse were at the station at 9:00 pm and with shorter days coming, it was dark enough to put their plan into action. Sure enough, the cellar door was unlocked, the padlock… laying there beside the door.

Lifting the door carefully, lest it squeak, they entered and went down the steps to the ground floor and found the hall. Creeping softly, they reached the stairs and climbed slowly, one step after the other, scarcely breathing.

A nightlight lantern hung to the right at the top of the stairs, but they were to go left. The reflected light shone all the way to the end, and actually glinted softly off the bunch of keys hanging on the wall.

Opening the cell where Slim was, Robert woke him by clamping his hand over the smaller fellow's mouth. "Shhh! We're here to break you out. Spike's next door gettin' your gun. Horses outside. Just follow me and we'll get out."

Slim, barely awake, finally realized what was going on. Still in his prison garb, he attempted to step where Robert had stepped. Spike met them in the hall with not one gun, but three, handing two to his partners.

At the top of the stair to the collar, Deputy Jones yelled, "Fire!" and let loose with a blast that splintered the wall beside the escapers. Robert pushed Slim toward the stairs and tried to follow but slipped and slid to the bottom.

Deputy Collier caught Slim by the collar and pulled his arms back, making the elbows touch. A short rope was wrapped around his elbows and he was forced to the floor on his stomach. A second shot from behind caught Spike in his left shoulder, permanently disabling his left arm.

He was an easy catch for Deputy Marshall who didn't even have to tie him, but instead attempted to staunch the flow that showed red even in the dim light.

Deputy Comstock grabbed for Robert, not being able to use his gun in the close space of the halls. Robert slithered away and dived headfirst through a window broken by the barrel of the gun given him by Slim.

He received several cuts, but managed to reach the ground on the outside. Unfortunately, Deputy Comstock was of a girth that would not go through the window, so by the time he reached the door, Robert was just a moving black dot in the dark, the sound of hooves echoing on the silent road.

The two captives were locked in the cell and the guns returned. The four deputies looked at each other. A partial success. The good thing was, only one successful escape meant only one person, and that was not a gang. He could be found because one alone, with a horse, could hardly make it through an Arkansas winter.

Constable Ike would be a little bit disappointed, but there were no injuries among the deputies. Robert had been injured, but likely not seriously. It should lay him low for a while if they could find where he would hole up.

Near morning, Robert limped into Hidden Cave, his bloody shirt plastered to the slice of raw skin over his ribs. His exhausted horse stood with his head hanging, dangerously near unable to restore his breath.

The wounded man did what he could with limited resources and a gash on his left hand. Also on his right leg, along with the stabbing jabs from the broken window. He really had no idea how serious his cuts were, but they were bad enough to make him mad. Really mad, and that lying fool who lived on the bluff would pay. He would pay the worse price ever to be thought up.

And Robert had time to do a lot of thinking. By morning, he was almost ready to wish he had been shot, and therefore moved to a bed in a warm infirmity. Almost... but not quite.

When his horse had recovered breath, he yanked himself loose from the tree, separating the knot his rider had been too injured and exhausted to secure. He began to graze and moved on down to Blue Lake where the grass was still succulent and green.

HOUSE ON THE BLUFF

Burley heard the news with mixed feelings. The trap was such a good one, it was a shame it did not net everyone, but the deputies certainly did their jobs. Deputy Potter had been stationed at the cellar door, and had watched them enter. If Robert had not gone through the window, he would have been caught. Oh, well. That did not mean the plan was not a good one.

Burley had about a dozen things that must be done immediately, it seemed, so he went to work on them. Robert, however, was never far from his mind. Burley knew it would be himself, eventually, who had to end it, and he might be the one to fire the fatal shot.

Planning his next move, he wished he knew how seriously Robert was wounded, and if he actually went back to Hidden Cave that seemed to be the favored headquarters. Assuming the wounds were not serious, he would be up and around in a week or so. He might still be there recuperating and if he, Burley, went near there and fired off a few shots, it might spur him to action... somewhere. A weak plan, but he had no other.

Just now, he was cleaning his cider press under the waterfalls. Cleaned and the gears oiled, it could be stored for the winter in the rear of the cave with his 37 jugs of cider. The rest of the apples were taken to the cabin and some would yet be sold.

September and October were usually good weather months. He hoped at least half the cider jugs would be sold, and then maybe a few in the winter by those who particularly requested one.

Frenchie was now lounging against a convenient tree watching. He stopped often, enjoying seeing his sister as she took charge of the bluff and the man who thought he owned it. So far, Burley did not realize what a gift he received when Annie moved in.

"Burley," he began. "Did you have occasion to play the game of checkers?"

"Checkers? Law, yeah, that was the favorite thing for fellows with no money to blow when the weather kept us off the river. Must'a played a hundred games... maybe more."

Frenchie nodded. "I just wondered. Cold weather is going to set in, and the nights get longer. You'll not want to stay down here in the cold, or stuff yourself in that wagon. You'll want to go enjoy some of that wood you will furnish the cabin with. Annie and I used to play checkers a lot and she always beat me. That's something I keep in the van just in case. Could be you'd be glad to have a few games on a evening of freezing November rain." Enough said. Burley wasn't slow.

He nodded. "Leave me off a set when it's handy. Just hand it to Annie." Then he packed away the press and worked on the enclosure for the goats. Needed to be wolf tight. Goats could pretty well protect themselves, but not in cramped spaces. Frenchie wandered off.

Burley waited for two solid weeks, but thought of no better plan than to flush Robert out, or satisfy himself that he had left the county. Finding Joker and showing her the plaid shirt, he told her "TRACK."

The canine took a sniff and lifted her head, flopping her ears. She looked at Burley, and he headed toward Hidden Cave over the trodden-upon grass of many trips. About an eighth of a mile, almost within sight, he took several shots toward Blue Lake. Joker looked at him for further instructions. She had told him he was on the right trail, but he had stopped and told her "SIT." So she sat.

Easing from tree trunk to bush, he came closer, telling Joker to "HEEL." Joker didn't want to heel, but she did… almost. When he was close enough to see the huge tree at the cave mouth, he saw a movement in the lower limbs, and then a spot of blue among the green leaves.

It was working. He was actually climbing the tree and of course he had a gun. He was waiting for the stupid neighbor to boldly walk into the cave, and he would put a bullet through his head. Who would expect an injured man to climb a tree? Or who would think he would still be there… as apparently he was horseless?

Burley waited. Joker was young and eager, and begged to attack. A delicate whine pled with the human, but he said "STAY," so she stayed. Burley thrashed around. making a bit of noise and then yelled, "Deputy Jones, you there?"

Pausing, he yelled, "Good. I want you to slip around and put a few bullets in that big tree. I don't think anyone would be so stupid as to climb up there, but we need to make sure." Waiting a bit and making more noise, he lowered his voice. "From here?"

Back in his normal voice, he answered, "No, go on in closer. I'm holding the dog back, but he might be still inside. Go ahead and shoot."

With that, Burley lifted his shotgun and aimed at the very top of the tree. The suddenness of the sound and the nearness startled Robert who attempted to scurry to the back of the thick trunk, but there were no handy limbs. Seating himself, he scooted and pushed off the limb… feet poised to land on a lower limb. A small bushy branch gouged his injured leg through his torn pants and threw him off balance. He landed a-straddle of the limb grasping for a hold and the gun slipped from his hand. Bumping against a limb, it discharged, the bullet hitting the worn sole of his shoe and stopping somewhere at the top of his toes.

He screamed in pain and caught a lower limb, breaking his fall to the ground on his rear and both hands. His shoe was red from the flowing blood.

Burley ran to him, pulling his bandana handkerchief from his pocket. Circling the wounded leg, he tied it off just above the ankle. So what did he do now? He stood, sighing heavily. There was no way he could carry the man up the hill for help. No one could possibly be close enough to hear him, but… maybe someone fishing on the lake.

Picking up Robert's stolen gun, he fired it from one hand aiming at the air above, and with his other gun, he fired another direction. He looked at the whining, begging Joker itching to take a bite of the person before her that had stolen milk from Annie's cow.

Small idea. Tiny change. "Joker? SPEAK!" The confused dog understood him. At least that was something. She raised her muzzle, tightened her muscles and drew in a breath. A shuddering bark issued behind the white fangs, and she ended with a long whine, a gasp, and another bark.

Burley waited, and wonder of wonders, an answering shot sounded. Then another one. Burley fired again, and was answered immediately. Then the sound of someone coming through the brush from the direction of his house. Joker eyed the human, hoping for more orders.

Then, bursting through the trees was the head of the Appaloosa stallion, the favorite of Constable Ike. Burley watched with unbelief as his friend, and a source of help, stumbled through the brush and vines to his side.

"Heard the shots. Thought it might be… What is that?" and he stared at the man on the ground groaning, staring at his bloody shoe.

"That's… that's Robert, isn't it?"

Clearly Robert was not going to be able to walk, or even to ride. It took a bit of scrounging, but a couple of dead poles were located, and a travois sled was made from contents of the cave… a canvas tarp and some bedding.

Working their way to the bluff was not an easy trip. It took dragging the travois to the edge of the lake where there were fewer trees, and going all the way to Burley's part of the water. Climbing where Burley had cut trees for building his fences and corral, they managed to get him up to the Ridge Road.

Loading him on the wagon, they headed for the station and the infirmary where he could be patched up. Didn't deserve it, ought'a be left to die, but they didn't do things that way.

Then Ike burst into laughter, and explained, "I was just comin' over to you with a badge to deputize you just in case you had a chance to do somethin'… just a protection in case you had to shoot his head off."

Burley was not impressed. "Keep your tin star, Ike. I'm out of the business. This here is the period-paragraph of my life. I got a year'a work ahead, and this'n has done set me back a month."

"Figgered you wouldn't take it. Needed to ask, anyway. Likely it'll be a few days before another problem arises."

They clumped along in the gathering dark, each man with his own thoughts. Ike first, "I was just thinking. What makes fellows like Robert, Spike, Shorty and Slim? Bad all the way through. What's to become of fellows like that?"

"I thought of that, Ike. Made me wonder if they were balanced off by Robert's brother, James… Johnny Langley… uh, Simon Turner and Sonny Simmons, the young man they hung."

About ten minutes of silence, then Ike, "Yeah, and young fellows like the ones you mentioned… they'll be payin' a lifetime'a taxes to pay for food and bed for these fellows for the next twenty years, at least. Ain't fair.

"Burley, I wish you'd reconsider takin' this tin star. Stuck out here in nowhere like you are, and like you seem to be diggin' in, it takes time to get to you. If you had the star, you wouldn't need to wear it or anything. Just have it in case you need it. Take it and think about it. If you really don't think it's a good idea, I'll take it back next time I see you."

Burley felt the metal star being slipped into his shirt pocket. He sighed… and left it there.

Ike continued, "And if that horse wanders in, keep 'im and use 'im if you can. He'd be the one stole from the fellow they hung."

Burley found a bed in the jail, and slept till morning. It had been a long day, week, and year.

Still exhausted in the morning, he settled in behind Brownie and Stray. He'd tried to leave Stray with the county, but Ike refused. "Along with that star, you'd get the use'a some horse. This way it knows you and you'll keep it fit."

It seemed natural, as soon as he had loosed the animals onto grass, to head for the cabin and the angel in charge of it. She had hot tea ready until the pancakes were browned. Almost too tired to eat… imagine that! Two hotcakes later, he was stretched out on his bedroll in the covered wagon.

A couple hours later he woke up. He found Annie Jo in her stand, ready for business. On the counter, however, was a fold-out checker board and a lively game of black against the red. Both sides being played by herself.

"Playin' with yourself?"

She looked up with a grin. "You seein' someone else here to play with? We had a game at the farm and Frenchie played with me when he was there. After that, it was just me and myself, and Pa readin' to himself and me." She picked up a black and jumped two reds, and continued, "He came by and left this. Said you ordered it for times you couldn't be outside, and for winter evenin's."

Burley scratched his black curls and congratulated himself for being so far-thinking.

OCTOBER

Time was getting short. October in Arkansas was a wonderful month for working, and that was a good thing. He located his sharpening file and the hand saw. Bringing down trees full of sap took a toll on blades, but it was time to bring down trees again.

He had tromped the woods near the cabin, carefully sighted the elevation in relation to the top of the falls and made a decision. He'd hitch Heppie, being smaller, to the poles and drag them into place, but first he needed to go to the mill.

Young Simon Turner was a big help and totally worth his pay. Hire someone, and you buy a piece of his life… the way the big river had bought his own boyhood. In addition, Simon could bring up a load of boards for the walls when he came. The windows (an expensive lot of them) would be ordered out of Eureka.

This would be the final building for the year, but one of the most important ones. Frenchie had engaged him into conversation about where he would be in the winter… the cave being too damp and the wagon too tiny. Burley sort of figured he was angling for information as to when he could expect a wedding.

Burley wasn't telling.

He was, however, making active plans for the winter. Every country lady either had, or wanted to have, a summer kitchen. It was there that the canning was done, and often summer meals were cooked and carried to the table, avoiding the steamy kitchen and hot house.

Annie would have one, but instead of open sides to make it cooler, it would be surrounded by windows. And a door on every side. That would provide the breeze, but closed off, the building made another room. It would, of necessity, have a stove required for the canning, and the same one would provide winter heat as well.

That bedroll and his other possessions would spend the winter there, cozy and handy for all the winter work he had filed away in his mind. The garden being the most important.

Hence, the need for Simon, his lumber and his muscles and time. Get the rafters up in a day, and he could finish the rest himself.

While grinding away on the saw teeth to sharpen them, the van pulled in from the road. Frenchie stepped out with a bucket which he deposited by the roadstand. "Sweet potatoes. Zennia said she never saw the sight of the way they produced. Said the Gardners sliced them and strung them on a cord to dry over the clothes line. Said they were perfect for pies, and easy to store… and the rats didn't get to nibble on 'em." Then he ambled on out to check out the saw-sharpening activity.

"Friend, I'm gonna offer to do you a favor. While down in Eureka at the stationer's store where I get Annie's tablets, I saw something she would really like. It's going to be a sacrifice to offer this to you, because I really wanted to give it to her myself. You need to put down that old saw and follow me to the van."

Burley obeyed. Put that way, how could he not?

Frenchie opened a box and took out a piece of cut glass… maybe a bowl, or a vase, or a… it could have a lot of uses. It was heavy, and there were deep facets cut in geometrical designs. The flat planes reflected light in every direction, and a slight movement of the head produced a whole different pattern of shapes. Burley stared, transfixed. Immediately he saw it in his mind, setting on the tall box where Annie kept a kitchen lamp and sometimes her Bible.

Frenchie watched Burley's face and knew he was sold. The Watkins Route man was not through, however. He was a salesman to the depth of his soul and the top of his head down to his shoe soles.

While Burley stared, he opened another box. Sticks, they must be, all in vivid colors. Held together in a bundle, one might imagine a bouquet of spring flowers. "Watch," Burley was told, and the bundle of sticks was stood upright in the vase, where they fanned out like a pinwheel, the colors showing through the glass, flashing colors behind the sparkling facets.

Burley caught his breath as though it had been a trick of magic. The salesman waited an appropriate length of time to give the demonstration its proper due, then he took out a random three of them. Red, purple and green. Turning them so the end faced his audience, he explained. "The lead in these pencils is the same color as the outside. If Annie had these, she would have a whole winter of entertainment."

Burley took out a yellow and a blue. Sure enough. Colored lead.

The salesman continued, "And these are not sharpened with a knife that might waste the lead. They have this little ball, and the end goes in here, and the ball is twisted around. Then it opens up to take out the sawdust." He allowed Burley to examine several more of the pencils. There must have been at least three dozen.

"I'll have to admit, they were expensive. I know, however, that some things are more important than money. Also, I know my sister. If she was offered the choice of this or a ring, she would take this in a minute. I also know, in addition, that you can afford both for her when the time comes."

Burley cast a puzzled look at Frenchie. When had he ever said anything about a ring? Maybe he thought about it, but he was certain he'd never said anything. It was a bit concerning to have one's mind read so accurately, but then, when would he ever have been where he could see a thing like this, even if he had known it existed?

Timing was important, and the salesman knew the time was now. "The thing is, I paid $6.25 for this and Annie is going to get it. From either you or me."

Six dollars and twenty five cents. The price of a pair of milking goats, and maybe three started pigs. Almost as much as the windows for the summer kitchen.

But truly, what was that against the smiles and the little things she did for his comfort? Clean socks, for instance. And laying that aside, how much was it worth to see those snappy black eyes over a bowl of oatmeal with honey? Or that mop of hair pinned to the top of her head that never stayed… that slid gradually down toward her ear.

Or the exasperated look as she snatched the pins that should have held it up, and put them on whatever flat surface was handy, so she could continue doing what she was doing?

Or the vision within his mind of her, of a winter evening, in the glow of the lamp lights bent over her tablet? He could see in his mind how she would squench her eyes while selecting the next color?

Adding to that was the way she ran the stand, the proceeds being far more than he had expected. What was the value of that?

"I'll take it. Do you have rings, too?"

A sad smile and a shake of the head. "No, friend, that is something you'll have to do for yourself. The market for a ring you would want is not enough for me to invest in stock. Fact is, if you doubt your skill in selecting it, you could take her to Eureka and let her pick it out. Then plan on spending the night in the hotel. Eureka has a good one."

After a chat with his sister and a fast game of checkers, he was on his way. A fellow had to work, didn't he?"

As he passed her Note Tree, he glanced at the paper.

"Will a man rob God?" (Malachi 3: 8,9,10) As a tyke, he had wondered how someone could rob God when they couldn't even see him. Pa had explained to them both that a penny from every dime was not theirs, but was God's. The neat thing about it was that if a person returned to God what was God's, then really good things could happen, and he was protected from certain bad things. That was also when he learned that heaven had windows and that God could open them up and toss down good things. Then, he had pictured candy, but in later years he realized how much was more important than candy.

Pa had a way of making things real, and it would be fun to stick around and hear Annie Jo explain that to some bewhiskered old codger, but he bet she could do it. He couldn't wait, thought. A fellow had to work, didn't he? He even remembered something about that, too. "If a man would not work, neither should he eat." (II Thes. 3:10)

He picked up the reins and flicked them softly over the horses' rumps. "Get up, Hobo! Move on, Lazybones!" And the Watkins Products began to move on down the flint stone-covered road.

NOVEMBER

One thing about November in northern Arkansas: you never knew what was next, but you knew you needed to be prepared for anything. The first week was drizzling rain out of a bank of gray clouds the height of Echo Mountain.

After piddling around in the cave for two days, Burley put on his sheepskin-lined Macanaw and his oil-skins and put windows in the summer kitchen. He was going to need it any minute.

Then the second week, the weather thought it was October. He sledded a half a dozen jugs of sweet cider to the stand, and Annie set out her other wares. With no rain falling, she decided she could put up another paper verse. There was that one... one of her favorites... that she had been saving. It read in part, "... thou shalt heap coals of fire on his head." (Proverbs 25: 22 & Romans 12:20)

Pa had explained to her that it was such an important verse for getting along with other people that it was written by the wisest man, Solomon, and repeated by the letter-writer, Paul. She pictured someone scooping coals from the stove with the stove shovel and trying to make them stay on someone's head. She thought she could even smell hair scorching.

But that wasn't it at all. Those dots in front of the first word meant that something important was said first. Solomon was explaining how you could destroy an enemy by making a friend of him. No matter how mean he was to you, you must feed him if he's hungry and give him water if he's thirsty, and most times he'll feel so bad about being mean to you that he'll stop. Pa said that was easier and more effective than giving him a bloody nose, even though that was what you wanted to do.

Only three people stopped by to read it. No matter... she'd put it out again maybe next May.

Burley went into town with the wagon and brought back a stove, identical to the one Annie had chosen for the kitchen. She must have liked it, so now she would have another, and he would have heat for the winter nights. He also brought several pieces of iron pipe which he hooked together and lowered one end into the waterfall where it came out from under the rock. He put the other end right by the door of the summer kitchen so Annie would have water to do the washing and to can the vegetables next summer.

After he buried the pipe, he began to plow the garden spot. Two horses came in handy because the tough dirt had obviously not been moved since God made it.

It was the third week in November that another little matter was taken care of. He couldn't actually remember saying any words, but he must have, because he ended the day being engaged to be married. Next spring.

He brought the vase and the pencils up from the cave and her squeal of delight likely echoed across Blue Lake and maybe farther.

Burley was amazed that it sparked even better in the light of the two kitchen lamps than in Frenchie's van. He also told her they would make a trip of Eureka Springs so she could pick out the ring she wanted thereby producing another squeal of delight. He said they would go the next time it looked like there would be two good days in a row. For weathers-watchers, which took in almost everybody, that meant a spell of cold rainy days which, when they passed on, usually left two to four good days.

Frenchie would bring his buggy and spend the night on the bluff to take care of the animals. He said he wanted to see his sister waited on for once in her life full of waiting on other people.

The very idea of this brought on an even greater surge of ambition for the stand. Annie remembered the little fall activity that she learned from her foster mother. Fall brought sore throats and December brought coughs and sniffles. One of the best local remedies was slippery elm tea. For children, her mom made hard-candy honey drops with a quantity of slippery elm.

Older folks mostly liked the warmth of the tea, but children liked sucking hard candy. So, if she had the honey drops wrapped in wax paper and packed in a pint jar, there are those who would likely buy them rather than make them because they might have to buy the honey, and getting the recipe just right was tricky.

Annie tromped the nearby trees and found oak, sycamore, dogwood and a lot of nut trees... no elm.

Burley nodded sympathetically at her plight and offered to help. "For that matter, old Ugly Face could lead you right to an elm, maybe the largest one in Carroll County."

When he said 'ugly face,' Joker alerted and stared expectantly into Burley's face. Annie moaned, "See? You've gotten her to think that's one of her names!"

Burley grinned and stroked the dog over her face wrinkles, and smoothed her drooping rag-like ears. "You could show her an elm tree, couldn't you?"

With a toss of the head, Annie pronounced, "Then if she can take me, who needs you?"

Whereupon Burley retorted, "You don't need me, but you might need the old plaid shirt you tried to wash."

So with her knife, her pail, and her 22mm gun, she started out, following the excited canine. For a fact, though, Annie would likely not have needed either the dog or the shirt. The many trips through the brush had created maybe not a trail, but certainly a marked path through broken sprouts and wilting vines.

While Annie sliced through the rough outer bark for the sap-rich layer, Joker sniffed and snorted, and cast about for a better scent leading away from Hidden Cave, and when she found none, she flopped on the ground, lowered her head on her paws, and watched her human. She could have stood or sniffed other scents, but she sensed that would be a waste of energy.

While they were gone, Burley busied himself on the chicken house she had not asked for, but he knew she was eager to get. So far, her eggs were dropped off only when her brother came passing by.

Keeping an eye on the sky, he noted the cloud bank building in the southwest. A wind shift and a chilly bite in the air. A shiver in the remaining leaves in the tops of trees. He nodded; a norther was coming for sure. Good to get the pen for the chickens.

Spring was the best time for starting chickens, preferably just after being hatched. Zennia would notice a hen going 'broody' and he would be ready put her up while she hatched a brood. Several incidents like that and Annie would have her flock.

He had brought home a roll of what was called chicken wire. It was a mesh with small hexagon-shaped holes about an inch across. That would fence in a 'night pen' to keep marauders from finding a way into the hen house in the dark.

In the daytime adult chickens were not a very easy catch for coons or possums, because of the flutter and the squawking that attracted other chickens and this year, would attract a bored bloodhound.

He was just tacking the last of the fence to the post when Ike rode in, pulling him up short from his speed. "Need your dog, Burley. Got a situation about a mile and a half down, and I've got Deputy Comstock on the road with a two-wheeled sulky we put together for Ugly Face."

"Bad news, Ike. Annie has the dog down in the woods."

But there through the brush came Annie, joyfully swinging her pail, and the bored dog, plodding dispiritedly after her.

Ike brightened, "There she comes, Burley. Get your star and horse and come on. Don't want the trail to get colder. Ugly Face is to ride in the sulky, so she won't be tired. Don't know how far we have to go."

The next little difficulty was getting 'Ugly Face' to get into the sulky when she had four good feet, and the flimsy little two-wheeled rack had no scent at all. Turned out, Burley had to get in with her and lead Stray on a tether.

Burley stared back toward Annie as they pulled away, and Annie waved. This... he reminded himself... was the reason he did not want that star. But that didn't seem to matter... he had it.

Ike, riding beside, tried to explain. "Got one dead and one on the loose. Headin' for Echo, we think, and we shore don't want him there. Thinkin' with Ugly Face we could head 'em off before Meadow Creek forks."

Burley nodded. Some things had to be done, and he had the way it could be done quicker. He reached out to the dog and smoothed the hair on her wide forehead, allowing his hand to slide down her back. She obligingly settled onto the slatted floor of the sulky and waited. Surely something better than that old empty cave was in her near future.

It was mid-morning the next day when Burley and Stray returned, soaking wet and cold, followed by a floppy eared creature with a satisfied expression. He put Stray in the pen, and Joker scratched on the door of the cabin.

Burley took himself to the wagon that seemed toasty warm and dry after the cold, hungry night. Dried out and somewhat thawed, he joined Annie in her warm kitchen.

"It was touch and go for a while there. He cut through the line and got to Meadow Creek that was already raging deep from the drain off Echo. We thought we'd lost for sure, but I said 'let's try 'er across the Creek.'"

He sipped fragrant coffee from the thick mug. "Ike said it weren't no use, no dog could track after that water, but I talked 'im down. We, me and Ike, that is, picked up that dog because the water was to our belts and the current was strong. That Ugly Face… she was casting for the scent a'fore we got her across, and she headed out up stream. We must'a been a hunnerd feet up when she picked it up again. We mostly had to run to keep up. Finally, we hung back and let Comstock go with 'er. Caught 'im about a mile up."

Burley paused and shook his head slowly. "Caught up to Comstock and that dog, 'er with a jaw full'a shirt even though Comstock had 'im in cuffs. Big fellow. We hobbled his legs with a rope and made 'im walk till he sat down and wouldn't move.

"We came up that last hill pack-saddlein' 'im in our arms, tradin' off every little bit. Got up to Ridge Road and tied 'im in the sulky they made for the dog. Last I saw was them high-tailin' it down the road in the rain, Ike grinnin' like a Halloween pumpkin."

Annie had listened, chin in hands, elbows on the table. "Good job! Joker was a good help, right?"

Burley sighed. "Good and bad. That beast is such a good tracker, Ike'll be forever here after me to get her. When you got that tin star, your time ain't your own… that you can count on."

He sipped the coffee and stroked the huge forehead of the beast that was 'good and bad.' She pushed her head against his hand. That trip was a much better trip than the one to that old empty cave.

The watched-for November storm came in and lasted three days. High winds, intermittent cold rain, and it brought down all the leaves that were still hanging on the trees. Only the oaks were still clothed in leaves the color of toast. They usually hung on until the new spring leaves pushed them off.

Burley donned oilskins and did what he could. The milking goats had to be locked in the cave. Goats do not weather well in the rain, but they voiced their complaint in the best way they could. A constant chorus of 'Ba-a-a-a-a-a'. One thing for sure, their eventual house would be farther from the cabin.

He finished the interior of the new room and installed the new bed with the beautiful iron scroll work. He built a closet against one corner that was roomy enough for a lot of dresses with ruffles, and he watched the weather.

On perfect schedule. The rain moved on east and the sun came out. Air bright and chilly. Frenchie appeared with his buggy prepared to stay overnight, and, wrapped in lap quilts, the couple from Burnt Tree Junction headed west toward Eureka Springs. The weather was just too beautiful for words, but they had a lot of them in the hours it took to reach the cut-off that headed down the hill into the town.

They walked everywhere and saw everything. Annie easily picked out the ring she wanted, and they ate at the hotel… someone bringing food to her. Imagine that! Whatever she wanted to eat they apparently had ready, and there it was!

She was shown a lovely room, and the door was closed, giving her the key. She sat at the window looking down at the street lamps all down the street and the reflections in the windows of the stores.

Then, droopy from the activity of the day, she crawled into a bed between sheets that she had not washed. She thought of Joker, and her last little bite of shirt and remembered Burley telling her brother, "If Ike comes by and wants the dog, let 'er go. She's far too good'a tracker to be kept only a pet."

So Joker might not be looking for that last bite. Annie sighed at the thought. She wasn't certain she liked it, but Joker was only doing what she was bred to do. Then a smile, as she remembered that was what she, as well, was doing. The notes on the tree worked well.

The next day there was one thing she wanted to do before they went home. She could be parked at the catalog store while Burley took care of this and that, and she'd see what their dresses looked like. Maybe she'd make a new one or two. There was time in the stand to do the sewing.

The next day was just as beautiful. The winter birds, chickadees, cardinals, thrushs and titmice were everywhere. Even a few blue jays hawking to each other in the trees. Northern geese were arriving to winter on the many lakes.

Burley asked her, "Did you see anything you liked in the catalog?"

She paused, and he turned to her with a puzzle in his eyes. "Well, I saw a lot of things I liked, but what I really liked, and want, is the catalog itself. The catalog people send the catalog to the catalog store, and we come and order things and they make a little money from our order. If I had a catalog, I could order for myself now that the mail hack comes by every week."

Burley was silent, thinking. "And what might happen is that other ladies would hear about it, and you might have a lot of company."

"Hey! That would be great! I could make out the orders for those who don't read and write very well."

Then Burley. "If you did that, then you'd need to charge a little bit."

"Oh, no! Not for neighbors."

"Yes, because we are all human. When we have to pay, at least something, then we put a greater value on what we get. And if you always did things free, people would begin to think that was just your job. Your time, your paper and your pencils are worth something, along with the three cent stamp you'd put on the order."

Well, yes, Annie had to agree. But still, she'd have the catalog to look at and one could learn a lot of things from that big, fat book of pictures. And if the catalog people sent a book to the store in Eureka, why wouldn't they send one to her? For a three cent stamp, she could find out.

And she would.

MARCH

Winter was over. A lot of changes happened over the last three months. Annie had spent a lot of time with her drawing pad and the multitude of colored pencils.

First off, she started with the local flowers. Amazingly, she had four shades of green for the vegetation. Wild roses, buttercups, daisies and sweet flag blossoms appeared on paper in all their lovely color.

Tame plants like daffodils, pansies, tulips and zennias. And hollyhocks. Especially hollyhocks. When the right time came, she'd transfer some of the hollyhocks from the farm and surround the house.

But there were other things. Necessary household duties always took longer in the winter, and there was the problem of getting her washing dry. But hey, there was the summer kitchen! A few lines from one wall to the next, and emergency drying could happen.

She hung thick quilts over the many windows so more heat could be held for Burley's bedroll. He was working so hard, all he wanted to do was eat something warm, do evening chores and fall into bed.

He spent a lot of time with duties on the apple orchard. That would be the money-maker, and such a time-consuming project. So fortunate that it could be held over until winter.

The orchard trees were scattered helter-skelter over about an acre located on a steep, up and down stretch of land. It seemed, for all the world, that there had been a picnic of sorts with apples as one of the foods. Then, full and frisky, a group of boys (?) had a contest of pitching the cores downhill. The fertile soil had grabbed onto the seeds as they fell, and some trees were as close together as four feet, and others might have room for another tree in between. To his best count, there were twenty eight bearing trees.

The wonderful part of it was the parental reseeding. The mature trees had born apples that were not harvested, but fell and often took seed where they fell. Some were as tall as two feet, others a few inches.

This, Burley had decided, was the nucleus of the new orchard. He chose a small plateau and fenced in a space for 24 trees, preferably 1 ½ feet high, that way gaining an extra year. Most apple trees bore at five years, so if the transplanted trees grew, they would bear in four years... maybe three.

In northern Arkansas the ground sometimes froze, but usually not deeply. When the ground was dig-able, and he had a spare moment, he dug the planting hole and poured in decayed leaves and black dirt. The winter moisture would send nutrients deep into the soil, and increase the survivability of the new trees.

As for Annie, the 'thought' seeds sewn at the catalog store landed of fertile ground, rooted and blossomed. She took sheet of paper and wrote:

Dear Mr. Montgomery Ward,

I really like your catalog but I have to go all the way to Eureka Springs to see it. If I could have one of your books, I could order by mail now that we have postman delivery every week. We didn't have it until we got the new graveled road.

I also have neighbors who might like looking at your book if I had one because where I live, it is handy for everyone. I live at Burnt Tree Junction, Highway 62 Eureka Springs, Arkansas.

Yours truly, Annie Jo McFey

P.S. I ordered all the furniture for my new house from you and it is beautiful. I will really appreciate it if you can send me a book.

Annie smiled to herself as she walked to the new mailbox with the letter in an envelope, and 3 cents in a small bag to pay for a stamp. It was so convenient that the postman carried stamps he could sell when those on his route didn't have one. The three cents per stamp was all that was needed.

She lifted the red flag on the side of the mailbox that told the postman that there was something to pick up. So, now it was up to the catalog people.

So amazing it was that in only three weeks, the fat book was crammed into the mail box. The weather was drizzling rain but Annie saw that the red flag was up. That meant… maybe…

Ann hugged the book under her oiled cape. It must not get wet. It took its rightful place on the dining room table where she looked at a few minutes between duties. Some of the pages were even in color, like the advertisements for cloth for dresses, curtains and a few other things.

She was sitting with her nose in the book when her brother came by bringing eggs… Zennia couldn't think of ways to use them all, and there were a few bones for Joker.

Hmmm…. say, his plan worked even better than he had hoped. He wanted, somehow, to release Annie from her cage of more than a decade, and he had not only released her, but he had seen her take flight.

Imagine! She had left a comfortable, established home and started from grass roots, like the original settlers, and seemed to be having a blast. Discomforts seemed as nothing. She took an idea and ran with it.

It was only a week later when he stopped off with another gift. He had a circle of wood sawed from a tree with a diameter of a foot and a half. He marked out the letters and applied his torch. His burned letters spelled out:

HAVE CATALOG
Will Order

The message was burned on both sides of the sign, and a pair of chains were attached to hang it from a limb. It would be easy to put up and take down if she wished, and the message on both sides would be seen from whichever direction the traffic came.

Annie squealed from delight at the sight of it, and promptly ordered 10 stamps, 3 cents each, for the orders she would get. It was not likely anyone would have the stamp, and she would just add it to the 12 cents she would charge for the service, making it a dime and a nickel.

The charge seemed a bit high, but that would encourage a customer to order more than one item at a time. She might find piddling little orders to be a bother, but it would be nice to have ladies stop in to look at the catalog and make up their minds.

Back in the first part of December, a note was mailed to Preacher Phil over at Dead Horse Springs. Not knowing where he would be next, it was good to give him a heads up that he would be needed the last week in March to join Burley to his lady, as he had predicted.

The white fabric and lace to make her new dress came wrapped and addressed to Miss Annie McFey, Hwy 62 Burnt Tree Junction, Eureka Springs, Arkansas.

It was cut out on the dining room table, sewed in stages as she had time. As each stage of the dress was finished, it was hung on a hanger on the parlor wall. Burley saw a finished sleeve appear, its lace ruffles gathered to fall just above her elbow.

He saw the skirt take shape, one ruffle, tuck or gather at a time. When he came through the parlor, he got the habit of glancing in the direction of the white dress… growing and taking shape. Its sight was so reassuring that he found himself heaving a sigh of pleasure just at the sight of it. It really had not been a dream or his imagination that this lovely person had consented to marry him.

He could promise himself a lifetime of the dark eyes that not only looked at him, but seemed to see through him, encouraging more words. It seemed to give importance to his most casual remark… and the whisper of a smile that attended the gaze.

He might very well be treated to the black hair framing the smile and the eyes. When it became proper to tell her he preferred it hanging down, it might be worn that way more often. It could happen.

When he saw the dress hanging all the way from the hanger to the finished hem, it was about all he could think of. His many duties and the new apple orchard served him well as a temporary distraction. There were times that he realized pleasures like this didn't just happen, they were specially created or orchestrated from a Higher Power. Certain to be.

The wedding party, when it finally arrived, consisted of Frenchie, Zennia with Charlie and Lily. And, of course, Brother Philemon Darkhorse.

As Preacher Phil put the ceremony in place, he stood Burley and Annie face to face. Burley was to take Annie's right hand in his right hand, and her left hand in his left hand. Hands crossed at the clasped fists were his symbolic way of saying that marriage meant that at all times, they would lean toward each other from one side, and hold each other up on the other. The patterns of their arms created two triangles and that geometric figure was the world's only totally ridged structure, and the solidest structure the world could create.

The tall man with the black, black hair held his Bible open before him, but he repeated from memory:

"Have ye not read that he which made them at the beginning made them male and female,

"And said, 'For this cause shall a man leave father and mother and shall cleave to his wife: And they twain shall be one flesh?'

"Wherefore they are no more twain, but one flesh. What therefore God hath joined together, let not man put asunder." (Matt. 19: 4-6)

Closing the Bible, he held it at his side and said, "In view of what I have just read, I now pronounce you husband and wife."

Burley, who had held his breath through most of the ceremony, let it out slowly and looked at the braided crown of black hair under a film of delicate lace. It was over. And he had won. The skin of his arms and shoulders rippled at the realization.

As the afternoon wore on, Charlie and Lily were put to sleep in the buggy, and the wedding party retired to the house to coffee, cake and various other goodies.

Entering the house, Burley's first glance was toward where the dress had hung, and there was only the hanger on the peg. He smiled, sighed a breath and took his place at the table.

As darkness fell, Brother Phil betook himself to the covered wagon, a place he had used a couple of other times. Handy, it was… just about half way between here and everywhere.

Frenchie brought Hobo from the corral and hitched him to the buggy. On the way to the farm, with Zennia at his side, he promised himself, *old Burley made it, and I'm next.*

When the sound of the buggy faded in the distance, the newlyweds turned toward their cabin. Burley shyly reached for her hand, and found it.

Joker, a pack animal by nature, saw that her 'pack' was safely in the house, and took her own place on the stepping stone rock. Sighed, lowered herself to the rock, sunk jaw onto paws… and eyes almost closed.

Burley found useless activities in the kitchen, finally blowing out the light. He entered the bedroom, heart pounding and blew out the wall lamp, leaving only the candle on Annie's night stand.

He looked in her direction, and startled as the loud sound of knuckles echoed through the wall. He groaned and went toward Ike's voice as it came through the door.

"Burley? Grab your boots and star. We got trouble at the lake. Won't need the dog. Deputy Potter's gettin' your horse and he'll show you where to come. I'm headin' on out."

Burley tossed the saddle on Brownie, strapped on his gun, told Joker to stay and wheeled into stride with Potter, who tried to fill him in.

"It's a thievin' migrant family, seems like, and they're in one'a them bluff caves that has two entrances. Got Jones and Comstock down there tryin' to hold 'im in. Don't know fer sure how many are there."

It was a night of a full moon, and the trail angled off Ridge Road about a half mile from the Junction. Single file they descended to Blue Lake, black in the distance. Burley tried to listen to Potter... tried to blot from his mind the picture of the black hair spread over the white pillow... tried not to remember the glow of the soft candle light on a beautiful face.

He was doing what had to be done. Ike would never have called him if it had not been necessary. He swallowed hard, and attempted to guide Brownie down the steep trail. At the level, he pulled up beside Potter.

"Just right up there," Potter yelled, motioning with an elbow.

Bad news at the bluff. Somehow, someone had slipped through, obviously crawling on his stomach through the grass. Maybe gone for help, but he was surely gone. Didn't know if it was Pa or one of the boys... maybe the girl that rode with them. Someone had to be somewhere with the extra horses.

Comstock still held at the upper opening, having pulled up dead brush as an aid to help block the entrance. The moonlight was bright, but the opening of the cave was dark, and anyone trying to enter would be a silhouette.

Jones indicated where he thought the escape had happened. A row of several short, scroungy bushes could have made cover in the grass. Ike looked at the three men waiting for direction when the sound of an approach from above the bluff.

Dreaded glances looked upward and a face appeared. Even in the moonlight it was unmistakable. Dark furred, furrowed face, eyes that reflected the moonlight and ears that hung low.

In a loud relieved whisper, Ike said, "Ugly Face! I said not to bring her… I was wrong." Joker had known he was wrong, and after waiting five minutes when told to 'stay' she loped after the horses. Speed is not the forte of bloodhounds with their bulky bodies, but the timber wolf inside her had persevered. She was less than ten minutes behind them.

With a leap down, she landed beside Burley and looked up. Ike could have hugged and kissed the dog, but he didn't have the time. "Burley, take her over to the bushes. It's our only chance. We'll deal with this here. If you find him, fire off a shot."

Joker followed Burley, nose down. She snorted to clear her nasal passages and the human told her in a soft voice, 'track.' She did.

Ike gathered his posse. "Listen. I'll cover with shots across the opening and you two slip in and stay in the dark, Jones left, Potter right. I'm comin' after and we'll push 'em together toward Comstock. Then we'll know the inside shape'a this place. You hold fire till I say, or you'll be firin' back'a us. When you fire, aim to your feet. They'll not know that. Go easy and hang to the walls."

And the shots flew ricocheting off rocks as the two deputies disappeared into the cave with the marauding family, whose size they could only guess. Six sons? Seven?

Joker snorted a couple more times and turned her face toward the hill, nosing out a path of sorts that the escapee would have taken. Around rocks and through trees and vines she climbed, Burley a step behind her. Some distance ahead he heard the snuffle and squirm of a group of bored horses.

In a stage whisper, he commanded the canine, 'stay.' She didn't want to stay and looked back to make sure what he said. He repeated the command. In a silent pose, the man and the dog stood, trying for a mental picture of where the human would be, because for certain, there would be one. Horses were a valuable means of escape. Couldn't let them be taken.

Joker raised her head and casted for the best scent in case she was permitted to go. Then he said, 'go,' and she did.

Her eyes were multiple times better than human eyes, and she saw through the low bushes where he could not have seen. She knew where the human was, and it was the kind of human she had never tracked before.

The bloodhound had brought her to this point, but the timber wolf inside her took over. With a wolf's leap, she managed to lift her thick body and whirl to the left… and downhill. A minor adjustment on the ground and a scream, definitely female.

Biting for blood was not in her nature so much as grabbing skin, which in the case of humans was that loose skin of fabric they wore. The scent she had been given was now in her mouth and Burley clawed his way to her.

The woman (girl?) was lying face down with Joker astraddle, the straps of overalls in her teeth. When the human struggled, Joker pushed a growl from her throat through her teeth, occasionally grabbing for a better bite.

Burley bound her elbows together and stood her up, tying her to a young tree. She had loosed one of the horses, so he brought the animal back and secured it with the rest… maybe six in all.

Untying her from the tree he pushed the rope through his belt securing her a scant two feet before him as he marched her back to the cave, following Joker who was wagging her head proudly. Success! She loved it!

Back at the cave, there had been an injury. One of the sons had attempted to crawl under the gunfire and had bloody mess on the calf of his right leg. Pa and one son had elbows touching and tied, and two sons were being put in a forced pack-saddle carry for their wounded brother.

Deputy Potter led the parade, trailed by the outlaw family. Comstock rode out-rider to the left and Jones to the right. Burley and Ike were in the back, all the animals struggling upward with rolling rocks, brush and low tree limbs.

"We'd'a never made it without you and that Ugly Face. That girl'd'a loosed the herd'a horses and thundered down on us. Good thing you brought her along, anyway."

Burley thought for a couple of seconds. Should he take the credit…? No, pretending was not his style. "It wasn't me, Ike. I told 'er to stay but she don't always mind me."

It was past midnight, and the posse was tired. Ike made the decision to use the Jud Carmichael's barn. He had good tight stalls, and the outlaws could be tied in. He'd leave Comstock and Potter to guard until morning, and he and Jones'd go back for the animals. Couldn't leave them tied down there, and he was still this close… only a mile or so.

"Go on home, Burley. I know'd what day this was, and I wouldn't'a bothered you… but…."

"I know, Ike. You had to."

Burley turned Brownie toward home and his bride, walking the animal because the climb had been fierce, also for the panting Joker, trotting beside them.

He dragged his feet from the corral where he had taken Brownie and climbed to the house. The bright, full moon had sunk to the west and glittered on Blue Lake… amazing that he could see it from here.

He entered the house and Joker flopped onto the stepping stone. Jaw on paws, eyes lowered to a slit.

Burley removed his shoes so he would not wake her. He'd just stay here on the settee though it was a foot too short. But he'd just take one peek into the bedroom.

The candle had burned down to its last inch, but the light glowed on her skin and shone on the hair flowing around her shoulders. She sat, resting against two pillows, and her dark eyes were trained on the door.

"Burley…?"

"Annie…!"

JUNE

The three months after the wedding had been about too busy for words. Everything had to be done… yesterday!

Gardens didn't happen by themselves. They had to be planted and tended… somehow, while still watching the stand. Pigs were to be turned into jerky and the young apple trees planted. The goats had produced kids who were turned into food.

Half-grown chicks scratched in the leaves, and more were being hatched. She still did not have the guinea hens she wanted.

Those speckled, noisy fowls presented a problem. They were almost wild, and needed a parent to show them how to survive. They also wandered a lot and roosted in trees.

If mature guinea hens were moved, they were just as likely to find their way home… as not. If guinea eggs were hatched by hens, the hens were not good teachers on how to live wild. Just about the only way to move them was to wait until there was a 'broody' guinea hen and move her and her clutch of eggs to the new place, locking her in until the chicks were hatched.

Guinea hens were good mothers, and they would know they couldn't take their chicks home…that their chicks couldn't make it that far. So they must stay at the new place until the chicks were on their own… and then THEY would not move.

So her brother with his van route was putting out the word for a broody guinea hen, but none had been found yet.

He still stopped by, often with young Charlie along. With him out of the way, his ma got more done, and spring was a busy time. Besides that, the little boy was fast becoming the son he never had.

When evening came, the owners of Burnt Tree Junction hauled their weary feet into the house and closed out the world. It was in June that Annie's field peas were ripe.

Goat sausage made wonderful meatloaf, and the milk made good soft cheese. The tomatoes were coming ripe, but the pervading aroma of the kitchen was that of the wonderful field peas.

The peas that were so hardy, one could plow all afternoon on their strength. It was the peas, along with peanuts, that held the south together during the deprivation of the war of the brothers.

Annie had slipped to the garden and gathered them. She shoved the meatloaf into the stove in her summer kitchen, grateful to keep the steamy heat from the house. During the winter, meals had accompanied lot of conversation, but now, sometimes, the weary pair was too exhausted to engage in small talk.

Windows open to the breeze, the day was finally over. Burley had removed his dirt-clod shoes on the back porch, his dirty socks with them. He hung his overalls on their nail, ready for another tomorrow.

Tossing his shirt into the dirty clothes, he moved on to the bedroom door. Annie was in her nighty, sitting up in the bed. As Burley came in, she looked up and began a sentence in one of her favorite ways.

"Burley, I've been thinkin'…?"s

He could play the game. "Thinkin' about what…?"

She fastened her dark eyes on him in her usual way. "You know that big tree out to the west that has those high limbs…?"

He nodded. "Yep. Seen it a lot'a times."

"Well, I was thinkin'. That'd be a good place for the swing."

He followed with a mental picture of the bench swing that was popular for courting couples, or a place to spend a cool evening after a hard day.

"Well, we could put us up a swing. Could be times we'd enjoy that."

"Uh, well, I was thinking more of a swing made with that little fine chain that has one board for a seat. A board about 14 to 15 inches wide."

"A board…" He struggled to fit his picture to her words. "Well, that board'd be…."

He stopped deathly still and looked at her, her hair fanned out over her shoulders and her dark eyes twinkling. Her mouth curved into a grin. A mischievous giggle escaped her throat.

"No! You don't mean we're going to have… Are you sure…?"

She nodded deeply and stretched her arms toward him. He was no longer weary and his feet no longer hurt. He grasped her hands and pulled her to her feet.

Clasping her around the waist, he felt her arms surround around his neck. He wanted to swing her around and around to express his profound joy, but there was not quite enough room in the bedroom.

He might have swung her anyway, except for the loud knuckle knock that rattled the front door. The door cracked open and a voice shouted through.

"Burley, I need you and Ugly Face. Grab some clothes and your star and hurry. Comstock's gettin' your horse, I'm goin' after your saddle."

Burley set Annie solidly on her feet, sighed and answered, "Coming, Ike." He picked his holster off the wall, and went for the shoes and overalls he had just removed.

It was when the three of them were rolling down the road, Joker in the sulky and the three men on horses, that he shook his head with dismay. It was at times like this that Burley purely hated that star. Tonight, he was almost ready to hate Ike.

But someone had said to him one time that 'true freedom was when there was nothing left to lose.'

He'd thought of that saying occasionally, but it had never meant more than it meant to him this minute...while he moved along Ridge Road with Ike and Comstock, and the animal that was pulling Joker in the sulky which she put up with. Only because she was mostly an obedient dog.

He swallowed the painful lump in his throat and felt the coolness of moisture form in his eyes. From the point of view of the saying, he was definitely not free because he had the whole world to lose.

Someone had to maintain peace in the dark of the night. It was a big county and there came a time that someone had to step up to the plate to keep it safe. To maintain some semblance of order... and mete out the punishment. It was something that had to be done sometime and that took the time and effort of someone.

Annie understood, and that made it easier.

A job was to be done, and if not now... when?

Someone had to do it, and if not him... who?

There was no one in the county who had more to lose than Burley, and maybe freedom was over-rated anyway. In the darkness of Ridge Road, Burley nodded in agreement with himself... while Ugly Face rolled on along, her muzzle drooling in anticipation of a hunt.

PART II

Burnt Tree
Junction

BROTHER PHIL'S ANGEL

GABRIEL

It really didn't seem like a dream. Dreams were made of sights he knew about, but he had never seen anything like what was now on the foot of his bed.

Six-year-old Otoe Darkhorse was intrigued rather than frightened at the hugeness of it all. Feet as long as his arm, it seemed. Overalls and shirt, so it had to be human, and when his eyes reached up to the face, there was Grandpop! Plain as day! But how did he get so big? And why was he here on the bed?

Grandpop had been put in the grave and here he was, out again. Otoe smiled with satisfaction… he'd been against putting Grandpop in the ground at the time, and here he was. Out. That proved that his opinion was correct. Grandpop was not someone that should be hidden in the dirt.

Work shoes, overalls, faded shirt. Smile under the straw hat. But as he watched, the shoes and overalls were fading away and Grandpop was wearing strap sandals and a shiny piece of metal on his shins. He had a long shirt made of cloth that looked hard and shiny… like Ma's soup kettle.

He had metal sleeves from his wrists to his elbows. And he was no longer Grandpop. He had a different face with a bigger nose and a different shaped chin, but he smiled like Grandpop. Small Otoe shrank back on his pillow in surprise, but he was still not frightened.

He watched, puzzled, and then the person started to speak. "Otoe… my name is Gabriel, and I have a message for you."

Message. That meant he was going to tell him something important, not just that it was going to be a sunshiny day. Sounded interesting, so he waited, taking in all the strangeness of this person… if he was really a person.

"Otoe, my message is to tell you that your name will not always be 'Otoe.' You will have a name change because you are a special person, and my boss, God, has things for you to do."

The small boy waited expectantly. He didn't mind the name his ma gave him, but it was interesting that someone would be able to change what his ma did. So, now he'd find out what it was going to be. "What is my new name?"

Gabriel smiled. He did not say he did not know what the new name would be, he just shook his head and said, "I cannot tell you. I can promise this, though, that when the time comes, someone will be here to help you, and you will not be surprised at what he says. It may seem like a long time to wait, but it will happen. I promise."

Hmmm. Well, Otoe knew about waiting. He'd waited quite a while for the special new shoes he'd wanted. So maybe he'd find out something else.

"How come you looked like my Grandpop for a while and then you changed into you?"

Gabriel smiled a nice smile and winked one eye, just like Grandpop would have done. "That is a good question. If I had first come as 'me' you might have been frightened. But if I came as Grandpop, then you knew there was nothing to fear from me. God always does things right."

Then Gabriel smiled again and told him, "I have to go now. We angels have a lot to do, but I am not leaving you alone. There will always be an angel with you, but most of the time you won't know it. I will be back to see you sometime. Just remember that." And while small Otoe watched, suddenly there was nothing at the foot of his bed, just like before.

So he wondered, *Did something really happen?* Maybe just a dream, but now he was awake. He slid from his bed and lit the candle. Leaning over the coverlet, he examined the place where Gabriel had stood. Clear as can be, two places where the covers were pressed down right where his feet had been, and they were much longer feet than Grandpop's feet would have been.

He stared, then stood and watched as the footprints slowly vanished, and there was no sign of them. He drew in a deep breath... put his fingers over his mouth in a thoughtful way and said, "Hmmmmmm."

When the boy was eight, he saw Gabriel again. It was one day when he had to miss school because the corn must be harvested, and the stalks cut in pieces for the cows. He was just a little out of sorts... school was such a wonderful place and his parents wanted him to go, but someone had to help with the work, and his younger brothers were too little to use the long, sharp knife.

So, there was Gabriel... standing right in the corn rows in front of Otoe's machete blade. Whack–whack-whack, and three stalks were down and placed neatly in the pile to be picked up.

The angel smiled and told him, "I just needed to stop by to let you see me because I don't want you to forget that you are chosen. That means you will have help deciding what to do with your life."

"Gabriel, I have a question. What does it mean to be chosen? And why me?"

"I'll remind you that I already told you why you are chosen. It is because you agreed to be chosen."

"When was that? I don't remember sayin' nothin' like that."

"You didn't have to say anything. God sees into your heart and he knows your mind. It was not necessary to say it in words."

"Hmmm, well, what does it mean that I will have help? Are you here to help me chop the corn?"

The angel threw back his head and laughed, and the sound was strangely like Grandpop. "No, I am not here to chop corn. You know how to do that. I am here to make you remember that I and the other angels are real, even though you can't see us. I was sent to remind you that what you are learning in school is going to be very important to you. You must do the very best you can."

"But… I always do…."

While he was speaking, there became only a row of corn before him. Kneeling quickly to the dusty ground, he saw the footprints of the strange footwear. A tiny shiver passed down from his head and into his arms. The hot April sun was pushed away for maybe a half a minute.

Otoe nodded, to no one in particular, grabbed a cornstalk in his left hand and swung the machete with his right hand. Whack-whack-whack and three more stalks were put on the stack.

OTOE DARKHORSE BECOMES TWELVE

This was the last year that the boy could attend school. He was savoring every minute of it. It was while he was coming home from school, stopping occasionally to pull muscadine grapes from the vines, the angel appeared once more.

"Sit down, Son. We must have a chat. This is an important year for you because you will receive a gift. You will be invited to hear a stranger who wants boys and girls your age to hear stories from his book called the Bible. You will go, but you will not say anything to him until he speaks to you privately.

"When you get that gift, you will know that is what you will be studying when you have no school lessons. You will be studying in your mind while you do chores, go after the cows, chop kindling or draw water for the animals. The words in that book will be with you and inside you, and they will help you."

"When will I see the man?"

"I must not tell you. It is a test of faith that you wait, and you will have many tests. It is only left for you to do what your head says for you to do. One thing… you must test the thoughts in your head because God's enemy, Satan, also gives thoughts to boys like you. Sometimes you will have trouble deciding which is which."

"What if I mess up? Will God not like me anymore?"

With a wide shake of the head, the angel said, "You will not be permitted to make a mistake, if you trust and think. (Isa 35:8) There will be a way, like a highway, and it will be so clear to you that you cannot miss."

And then he was gone. The boy continued to sit on the stone and stare into the sky watching the puffs of white cumulus moisture drifting past. *Why, just when we seem to be getting somewhere, does he disappear? He seems to think I'm smart... or something.*

Then a thought came into his head. *This is a test of faith. I must not fail it.* He knew about tests, and he always made sure he was prepared. He also knew about faith, but it was rather hard to get words for it.

He looked quickly around, but saw nothing except a packrat stealing from the muscadines he had been picking and putting in his cap. All of this was just his good imagination. Of course it was!

Oops! That... without doubt... was the other angel who was not Gabriel messing with his thoughts, because the thought just entered his mind like a muscadine entering the rat's mouth.

Nodding, he began grabbing handfuls of the tarty, wild grapes and tossing them into his hat. His ma liked to get them for jam. Yes, it was time for that other angel to put in an appearance inside his head, because Gabriel came and went so quickly. *Thank you, angel. Stick around close, will you? I have a lot of questions.*

It was during the two week Christmas vacation that word was circulated from every direction. Children from eight to twelve were invited to the schoolhouse for stories. Older people could come and listen if they wanted to, and if there was room.

Right! Now I will get the gift. The boy was certain the storytelling was just for him.

The storyteller was old... way over fifty years... to Otoe's calculation. He had wrinkles of the kind caused by smiling, and when he told stories from the Book, it was just like he had been there when they happened. Otoe's sister was with him, and they glanced at each other, nodding and smiling eagerly. This was fun! Really fun! And it would happen for the five whole days of this week.

While enjoying the stories, he wondered when he would be told of the gift, and felt pangs of impatience. The last day came, and they were dismissed. He asked his sister to wait while he thanked the man for the stories as his mother would want him to do, and when he walked toward him, he knew he was doing the right thing.

The old man with the good wrinkles nodded and smiled. "I rather thought it would be you. I was waiting for the chosen young man to come to me so I would be sure. You must come here tomorrow without your sister, because I have been told to see you alone."

"Who told…?"

"That is not important." The man patted Otoe's shoulder. "Tomorrow it will be clear. Go now and take your sister home." The man turned and walked away, and Otoe returned to his sister with his mind in a whirl.

He thought morning would never come. Immediately after breakfast he ran to the schoolhouse, intending to sit and wait for the man, but the man was there waiting for him. And he got right to the point.

"Young man, you are the reason I am here. Yes, I had stories and entertained your friends, but I have something for you. Two things, really.

"First, I was told to offer to share my name with you. For some reason, God wants you to have another name. The same thing happened to me, and I was given the name Philemon. That is the name of one of the friends who got a special letter from Paul, and the letter became part of this Book. It has a special meaning and I am told to share the name with you.

"I know that the name may seem strange to you, and if it does, you may shorten it to Phil. Its meaning is 'friend, trusted one, obedient servant and helper.' Mostly, helper. I know that you want me to tell you how I knew to do this and I don't know. But this I know, you must, from this moment on, be named Philemon. If people do not believe you, it doesn't matter. If they won't call you that, it still doesn't matter. It is true, and you must believe it.

"Now, the other thing." The old man's smile disappeared and he sighed a long, loud sigh. "My old papa, who is gone, had a Bible that he read and re-read, and he wrote notes on the pages, and in places he made a note telling of another interesting place to look. When he died, the Bible became mine and it is the most precious thing I have. I made a leather bag for it to protect it, and I would not use it because I thought it might be damaged.

"I bought another Bible to use and kept Papa's Bible to remind me of him. But now I know I must pass it on to you. I was told that it was to be given, and I said I would gladly give my newer book. But then I was told that it must be Papa's Bible, the one with Papa's notes, and I would see who it was for when I came out here on Ridge Road."

He paused, swallowed hard and wiped his eyes. Otoe, now Phil, bravely asked, "Sir, who told you to give up your papa's book?"

The man looked sad and said, "I can tell you, but you will not believe it. It was a very tall man who appeared suddenly. He frightened me so much I could hardly look at him. He looked rather like a soldier, but was dressed in strange, shiny clothing that looked like metal. See, you don't believe it."

"Oh, yes. I really believe you. What was his name...?"

"Oh, Son, I was too frightened to ask. He just said I was to give you Papa's Bible because you were chosen to have it, and the marks on the pages would be valuable to you. The big man said that all these years, I was just the keeper of the book until you reached twelve years old."

Young Philemon shuddered and pulled himself into his bright blue, go-somewhere-special shirt. He clasped his hands to keep them from shaking. His teeth chattered, and he could hardly push out the words.

"Mister... sir...? I know that big man. He is an angel and he told me four years ago that you would come. His name is Gabriel."

The old man nodded. "Gabriel. Of course. Gabriel, the announcer, the one whose trumpet heralds the good and bad. I should have known. So I'll tell you the last thing. The man, Gabriel, told me that the scribbled notes of my papa would help you because there was no teacher here for you. He said the book was of no value to anyone while hiding in my leather bag when it contained something you needed."

He reached in his pack and brought out a bag made of new leather, smelling strongly of the leather preservative. Carefully, he untied the clasp and took out a book with a worn leather cover. He opened it, and the delicate, tissue paper pages were covered with tiny, handwritten notes. In ink.

Phil raised his hand to his lips to keep them from trembling. His heart beat within his chest so strongly it seemed to be pounding against his ribs. He forgot to breathe, and suddenly gasped for breath. This could not be happening. In 1910 northern Arkansas the whole Bible was only for the very rich, and was as scarce as hen's teeth, so to speak.

This whole incident, of course, could not be happening to the young mountain boy. Still and all, it made him swallow again and again, so he might be able to speak, but he had no words.

"Son," the man began, "I can see how you feel about this gift. I was thinking of the average twelve year old boy and why would he deserve this most precious thing I have. Now I see. It is now yours, and I needn't tell you to take very good care of it. I know you will. I will also say that I know your life will be a hard one and full of disappointments and puzzling confusions. I know, also, that you are a chosen one. These mountains must be needing someone like you."

He tied the leather strings around the bag and handed it over to the boy. Phil steadied his hands to accept it, feeling the wonderful weight of it on his palms. His. He would be through school in three months, but now his studying could continue.

Feet seeming not to touch the ground, he followed the well-trod path to his house. It was then that his head received an idea, totally foreign to what he would have thought. The little house in the side yard. It was a small cabin used for his Gran when she got older, and was now used for storage.

The commandment that came from nowhere was there in his head. "Request to be permitted to move into the cabin, at least at night, so you will have time and privacy for your study. You will soon be looking for a job with someone who needs a strong boy, and you are nearing thirteen. The perfect age."

Angel…? Is that you with that idea…? Are you tellin' me I can get a job for money? The angel did not answer, so Phil decided that this was another test of his faith. Certain to be.

THE SECOND IMPORTANT GIFT

Philemon at age thirteen had two sudden thoughts. One was "there is no way for me to tell the world I am ready to work for money." The other one followed quickly, and advised "a strong boy of thirteen would know how to advertise."

Advertise…? That was for grownups who had something to sell. *Something to sell…? Well, that's me and my time. Who's a grown up…? Someone with something he owns and wants to sell it.* So young Phil talked to his ma.

"Ma… I'd like to work for cash money. You got other boys comin' up for work on the farm but cash money'd be handy. If I could figure how to let people know that I work good, I could live here and give you half of what I earn to make up for bein' gone…."

Ma sat across from him at the round table. (Round tables were able to seat more people… an important feature for a lot of families.) She had set a steaming cup before each of them when he said he wanted to talk. Waiting for tea to cool to sipping temperature encouraged real conversation… not just rapid words back and forth.

She waited after hearing his plan. Mothers must exercise patience, so she blew a soft breath into the steam and lifted it to her lips.

"…so I thought of, well, it wasn't me, but the thought came in my head. Up on Ridge Road where the sign is for Burnt Tree Junction, there's a tree that folks nail messages to. The lady that tends the stands started it with her own tree, but she pointed out another tree that had pegs for folks to hang their notes."

Ma nodded encouragement. She had supposed that her first born had a plan already, and she had only to wait to see how she fit in to it.

"So I was thinkin', Ma. If you was to agree with me that some neighbors could come to the house some evening… maybe after supper and before dark, I could tell them stories from my Bible. Not many folks have one, and it's just packed full of things that happened to people. And there's the second part that talks about God, Jesus and a man named Paul who spent his life just telling people what they didn't have a chance to know."

Ma was following closely. Visits! It was so difficult for neighbors to get together… like when each would be available. And at home. If she was to know… for sure… that company was coming, she could have tea (or maybe coffee) ready and certainly cookies that her daughters loved to bake.

Entertainment on the mountain was practically nonexistent, and a story teller was a prize. She nodded, being positively certain that her son could tell an interesting story from the book that was such a special gift. Then, after the story, they could eat and drink and talk until the neighbors had to go home. All of this zipped through her mind, all in a piece, and she knew it would happen.

"Yes, Son. Make your sign and tack it to the tree. I'll talk with Pa but I know he'll agree. We'll set a date for the first story time and see what happens."

Phil left Ma and went back to his cabin, his fist full of a generous slab of buttered cornbread. Ma's cornbread was perfect when hot, cold, fresh or leftover from yesterday. He smiled between bites. It was wonderful to have a ma. What did fellows do who didn't have one? That was a thought too awful to think on.

So he located two pieces of cardboard from a packing box. With crayons he worded the first sign as best he could.

Story teller with a Bible invites neighbors to the Darkhorse Farm at sundown on Saturday, next. Come for a story, refreshments and conversation.

Then with a sigh and deep breath, he began the second sign.

Strong teenage boy wants day work. One day or five. For overnight jobs, I need meals and shelter for a horse and myself, preferably together. Reasonable charge. Phil Darkhorse.

Reading over his efforts, he nodded with satisfaction. *Gabriel, am I doin' the right thing? If you'd show up and help me, maybe I could do better.*

But then he remembered with a grin, it wasn't actually Gabriel who gave him these ideas. It was more like that other angel (?) that Gabriel said would always be with him. So far, Gabriel had always shown himself when he came. The other angel (angels?) remained hidden inside his thoughts.

152

Ma was almost giggly with excitement when three different wagons pulled into the yard. Neighbors! Visits! What an evening this would be!

The first wagon had neighbors she did not know. The man came to the door, "We been hearin' a storytellin' was happenin' and the fellow up at the junction pointed us here. Did we hear right?"

Ma pulled them into the house faster than a pair of hands could pull taffy candy. She brought in chairs as far as they would go... youngens on the floor... and they waited expectantly.

For his first storytime, Phil chose the story of David killing the Giant. It took almost a half an hour, and the applause was enthusiastic, especially from the children. Two hours later, in the pitch darkness of night, the last person left with an invitation to come again next week.

It was two days later that a fellow on a horse galloped into the yard asking for the boy named Phil. What he had was a field of cornstalks to be brought down, hauled to the barn and chopped. Thought it would be a two day job, but maybe three. Could Phil do it?

"You bet, man. I'm the best corn chopper you'd find in this county."

The man on the horse was Simon Turner whose family operated the lumber mill across Ridge Road and down by Blue Lake. Like most farming families with businesses, there were times that a workload happened without a worker to do it. Phil spent his first week on the job, but insisted he had to be home on Saturday.

After about the third Saturday, the other ladies who came to the storytelling looked at Phil's ma with a bit of... maybe not envy... but clearly a tiny twinge of jealousy. All that wonderful company, showing off her baking skill and also owning the son who made the evening so entertaining... especially for the children.

The answer to this jealousy would be to scatter the meetings around, which drew a lot more attendees. The only problem at this time was the smallness of some of the houses, and the weather was not always permissive of using the yard.

It was after years fourteen, fifteen, sixteen and seventeen that Phil knew, for a fact, that he was good at speaking before people. His stories became even more interesting, and he felt a confidence that he could never have expected to have.

At various times he felt as if he had a message from his angel, but it was hard to be sure. *Just a test of faith*, he told himself, and carefully sorted these messages away from the ones he knew, positively, were from the other direction. Those were not to be listened to.

It was at age eighteen that he heard, it seemed, another voice. It seemed to be a dream, but he dreamed that he was in his bed, thinking of nothing, when a beam of sunlight flashed across the room and against the far wall. A voice said, "Today you will receive another gift."

Hmmm, now what would that be? Not the Bible, because that was years ago, and the voice had said 'another.' As his mind woke up, he remembered the voice, and chuckled at the ridiculousness of it all. Today he was going to work for old man Pennyworth, clearing brush from his yard and driveway. The old man was shaky and had trouble even standing while using his cane, and there was no way he could handle a hatchet or an ax to do his own clearing.

Phil had offered to do it for nothing. It would only take a day, and a short one at that, and it was sorely needed. The brush had grown up over the past years, as it does everywhere in northern Arkansas, and the man was so the old that he could hardly make the trip to his privy without risking a snake bite.

Phil would work for free, but the old man would have none of that. The man had no money. He did, however, have an old mare he had turned out to pasture to die, but she had seemed to be surviving without care. The mare's name had been Dolly, but had turned into 'BOB' for the last couple of years.

'B-O-B' for Bag of Bones. The old man chuckled and said she got that name because even though she ate all the time, she couldn't seem to put on flesh. Old Mr. Pennyworth's eyesight had dimmed drastically, but he could manage his cabin and the milk goat he tied from place to place, so he'd remember where she was and she would not wander off.

Of course, BOB could no longer plow or pull a wagon, but she might be able to pull a dog cart to haul his sisters around… couldn't she? Would that be a help at his house? The old man so hoped that would be payment enough.

Phil assured him a cart horse would be handy. The old man seemed bent on some method of payment, and Phil could take care of the animal in Pa's pasture, and put her down when necessary… when she got too old to live.

It would have been a short day for Phil, but the old man wanted to talk, and followed him around like a pup, stopping him often to say something. So it was lowering dark when he finished.

He was told by the old man that just back in the pasture was the old nag, and Phil would not mind to get her himself, would he?

Phil was tired, and he'd just as soon not go to look for the horse. He couldn't, however, disappoint the old man. As he went through the corral gate and into the pasture, the words came to him again. "Today, you will receive another gift."

Weary as he was, Phil had to chuckle. An old nag in her last days… a gift? Maybe the thought came from the 'other side' angels meant to disappoint him and damage his faith in God.

The words had not, for a fact, come from Gabriel. It was just one of those times when it seemed someone was speaking to him without words. He prided himself that he was getting good at sorting from which direction the thoughts came.

Oh, well. He'd get the old nag, and when he actually saw her, in the gathering dark, his hopes of riding her home evaporated. More possible would be him carrying the animal. But he walked her back to the barn, and she followed willingly. He found the saddle that the old man wanted him to take, and it was a rather nice creation of tooled leather. Lots of use in it still.

Maybe that was his gift, and if it was, it was something he could certainly use. Speaking out loud to the inner voice, he said, "Thanks for the saddle. BOB should be able to carry it home." His words had echoed around in the empty barn, shingles missing, and corners festooned with dusty cobwebs.

With no thought of mounting, he led the animal beside him, and she seemed willing to be led. One foot after the other, and the young man and animal reached the Darkhorse Farm.

He put BOB in an empty stall, removed the saddle and poured a scoop of chopped corn into the manger. She lowered her head and attacked the grain, obviously still having enough teeth to chew it. Poor old BOB.

As he walked past her to go to his cabin, he ran his hand down her puffed-out sides. Bloated. Obviously. Maybe he shouldn't have given her grain, but it was too late now. With a sigh, he headed for his bed.

He was awakened in early dawn by the raucous discussions of a family of crows, choosing to use his roof as a meeting place. He rubbed his eyes and thought of the saddle.

He had no job for today or tomorrow, and it would be a good time to oil the dried-out leather of the saddle. Linseed oil would be first, to soak into the seams and soften the leather. Then after an hour or two in the sunshine, he'd apply melted beeswax to the warm leather. He'd soon see if it was as good as it had seemed.

Entering the barn stall he was greeted with a conversational whicker through the old mare's lips, then she returned to her duty of washing her newborn son who stood beside her on wavering legs.

WHAT was going on?

The 'bloated' abdomen had obviously sheltered a foal. Bless the old nag! She had managed to get herself bred, and there was no sire in the pasture with her. Well, animals were known to jump fences when properly motivated, and if the sire of this little animal jumped the fence, he must have been in good shape. Hmmm, well….

Leaning on the stall wall, he watched as the old mother proudly nudged her son toward his first meal. Big fellow! Just look at that! Big as a colt a month or six weeks old! Black, he seemed to be, but the stall was dark. What an animal! Perfectly formed, too. And all his!

How did that old wreck of a mare manage to produce this small example of perfection? And if this was a gift from God by the angels then it must mean that he was going to need it… in a year and a half or two years…? That is when the animal would be able to carry a full grown man, like Phil was becoming.

Well, now, didn't he have a story to tell at the breakfast table… and he would have the delicious duty of selecting a name!

There was always Blackie, Buddy, and other friendly names for a horse, but this gift horse was special. Thought would be required to reach the exact right name, and he had a saddle to restore while he was thinking.

He painted on the melted wax, flooding it into the seams to protect the threads that held the saddle together. Relaxed in the September sun, luxuriating in the knowledge that the saddle and the colt would have required at least two months of his earnings if he had bought them, the thought jammed its way into his brain.

Sergeant!

Sergeant. His Pa's old dad had told stories of the war between the brothers, north against south, and destruction was on all sides. He had been conscripted into the Battle of Pea Ridge that was fought just down the road. It had been one of the last battles, and one of the bloodiest.

It was the sergeants, the old man had said, that fought the war. The generals sat under roofs and gave orders, thinking they were fighting the battle, but it was the sergeant that faced the blood and death of the battle. He was the one who worried about the food supply, the ammunition shortages and the soldier whose shoulder had caught stray grape-shot from a cannon across the ridge.

It was the sergeants who fought the war, carrying wounded on their own backs, ripping open a shirt tail for a bandage to stop the blood. Putting a bloody, scrappy note in his pocket to, hopefully, deliver it to a ma, girlfriend, wife, or a small daughter… something to remember their soldier by. It was the sergeant who racked his brain to remember where on the sketched map was the cave where his men could ride out an ice storm.

This horse was a precious gift and would be a friend for many years. 'Sergeant' he would be. A magnificent stallion, shining and polished from head to tail to hoof.

And now BOB's tongue lovingly caressed him while he lay curled at her feet, belly extended from his meal. Phil was finished with the saddle that was now catching the last of the sun's heat, and he stood at the stall watching. The miniature ribs of the colt expanded reassuringly as he breathed, his ma whickering tender caresses over his head.

A pleased sigh, and Phil turned away. A mare like this deserved another scoop of chopped corn, and a bucket of fresh water delivered to her so she would not have to leave her son.

As he poured the corn in the manger, he made a decision. BOB would again become 'Dolly' to the end of her days.

NEW ANGELIC ORDERS FROM ABOVE

When Sergeant reached the age of two, he was filled out and strong, easily carrying his owner and friend. Occasionally Phil reminisced with sadness the demise of old man Pennyworth, who would never know how great was his gift.

For the first month or so of Sergent's life, Phil would have the feeling that he should stop by and assure the old man that he had, really and truly, paid for that day of work. Maybe it was an angelic suggestion, but Phil thought it was more likely just his own thoughts. He had really liked that old man, and he grinned as his mind presented a picture of the grizzled old head thrown back in laughter, his toothless gums open to exposure and his bony shoulders shaking with mirth over a memory from his younger days.

A good old joke BOB played on her owner! Jolly good show, and now the helpful young man had a colt that would bring money. Phil thought of it several times, knowing the old man would enjoy the knowledge, but there were other things to do, and it took Gabriel standing in the way to center his attention.

It had been over a year since the heavenly warrior had put in an appearance. Over the intervening years, there had been several conversations. Like:

"Gabriel, are you the real Gabriel in the Bible?"

"Why would you think I wasn't?"

"Because you spend so much time with me and I am so unimportant."

"Why do you think you are not important?"

"I'm just a mountain boy and there's not much I can do. I know you said I was chosen, but I still don't know what for."

"Have you been told to do something that you did not do?"

"I hope not. I certainly didn't intend to."

"So, think about it. If you have not disobeyed an order, then you have done what you should do at this time and at your age."

"Oh. But I just talk with neighbors and save my money like I was told. I got two wonderful gifts and have done nothin' to repay for them."

"What says you have to 'repay' for a 'gift'? God gave his only Son and there is no way you could possibly pay for that."

Phil thought a minute. Their conversations always went that way, making him feel a little foolish for asking questions.

Another time, Gabriel told him, "You will go over to Berryville and buy a tent with a floor in it just big enough for you to sleep in. And see if there is a small dog someone is giving away."

"How will I find the dog when I don't know anyone in town?"

"The classified ads, don't you think…?"

"You're saying I am going to need a dog?"

"Small dog. Terrier. English rat dog."

"Oh. What else?"

"You're going to need two mules, but not yet."

"Two mules…?"

"Are you questioning me? I'm here to make sure you are hearing words from the Boss. The Boss doesn't like to spring surprises when they aren't necessary. Yes, two mules… but not yet."

Somewhat chastened, Phil silently bowed his head.

And now Gabriel was back. "You must stop by the house of old man Pennyworth. Today."

"Yes, of course. He'll be glad to know about the colt."

"He already knows. There is another reason to stop by the cabin."

"What is it?"

"If you were supposed to know, I would have told you. I keep telling you that your trust and faith must be kept strong."

Phil was just coming home from a three day job chopping wood for a cook stove… and that meant each chunk required a lot of splits. A lot of bending over, and a lot of lifting the ax. He was tired and wanted to go home.

Sergeant was stepping lightly along Ridge Road, and turned without direction at the lane that led to old man Pennyworth's cabin.

Apparently the stallion had been listening to the angel, the thought crossed Phil's mind. Wouldn't put it past Gabriel to tell the animal first, just to make sure his owner did what he was told. After all, Balaam's donkey, in the Bible, had to correct his rider. (Numbers 22: 28)

As he turned in at the ancient and dilapidating gate, a pitiful sound met him. Goat! Bleating pathetically. Injured by a timber wolf, maybe. Something, for certain, was bothering the animal. Sure to be.

Bypassing the house he turned toward the corral and the bleating goat hardly had a voice left, but was agonizing over the pain of a bursting udder. Another few more hours and she would be gone. Forever. Dead.

Leaping down from Sergeant, he knelt by the goat and began milking onto the ground. Then he heard the weak bleat of the kid from the adjoiing pen. Leaving the goat, he leaped the fence and gathered the kid in his arms. Kicking open the gate, he put its hungry mouth to the udder, and stood back watching the little one slurping and sucking, wads of milk-foam dripping down his chin.

Leaving the animals, he went to the house. The knock aroused no one. He opened the door, and found the old man still sitting in a chair, arms lying across the table. The lifeless hand had upset the tea cup, the liquid now having soaked his sleeve and dripped onto the floor.

Phil checked the artery at the man's neck. Cold. No action. Dead. The old man had clearly died at his breakfast table leaving the goat unmilked. Well, that changed Phil's plans.

The goats, mom and baby together in the corral, would last… for now. Next he checked for a buggy, wagon or dog cart. He found the old but well kept buggy under a large canvas tarp.

Wrapping the man in the tarp he put him on the back seat of the buggy, brought Sergeant to the shafts and harnessed him in. Now what?

Almost twenty year old Phil had never experienced anything remotely like this. What to do…? Maybe back to the junction and ask the deputy that lived there. Or take him home and ask Pa. He'd never heard of the old man having family. So….

Something must be done immediately. Take him home. Yes. And then report the death…? Ma would know.

Early the next day, the old man was stretched out into a hastily made box and put into the Darkhorse family graveyard. Ma wrote down everything she knew about him and put the letter in the mailbox for the carrier. He came down Ridge Road once a week now. Real handy.

Phil wrapped the buggy in the tarp, and pulled it into the shed. Then went for the goat, bringing her back in the dog cart, the small two-wheeled farm vehicle, four feet by four feet square. Those carts were so handy for the mountain farms.

He went to the junction and reported the death and the empty house that would now belong to the county. New neighbors might soon buy it. Good house and barn. Plenty of pasture, but needed more brush chopped. Not his job, though.

Perhaps there would be new neighbors not too far from the Darkhorse Farm. Maybe friends for Ma.

DEAD HORSE SPRINGS

Dead Horse Springs was located on a ridge plateau just east of Eureka Springs. What kept it together was the several top-of-the-mountain springs that freely flowed their sparkling water as they had for eons, and would possibly continue as long as the earth lasted. No one remembered how the 'Dead Horse' got there, nor did they care.

The streams from the springs joined together and passed through the small town of Wishbone Hollow, and then into the Mulberry River.

Dead Horse Springs was composed of seven houses more or less within yelling distance on a clear day, and another 10 or 12 sprinkled a bit lower down the ridge. Wonderful land there, hilltop view and an unending supply of water. The thing was, it was too far from Eureka Springs or Wishbone to travel there except when absolutely necessary. Ate up a whole day of travel, there and back. It was just the way of things, and one couldn't have everything.

Going down the mountain for a shopping trip was one thing, but going every Sunday for church was out of the question. Why, a body'd be midnight getting home from the night service. No matter. There was an answer.

The Parnell farm was the flattest, and had the best centralized location, being situated on a lower step of the mountain, and on the marked road down to either town. Mr. Parnell had more land that he had the need to farm, and it would be a plum in his hat to get to deed a couple of acres, maybe as many as five, to build a church, and eventually add a parsonage for the preacher, the preacher that would certainly be difficult to obtain.

The best they could hope for, without an outright gift from God, was a beginner of a preacher. But then, even preachers had to start somewhere, and the people from Dead Horse Springs were of a tolerant nature.

In addition to that, there were those who had been church attendees before coming to the Springs, and fervently wanted to continue to "assemble themselves together, as the manner of some is," (Hebrews 10: 25) if they just had a place.

So the Parnell land was set aside and the building begun. They were aiming for a 100 person capacity plus an office and two small classrooms. A very ambitious venture for such a small community, but the farm work slacked down in the winters, and in three year's time they had put the building together, chopping the last shingles from cedar chunks and oiling the plank flooring with preservative.

During this time they had put out hopeful invitational tentacles to attract interest from somewhere. Anywhere, in fact. Nothing usable so far. For the older folks, an assembling of themselves together for a reading of the word would work as a temporary measure, but not for the youngens. A teacher/preacher must be found.

Children under ten (and there were quite a number) were the ones to reach if the church on the hill was to continue and grow. So when the last shingle was tapped into place, and the oil that would not soak into the boards was mopped away, prayer began in earnest.

"God, do you see us down here? We done all we could, and now we could use a little help." Surely God could see them, being up there on the hilltop right in front of him.

For a fact, God did see them, and he watched their ambition. He saw their fervor, but he had a special plan for them. The guardian angels had been on the job, but this was an errand for Gabriel. Gabriel, of course, had known all along what would happen.

Over on Ridge Road it had been three days this clear October weather had produced, and no one came wanting day-help. Phil wandered restlessly as a petrol winging over the waves of the ocean. What gives here…?

He had pulled the buggy out into the sunshine and cleaned it inside and out. Repainted the wheels and the undercarriage a shiny black. He had painstakingly oiled the hardened leather seats into pillow-softness.

So now, it was mid-morning and he was debating whether to take it for a spin to circulate the grease he had forced into the wheel bearings… or put it back in the shed and find something else to do until someone needed him.

He was sitting there still debating when he saw the handsome pair of bays as they tossed their heads at the flies and brought the buggy they pulled down into the yard of the Darkhorse Farm.

Hmmm, well, finally. A job. But Phil would never have guessed in a million years what the job would be… He leaped lightly from the buggy seat and headed in their direction.

"Can I help you, sirs?"

"Parnell, here… and this gentlemen is Mr. Kilpatrick. We've come looking for a young man by the name of Philemon Darkhorse, and were directed here. Would you, by chance, be that person?"

"I am, sir. Would you like to step up on the porch and sit? What kind of work would you like to have done…?"

Mr. Parnell looked at Mr. Kilpatrick, who nodded and began, "They tell me you are called Phil, and I will use that name if you don't mind. For the past months we have been hearing about the way you tell stories to children on Saturdays, and that you are very good at what you do."

Puzzled, Phil leaned forward, chin in fists, the better to study these men who were talking so strangely.

Mr. Parnell took over. "Perhaps we should explain a little about ourselves. We are from over at Dead Horse Springs and that is, as you know, almost seven miles over Ridge Road, and another mile north. We have just built a new church building and do not yet have a pastor. Mr. Kilpatrick will continue."

With a nervous clearing of the throat, the first speaker picked it up. "Yes, and while we work to get a pastor, our new building sits empty. That cannot be pleasing to our God. When we prayed for an answer, some of us, many actually, were to learn of a young man who was very well studied in the entire Bible, and was having much success with children.

"Now, we know you are very young and would not be seeking something permanent just now… but we thought we might offer you our pulpit for a time, say, during the four winter months. If you were available, there would be bed and meals and a small stipend for your services. Mr. Parnell…?"

Mr. Parnell nodded. "Meals would be served at my house, being just a few steps away. We learned that you have roomed away from your parents, and we supposed it was for privacy and study. Therefore, we have outfitted our office in the church building with a stove, bed, study table and chair. Whatever you would need additionally, we would provide."

Mr. Kilpatrick again. "What we would love to have would be two dissertations on Sunday, and another service on Wednesday evening for the few who live close and can come." He paused, watching Phil to see how it was going.

Phil felt the blood draining from his face as he drew in a breath and let it out. "But, sirs, I've never… I mean I can't really do…" And then he ran out of words.

Mr. Kilpatrick again. "What would it be than you could not do? You read stories to children and explain them wonderfully, we're told. We have children who would love to have stories read… especially by a well-read, handsome fellow like yourself. What would it be you could not do?"

With an encouraging smile, Mr. Parnell added, "If it's the meals you're concerned about, my wife is an excellent cook… positively the best. And there is this, there will be other families who will want to come to my house and bring the evening meal, just to get to talk with you and perhaps ask a few questions. So many of us have had no opportunity, and sometimes hardly the time, to study for ourselves. We hoped to glean from your years of study. We hear it has been almost a decade since you received your Bible."

Phil's head was reeling. How did these strangers know so much about him? Who's been talking to them... and them so far away? It was beginning to give him shivers of fright. Like maybe he had been tossed into the swimming hole with his hands and feet tied. Breathless and scary. He looked from one to the other, the silence looming heavily.

A squeak of the screen door signaled another person entering the porch. There was Ma!!! Her tray held steaming tea and her poundcake cookies that almost dripped jersey-cream butter.

She smiled above her snow-white apron as she scooted onto the edge of the near chair. "So pleased to have you gentlemen stop by. We have so little company being back from the road, the way we are. I know you have come a long way, and it would be my pleasure if you would help yourselves to the cookies."

Chewing cookies gave the three men a short reprieve from speaking. Ma continued, "I'm so glad my son was home today. He's away so much now, I don't get to see him a lot. But I know... he's a man now, and it would be time for him to use his talents.

"So I'll just slip back to the kitchen, and not interrupt your business talk. So pleased to have you, sirs." And she was gone, leaving Phil alone and forced to speak.

He drew in a breath, and began. "Sirs, I am so appreciative of this offer. I'm thinking you may have been given the wrong information, and I wouldn't want to disappoint you. So sorry you had to come so far just to be disappointed."

Mr. Parnell took another cookie, and looked pointedly at his partner. Mr. Kilpatrick took the hint. "We're not disappointed yet. We were of a mind not to tell you this if we didn't have to, because we didn't want to cause you concern, but this is what happened. During the last week, ten days ago, actually, three different members of our community had a dream. In it they saw a huge man that looked like pictures of a Roman soldier, with armor on his arms and shins and a shiny helmet. This man told the dreamer that it was time to go to Burnt Tree Junction and ask after young Brother Philemon Darkhorse, who preferred to be called Phil. The big man said the young man would have the answers to our needs for the winter."

Mr. Parnell was nodding during the whole speech. "Yes, and one of them dreamers was my wife who never remembers her dreams, and she woke me up scared, and told me what she dreamed. Later we heard of the others."

He paused, "We wasn't wantin' to tell you, but you wasn't seemin' to see what we meant. I'd not want you to be spooked or nothin', but from what my wife described, I thought I'd do what that big man said... not wantin' to tangle with him myself."

It was Mr. Kilpatrick's turn to nod. "So you see what we're up against. It seems to be took outta our hands. That don't mean we won't welcome you with open arms. Our youngens heard us talkin' and they're in a hurry for you to be there. It seems what it is you got is what our church needs just now. We voted on four months, but that ain't firm. If you come and find you don't like it, there'd be no problem."

Phil raised his head and trained his dark, dark eyes onto the blue eyes of Mr. Parnell and the gray ones of Mr. Kilpatrick. "Yes, I will come. I will be ready the first day of November, 10 days from now. I will be glad to do my best for you." He pressed his lips together, to firmly hold inside his head the knowledge that he knew just exactly who that 'Roman soldier' was.

With that, the talk lightened to the weather, the crops, and the new animals. "Seems you got good transportation," Mr. Parnell jabbed his elbow toward the shining buggy. "Single horse shafts... I'd say you got yourself a young stallion just rearin' to go."

Mr. Kilpatrick arose, as a signal the meeting was over, and Ma appeared like magic. "Such a lovely day to be out on the road. I hope you gentlemen had a good visit, and it was my pleasure to serve you." With that, she smiled, picked up the empty tray and left.

Phil walked them to their buggy, signaled farewell, and watched the team circle in the yard and pull out on the driveway, leaving tiny dust puffs in the dry dirt. Then he sighed and turned toward the tiny cabin that had been his castle and sanctuary for the last number of years. He needed to have a talk with someone, and when he opened the door, the 'someone' was sitting on his bed.

Phil was so full of terror, it spilled over when he opened his mouth. "I can't do that, you know that! I can't go all the way over there and talk with youngens I don't even know…."

Gabriel butted in, "Are they made out of different stuff than the ones hereabout?"

"It's not that! It's just… I'm not ready for anything like this. You're the one that told them about me. Why did you do that to me?"

"Because you are ready, and because my Boss told me to. Those who are chosen have to do hard things. You are chosen, and this is your first hard thing. The hardest part will be to get your stubborn head fixed in the right direction."

"I don't think I'm so much chosen. I never thought I'd have to do something like this. I really can't."

"Are you saying God, who made you, doesn't know you inside and out? Now, I can tell you this, He don't usually send me to talk with humans like I've had to talk with you. The Boss, who runs this world, works things out for the good to everybody who loves him. (Romans 8:28) And you're part of the workings that will be good for you, as well as the folks at Dead Horse Springs."

"…but I didn't know it would be this way."

"What would you have done differently if you had known?"

Phil stood by the door looking down at the toes of his best everyday shoes, not his plow shoes. The angel continued, "Why do you think the Boss made that other Philemon come all the way up here on the ridge and give away what he loved best… just for you to enjoy? And that handsome stallion you have, and the good buggy from Mr. Pennyworth? And look at the good name he gave you. Was that just because you were such a good boy?"

Phil scrounged his head for an answer. "Mr. Pennyworth didn't give me the wagon."

"Oh, ye of little faith. (Matt 6:30 and 8:26) The old man would have given you the buggy if he had remembered he had it. He wasn't permitted to remember, because you were going to need it to bring him out. It's really hard to get through to you. Be glad you haven't been struck blind like Paul. (Acts 9: 5) The Boss really works hard on some of you humans to get you to use your inside eyes. Now you must remember that part about using inside eyes, you'll need that when you teach about Paul."

Phil raised his head and looked into the shining eyes of his inquisitor. "I'll do it." He wanted to add that if he was a failure, it would be Gabriel's fault, but from the look in the angel's eyes, he decided to keep the rebuke to himself. "I said to 'em I'd be there in November, and I will. Sorry I had to be such a bother to you."

The angel managed a lopsided grin. "Don't flatter yourself. There are a lot of humans even harder-headed than you. At least you studied all on your own, and some of the chosen have to be battered into preparing themselves. (II Tim 2:15) You studied and you are prepared in the very best way. There is one more thing to say, and it is that God said 'open your mouth, and I will fill it.' (Psa 81:10) That should give you confidence."

"I have a question. Are you the only Gabriel?"

"I'll answer, are you the only Phil? The fact is, I do what must be done. You are not the only problem God has. It takes a multitude of angels to take charge of humans. When you need to have me, I am there. If I am not there, then you do not need me. I'm not the only one in charge of you, you know."

As Phil attempted to digest those words, the vision before him became dim and the colors melted into the faded pattern of the quilt covering his bed. He was now alone. Phil sat down wearily on the bed, leaning forward on elbows, chin in hand.

He glanced toward his beloved Bible, and his mind said, *When you get to the Springs, let your first talk be about Samson, and how he kept being disobedient. Stress on how God forgave and forgave, but his life was destroyed in the end and his usefulness was gone... Much better to listen to God than fight back.*

Phil eased back, resting his head on the pillow. That was the other angel bringing thoughts. It had happened so many times for his Saturday stories. He would think one thing, and the other angel would bring up an entirely different part of the subject, furnishing new angles.

So he would be going to Dead Horse Springs, and must manage to be presentable most of the time. No more plow shoes on Sunday. He needed a decent looking overcoat for winter. Shirts.

Maybe laundry was taken care of. Sure to be. He would have time to go down to Eureka or Wishbone for haircuts. None of that should be a problem.

He moved to the chair by his table. He was now reading in Paul's letters to the churches, being the third time he had read from Genesis all the way through.

Paul. Lawyer, and an educated and wealthy man, but he used it all for God. He was repaid by being locked in prison so he couldn't go to the churches. It seemed a mistake, but was really a blessing for the world... blessings that would last until the end of time. Paul didn't say, "Well, if I'm in prison, I can't visit the churches God wanted me to start." What he did was write letters and they were something to be saved and read by millions. What looked so bad had good in it.

Dead Horse Springs? Didn't matter. Good or bad, he was going. Like Mr. Parnell, he didn't look forward to a tangle with Gabriel.

THE WINTER OF 1911

The church at the Springs was bright with windows and fresh with the smell of new wood. A stand was made for his Bible, and it was just the right height. There were two rows of benches from front to back, and a potbellied stove between them.

Four wall sconces down each side held the eight lamps for night services. The two on the wall beside the pulpit stand held two more lamps. Well lighted, for a fact.

The tiny office-bedroom was about the size of his cabin at the farm. A lamp for his personal evening reading. Cozy.

The first Sunday morning there were six families, forty three persons in all, counting the Parnell baby. They sang a few songs they all knew, and it was his turn.

He opened his mouth, and God filled it with the life and disobediences of Samson, and the fact that he had paid dearly for the mistake of disobedience. He just didn't seem to be able to learn. That led into the parable of the sower, and followed into reaping what you sowed. All the farmers knew about that.

He stressed the certainty of reaping exactly what was sown. (Gal. 6: 7, 8). He ate a hearty meal at the Parnells' table. Food almost as good as Ma's. It wasn't until he was back in his room thinking of the night subject when he realized that he had never really thought of putting the sower and the reaper with the story of Samson. Apparently, he had opened his mouth, and it had been filled.

He looked up at the boards of the ceiling. *Thank you, whoever it was that followed the Boss' orders.*

At the end of the first meeting, a song was sung about 'Till we meet again' and Brother Hanover passed his hat. Most attendees put something in the hat. Phil waited patiently, thinking this was not his part of the service... but it was.

After the dismissal by Brother Parnell, Brother Hanover came to him, emptied the contents of the hat into his hand and transferred it to Phil's hand. Phil stood looking at the handful of coins not knowing what to do next.

"Yours," Brother Hanover advised him.

"But I... I don't need to be paid," he stammered.

"Ain't pay. Ain't 'cause'a you it was give. It's God's part'a our money."

"God's part?"

"Preacher Phil, ain't you read Malachi? Dime outta every dollar belongs to God."

Yes, he'd read Malachi and some of it he didn't really understand. Like in Chapter 3 about tithes and a storehouse and windows in heaven being opened to pour down blessings on the obedient. Sorta mysterious, but these people seemed to understand it.

Brother Hanover decided to further instruct the preacher. "We bring God his money for the blessin's. We want them windows of heaven to be opened and send us more'a them blessin's. That's how we got this here buildin'. That's how we got you for our youngens." Figuring that to be enough of a lesson, he jammed the worn hat on his head and left... Brother Phil staring speechlessly after him.

And after the first of the year, the next year's crops needed to be planned. Phil, now at home in the Springs, found himself offering to follow the mule through the first spring ground-turning, to help gather rocks from the fields that worked up every winter, and to follow along as extra hands on fence mending.

The farmers took his help with cheerful thanks, and in the course of it, Phil learned how to create an easy and familiar way with adults, even though he had barely passed twenty.

While helping at the Argosy's, little Troy insisted 'teacher' come and see the new puppies. Terriers, they were. Black and white, roly-poly and adventurous as they explored the box where they were kept.

"What will you do with all these puppies?"

"They done been spoke for," small Troy advised, sadly. "All 'ceptin' that'n. She's the runt and no one ever wants a runt."

"Does that mean you can keep 'er?"

"No, preacher. Pa says he'll take care'a the problem. I don't like to think how he's gonna take care'a the problem, bein' that nobody wants 'er."

The soft voice spoke in his ear. "That little bit of doggy is yours. She was made special for you."

Phil's mind spoke back. *I can't take a puppy everywhere I go. You know that.*

"What I know is," the voice told him, "that your ma'll keep her when you can't. Dogs got good ears and terriers have the best. Times you'll find you're gonna need her."

Phil nodded to the voice. He didn't have to be hit over the head to take something so cute as that runt. "Tell you what, Troy. If you take good care'a her till I have to leave, I'll take her with me and then you'll always know where she is. Your pa won't have to bother with 'er. That be OK with you?"

"Oh, yes, preacher! Can we shake on it?"

"Most certainly," and he took the small hand into his large one and shook as Troy smiled widely enough to show the dimples that would be embarrassing to him in another ten years.

Phil lifted the scrap of a dog from Troy's reluctant hand. Cradled in a left hand with outstretched fingers, the little critter when curled up seemed not much bigger than Ma's huge breakfast biscuits.

A stroke on her back with the right hand, and the small black head lifted, the brown brows twisted quizzically on each side of the white stripe from forehead to nose, and the bright eyes like chocolate drops gazed intensely into Phil's eyes.

"Little Bit, that's what you are. You and me… we're gonna be pals for a long time."

Troy studied Phil's eyes for sincerity and seemed satisfied. "I been feedin' 'er special," he admitted. "The big'uns, they was knockin' 'er around. She eats good from a big spoon, and licks butter from my finger."

Phil grinned. He'd bet she would. Troy was going to miss this tiny bit of caninity, but it was for the best. At least, that was what the angel had said.

Preacher Phil would never have believed that four months could pass so quickly and the farmers were already putting in the spinach and radishes, along with onions and turnips.

A pastor had been found. A young fellow from one of the schools was ready to take his place.

There had been an important thing happen over the winter, though, and he had never given thought to needing it. Now, he saw how important it was. He needed papers.

He needed a Religious Organization to back him with the papers assuring that he knew what he was doing. He needed papers to perform marriages… imagine that, Ma! In the tiny town of Wishbone he found a leather shop that stitched up a folder for his papers and the addresses he needed to keep. Life was getting complicated.

It was during his last month that he had been contacted by a scribbled note. Would he contact Burt Hollander at the end of Wolfpath Lane in two weeks? Maybe for a day or two with his 'talking like at Dead Horse Springs.'

The note had been sent on to him by his ma, and he read and re-read the note, turning it over in his hand. Should he? That Wolfpath hollow was said to actually be crawling alive with wolves. Be no way to take his fancy buggy back down there. *Well, Sarge? You gonna be ready to tackle it?*

But the decision was really not his. The soft-spoken angels were warning him not to tell himself 'no'… that he must remember who he was… a messenger and servant of God.

As spring approached, he found himself offering help in every way he could. He began to feel that he was leaving behind about a dozen fathers and about twice that many brothers.

The day before he left, the Parnell children presented him with a small, high-sided box lined with a scrap of an old wool scarf. March, in the mountains, was windy with a bite in the air, and the puppy must not get cold.

So now it was time to put Sarge between the shafts and get on down Ridge Road. Last stop was to pick up the pup.

Troy was placidly swinging in the porch swing, the pup snuggled on his lap. After the preacher had a few words with Pa, he followed Phil to the buggy and handed over the dog. Pursing his lips in a hard line, he removed a glove that was sorely ragged and all fingers gone.

"Ma said to give you this for a while 'cause it smells like me and Little Bit might sleep better. Just for the first little while, Ma said."

Phil solemnly took the scrap and tucked it into the box. The 'little boy' smell of it would be a help to the pup. Certain to be.

The jiggle of the buggy and an occasional word from her new owner, and the pup nestled and dozed, never knowing or caring that this trip was the first of many she would make with this human.

BULLETS, VINES AND THE GIRL ON THE FLOOR

Ma wasn't too excited about Wolfpath as a destination for her firstborn. That valley had trees one hundred feet tall and twisted with vines from top to bottom. But Pa told her to stay mum, the lad must make his own decision and an invitation was an invitation. Well, there was one thing she could do.

"Son, you wear your biggest straw hat, less'n a snake drop outta them trees and land around your neck."

Phil nodded. Easy thing to do for Ma, but his own mind told him the snakes might not be the worst threat. Here he was, on a magnificent black stallion with no protection but the 9mm Walther concealed in a saddle bag. A robber could jump out and shoot him for the horse, or just leave him alone without transportation out of the valley.

So… should he risk it? Was the invitation for real? What could he do in just a stay of two or three days, as the note said? With a sigh, he knew arguments were useless… he would go. First he would make a trip and look over the prospects. And maybe he could promise to come maybe next year.

Phil tossed the question back and forth, catching it first with his right thought, then with his left, all the time knowing it was only a stalling tactic. He didn't want to go, but being chosen (i.e. being an obedient servant), did he really have a choice? Of course not.

He had no thoughts toward looking around to see if someone was interested in his trip and wanting to give him trouble, and if so, when it would be? Why ever would anyone be interested...? But someone was.

Sarge was brushed and fed and clothed in the striped saddle blanket with a concealed pocket for the Walther and another for the ammo. Just precautions any young man from northern Arkansas would take before a foray into unfamiliar territory. He tossed the attractive saddle onto Sarge's broad back.

He glanced around and toward the sky, giving his angels (Gabriel?) every chance to call a halt to this travesty... this example of utter stupidity... but there was no reprieve. Swinging himself upward, he landed comfortably in the saddle and Sarge turned to look at him. An interesting habit of the animal.

"Git up there, Sarge," and they were off with a trot. It was near noon, and Ma had insisted on his taking a ham sandwich, though there was plenty of time to be back for supper. From the hand-drawn map, it seemed to be not more than 6 miles each way... though it was hard to tell from the up-and-down terrain and someone else's hand-drawn map.

He turned at the indicated cut-off and ducked into the little-used road (trail...?) pushing back the muscadine vines hanging from the overhead limbs. The roads on either side of Ridge Road, of necessity, went downhill, some more so than others. This one took pleasant hair-pin-type curves. Not bad at all. Down... down... down... was there ever a bottom to this hill? Likely not until it reached Wolf Creek.

About a half mile off the road, a trail angled to the right, back up the hill heading east. Sarge hesitated at the cut-off but Phil urged him on. He needed to get this trip over with.

As he made his way along the narrow trail, he sensed a presence beside him. Looking back, he was startled by the sight of a huge horse, actually dwarfing Sarge. The other horse was plunging along in the brush, but not moving a limb or waving a leaf or blade of grass. The animal was outfitted with the metal headgear and draping sheets of mail like a Roman war horse.

Sitting firmly astride the animal was the helmeted and shielded angel. The afternoon sun glinted off the metal breast plate and shin guards.

"So you finally decided to go," Gabriel commented. "Took you long enough. Did you not remember about 'preaching the word' and 'being instant in season and out'? (II Tim 4:2) You had a little doubt, there for a while, but your faith won out in the end. Good for you."

How was Phil to answer that? His companion continued.

"You did well at Dead Horse Springs. We were sure you would. You learned about tithes; that you hadn't understood and now you do. You learned humility and how to accept praise, passing it on to the Boss. We think you enjoyed yourself at times, and that is good, because there are very few places like Dead Horse Springs. Someone once asked Jesus why he ate with sinners and bad people. He answered 'They that be well need not a physician, but they that are sick.' (Mat 9:2) From here on, life may seem hard. The world has a lot of sickness and not all of it is in the body."

Phil thought about the hardness. Like this trip down Wolfpath Hollow?

Gabriel turned his shining eyes toward Phil. "No, times will be a lot harder than Wolfpath Hollow. The chosen ones agree to be lowly servants, and that is a tiresome and often thankless job."

They rode side by side for a while, the angel's horse passing through the bushes without riffling a twig. "Good little dog you have. You'll likely see the time she saves your life."

That gave Phil a grin. The little creature that fit in his overcoat pocket could save a life? But if the angel said it… who was he to argue?

Then the immense white horse faded into nothing, taking the angel with him. Phil guessed that the visit was just to show him he had not been forgotten. And that he was where he should be on the path.

Sarge made his way skillfully down the steep rocky trail, snorting at the smell of moldy dampness just ahead.

Finally the trail seemed to level off. The trees were 80 to 100 feet tall, watered by Wolf Creek, and the tops of the trees intertwined thickly with vines and their own branches. Dark… cool… and slightly musty, with an overlaying smell of fish and other water creatures. Underfoot, the leaf litter was thick and damp, issuing its own earthy aroma.

Sarge snorted, sneezed and shook his head, and Phil thought, *me, too,* but he pressed on until a scream from the underbrush startled the stallion who reared and neighed, almost tipping Phil from his back. No matter… he hung on.

Someone grabbed Sarge's bridle and another person clasped onto Phil's leg and pulled. A third person helped and they succeeded in pulling Phil from Sarge's back and standing him in the leaf litter with his arms held behind his back and a rope twisted around his middle and quickly tied.

"Got 'im!" someone yelled in triumph.

"Easy as fallin' off a log," announced another young male voice.

The third person wrapped a sweaty bandana across Phil's eyes. "Yep, and we'll see how lucky he is now."

"Good enough for 'im. Sashayin' around the Ridge in that spiffy buggy he done nothin' to earn."

"Yeah and that high powered stallion. He's got this a'comin'."

"So let's get it over with. Bring 'im over to this skinny tree. It'll let us git 'is hands tied behind."

Phil felt himself led by a tug on his sleeve and encouraged by what seemed to be a kick in the rear.

"Hey, fellows… take a gander at them boots on his feet. Reckon they'd fit one'a us?" That was met with a burst of raucous laughter that would have been the envy of a flock of crows.

Phil felt his hands being extended behind him around a small hackberry tree and tied together. He knew it to be hackberry because of the sharp-edged roughness of the bark. A rope that felt like rawhide tied his feet to the bottom of the tree.

"Now take off the handkerchief. He ought'a get to see who wings 'im 'afore he stops breathin' altogether. Will? You got them sticks ready so we can draw lots for who gets the head-shot?"

Now with his eyes uncovered, he saw the three young men, about his own age, eagerly engaged in drawing lots. It seems that Will was the winner.

"Now, Will, don't you kill 'im with the first shot. Just get 'is hat, 'cause he' ll not be needin' it no more." More laughs.

"So, Slim, you get the right hand and I get the left, and then Will can do 'im in. I'm guessin' it'll be days 'afore he's found, and after the wolves get through, nobody'll know who he is."

"Yeah, well, let's step back to make it fair." That was also met with laughter.

A stillness ruled in the dim light of the glen, as 'Will' knelt behind a sapling and took aim. Phil looked up into the thatch of leaves… *Where are you, Gabriel? Is this how it was supposed to end?*

The sound of the bullet was deafening in Phil's ears and the new straw hat jiggled but held fast to his head. Apparently he was still alive. Great Grandpop had told him you never heard the shot that took your life. Young Phil had wondered how that could be, because when one was dead, it was not possible to ask if he heard the last shot. Or even the first one.

The report of the gun bounced back and forth between the mountains and up and down the valley. Sarge reared, screamed and tore off through the vines and bushes, snorting in terror.

Slim beat his fist against his forehead. "Now lookie what happened! We was to get that horse, and now it'll take a day to hunt 'em down, the way he was a'goin'."

But Will was not worried about the horse. "Fellows! Lookie out there a'comin' at us. Run for your life! That big shiny fellow's got a sword longer'n all'a us put together."

Before Phil's amazed eyes, his three tormentors disappeared into the shrubbery like rabbits down a hole. No trace. Not even a waving branch.

He looked quickly around to see what horror was advancing on himself and saw nothing. Even the swamp birds had resumed their singing. Not a wolf or a snake… or a wild hog or anything to be frightened of. Hmmm…

And here he was tethered to the hackberry tree like a pig on a spit over a flame. Maybe worse, because no one knew where he was. It would not be long until there would be a cramp in his legs, tied so close to the tree as they were, causing his body to pitch forward.

And his hands, resting against the rough, sharp bark of the tree would soon be raw, and he could not hold them away from the tree trunk very long at a time. Leaning forward because of the hat brim, he felt it slide gently down toward one eyebrow, and he had no way of removing it. Shaking his head did not knock it off.

Adding insult to injury, a swamp mosquito bit him on his uncovered wrist. Where were his guardian angels? *Gabriel? Where are you?*

How long would it be before he fainted, starved, or just pitched forward from exhaustion and injured his hands on the bark?

Thought after thought passed through his head. At least he was not stoned, as was Paul, when he just tried to help people. Though, come to think of it, stoning would be quickly fatal, and he could be days, maybe, before he was dead.

What had he done that was wrong? How had he angered God? Surely if God was mad about him for some reason, it would have been told to him… like when he really didn't know what tithes meant. Gabriel had told him that he had extra angelic help because he had no human to teach him. So where was that 'teacher angel' now?

As the hours passed, the swamp became dimmer. A full moon was overhead but precious little light filtered through the thick arbor of leaves. Hunger began to set in and discouragement was thick around him. His arms ached and both legs were screaming with muscle cramps.

And to top it off, he could see small, beady eyes glowing not far away. Not a deer or a rabbit. Too low to the ground. More like a snake. He breathed as softly as he could so whatever it was might not know he was there.

His attempt at being invisible was not successful. The pair of eyes moved forward in little jumps… not like a snake; that would move smoothly.

Then he could see the little glob of dark fur as it moved closer and closer toward him.

RAT! PACKRAT! Of course. Well, he wouldn't attack something so large as a human. Not with all the insects, crickets and beetles in the leaf litter.

But still it approached. Then there was the sound of small grinding teeth and a faint vibration of movement around his boots. Was the rodent actually eating the boots off his feet...?

But then he realized it would be the leather ropes. Braided strips. Rawhide made good ropes. He'd made them himself, though they were a lot of trouble. Hides were sliced in strips about ¾ inch wide, soaked, and braided tightly while soft and wet. Then they were squeezed into a cylinder shape and allowed to dry. Took a week or more of sunshine to dry them into a tight stick. Then they were oiled to make them softer.

Made a most useful rope before hemp ropes became easily available. Thinking back, it would have been leather ropes they used to tie him, and after the ropes were used a lot and handled, they picked up the salt from the sweat of human hands.

So there was the wad of dark fur and stiletto teeth sawing away at the ropes that bound his feet. Phil fought against the leg cramps that almost made him scream from pain. He must do nothing that discouraged the little rodent from his gnawing. Even weakening the rope would be a help, and then maybe Phil could break it. Somehow.

Suddenly a release of tension as the rat severed the rope. AHHH! Relief was palpable! The cramps eased away as he heard the rodent dragging the rope across the leaves. A sly grin crossed Phil's face as he thought of the rat being a mama and bringing home supper for the babies in the nest. Salt and oil soaked animal skin would be an excellent meal.

Then he ungratefully wished it had been his hands that were loosed instead of his feet. Fact was, he could then have untied his feet by himself. But then, being able to stand straight and brace his legs, took a small amount of strain off his sore hands.

Very little reflected light filtered down, now, and the damp, darkness seemed to be closing in. He saw the beady eyes again, hesitating at the edge of the shrubbery. They advanced, and another pair followed, both coming toward him. Coming for his leather boots...?

No, they were scurrying up the tree. One climbed onto his arm and clutched his wrist with sharp little claws as he began to gnaw on the rope. The other rodent dug its toes into the hip pocket of his pants and helped with the gnawing. Where the hip-pocket rat's claws dug into the skin, it began to tickle, causing Phil to shiver.

With every small movement of Phil, the rodents stopped gnawing to assess the danger... then resumed.

Phil rationed his breath and pictured a kitten playing in his hands, their tiny claws not particularly painful. Then came a push against his wrist as one of the rats jumped away. A loosing of the rope freed one hand, then the other.

Freedom! Wonderful freedom, and with one hand upward, he adjusted the straw hat from its awkward and irritating position. He stepped away from the tree and massaged his wrists and hands. Relief. He heard the little beasts scurried away with their prize.

But now here he was in a dark forest with no clue as to direction or how far he was from the trail. He could be ten feet away from the path, and it could disappear. And the hoodlums would have captured Sarge by now. Phil found himself hoping the animal bit his captors... or maybe kicked them soundly.

So he would wait for morning, moving fairly constantly to avoid attracting snakes. A dark swamp like this could give a fellow the heebie-jeebies. He heard noises on every side.

It was nearing morning when he heard, for certain, the approach of several footsteps. Solid movement in the trees and bushes.

Tormentors back? Certain to be, but where could he hide? He frantically cast his eyes about, but there was no escape. If they were coming back for him, he might as well face them bravely.

He turned toward the sound, lifted his chin and stared... as the bushes parted and a long, black face appeared. Two fur-covered ears swiveled toward him. Then a soft whicker of greeting as he pulled his feet from the thatch of vines and high-stepped into the small clearing.

"Sarge! Good fellow! You're back. How did you get away?" But it didn't matter; he was here. Saddle intact, Walther still in its hidden holster, and reins dragging across the dead leaves.

Phil hugged the long face and the rubbery black lips reached for fingers to nip gently. Whispery whickers rippled soundlessly in his neck muscles as he pushed his head against Phil's shoulder.

"Say, old boy, let's get ourselves out of here. You got any idea of which way is which?" He swung up into the saddle, feeling the comfort of it more than at any time in his life. Sarge had got away and come back! What a horse!

Feeling his master settled, the animal walked resolutely forward and parted the bushes, revealing the trail they had come down. Without direction, he turned into the way they had come and began to climb the steep grade backward toward Ridge Road.

It was when they passed the cut-off trail where Sarge had halted on the way down, he halted again. A sound. Not really a scream, but more of a dispirited high-pitched groan... but there was no one near.

Parts of a fence were visible, and the trail climbed upward toward a small plateau, it seemed. Certain signs of human habitation. Sarge, who had paused, began to climb up the path toward... what...?

Not more than a hundred feet farther was the house. Fairly good house. Painted. No signs of life. No barking dog.

He continued up to the porch, wrapped Sarge's line around a porch post, though why, he couldn't have said. Sarge wasn't going anywhere without his master.

Phil knocked. No answer. He pushed against the door but it didn't open. Carefully he turned the knob, and stepped inside. He was met by the blast of the smell of... a dead body? Gagging, he looked through a couple of doors and saw the source of the smell.

The man was spread-eagled across the bed. No signs of violence, but he was unmistakably dead. A jug with an inch of liquid was by the bed.Phil backed up and out of the room, pulling the door shut behind him. Too late, of course, the whole house reeked already.

He moved through the well-kept parlor and on to the kitchen, and was met by the pathetic groan from the floor. There, lying sprawled was a woman...girl...? Some female, anyway, in an ill-fitting dress.

Coming closer, he saw the drawn face of a girl… maybe eighteen, maybe sixteen. Hard to tell. Skin drawn, mouth open, lips chapped. The eyes opened and looked at him in pitiful agony, wanting to say something, but having no voice.

Around her wrists were handcuffs similar to those of a deputy constable. A metal chain attached her to the legs of a massive iron stove. What… in the world….

REBECCA JONES

Hungry! She had to be starving to death? How long had she been there, and why? Questions would wait. She needed help now. From where she was, she couldn't even reach the water bucket. He knew that a person died from thirst before from hunger.

Dipping stale water from the bucket he came toward her, but she could not swallow. Her eyes pled for him to understand. He did. Locating a spoon, he tipped water a few drops at a time, onto her dry and stiffened tongue, to move finally down her throat. Ten minutes of this helped a lot.

Now food. What would Ma do? Egg custard, that's what. But he didn't have time. Looking around, he saw the key to the handcuffs hanging over the water pail. He loosed her but she did not attempt a move.

Poking sticks into the iron cook stove, he lit it and looked around. There on a shelf was oatmeal. Another of Ma's rescue foods. No time to cook. There were cows in the corral, and surely there would be a drop of milk somewhere among them.

Taking a handy kettle, he stopped at the henhouse on the way, and from a nest heaped with eggs, he took three and put them carefully in a pocket. The nearest jersey cow was agreeable to a stranger taking her milk, and he quickly squirted about a pint into his kettle.

Back in the kitchen, he tipped out a cup of milk into a bowl and broke an egg into it. Seeing the sugar bowl nearby, he added a teaspoonful. Whipping it into a yellow froth, he knelt on the floor by the girl's head. She followed closely with her eyes… seeming that that was the only part of her that she had the ability to move.

Lifting her head slightly and propping it against his thigh, he dipped a teaspoon into the egg mixture. Patiently, he leveled the spoon, allowing the mixture to slide past her swollen tongue. Somehow she managed a weak swallow.

Careful, careful, so she wouldn't choke, he spooned the cup of liquid into her mouth with very little spillage. Sensing that regardless of whatever got her in this shape, she would not be able to accept much food for a while. Laying her back, he found a pillow from the parlor and propped her head more comfortably.

Putting on a small kettle with water, he added salt and sprinkled in the oatmeal. To his own hungry self, the aroma of cooking oatmeal seemed a bit of heaven all by itself.

Taking the finished cereal from the burner, he set it aside and went back to the eggs. Finding the egg basket, he started for the door, but came back and set the iron skillet over the hot burner. He felt that he could eat at least 8 eggs himself… maybe 12. In the henhouse, he emptied the nest into the basket and returned to the kitchen, puzzled thoughts chasing themselves.

WHAT was going on…!!!

Whoever would chain her to the stove and hang the key out of reach? How long had she been there (surely a week or more) and how did she survive without water? And what a mess she was in….

Anyway, he was here now, and he would have to decide what to do. She had to be taken away, of course. He needed a buggy or wagon, but didn't see one. He saw a dog cart, but she was certainly not able to stand or sit. She was limp as a dishrag.

Sled? Apparently not. How did this man get around? How did he manage with her in a dog cart? Too many questions. No answers.

First, get the girl home to Ma. In the corral he found boards and poles, apparently intended for winter wood. Selection two of the smallest and laying them aside, he decided they would do… but first breakfast.

He found the lard and tossed a liberal glob into the iron skillet. Breaking egg after egg, he thought he could hardly wait for them to cook, maybe a whole five minutes! Could that girl eat scrambled eggs… maybe not. But there was the oatmeal, that would work.

Scooping eggs into a bowl, he ate while cooling the oatmeal, whipping it to be positive there were no lumps. He felt the girl's eyes following his every move. Well, when she could speak, she could answer a lot of questions.

Kneeling beside her again, he lifted a half a spoonful to her lips. Hey, she was much better. She even managed to move her tongue. A little. It was slow, but he was able to get about a half cup of the cereal down her.

Another eggnog? Maybe not. Maybe he should work on the sled. Looking at her, he smiled and said he was going to help. He would be right back. The blue eyes frowned with fright. "Don't worry. I'm here to help, and I will be right back." Patting her hand, he left.

Travois sled would be the answer. It would be hard on her, but it was the only conveyance available that could negotiate the trail and keep her flat. Finding canvas and straps and a wealth of rope, he put the sled together, and located lines to attach it to a harness around Sarge's ample chest.

That ought to do it. Back in the kitchen, he finished the eggs. Cold now, but still delicious. He located a thick quilt to put on the canvas, and a belt (belonging to the dead man?) to fasten her against the jiggles as they made their way down the slope to the Wolfpath trail.

Back in the kitchen, he scooped a large bowl of oatmeal into his empty stomach, and prepared to feed the girl the rest of the milk with two beaten egg yolks. Then he put in another yolk, just to be sure. A little more sugar.

Back on the floor, he manned the spoon until she had obviously had as much as she could handle right now. He certainly didn't want her to upchuck on the way out of here.

Finally ready, he scooped her up in his arms… surprisingly light. No wonder. No food that she could have reached.

Laying her on the quilt, he pulled part of it over her. On second thought, went to the bedroom and battled the stink until he found another quilt. And another belt.

A quilt on top, and a belt under her arms, and one at her knees, he told her, "I'm sorry but it's going to be a hard ride for you. This is the best I can do, but I have to take you where you can get help." He was encouraged by her feeble attempt to smile.

184

This had been Sarge's first venture with a travois sled, but the dragging poles at his side did not seem to bother him at all. The lower tips of the poles slid over the rocks and tree roots with a decided juggle, but the girl was able to lie straight, and that seemed important to Phil.

Sarge took small steps and pulled the travois to the trail. Turning away from the rising sun, the stallion started up the hill toward Ridge Road. Phil walked beside him, speaking encouragement and patting his muscled withers. He pulled steadily ahead, his mobile ears swiveling in answer to Phil's encouragement.

On Ridge Road he made better time and gave a smoother ride, and it appeared that the girl had actually gone to sleep. Her head had tilted sideways, and eyes closed tightly. Good. This could have been a scary ride.

On the way to the lane to Darkhorse Farm, he passed by the corner called Burnt Tree Junction. A deputy with a star lived there, and Phil stopped long enough to report a dead body. The county would have a responsibility to the dead, just as he, a 'chosen' servant, had to the living.

The sound attracted Ma. Of course it would. He had been expected home last night and had not come. Something wrong. Sure to be. Her son would have told her if he expected to be away all night.

One look at the girl and Ma was hooked. Anyone or anything that needed help needed Ma. And she knew it.

Even the scrap of a pup had taken her eye, and she had quickly learned that a couple slices of fried side meat and a half a cup of cream gravy answered all her ills.

With this girl, it would take a little longer. Ma began her triage inspection while the girl was still on the travois sled. Pulse. Faint but regular. Arms. Head....

"Oh, Son, she has... her head has... company!"

Phil hadn't noticed, but he was sure Ma was right. Ma just couldn't bring herself to say the words 'head lice.' Neither could she say 'bedbug' or 'maggot.' Ma knew what to do, but there was no way such creatures should be let in the house, and it was obvious this girl could not sit up to withstand an attack of lye soap on her head. Hmmm... Ma bit her lip and studied the situation.

185

Phil helped. "Ma, she could use my cabin, and I'll sleep on the porch. Then you can fumigate the whole cabin when it's over."

Ma was a genius with sulfur fumigating candles and lye water floor scrubs. She nodded that the problem was taken care of. "Son, when you transfer her to your bed, see you don't pick up no ... company."

"Sure, Ma."

It was two days of rest before Ma would allow the girl to be interrogated. Phil did not sleep on the porch, either. He moved his bedroll to the ground by the cabin door in case she woke up terrified. It didn't happen, though, thanks to Ma's relaxing tea and the girl's total exhaustion.

Ma let Phil continue to feed her. 'Company' would be a lot easier to get out of his hair than her own. On the third day she wrapped a towel snuggly around her head and advanced onto the cabin with warm water and lye soap.

Assigning her son to hold the girl's shoulders in the event she should faint or be scared, she applied the bar of lye soap to the assaulted hair follicles. While doing so, she found the sores caused by the tiny beasts' bites and the subsequent scratching. No matter. She had the answer for that.

Melting the wonderful stuff called petroleum jelly, she anointed all the scabby clusters and wrapped her head in a towel for the day. She was moved to the front porch bed and permitted interrogation.

Little by little, and in spurts and silences, it came out.

The girl had no name that she could remember, other than 'girl.' Her childhood caretaker, that she could remember, was a woman who said to call her 'Lucy.' Maybe it was her name.

Lucy had been abducted, blindfolded, and brought to the house at age thirteen. She was made to do all work, and threatened pain if she attempted to leave. The man said she was a long way from her home... another state, he said. That was all she knew.

She took care of him in every way he demanded, or she was beaten. Somehow she had lived, and was maybe about thirty when he came in with a little girl that Lucy thought might have been four years old.

He had said nothing about where he got her, and Lucy didn't ask. In fact, she wasn't sure what the man's name was. She just did what he said and had meals ready on time. When he was gone for a few days, she tended the stock and whatever else needed to be done.

Though she was so sorry that the little girl was stolen, she was pathetically glad for the company, however young it might be. She loved the girl and taught her to help with the work, as the man had told her to do.

For some reason, maybe the trauma of the kidnapping, or maybe that she was just too young and too many things happened, the girl couldn't remember any name but 'girl' and had no memory of her family. She had clung to Lucy like a barnacle to a sailing ship and somehow survived.

She learned to do whatever Lucy could tell her, but Lucy had no education and the girl had no words except the ones Lucy had. She saw no other people, though Lucy said there were a lot of people in the world. Lucy had been afraid to try to escape, and she was beaten severely at every opportunity the man could think of.

The 'girl' made a life as best she could, not actually knowing anything different, except what Lucy told her, and she certainly had no way to escape. The man brought food, and he came and went, and sometimes he brought a jug home with him. Lucy always liked that because he would be occupied for a day or so, and then he slept for hours and hours. Leaving her alone.

It was then that Lucy would bake cookies for the two of them or make something they both liked… something that was forbidden when the man was awake. It was when the 'girl' was about twelve that Lucy began to weaken. She had no idea why, but she struggled on because the man beat her and called her lazy.

The 'girl' did all she could to keep Lucy safe… and alive, but the man was merciless. Lucy was beaten so much, she eventually gave up, though she was distressed to leave the 'girl' alone with the man.

And then came the time she could go no farther and she just laid down and stopped living. She just quit breathing… the only way she could escape.

The 'girl' was beaten severely for letting Lucy die, and was ordered to 'bury' her.

Where…?

With a shrug… who cared!

From that time onward the girl was expected to run the house like Lucy did, and she tried. The difference was that Lucy did not fight back, but the 'girl' could not hide her anger and hatred. The man knew she hated him, so he took special measures.

When he brought home the jug, he would chain the 'girl' to the stove legs so she couldn't reach the guns on the wall. He thought she would kill him in his sleep, and she might have. She hated him so much.

When he locked her to the stove, he hung the key out of reach so she couldn't get loose until he sobered up. He turned the calf in with the cow and let the other livestock go while he slept it off.

So this time, he had locked her up and when he went to bed, he just didn't get up. On the fourth day she had become desperate. She had eaten everything she could reach which wasn't much. She had begun to drink the water from the stove reservoir, and when the days strung on, the water level sank lower, so she made herself drink less.

She had screamed until her voice was gone, but the next day she screamed again. She wasn't sure, but thought it had been ten days when she couldn't get up from the floor, and she had occupied herself with crying. She tried to see how noisily she could cry… just for something to do.

Phil listened, and nodded. There was a chance that Sarge's ears had picked up her moans as they first passed the cut-off, but Phil's mind was on the difficulty of the trail and concern as to where he was going. Turned out, he had reason to be.

But it was less than a day later that he was back by and found her. And now there was the body that was removed and neither she nor Phil had cared what was done with it.

There also was, however, the farm. Considering all, the farm had been well kept, animals were healthy. There was a saddle horse for transportation and two mules for the farm work. There was the dog cart for bringing in whatever would not fit a saddle bag.

Somehow the taxes had been paid. The county annually received seven quarters taped to a cardboard and mailed in. The property had been settled by a James Jones, but there was no knowing if that was this man's name.

The girl had no name that she remembered, and she begged Phil to think of a name for her. She deserved a name, she insisted, and he agreed. Thinking of the women's names in the Bible, he settled on Rebecca, one of his favorite ladies in the book.

Last name? Well, after a lot of consultation by the authorities with the girl and with Phil, who had found her, a decision was made. Considering her totally unique situation, they put her on their population register as Rebecca Jones, adopted daughter of James Jones, owner of the farm. That was the easiest way to reward the ill-treated girl, give her a background, even if it was made up, and legitimized her with the pretend 'adoption.'

That still presented problems, but Phil was ready to work on them. The girl had to have a life.

The man should have been drawn and quartered (if he hadn't already killed himself) for what he did to the woman and the girl. There had to be some good in it somewhere, and there were places in Berryville where they let girls stay until they could take care of themselves. That might be an option for her.

Ma was sympathetic, but she had a family to take care of, and didn't need another person. She sent Phil and his fifteen year old sister to the city to pick up needed garments for her. A couple of dresses and various unmentionables. And shoes. They had slipped the sister's shoes on her feet, and they fit, so the sister could pick out the right sized shoes.

Rebecca, however, was entirely too fragile to make the trip. While in town, Phil checked out the facilities. There was a large many-roomed house called a dormitory for girls who had no family. Yes, they would take her and help her any way they could. Matter settled.

Rebecca, herself, was concerned by her lack of words. Her own baby-talk and Lucy's minimum vocabulary left her severely hampered. She begged to be talked to so she could learn and not be ashamed. Phil almost convinced her the 'home' would be a good place to learn words from the other girls, and he would see about her farm.

A notice on the tree at Burnt Tree Junction produced an old man who begged for the job of caretaker of her farm. He and the old lady only needed a place to stay until they were called home to their final abode.

"Please, Mister, let us try. We'd not need no money, just a roof and milk and eggs."

"But it's only temporary," Phil insisted. "It belongs to the young lady, and she'll make the decisions."

"But try us until then. Please, Mister."

So Zeke Conway and Mamie moved in. Changes. Removed the smell of death, milked the cow, took care of the pig and chickens and sang as they went about their work, confident that the 'young lady' would eventually let them put up a little cabin and live out their lives on the property. Mamie even stitched cheerful new kitchen curtains in yellow checked and flowered fabric.

At the home, the 'young lady' was in a daze for the first weeks… like suddenly finding herself on a strange planet. But there was wonderful food that she hadn't had to prepare, clean bed and pillow, and most strangely wonderful, a lot of people who spoke. Words. Precious words that painted pictures in her mind and the girls were all about her in a dizzying array.

Lucy had given all she had to the little waif tossed into her care, but she did not have many words, herself, and sometimes Rebecca wasn't sure that what she had were correct. She could count, and add on her fingers, and could read directions on boxes. Most times. But here at the school, everyone knew a lot more, and Rebecca was determined to catch up.

When he had reason to be in Berryville, Phil checked on her. She couldn't have been more joyful to see him if he had been a long-lost brother! Having nothing to go on, the staff determined that she was likely seventeen, and gave her a birthday. May, the first. Legally, she should be dismissed on her own at age eighteen, but Rebecca was a unique case. She should stay a year longer to catch up. It was decided.

Surprisingly for someone who had been so mistreated, she occasionally wondered about the farm. Her desire to return to something she knew fought with her determination to catch up with her life.

There was the time that Zeke and Mamie came to the home with Phil. They wanted to assure her they would take good care of the place, and they'd love to have her come anytime. Then she could see how well they took care of everything.

Maybe sometime, the home said. She couldn't just come and go and continue in their care. Maybe next Christmas.

Little Bit had made her place on the Darkhorse Farm. Standing 7 ½ inches at the shoulders, she commanded a presence, and her nights were spent in the separate cabin with Phil. It was clearly time to start training her to be observant, and to be praised for announcing that she had heard a strange sound.

Phil knew he still had to go to the farm that was drawn on the map the three fellows left for him. Even if they were 'lying' when they made it. Phil had told Ma that he hadn't made it there yet. There was Rebecca to rescue… remember?

But there were arguments in his head about whether he should actually go, when the whole thing must have been a hoax. Sometimes it was very difficult to tell which voices spoke from which side. Gabriel had told him to be careful, and that he would know… but he wasn't so sure.

And one thing about it. If he went, then he would know, and not knowing when that trip would be, the fellows with their pistols would not be the welcoming party. Starting early, he could make it in a day… easy. He prepared a basket that he could attach to the edge of Sarge's saddle blanket for Little Bit. She had to learn sometime, and this trip would not be overnight.

Nothing much got past the pair of beady-bright canine eyes. The white strip painted down from between her ears to her wriggling little nose pointed importantly first this way and then that as Sarge negotiated the over-grown path.

The tall trees at the bottom and the musty smell of the leaves made Phil shiver and put a tiny, apprehensive growl in the pup's throat, but they waded through Wolf Creek and began the climb on the other side. The path stopped at a well-kept fence around a spacious yard. Large house with a northern view that may well have reached over the state line into Missouri. The house dogs, a pair of redbone hounds, announced his arrival and were answered by a series of snappy yaps from behind the saddle.

A man of an uncertain age came to meet him. "Help you… sir?" was the polite greeting. "My name's Burt. Burt Hollander."

Burt studied the note with great interest, and nodded his head. "Yeah, well I got no idea how this got made, but it done me a favor, anyway. I heard about you but didn't have no way'a knowin' how to reach you. Didn't know if you'd be interested, with us bein' so far back from Ridge Road. We mostly deal the other direction. Over t'ord Missouri.

"I know preachers and what they say, and we have a passel'a youngens that need teachin'. Us grownups, too, could use a some learnin'. The little school down by the tracks is doin' a good job but they ain't preachers. Didn't know how you worked it out… what you did…."

Phil took a deep breath. So far, so good. "Well, I can come if there's a place to speak. Maybe for a few days."

More nods. "We got a brush arbor the youngens use for get-togethers. Needs new branches, but it's got split log seats. Just my youngens alone'd be a houseful, and they's neighbors that'd want to come. See down in that valley?" and he waved an arm to the north to a wide expanse of trees and cultivated fields. "We farm and sell to the Santa Fe to go to Eureka and on west. We sell whatever's ripe at the time, and beans and squash all winter. Does good, but we're a long way out from everywhere."

A pause and more nods. "Be grateful if you could put us in line for a few days… maybe longer. We can put you up in the house. Loads'a room."

"I have a tent, except when it rains. Have my little dog along, her bein' trained for a watch dog."

Burt Hollander knew a joke when he heard one, and answered with an appreciative guffaw. Seems it wasn't a joke, though Phil had to smile at the pup's head above the basket he had fastened onto the rump of the stallion, and the two long-legged, flop-eared hounds milling around Sarge's feet.

He explained. "Mostly, I want her to make a noise and wake me if she hears somethin'. I'm pretty fair with a gun, but I sleep sound. During summers, I expect to spend a lot of nights on the ground."

"Makes sense. You'll be fed, though. Food's what we got mountains of."

So the date was set, and on the way back to the Ridge Road, he stopped in at Rebecca's farm. "Need to take one'a them mules. Need a bit'a haulin' and I'm figurin' you'll not be needin' anything plowed."

"Take 'em both, preacher. They work good together."

So the two mules trailed Sarge on a tether, plodding expertly and sure-footed up the hill.

Turning down the lane, he was met by a harried young man on a sweaty mare. "You the preacher...?"

"Uh... yes. Can I help?"

"Yes, sir, you can. Got a dyin' man, my old granddad. He's beggin' for a preacher. Thinks he needs to talk to God, and don't remember how. Somethin' he heard when he was a boy, and plum forgot. He's painin' somethin' awful, but says he ain't gonna go till he knows about God. Can you come? It's down in Devil's Canyon, about four miles, maybe four and half."

Phil listened, and his first thought was *Gabriel, where are you?* But words whispered (?) in his ear were, 'You don't need Gabriel. You got the answer right in your head.'

To the young man, "Come back and rest on my porch while I change clothes and get my Bible. Need to leave the pup and put the mules to pasture."

The road down to Devil's Canyon was steep and rocky, but wide enough for a wagon. Phil guided Sarge with his mind whirling. *What do I do first? I don't even know what I'm doin' and I shouldn't even be here.*

In spite of the heat, he shuddered and shivered at the certain knowledge that the words in his mind came from the wrong angels. Here he was, on his fourth trip through the Bible, and of course he knew what he should know. He just had to figure out which part to use for a dying man.

First there'd be that promise in John 3:16 about God loving all humans so much he let his son die for them so they didn't have to pay for their own sin, no matter how bad it was. All the human had to do was ask… and believe in the answer.

And there's different kinds of believing. You could be inside your house and if someone said there's a shower comin' on, and you hear drops on the roof. That's believin'.

But if you're in a valley and there comes a waterspout just up stream, you'd find yourself swimmin' or drownin'. That's real BELIEVIN'.

Then next would be the askin' and God promised anyone askin' would be receivin'. God hears every voice askin' for forgiveness.

After that, there's the knowin' that you been heard. That'd be important for a man on his death bed. The best verse would be John 16: 24: "…ask, and ye shall receive, that your joy may be full."

That's another commandment. You gotta be happy about it when you get forgiveness. It cost God a lot to give you forgiveness, and every old farmer knows about costs.

The young man's stallion disappeared into a leafy thicket, and Sarge followed, joining in a well-trimmed path with a trio of cabins just ahead.

"We're here, preacher. It's the third cabin. Ride up there and I'll take your horse."

He did. Eager arms beckoned him to the sick bed of the withered old man.

"Is that the preacher…?" the old voice croaked.

Phil bravely (much more than he felt) moved over to the bedside and took the low stool provided. "Mister, they tell me you forgot how to talk to God. Well, God never forgot you, and he gave you the brain to ask for help."

After a pause, "I'm here to help. First off, Jesus done paid the price for anything you ever done. There weren't any sin that slipped past 'im. Is that right?"

The old head found the strength to nod.

"Then he's waitin' for you to ask, knowin' you'll get what you ask for. Just say, 'Please forgive me, Lord, for all my sins." The old man did so.

"Now, mister, we know God don't lie, so that means he told the truth and your sins aren't anywhere, anymore. They dried up like mist off the lake. They puffed off like smoke from a chimney on a windy day. How does that make you feel?"

A short pause, and a toothless grin, rearranging his cheeks into a mask of wrinkles. "I feel good, Mister! I knew there was a way, but I forgot how it'd be easy to do. I thank you for comin' all this way." The eyelids drooped and a tear oozed down his wrinkles onto the pillow.

Phil stood and turned to the family, facing a wreath of relieved faces. "Come on in the kitchen, Preacher Phil. We was just settin' down to eat when my son came in with you. Looks like Pa'll doze for a minute. Been doin' that for a couple'a weeks… when he wasn't yellin' at us to find 'im a preacher 'afore it was too late."

Fat sausage patties and steamed ears of field corn graced the table. Squares of cornbread and a bowl of greens with hard-boiled eggs decorating the top. Phil had forgotten how hungry he was, but that didn't last long. Topped off with cool milk and a slice of apple pie.

"Preacher, you don't know how glad you made us. We almost didn't know to do with the old man. Scared, he seemed to be. I sent Cliff up to the place they named Burnt Tree Junction, thinkin' they might know how to reach someone. He sent us to you."

Phil was still chewing his last bite of cornbread slathered with sorghum molasses. One of the men took up the conversation.

"Preacher Phil? Would there be a chance at havin' you here for a while? We got youngens not knowin' nothin' about God, and us not knowin' enough to tell 'em. We ain't got no buildin', but we could put one up. By next spring it'd be ready, but we'd like to have you sooner… maybe for a day or two?"

Before leaving, Phil stepped in to have a last word with the old man, but immediately saw that the last word had already been spoken, and it had left a faint smile among the wrinkles. The old pa was long gone, and now the family was left to deal with the remains. Phil sighed with a sudden bout of weariness but it was a GOOD weariness, unlike any he had ever experienced after chopping corn.

Climbing out of Devil's Canyon was a long, steady haul and he let Sarge take it at his own pace, also stopping twice at a shady spot of grass. There was no hurry now.

While he sat, stomach comfortably full, on a rock in the shade, he was joined by the tall armed man, whose massive white steed stood by, switching flies. Gabriel asked, "Well, do you think you will be so frightened again, of saying the wrong thing or not knowing what to say?"

Phil wanted to say 'no' but was truthful. "I suspect so, but I'll live, same way as I lived this time. It don't get no easier, does it?"

The angel answered, "No, it doesn't. But you will always have the strength to do it. Like down at Wolf Creek."

"Yeah, well, I almost got my head blowed off down there."

The angel shook his head. "No you didn't. You had nothin' to do with any of it. What happened was that you ruined your new hat, but you saved it as a reminder. Good thinking. Satan just wanted you to fail, and we had a small showdown. .. him, me, you and God. But a pair of woodrats saved you. That should have been a humbling experience. I notice you're not telling anyone the whole story."

Phil nodded, picking up a blade of grass to run through his fingers. "Now I got two places wantin' me to come. I guess that's good."

"It's good, but remember, it's not you they really want. It's what you can tell them. You, without God, are just another young man who lives off Ridge Road. Don't forget, God sent a pair of rats to save you. You without God are nothing, but with God, you're worth the whole world."

A hawk flapped overhead, diving to the ground for a snack. Rabbit… rat… snake or something.

"Gabriel, I got a question. Why do you spend so much time with me? I don't think you treat everyone like you treat me, or is it 'cause of somethin' you know but can't tell me?"

A pause as the angel looked around. "You're right. Most people are able to listen to their inside voices when they try. You, on the other hand, sometimes need something you can see.

"You remember Paul before his name was changed. He was rich and educated, and he tried to help God, but he did it the wrong way and wouldn't listen when God tried to talk to him. God had to strike him blind in his outside eyes, so he could see with his inside eyes. He really had no one to teach him about what God expected him to do, much the same as with you.

"You have your inside eyes, but they are not yet enough to give you strength to do what you have to do. Sometimes you need something you can see to remember which way to go. You always liked the stories about Roman soldiers, so that was a good image for you. You see me as strength, and that gives you strength."

With a sigh and a nod, Phil could see it all. Yes, seeing Gabriel gave him strength. He turned to thank the angel, and there was no giant Roman soldier, and no magnificent white stallion armed in silver. Just the road that stretched into the faint blue of the mountain top. Time to go.

He stood and Sarge came to him. Springing himself aboard, man and horse headed on up the hill toward Ridge Road.

Then as his thoughts and re-thoughts of the last hours passed through his head, Phil remembered the plan of salvation as he had memorized it on the way down this hill. When he had looked at the man, he had said nothing of what he planned.

Example of 'open thy mouth wide and I will fill it'? (Psalm 81.10) Presumably his mouth had been opened wide enough. He needed to remember that.

THE EDUCATION OF LITTLE BIT AND OTHER THINGS

Along with his other thoughts, Phil decided he'd tell Ma how much he appreciated her. Handier than a pocket on a shirt, she was.

Here he brought home a pup when the family had plenty of dogs. Ma did not question him about it, but just began to take over the care of the little terrier when Phil suddenly had a trip.

And Pa. Here he dropped off two mules with no explanation. He did not even remove their tethers and put them in the corral, knowing Pa would take care of them, and ask questions later. Not that Pa cared… he just liked details.

And those two animals. Gabriel had said he would need to have two mules but don't get them yet. Would these do? Would they be the ones he should have? Now was apparently the time when he should get them. It should be Rebecca he was borrowing from, but she had her plate full of the catching up on learning that she had to do about, working with words and what they meant.

And also there was Little Bit. She needed to be a 'watch dog' in the strictest sense of the word.

Not an attack dog, or a growling dog. Or even a 'chase down' dog. Just a watch dog to alert him of the presence of rats attracted by something to gnaw, or snakes looking for a warm place on a cool night and deciding that Phil's sleeping bag would work just fine.

More than one camper had died in his sleeping bag by a snake looking to get warm, and when he was warm, he decided he needed something to eat. Humans were hard to swallow so he left them dead in their bag.

First off, he needed a snake as an object to teach her she must bark when she saw one. He had never in his life trained a dog to do anything but hunt, so he'd just have to play it by ear. And he needed a snake.

Shouldn't be hard. Anywhere in the pasture one was likely to see a snake. It didn't have to be a poisonous one. Just something that looked and smelled like a snake.

He had begun to take her to the cabin and now he let her sleep on his bed. Just as well that Ma didn't know about it.

The pup took readily to the change, but when a squirrel leaped from a tree to the window sill, Little Bit erupted into a volley of squeaky barks that had Phil awake in seconds. Looking good!

He'd just as soon that she didn't back up and sit on his face, but he had to admit, it got him awake, and his sound sleeping was the main reason for needing her.

THE HACKBERRY TREE

The week at the Hollanders' was a picnic… in the literal sense. A massive hackberry tree shaded the brush arbor that sheltered picnickers from the sun, creating a layer of cooler breeze between the late August sun and the layer of leafy branches of the arbor.

The thing with arbors, they were temporary as in they needed regular maintenance. Heavy ropes had been attached to solid trees and a network of cords, wires or smaller ropes were stretched to hold the leafy ends of shrubs, smaller limbs and sprouts. Eventually, however, the leaves withered, dried and tended to crumble and filter down on the revelers as well as into the potato salad and lemon pies. Couldn't let that happen.

So, when there was a need for the arbor, the roof was examined, and usually required fresh branches. A bit of a trouble but considered worth it.

That had been done when Phil arrived with Sarge and Little Bit in her basket, and the two mules belonging to Rebecca. The mules were loaded with the small, one-man tent, a sleeping bag, a lantern with an extra bottle of oil… just in case.

(Jesus had things to say about having extra oil. The parable of the ten virgins pointed out what could happen if the oil was used up before the feast. Mat. 25: 1-13)

The animals were turned out to pasture, and Phil was set before a hearty meal. It appeared that there were a number of grown children, and even more children from the neighbors, and grandchildren. A mob, actually.

Phil found a brave streak inside himself and set a rule that Little Bit must not be touched unless he was around. He explained it in a way they could understand… that Little Bit was in 'school' learning how she must act in a group. And that extra petting interfered with her lessons.

He set up his tent beside the arbor, though he was invited into the house. Some things go well, and the five days with the Hollanders was one of those times. The children loved the stories, demanding favorites be repeated.

One morning at dawn, he was aroused by the tent being shook. He startled awake and peered out into the face of two children, about three and five. They demanded that he 'come and talk.' Before Phil could decide what to do they were rounded up and carried off by their parents.

The other disturbance was when Little Bit, who was doing well with her lessons, alerted herself with a different smell. The lantern was set up in the tent and allowed to burn all night to discourage small fur-bearers. In the dim light she lifted her shiny nose and widened her brown eyes. Standing on four stiff legs and a tail as still as a whisper, she stared at the tent entrance.

A face had appeared that she had never seen before and likely hoped never to see again. It crept bravely forward toward her basket though she managed a small warning growl in her throat. The thing paid no attention.

Its long nose, whiskers and tiny eyes continued to approach. Little Bit decided this was no snake or rat to be easily frightened off, and she backed up out of the basket and stepped into her master's face.

The tiny claws dug into Phil's cheeks, bringing him suddenly upward, sending the terrier rolling toward the beast. Sensing that she was facing certain destruction, she turned her nose upward and let out a howl of immense proportion… considering the size of the source. The beast stared at her, and decided there must be better luck elsewhere but before it could leave, Phil was out of the sleeping bag.

With a chuckle, he seized the rope-like tail and lifted the animal, tossing it out of the tent. So now Little Bit had met a possum, and learned that they did not attack… maybe. Phil picked up the trembling mite of a canine and hugged her, stroking her fur and telling her she did the right thing. Tucked inside the bag with him, however, she spent the night with her eyes open.

Good thing, actually. The worst trouble with sleeping bags and the ground was the snakes. In the hot summer, it was not a problem, but in the spring and fall the coolness of the night slowed their metabolism and using their heat sensors, they looked for warm rocks but would settle for a warm body inside the bag.

Then it was time for school to start for the Hollander children, and Burt Hollander made arrangements for another session next summer. And into Phil's hand he put a $20.00 gold piece. God's money, he told Phil.

Something else had been happening over the summer. The young men who had put a bullet through the new hat were busy young men. Two more had been added, and Will had departed, leaving the group of four who would again take up the problem of getting even with the fellow who got everything without working for it. The fact that they, themselves, did not work did not seem to interest them.

It took weeks of talking and planning, and finally deciding on a way that they could do him in without attracting the huge fellow on the massive white horse. It would also be a way that they would not be held responsible if the 'preacher' didn't come out alive.

Fact is, no one was likely to notice him being gone but his family, and they'd have not a clue as to where he'd gone. He was such a gad-about, he was likely to be anywhere and not missed until it was too late.

Their plan was an excellent one, but it had its dangerous side. They needed to catch some of the members of Ridge Road wolf pack without shooting them or damaging them in any way. Six animals would be wonderful, four would be all right, but with the difficulty they had catching them, they decided three were enough.

Wolves were smart about traps, and they were quick to chew their way out of snares. It took ingenuity. A trap was made within the walls of a wire and brush fence circling a hackberry tree. The low, tunnel-like trapdoor was strewn with raw meat all the way into the circle, and the bait was scattered liberally around the circle.

Wolves can smell blood from far off, and after about 20 hours waiting, the pack was attracted. The old ones were suspicious of the man-made contraption, but the young ones were hungry.

When three of them entered the trap and were consuming the food, the gang fired off a shot and the pack was gone… all except the three who were shut inside the circle.

The timing was exactly right for the gang. Leaving one of their number to toss in previously caught rabbits, the others found Phil on Sarge returning after an errand in Berryville and a stop-in on Rebecca. He was deep in thought about the girl. She could hardly be seen as the same one she was almost a year ago. Purely amazing, it was.

Today, with sparkling eyes, she told him of the Sunday Lady who made music on the piano and taught the girls some songs. There was 'The Sweet Bye and Bye' song, that Rebecca didn't really understand, but loved the tune.

Also 'Amazing Grace,' and one of the girls had wondered what 'grace' was. The Sunday Lady explained that grace was a word for a bundle of love freely given to another person expecting nothing in return for it. And the word in the song meant that God gave a big bundle of grace to humans when he offered to forgive every wicked thing they did, if they just believed in his son and let him help them.

That song was nice, too, but her favorite was 'Rock of Ages.' Could she sing it for him... maybe just a little piece of it..? Of course she could, and it set Phil to wondering, dazed at the music coming from the girl with no education.

No bird in the trees could have excelled the clarity of her voice. She whispered to him that the Sunday Lady said that she had 'a very good ability to stay on the tune.' She glowed with pride over the small praise.

"When I sing 'Rock of Ages,' it makes me... feel... Well, I... don't hardly have words to tell about it."

Intrigued, Phil asked, "Can you try to tell me?"

She dipped her head soberly, took in a deep breath and began. Haltingly... word by word... she explained the Rock in a way that no other could, unless their life had been like hers. Maybe only a dozen sentences, but she was clear in the knowledge that the song was written for her... and that this new Rock was sheltering her all by itself.

As Sarge clipped along Ridge Road toward his barn and feed bag, Phil turned the girl's words over and over in his mind. How could she manage such clear descriptions with her lack of words? How amazingly far she had come!

Darkness had fallen but the road was clear and he was almost at the cut-off for his home when loud yells stopped Sarge. He reared on his hind legs and whinnied at the top of his voice as human figures emerged from the trees on each side of the road bearing blazing torches.

Advancing onto Phil, one of them grabbed Sarge's bridle and was immediately shaken off but not before Phil's leg was grabbed and he was dragged from the saddle.

Falling off balance on his hip and right arm, he was tackled by many hands and a sack pulled down over his head, gathered in at the neck. His hands were yanked behind him and bound together. He was pulled to his feet and tossed over a saddle, stomach down, and strapped tightly, dead-man style.

In mere minutes, the horse was running and Phil was bouncing on the saddle blindfolded and tied, and laying helplessly over the saddle on his stomach.

Strange how unrelated thoughts can intrude in a moment of terror, and Phil had a passing thought that he was glad Little Bit was not on this trip. Then he turned his thoughts back to his own plight. What was going on this time?

Then he could feel himself pitched sideward as the road went sharply down hill. Leaving Ridge Road, of course. Thinking back he tried to visualize how far he had come before the turn-off… just in case he had a chance to get loose.

It seemed to be a rocky path as the horse fought for footing, and as leafy limbs brushed over him. It might not be a path at all. These fellows were getting better at abduction. Darkness was a good idea and leaving no beaten path was another one.

Finally the path leveled off, and the animal moved with more confidence. There was low conversation, but being inside the sack kept him from understanding the words. He did have a clear thought, though. *Gabriel, I hope you're somewhere near here.* This was clearly another test of faith.

It was pitch black darkness when the animals stopped and there was considerable milling around. Also some disjointed conversation.

"Where at's the drawin' rope?"

"Over here. I ain't wantin' to light the torch again till I have to. We got a breeze stirrin' up, and we don't need to start a fire."

"You get the rope."

"Yeah, I hope it's tied good up there. If he should slip down in the pen too soon, it'd'a spoil all the fun."

"It's tight. I made sure. It pulls up to that limb we decided on that was strong enough. You know how tough hackberry…."

"Yeah, that's enough talkin'. Tie it around his waist and bring the horse over here."

"You givin' orders now…?"

"Sure am. Now get a move on."

Phil felt the horse rearrange its position. His feet touched something solid. A rope was pulled tight around Phil's ribs under his arms and circled again. Double tight. Were they planning to suffocate him?

But no, he was pulled upright and his hands were untied. He now sat in the saddle with both feet over the same side, toes touching the wood.

The most authoritative voice addressed him. "Now, mister Lucky Boy, listen to me. You're gonna be hoisted up in a tree, and there's likely to be damage to you on the way. There'll be enough light for you to see a limb, and you gotta grab it and hang on for your life till you get pulled higher.

"Here's the situation. That noise trompin' around below you is hungry wolves and you don't want'a be their dinner, so you gotta pull up in the tree. You got that?"

He felt what might have been a slap on his face. "I said, you got that?"

Phil answered through the sack, "I got it."

"That's better. Now I outta pull you up in the dark and let you find your own limb but I'm gonna be good to ya. When the torch blazes, you look quick for a limb to grab, cause the wind is too strong for the torch. Get ready, now."

He felt a fumbling at his neck as the sack was untied. Then it was jerked off, and a quick look up showed the hackberry tree with a rope hoisted over a high limb and tied around his waist. Directly overhead was a smaller limb, but hackberry limbs are tough. They are, however, very rough with sharp-edged bumps on every limb, no matter how small the limb is.

He believed the promise that the light would not last. It flickered like a candle in a gale.

"Here goes... get ready to grab!"

He felt himself jerked off the saddle and swung toward the trunk of the tree. With both hands upraised he grabbed for and caught a limb that bowed down but did not break.

Below him he heard the unmistakable snarl of wolves struggling over a kill, and he was sure the intended kill was himself. One of the leaping, snarling beasts actually bumped a nose against his boot.

In a desperate strain of muscle, he pulled up... let loose one hand... kicked at a lower limb, and caught a higher one. Not much higher, but a hackberry has a lot of limbs.

The bark on the second limb cut into his palms, but he could not let go. The other hand had to come up and he had to find a solid limb for a foot hold. It was then that the wind snuffed out the torch light, and he was in a tree full of barbs and snags and the wolf pack below him was leaping and snarling… and he didn't know how close they were. Too close… for certain.

So now, pulling his senses together for survival, he breathed deeply and sought for a higher limb for his feet. Had to. At least they'd left his boots on, but he was certain that was just an oversight.

Finding a limb that firmly held his weight, he loosed his hands and rubbed them together for a bit of comfort. His hands were full of blood. Must be… as slick as they were. Carefully, he swiped them, painfully, down his side and felt in the darkness for a higher limb, hopefully one that he could sit on.

His tormentors were out of hearing distance. Likely there was a cave nearby. In northern Arkansas, there was usually a cave nearby most everywhere.

Finding a suitable 'seat' he took stock of his position. Likely he would be there at least all night, so he must make plans. It was too easy to doze off, no matter how uncomfortable, and slip off the limb. There'd be no way to catch another one in the dark with painful, bloody hands.

Removing his belt, he felt for a limb close enough, and small enough to be encircled by the belt and have it still reach around his waist. That took a good number of minutes, and by then the animals below him had quieted. Willing to wait for their meal, seemingly.

Eventually the wind quieted, and Phil leaned against the tree trunk and dozed. At one point he felt a strong pang of loss for Sarge. Also the angel.

Gabriel, where are you?

The sun finally peeked over the mountain, and Phil knew he was on the south side of Ridge Road. That was something, anyway. Then he smelled bacon and coffee. His taste buds were suffering at the aroma and the knowledge that there would be no food for him.

Looking below, he saw the three young wolves roaming and circling the tree, occasionally looking up. Then one would put paws on the tree trunk, stare at him and snarl, hungrily. With a wry smile he sympathized. "I know what it's like, old boy. I'm hungry, too."

Then he amused himself with wondering what the hoodlums planned to do with him, and eventually came to the conclusion that it was nothing. They were going to leave him there and he would eventually fall, and the wolves would take care of the rest. So… how long could he stay here when absolutely no one knew he was missing except his folks, and they would not be concerned. At least, not yet.

They would not be concerned for a day or more. So often something happened to keep him from being where he planned to be. They were now used to it.

The day wore on with the fellows wandering around below him and ignoring him as though he did not exist. The wolves leaped against the tree and against the wire circle bolstered with brush. They were totally aware of him.

And he got hungrier. Worse than that, he was thirsty. The dry October day sucked the moisture from the air, building it into a bank of clouds in the northwest. Fall storm brewing. Sure to be. It was time. It always came this time of the year, seeming to warn the landholders it was time to do what they needed to do before the winter winds came.

Today, his brothers would be bringing in the third cutting of hay. The barn loft would be crammed full, and the extra loads would be stacked on the ground and tarped. Hot, sticky job but oh, how he wished to be there with them.

When evening came, the smoke from the roasting fire circled the skinned rabbits on the spit and arose to his nostrils. The wolves were smelling it, too, and were whining and leaping against the fence. The tormentors lolled before the fire chewing on the bones of the roasted rabbits and sipping coffee. The aroma of the coffee was almost un-endurable.

He looked down and studied the animals. Three of them, young and healthy. When dark came, maybe he could creep down and maybe get over the fence. He tormented himself with the thought, knowing for certain the hungry wolves would have him down on the ground as soon as they could reach a boot.

That fence was made tight by fellows who knew the strength of wolves, and also the ingenuity of humans. The story of Daniel in the lion's den passed before his mind, and he remembered what Daniel said. He clearly remembered every word, for hadn't he read the story at least four times?

"O king, live forever. My God hath sent his angel and hath shut the mouths of the lions. They have not hurt me. I am innocent…" But somehow Daniel's words did not seem to fit the present situation.

As the storm seemed imminent, he nodded in appreciation of Daniel's faith. Was it that much greater than his own? Where was his faith, now? He decided to bypass Gabriel and contact God. "God, it is surely not time for me to leave the earth. I thought I had a lot to do but you are omnipotent and wise. If it's my time, I am ready to go."

He felt a shiver from his head through his aching hands and into his feet, numb from sitting for nearly 24 hours on the limb.

The shiver was not for the coolness of the raising breeze, but at the thought that his work on earth might be done, and he had thought there would be much more. He pressed his hands together, gently, because of the torn flesh and thought of Jesus with the nails piercing through between the bones. A lot worse than hackberry stickers.

Not only that, his numb feet were still in comfortable boots and had not been nail-pierced.

Oh, how weak I am, he thought. The wolves would make short work of him. He would not suffer long as Jesus had. But where was his faith?

Then he thought of Job, who, when he had lost everything, and he was told to just 'curse God and die,' he answered, "…though God slay me, yet will I trust in him."

That was the best… he decided… for him. It was certain in his mind that if he was 'slain' it would be the will of God, because God had power over all and could save him if it was his will.

So now it was time to put himself entirely in God's hands. If anyone should know all the ways God had of dealing with humans, it should be Phil himself, as he had already started his fifth trip through the wonderful book.

God, if this is the time you will take me, I thank you for the time in this tree. I had an opportunity to think and remember, and be ready to look forward to being with you.

The sky opened up and a shower of rain sluiced down in the valley. The tormentors scurried into their dry cave and watched the rain. It poured down through leaves, drenching every inch of Phil's clothing. The dreary valley managed a brisk wind, sending sheets of cold air all the way into the marrow of his bones. Darkness came early, and the wolves curled into a circle at the base of the tree, trying to sleep off the drenching.

Phil shook the rain from his eyelashes and looked as far as he could see. The valley toward the west was black with lowering clouds. It was, as folks always said, "settin' in for all night." Phil loosened the belt for the dozenth time and stretched as best he could. Had to keep the blood flowing. It wouldn't be warmer until morning. He'd wait. Then the protective belt went back on.

With the gale wind increasing, the persimmon trees began to bend. That Arkansas native tree was used to storms. Those trees won over the weather by bending until the wind was past, and then they straightened up, slender and tall.

The hackberry did not bend. Its iron-like consistency held it fast and the most that broke away from the limbs were the leaves. Phil's seating would be solid, whatever happened. Come morning he would still be in the tree and the wolves would still be in the pen.

So now, leaning toward the tree trunk he tried to relax. *It's in your hands, God.*

As darkness fell, the only light was the flashes of jagged lightening. The persimmon tree that was very close to the enclosure was bending almost double, and Phil leaned tightly against the hackberry tree trunk, glad for his secure belt.

He was soon to see that one could not count on earthly means of security. With a sudden crack of thunder, he felt himself cringe, unconsciously. With a snap, he felt the protecting belt give way and fall past him, down toward the wolves. The next lightning bolt revealed it, laying over a limb below him, totally out of reach. No matter. It would be broken now, anyway, and useless.

Squaring his shivering shoulders, he told the wind, "God is in charge. He knows how to make you stop. He did it on Lake Galilee, so you have absolutely no power over me. So just blow all you want to. God could shut you up with one 'Peace, be still.'" (Mark 4:39)

Those final words were thrown back into his face with a terrific gust that leaned the persimmon tree all the way over into the limbs of the hackberry. Hackberry limbs did not break... they were welded by sinew and sap to the mother trunk, but this time a limb broke.

The limb he sat on splintered at the connection with the trunk and tangled into the limber limbs of the persimmon tree. Phil felt a face full of persimmon leaves and nothing solid under his feet. Flailing his arms into the persimmon limbs, he caught one... bark smooth and slick from rain... and his blood.

Ignoring the pain, he clasped the limb with ragged and fiery blood-shot palms, and held on as if his life depended on it. It did. When the clouds sucked the wind back, the gust let the persimmon tree rise up to its tall stature, carrying Phil with it.

The broken hackberry limb fell across the wire and brush fence, and in the next flash, Phil saw the wolves dash up the limb and leap to the ground. Amazed, he watched them, now free, heading for the cave where they had no doubt spent many storms.

Not hesitating, he swung down... limb from limb... to the ground and ran as best he could. He was not more than an eighth of a mile away when he heard three shots and a scream. He paused not a second, letting the humans and the wolves battle it out without waste of breath or thought on his part.

There were two rules for a lost person in that part of Northern Arkansas. When looking for humans, follow the river. When looking for a road, climb the nearest hill. Roads followed ridges every time they could.

Some distance away he had heard the three gunshots followed by the wail of the wolf pack come to join those that escaped. He had a fleeting thought that something may have happened in the cave, but somehow he did not care.

He was no longer chilled, though he was still dripping wet. The rain had settled into a steady downpour, but Phil climbed. Rocks were slick and briars were scratchy. Low limbs dug into his face. No matter. Safety was distance and knowledge was the road.

Rain flowed though his drenched hair and into his eyes. He ingored it and ran.

Dawn was breaking when the terrain leveled. He climbed a fence and followed a row of dead cornstalks all the way to the road. He could have found shelter in the house belonging to the owner of the field, but he opted to move on.

He was much closer to Berryville than he would have preferred, but just knowing where he was lifted his spirits.

Plodding with one squelching foot after the other, he moved toward Burnt Tree Junction. Darkhorse Farm. Home. Scratched, damaged and bloody he walked. *Jesus, you were much more bloody than I, and it was all for me. You could have called a 'legion of angels' to help you, but you didn't. There were times I might have called for angelic help, if it had been me.*

And then he shivered, but not from cold. The voice was so plain, he even looked around. "You were surrounded by angels who bore you up when the limb broke. They loosed the belt to have you ready for the transfer. They loosed the wolves and made them more interested in the tormentors than in you. They helped you up this hill."

Phil swallowed hard, sniffed and felt warm tears on his face. Shaking his head from side to side, he told the air around him, "Oh, Lord, and I didn't even know!"

Someone walked up beside him, and he knew without looking that it was Gabriel. "Just had to tell you. Humans so often don't know when they are given help, and they think they were saved by their own strength."

After a few more squdgy steps, he told Gabriel, "I looked for you. I thought you would come."

"I was elsewhere. You did not need me, you had a hundred heavenly beings surrounding you. There was nothing that could have happened to you that God did not permit and direct."

Phil made the rest of the trip alone. Comforted. He was almost dry when he turned toward the farm, and saw his home.

Hanging a head over the fence was the beautiful, long, black face of Sarge, his swivel ears turned toward his master to hear any command. He lifted his head and sounded a long whinney of greeting toward the world in general, and toward his master in particular. He followed the whinney with a conversational, rubber-lipped whicker.

No longer as weary as he thought he was, Phil walked to the fence and stroked the silky face and patted the muscular neck as it pushed against the fence. "Sarge, how did you get home? You old fellow, you! Is there nothing you can't do?"

He opened the door and Ma greeted him with the question, "What you want first, Son, food or dry clothes?"

"Food, Ma. Anything you got handy."

Phil sat himself down in his still-damp clothing and watched Ma break a half a dozen eggs into the smoking skillet. Biscuits came from the warming oven over the stove, along with a slab of pink ham. She poured strong, leftover coffee into a mug and put it in front of him. The platter of food followed.

"I was lookin' for ya, Son. When Sarge come in without you, I said to Pa, don't you be in no hurry to go after him. He's got things to get settled... him and God. So Pa was gonna start out right after dinner... that'd be in a hour from now."

Smart Ma. A few things did get settled. Phil knew one thing for certain. The road before him was going to be rough, and there would be worse things ahead. No matter. There would be help when he needed it.

He bowed his head and muttered, "Thank you." What else was there to say... so he picked up his fork. He definitely knew what to do with it.

GOOD BYE, LITTLE TODD HOLLANDER

After he had eaten, Phil retired to his cabin. Exhausted, he changed into dry clothes. There were a lot of things to be done, and he sat back on his bed and attempted to decide what should be done first. It was four o'clock when he again opened his eyes.

He might not have opened his eyes then but his sister, now sixteen, was pounding on his door shouting "Sleepyhead! Are you a'aimin' to sleep through supper? Ma's made meatloaf and someone left you a note."

Phil bolted from his bed. "When did he leave the note?"

"Just now. Get yourself outta bed and you can catch 'im."

He leaped aboard Sarge without saddle or bridle and galloped up the lane. There was the messenger… just up ahead. Something about the rider looked familiar.

"Leon! Did you need to see me?"

Leon Hollander was the next youngest of Burt's grown children. Only Rosalie was younger. The family had been excited that Rosalie's baby was due momentarily. No matter that the child would be the 28th grandchild… he was eagerly welcomed and excitedly anticipated.

"Bad news, man. Pa sent me to get you to attend at the funeral."

"Funeral…?"

"Yeah. The little fellow was pink and healthy lookin' one day and didn't live till mornin'. Rosalie went to wake him up and he was… well, he… uh. It was too late. It's hittin' everyone hard. Pa said to get to you 'cause you'd come. The family needs words at the buryin' a Todd and Pa said special to ask you for music. Someone who could sing. He said you'd know what to do and what to say. Wasn't needin' no sermon or story… just words for comfort to us for losin' one of us."

"Oh, I'd… but, Leon, I've never done something like that."

"Pa said you'd say that so for me to say you're gonna do it a lot of times 'afore you die, and you ain't gonna start no younger. Says we're the place to start… the youngens knowin' you like they do. Time you get there, you'll have the words… Pa said. And Pa don't let himself be wrong…. about folks, that is."

Sarge snorted at a pesky fly, flinging his head wildly. Phil sighed, drew in a breath and looked at Leon, waiting expectantly.

"Best I can say is, I'll try. My family'll be there, of course, and my sisters sing, but I ain't in position to say how good they are. I'll ask around. Did your pa mention any song, specially?"

Leon shook his sadly. "No. Said you'd know what was right."

The bereaved uncle gave the time and date, and stated that the burying would be in the family cemetery on the north slope. Then with a swinging leap, he was in the saddle and disappearing up the lane.

Death was so final. He was small when old Grandpop passed on, but he remembered it… the total finality of it. No more stories about the war. Nobody else was there who could remember the awful things that had happened.

And all the babies in his own family had lived. There was not one of his siblings that the family could spare. But the Hollander family would now get along without little Todd. What would be the purpose of God taking a baby? What words of comfort could he furnish… and him only twenty two, and never having done a funeral before? Mostly the families just read the 23rd Psalm at the grave and sang about 'gathering at the river where bright angels' feet had trod.' What did that all mean?

And a singer. Bringing his sisters to mind, he couldn't picture any one of them singing… special-like. And why did they sing about gathering at the river, when that had nothing to do about nothing of losing a baby that wasn't even sick?

How about the Sweet Bye and Bye…? With that thought a flow of chill bumps passed down his arms.

REBECCA! Rebecca, of course. He could already hear that voice, clearer than birdsongs, flowing out over the Hollander's north slope toward Missouri. Across the track of the Sante Fe. Echoing at the small river that ran alongside the track.

It was November, and most of the leaves were off the trees, but the meadow would be covered with goldenrod plumes and the blue stars of fall asters. The leaves on the sumac shrub would still be scarlet, and the oaks would be all shades from yellow to red to brown.

He could picture it so clearly in his mind. All he needed now was 'words of comfort.' How does a fellow of 22 comfort an entire family…? Maybe three dozen persons plus an unknown number of neighbors would be there.

First, he must secure the services of Rebecca. Now.

Stretching an arm over the shiny black neck of Sarge, he hugged the animal, leaning his face toward the short hair of the horse's cheek… warm from standing in the fall sunshine. Arkansas always had wonderfully warm days sprinkled through the fall, and may the day of the burying be one of those.

Leaping aboard, he turned the horse by knee pressure and a slap in the neck, and he galloped back to the house. He'd have liked to head out to Berryville this minute, but better to wait until morning. Early morning.

From the basket of apples on the porch, he selected one for Sarge, and then led him to the corral. "Rest up, old fellow. We gotta go back to Berryville. Maybe we'll have better luck this time."

It was barely light on Ridge Road when Sarge climbed up out of the lane and headed east. The breeze from the north carried a slight bite of a chill as was expected in the dark of early morning. When he went after Rebecca, he'd take the buggy.

Then a shrug and a grin. He was already expecting that Rebecca would readily agree to go. It was something she had never done before, either. Should he warn her ahead of time that he would want her to tell how the Rock made her feel… to let her get used to the idea? Or maybe just let it be fresh, the way it was for him. He'd have to think about it.

Now, about his own words of comfort. As Sarge trotted on the hard-packed limestone flint road, he searched his mind. Total blank. Nothing but darkness in his thoughts. *Gabriel, where are you…? I can't do this. I really can't and I'll make such a mess the family'll hate me.*

No comforting presence of an angel riding beside him. He was alone, inside and out. No voices encouraging him. As he neared King's River, the turbulent stream that divided Carroll County, the sun burst through the tops of the oak trees, spreading warmth over his shoulders.

As he neared the school, he made his plans. First he'd tell the head mistress why he was here. This request certainly could not be normal for the school, but Rebecca was there voluntarily. It was not punishment. The school was just to help girls who were not so fortunate as to have family to help.

Whether or not, he knew he needed her. If he made a mess of words, perhaps her music would cover it up. Partly, anyway. A preacher at a funeral… of course it would be expected. What did he think… anyway? It was just that it wasn't supposed to happen so soon. But it would it be easier later? There was always a first time. Had to be.

As he rode through the gate, he was somewhat relieved. The battle of the angels was again going on so he knew help was near. The voices called demons insisted on their turn, but the protecting angels always won. Maybe. Sometimes it was hard to tell the difference, until he remembered that the demons had the worse liar in the world for a boss, so of course they lied. They had been trained to lie... trained by the best.

He tossed the reins over the hitching post by the door. *Have courage, Phil,* he warned himself.

The mistress at the home said, "Sing at a funeral...? Well, I understand she has an exceptional voice, but we... well, we try to protect all the girls until they can protect themselves. Rebecca has done so well...."

"Ma'am, I really need her. I am the speaker, and very nervous. If Rebecca is there, it will make up for me."

A wide smile on the matron's face. "I thoroughly understand. Sometimes a woman's skirt is a good thing to hide behind, after you've grown too tall for your ma's skirt. You must give me a minute to think. Meanwhile, I know you must be hungry, and the girls have just sat down to breakfast. You must join them."

Phil was startled, wide-eyed. Sure he was hungry, but to eat with a hundred and fifty girls... maybe two hundred? But he had no chance to escape.

Matron scooted the girls apart to make room for him beside Rebecca. Sugared oatmeal was set before him, and biscuits... flanked by the bowl of butter and pitcher of honey. And milk.

No one was more startled than Rebecca but she recovered quickly. "This here's the fellow that found me when I was chained to the cook stove and left to die. He's a really good fellow and stops in to see me when he can. I'm glad he got here in time for breakfast."

The girls were not shy, and there were enough words among them that he didn't have to think of any while he buttered his biscuit.

Then he was alone with the matron and Rebecca. "Brother Phil, would you tell this curious girl why you're here, after seeing her only three days ago?" To Rebecca, she whispered, "I think he's going to ask you to sing for someone."

Well spoken, Phil thought. "It's a funeral for a baby, Rebecca. I'll be there and my sisters too, and the grandfather of the baby specifically wanted a singer. Not just someone who could sing. He wanted a special singer, and you were the most special one I could think of."

Rebecca was leaning forward and looking into his eyes, biting her lower lip with her upper front teeth. What did that mean… that she was thinking it over, or maybe saying she didn't want to do it?

Phil nervously continued. "It'll be the day after tomorrow. I'd come and get you to spend the night. Then you'd be fresh for the funeral, it's a pretty far piece from where I live. It's quite a way back in the woods, but we can make it."

She nodded. "But I only know three songs good enough to sing all the way through. And there ain't time to learn no more. What song was he wantin' to hear?"

"Didn't say. Didn't mention any song, just that he wanted a singer. How about the 'Sweet Bye and Bye,' and 'Amazing Grace.' They'd both be good. And then for sure I'd want you to sing 'Rock of Ages.'"

"Three songs? You sure? I wouldn't want no one to get tired hearin' me."

At this the matron smiled. She had been turning from one to the other, studying Rebecca's reaction. What human would complain of a mockingbird's repertoire? Who could get tired of hearing the angels sing? Of course they would want three songs… if they had a choice.

With a wide shake of the head, Phil told her, "They'd not get tired. Absolutely not. All three songs if that wouldn't make you too tired."

"Shucks, no. I could sing a hunnerd songs if I just knew the tune to 'em."

The matron nodded with satisfaction. "Then it's set, and she'll be ready. We'll have her dressed appropriately, and it is my idea that it will be very good for her. Especially if it helps you. She loves to help."

And Sarge and Phil were on the way back home. Most of the day had been taken up, but it had been successful. For five whole miles he amused his mind by wondering how a person learned a song they didn't know if there was no one to teach it. There had to be a way.

Gabriel, that would be a good job for you. You certainly haven't been any help to me on this funeral, but you could tell me how I could get music to Rebecca that she hasn't heard before. I figure she's got angels takin' care'a her, but you'd be extra good at findin' a way.

Gabriel, wherever he was, remained silent and invisible. Phil nodded agreeably. No matter. Of course the important angel Gabriel was not his own personal servant assigned to fulfill his every wish. However, if one didn't ask, how could one expect to receive?

The next day Phil took his sisters down to where the hickory nut trees grew. By now the nuts would be on the ground with every creature in the woods after them. Humans had to be fast if they wanted any.

He took Scout and the dog cart. The nuts'd be heavy to carry back. He picked up nuts for a while, but the girls were so much better (and faster), he went back to the cart and opened the leather Bible case.

Words of comfort. Where are you, words? He touched the tissue-thin page… thin as a whisper, but oh! So many words. Notes for him from someone long past. Comfort words. Hmmmm.

It would be nice if they would just jump out in bold type. Scout, still hitched to the shafts, kept pulling the cart forward a few inches at a time, reaching for the next clump of grass. Squirrels chattered down at the thieves stealing their nuts, and pitched twigs down on them. Crows shrieked and disputed, but there were no words of comfort to be had.

Cart loaded, they climbed up the path. The sisters giggled and teased each other, argued and flung insults, then dissolved into giggle fits again.

Still no words.

Evening came, and he polished his shoes and brushed lint and dust from his best jacket, the one he bought for Dead Horse Springs. He wiped the seat of the buggy, and oiled the wheel bearings. He didn't need any squeaks to distract him.

He fed Sarge a cup of chopped corn that he didn't need, and patted his cheek. "Sarge, old fellow, get to sleep early. We got a long day'a pullin' tomorrow."

Sarge bobbed his head that he acknowledge the suggestion. Who cared anyway what humans said? If they didn't whip you with the reins, and fed you corn when you didn't need it, words didn't matter.

But words did matter, and Phil had none.

Rebecca had been ready and waiting in the matron's office. Beautiful Rebecca! He had never seen her 'fixed up' like women get when they're going somewhere special.

At the buggy, she held her hand toward him, and he extended an elbow for balance when assisting a lady. Obviously, she had been taught a few social gestures. Why was he surprised? Also, she wore shiny pumps with heels that made her an inch taller.

But even at that height, Phil saw how her yellow hair was twisted and pulled up, and a ribbon bow, black velvet and at least 5 inches wide, had been shaped and secured to her head to resemble a hat. Black against yellow. Striking, yet modest.

She seated herself on the velour cover over the buggy seat, crossing her feet delicately at the ankles. He climbed aboard and they were off.

He turned to her, looking her up and down. Really well put together, as far as he knew girls. Ma would be pleased. Skirt black, shirtwaist of delicate white with buttons and ruffles. Over her shoulders was a shawl of snow-white yarn. What a sight! One didn't openly stare at a girl… did one? Not unless one couldn't help himself.

Rebecca saw his gaze and shyly confided, "This here skirt's borrowed from Caroline, that her grandma sent her. My shirtwaist was made by Miss Mamie Conway that lives in my house. She made it all… even the lace. She says she'll teach me how to make lace when she gets a chance. She wants me to spend Christmas with her."

"Will you?"

"I'm thinkin' likely… yes. When folks want you just 'cause you're you, it makes 'em special. I ain't been much special to very many folks."

Now Phil found words. "The only reason you haven't been special was that no one knew where you were. The man kept you hid."

Sadness passed over her face. "'Speck you're right."

And now was the time to head for Wolfpath and the Hollanders. There was time for a light snack before they left the farm. Food would be served at the Hollander's home, of course, but it didn't pay to arrive hungry.

Phil assisted her back into the buggy, along with his oldest sister. A bit of relief there, as they would entertain each other. He needed to find words of comfort somewhere... anywhere!

The brush arbor still had leaves on the limbs, and the split log seats had been swept of leaves and spiders. The warm breeze blew up from the valley smelling of cedar, fall flowers and orchards.

It was Phil's time.

"Friends, this has been a good day for me because I am privileged to bring you music for your souls. This music is wrapped up in the person of Miss Rebecca Jones and she will now sing."

She started with 'Amazing Grace.' When she finished the song, Phil asked her, "Rebecca, what did they tell you about grace?"

She turned to Phil with a smile. "Grace is a little package of love that's given and does not have to be paid back."

"Thank you. Now your next song."

Stains of pure heaven came out. "In the sweet bye and bye, we will meet on that beautiful shore. In the Father's house over the way, is a land that is fairer than day...."

The song was a story and needed no explanation. Rebecca sat down and Phil arose to speak. He opened his Bible and looked at the family and their friends.

"My friends and neighbors, I have spent a lot of time looking for words of comfort. Sometimes there are none. When one steps into rain, they get wet. When there is ice, they get cold. When we lose something we love that is precious, we are sad and there is no comfort.

"There is, however, some other thoughts. Baby Todd was with us only for a minute, as compared to a lifetime. Many things happen in a lifetime and we forget most of them, but there is no one here who will not remember the time spent with Todd. Every minute of his short life will be fondly pressed into our memory.

"We will remember that we were given a beautiful, warm day, when so often the first part of November has ice shards raining out of the clouds. We enjoy the day, but tomorrow it may rain. That is the world God has given us, and we are thankful.

"Some things last, and others are fleeting, but there is a place where life is perfect, and that is where little Todd is. We'll see him again.

"I'm going to ask our singer to give us one more song. This song is special to her, and I think it will bring a bit of comfort."

Rebecca looked at Phil, nodded and stood.

She sang, "Rock of Ages, cleft for me. Let me hide myself in thee. Let the waters and the blood from thy precious side that flows be from sin a double cure. Save from wrath, and make me pure."

She finished it, and Phil asked, "Would you tell everyone exactly what you told me about this song?"

"Yes, I will. It was when I wanted to know what 'cleft' meant, I was shown in the Bible where a man named Isaiah said, 'Go into the clefts of the rocks, and into the tops of the ragged rocks for fear of the Lord and for the glory of his majesty.'

"That made me think when I was a little girl and was taken away from my family. In the new place I saw a rock that had a space just my size and I could crawl into it and no one could see me unless they were right in front of me.

"I crawled into the rock, and hid, but then Miss Lucy who took care of me told me not to do it again because it made her cry when she couldn't find me. So after that, I crawled into the rock in my mind. When things got so bad I thought I couldn't stand it, I hid my real self, and only my body stayed in sight.

"I was amazed when the memory of the cleft in the rock in my mind grew larger as I got bigger, and later I went to see it again. The real hole in the rock was really small. I was very surprised.

"Then when the Sunday Lady taught me that song, I learned about another Rock that had a hiding place that just fit me, no matter what size I was. She told me about the Rock in the weary land.

"So now when things get too bad, I go there in my mind, and cruel words just fly on by and can't find me. That cleft in the rock is just my size and it has no room for anything else. Anger can't get in there with me; neither can disappointments. I can't feel sorry for myself when I'm there because there is no room for self pity.

"I was really glad to find that cleft in the special Rock that was made just for me, and wished I had known about it sooner. But I'm grateful. I will never know my family because of what someone else did to me, but my sadness has no room to be in the Rock with me. Happiness and good memories don't take up any space, so I can take them with me everywhere." She hesitated and looked around, then continued.

"That's why I love the song so much."

She sat quietly down, and Burt Hollander stood. "Brother Phil, please ask her to sing the song again."

Phil nodded to Rebecca and she stood. "Rock of Ages, cleft...."

Phil began again. "There is a Rock for everyone. It is a hiding place, a rock in the weary land, a shelter in the storm. When sadness comes, and when it is greater than we can bear, we must flee to the Rock, regardless of where our body stays. The cleft in the rock is just the right size for each person, and gives comfort, and there is no room for sadness.

"So we say a fond goodbye to little Todd Hollander and let him go to where he has already gone. We can keep our good memories of him because they are within us, and there is room in the Rock for them. Let us bow in prayer."

Here Phil repeated the prayer from his training sheet. He felt he could have done no better if he had written it himself.

The small box was placed in a buggy and the baby's parents took him to the family cemetery. They stood around for a last goodbye. There is no good way to end a funeral, but this one was now over. It must be faced.

Burt Hollander took Phil's hand in both of his. "I could imagine nothing better than what we just heard. I knew you could not let me down."

Phil shook his head. "I did nothing. God gave us the singer."

And Phil, back in the buggy with his sister and Rebecca, turned Sarge to the south and headed toward Ridge Road. Some of the brushy overgrowth had been chopped away for their benefit, but it was still a long hill down, and just as long back up. He refused to glance into the darkness and tangled vines where he had been abducted.

The girls rode along in silence until they reached the road that trailed up into the mountains. Rebecca sighed, audibly, and pointed. "That house is where I grew up."

Then she pointed up. "Top of that bluff is what was my cleft in the rock."

Silence followed. What could one say?

THE PAINFUL PASSING OF PRESTON PARSONS, JUNIOR

Preston Parson, Junior ('Press', to his friends) had absolutely everything going for him. Money, looks and fawning adults.

Young Press was born in Fayetteville and was only two when he became fatherless. Preston Parsons, Senior, was caught with possessions that actually belonged to another. The legal owner of the possessions located them and retrieved them. The retrieval was aided by a Colt 45 and its owner being very proficient in its use.

The Colt owner then rode out into the sunset on a stallion that belonged to someone he didn't bother to ask. He sold the animal in the little burg of Westfork and caught the next Santa Fe engine going south.

Until he reached the town of Van Buren, the conductor and engineer had no knowledge of his presence. He then leaped to the siding, found his way to the ticket office and bought passage to Little Rock, leaving Preston, Jr fatherless. It was not that much of a loss. To almost everyone.

Octavia Davis Preston packed up her son and returned to her parents' home. Carlton Davis had a small farm just west of Burnt Tree Junction in a community called Garland, named after a former landowner.

The Davis' welcomed their only child with open arms, and the three adoring adults handed the two-year-old everything he could have dreamed of, and then some. He passed through school with only minor disturbances and pranks, graduating into a healthy teenager with nothing to do.

He had repeatedly threatened to 'run off' to some town where something went on, but then managed to find a group of friends much like himself.

Later, the neighbors and friends wailed at the injustices of life that 'took' from the Davis family the only young person they had. The one with everything. The one they had dedicated their lives to.

Actually, infection took him. That's what it was called, as that was the current word for anything they didn't have a better name for. The stubborn infection crept from his left calf up to his knee, and proceed farther with inflamed and painful red streaks.

Being in the next community from Burnt Tree Junction, the young man was not well known around the area, and 'Preacher Phil' was surprised and puzzled when a message was delivered to him.

His presence was requested to officiate at a funeral in Garland Community. News had circulated about the Hollander baby's funeral, and this pride of the Davis family requested Preacher Phil arrive with whatever he needed to furnish a suitable send-off.

Phil read the note and looked up. No Gabriel to give a hint. The messenger with the note had seemed nervous, so Phil asked directions and promised to be there. After all, he now knew how it was done.

He greased the buggy wheels and dusted off the seats. He would rather have saddled Sarge and traveled light, but something began to tell him that there were times that dignity rather than efficiency was expected from the preacher.

At the appointed time, Sarge was fitted between the buggy shafts. He lifted his head and swung his mane with pride, but he was definitely not a 'carriage horse'. Rump too narrow, legs too long, hooves too streamlined and with no fringe of hair over them. Nevertheless, he was a striking animal and looked good drawing the expensive and well-made buggy.

Fortunately, the 'singer' had not been requested, as there would not have been time for that, anyway. So… what would be his words of comfort? Losing a young man was rare. A catastrophe, actually. The 23rd Psalm, so appropriate for the elderly, would not work well here.

But a God-given memory of the life, up to now, was a gift. When a baby passed, it was a shock and a loss, but actual memories were scarce. In this case, however, there would be good memories. A gift from God.

So… the graciousness of God… and he actually had a copy of the words of the song 'Amazing Grace.' He could not sing, but he had been good at memorization and recitation of poetry… perhaps….

He turned Sarge at the proper lane… well-marked for his benefit, and traveled almost a mile. The home was a painted house, large and comfortable looking. There were buggies parked nearby, and saddle horses tethered to available trees.

He was met by an older man with a sober face. Grandfather of the deceased? Likely. And he was shown into the parlor.

These people held to the ancient practice of open casket centered in the parlor. Long-burning candles and perfumed air.

It would be expected that the preacher view the body… out of respect for the family… and possibly make a comment. As he was a stranger to the family, he would attempt to make no comment.

When he approached the polished wood of the box and leaned forward to look down, his own heart took a thump, the magnitude of such that he had seldom felt. Truly, his heart took away his breath, and for a moment the pine box began to whirl.

NO! he told himself. *Be strong. It is expected of a preacher, and you have a long way to go before you escape from here.*

The old man edged his way up to Phil and said, "We was thinkin' on a few words here, and you'd follow us down toward the buryin' ground. Then you'd pray a prayer."

Well, there was a certain small comfort in knowing exactly what the family wanted, but it did nothing to overshadow what he saw in the box. He had looked down and suddenly had the feeling that he was sitting on the rough limb of a hackberry tree in the sprinkling rain, viewing the campfire at the mouth of one of Arkansas' bigger caves.

He had seen that face before, but then it had been gnawing on a roasted rabbit haunch, cracking jokes about the 'preacher man' and how was he likin' what he got… him bein' the fellow that 'got everything for nothin' and had folks bowin' and scrappin' before 'im.'

The mental picture of the face had been highlighted by the glow of the campfire that looked cozy while Phil was shivering. The face stuffing its mouth, while Phil was hungry.

A deep swallow, and Phil's heart returned to rightful position, almost. And his breath became more normal, but it was achieved with intense effort on his part. He WOULD get through this, though Gabriel could have warned him if he had just chosen to do so… but on the heels of that thought was the one from the other angels that if he had known, he might have made an excuse not to come.

Words of comfort. Absolutely the only words still in his mind were the ones of a good memory. They would still work. These people likely had no knowledge of the situation between the deceased and the preacher, and what would he gain by telling them?

So he began. Small babies left an empty spot but not many memories. A loss, but few mental pictures.

This young man, Preston, was older and had lived longer. He had learned to walk… to talk… and do so many things. And there was the school. He had touched so many lives. People became richer by contact with each other.

Phil's mind played a scene in his head of himself stepping on tiptoe, carefully… only on good, solid stones as he crossed a stream of rushing water. No stones with slippery edges.

He WOULD get through this. The old man said 'a few words' and Phil would take him at his word. One stone and another… and he would be across the dangerous creek of social expectation. He continued.

Such a fortunate family to have been given this young man for these many years. There was no knowing the mind of God, except that he gave good gifts, and every perfect gift was from him.

As for the family, they could think of the good and perfect gifts they had been given, and thank God for them.

With that, he nodded toward the old man and closed his Bible. The old man stepped forward and told him, softly. "We got a friend'a Press' that'll ride with you to the buryin'. Ain't very far."

Phil nodded. That would be a help… but only a moment later he groaned within. Who were this fellow's friends, anyway?

When another person with a face he knew well… from the campfire and the roasted rabbit… appeared to guide him, Phil forced his hand forward, "Pleased for the help, friend." And he shook hands.

The ride was silent, except for the 'friend' jabbing an elbow toward where the buggy should be turned. Many were there already, and were gathering around the open grave. Two others were leaning on shovels and he recognized their faces also. From the campfire and also from the swamp at Wolfcreek.

No matter. He WOULD get through this.

The perfect graveside prayer that someone had constructed was right there on the card marking his place in the Bible… the place about the gifts of God. Phil's voice was firm and strong, and he looked at each person boldly, not lingering on the three he knew. Then he closed with the prayer.

With that he was released, and the three friends were joined with others armed with shovels. The chunk and rattle of dirt and rocks on the wooden lid echoed through the small fenced cemetery.

As he would leave, the old man approached him. "How much you charge for what you did?"

Startled and taken back, Phil dredged up the perfect reply. Squaring his shoulders, he stated, "I never charge for something I do for God."

The old man hesitated, rammed a hand into a pocket and brought out a fist full of loose change which he poured into Phil's hand. "That be enough?"

"If that is what you want to give God, then I would say it's enough, though it is not for me to judge. God does not send a bill here on this earth."

He actually bit his tongue to the point of pain to keep from retorting, "…but he could possibly withhold future gifts."

Phil gave the man a nod and his best 'preacher' half smile, climbed into the buggy, and tapped Sarge with the reins. The magnificent stallion stepped forward with the dignity of his breeding and led the buggy back to Ridge Road. He pulled it to the hill and climbed up the four mile slope toward Burnt Tree Junction and home.

Phil was empty. Totally drained. He had a fleeting wish for Little Bit to be on the bench beside him. Her furry, wriggling body would be a comfort. She would look up at him with a look that said she knew everything that was in his mind, and she sympathized. He was going to have to figure a way to bring her along on trips like these… because surely this would not be the last one.

Then, on a sudden urge, he shoved his hand into the pocket where he had dumped the handful of nickels, dimes and pennies. He'd just see how much the old man valued God.

As Sarge's slender hooves beat a tattoo on the flint of the roadbed, he spread the coins on his open Bible. Copper and silver… yes,… but there was a shining piece of… what?

Gold, as sure as my name's Preacher Phil. Gold coin… no, it was coins. Three of them. More than a man might expect to earn in half a year!

Now… something was surely wrong. He was not seeing clearly. But then he remembered that when taxes were due, and Jesus was asked about where to get the money, he sent them to the sea to catch a fish and said to open the mouth of the first one. There they would find the money for the taxes. Peter did that and the account was in Matthew 17:27.

If God could put money in the mouth of a fish, and make it the next one that was caught, then he could surely create just what had just happened.

Phil was still riding along, looking down at the coins when he sensed a presence. Gabriel, of course. Phil turned and looked on the sculptured face of the 'Roman soldier' and saw a twinkle in the eyes and a half smile on the face.

The angel uttered five words and they were enough. "Reached in the wrong pocket." Then he was gone.

Eventually, when the information about the death passed through the gossip grapevine telephone, and reached Ma's ears, she was dismayed.

"That young man you helped to bury, did you know he passed on from a wolf bite…? Infection. If I'd know'd about it, I'd'a told 'em what to do for him. Wish I'd'a know'd in time. He didn't need to die like that."

Phil nodded. "I know, Ma. But the ways of God are his own, and he don't need to be explainin' 'em to us. Could'a been a reason for that young fellow to be called to his reward..." He wanted to add, 'whatever that turned out to be,' but Ma would not like to hear that.

He did, however, separate out one of the gold pieces which he pressed into Ma's unwilling hand. "Just payin' my debt, Ma. You got no right to refuse. God gives and God takes away, and this time he gave to us both."

Ma turned to her son and viewed him through squinched and thoughtful eyes. There was more to this than she was going to be told... but no matter.

November eased into December. Trees were bare except for the oaks that held their leaves until they were pushed off by the new ones. Grass was brown and crisp. Small animals were hibernating or remaining near their dens.

Christmas was looked forward to, and handmade gifts were created. Rebecca was to spend the holidays in her childhood home with the 'caretakers.'

Phil would bring her from Berryville as he was invited to be there, anyway. The matron, having met Phil, decided the girls would enjoy a story about the first Christmas. It was such a wonderful event, it could not be told too many times.

The Sunday Lady had agreed wholeheartedly. The girls had practiced carols and the residents of Berryville could come for the program. It was requested that they bring one or two jars of vegetables for the kitchen. Meat of any kind was also appreciated and needed for soup.

For Phil, it would be the largest congregation he ever stood before, and the idea was somewhat daunting. The Christmas story. A new angle, or something not usually included. Special words. Well, he could do that.

There was something he had given thought to, and he sincerely wished for more information. He could then use it and say it was thought up by some other people. Or should he stick to what was always told? Thinking back, he remembered what he had thought of when he was young.

There was that Christmas story about the star that appeared before the wisemen. Even now, some small boys of his storytimes wanted more information. They asked hard questions.

"Weren't stars too awfully big to come down to the earth without squashing everything?" So how would Phil answer that?

This observation might be followed by, "If a star stopped over the house where Jesus was, how did it keep from catching it on fire?" Didn't they deserve an answer?

And it got worse. "A star is big and bright! How come everyone in the country couldn't see it and be scared out of their be-jabbers?"

Phil sincerely believed the words the other Philemon's father had penned in the margin in ink. It plainly said, "Remember that the ancient definition of star and angel are the same. They are each 'bright heavenly bodies'. It could as easily be believed that it was an angel that appeared to the wisemen as it was to believe in angels who were assigned to humans to take charge of them and 'keep' them. Why would it not have been an angel that guided the wisemen? It is known that angels can be seen or unseen, as the case necessitates and we are not sure a 'sky star' has that ability."

Such a lot of words and they were printed small, but clear. Phil had read it and re-read it, wishing he could see the original word meaning. Where did one find it?

The small boys in his storytimes had brought up this interesting thought over and over. He'd had the same puzzled thought when he read the story.

But should he, only 23 years old and a newcomer to public speaking, bring up something so controversial? But how would he keep from it? He must say that the interesting angle had been brought to his attention. He would say he was telling the story so each person could think about it.

He would state that an angel brought the news to Mary, an angel comforted Joseph about the baby, and also warned him that the king was going to try to kill him, and that he should flee the country. So… if the angel came three times with messages and direction, why would they not also appear to the wisemen to lead them, and not be a sky star that would scare everyone when it moved across the land?

That was it! He'd just leave it a question for everyone to take home. He was tired of reminding small children that God can do anything, and still leaving them with the three questions and possibly more. So unsatisfactory. Little boys liked magic, all right, but there needed to be a smidgen of believability. Why would not teenage girls be the same?

Yes, he would do it.

When the songs were finished and he had told his story, the way he intended to tell it, he followed with these comments.

"There is information available that gives an interesting view on the star that led the wisemen to Jesus. It is said that the original words 'star' and 'angel' had the same root word. Each would mean 'a bright, heavenly body.'

"The English words have some interesting meanings. For instance: if I should say to one of the ladies, I'm really tired, and would like a cup of tea, she would get it for me but it might be the wrong kind. If I meant that I was tired, and wanted to go to sleep, I might get chamomile to help me sleep. But perhaps I meant that I had something important and difficult to do, and the tea should be of another kind… maybe red zinger with hibiscus, mint and rosemary.

"In either case, it would be tea, though a different form of it.

"Or if it was cold weather and my neighbor came to me for help to fix his wagon. I might need a 'hand warmer.' It would help if I knew whether he was stuck in the mud or if he broke a wheel. Mittens would be warm enough if it was just to pull him from the mud, but to mend a wheel, I'd need the fingers of the glove. Both are hand-warmers." With that, he left both a question and a possible answer in their minds.

Treats were handed out, and people began to leave. When he had sorted Rebecca out from her friends, he gazed in amazement. She was ready, with a small bag of necessities. She wore a stunning cape of black and white plaid wool with a wide red stripe every so often. A soft, knitted scarf of bright red with mittens and shiny new shoes.

Giggling with excitement, she waved goodbye to friends and was helped into the buggy. Sarge was stomping and tail switching, ready to head home. It would be at least three hours.

Rebecca would spend the night at Darkhorse Farm and be taken on in the morning.

When he told her she looked lovely, she beamed with excitement. "It's the scarf! It's soft as a baby kitten! Miss Mamie made it, but she bought this cape. She looked in the catalog to see what girls were wearing and picked this one. It has fur on the inside, and big pockets. There are even fur-lined mittens to go with it."

Phil listened with interest, just to hear her bubbling talk, but that was not what he thought was lovely. Wisely, he decided not to explain.

When morning came and breakfast cleared away, Rebecca and Phil were again in the buggy, heading down Wolfpath, toward the creek. The cut-off came and Sarge turned without direction. Phil was amazed, at times, how the horse read his mind.

THE FARMHOUSE

The Conways were waiting in the yard, oblivious to the sharp wind. They almost pulled her into the house, with Phil tagging along behind. He had no idea what he would see… but nothing was like what he actually saw.

New, starched yellow curtains were ruffled at the windows. The table and chairs had been painted yellow, and a beautiful cream pitcher and sugar bowl were centered on a crocheted doily. The big iron stove was polished within an inch of its life, and the wall behind the stove held a row of shining kettles with copper bottoms glistening like so many golden moons.

Rebecca was pulled on to the parlor where the old furniture wore new covers and the floor boards were scrubbed and smelling of cleanliness. Small pillows were here and there. Rebecca was speechless.

The room where the old man passed on now held not one item that would remind her of him. A new bed with a beautiful coverlet was centered. Curtains matched. Braided rug added for a spot of color.

On to the room that had belonged to her and Lucy, and later, just to her. The iron bedstead she remembered was covered in blue paint. The windows were hung with a filmy white material and held back with ties. The wall was a light blue, as was the dressing table.

The whole room was more than she could comprehend so she brought her attention to the one item that took her breath away. A mirror! It had its own stand, and was so tall she could see her whole self! All at one time!

The mirror occupied a corner, and when she looked in it, she saw her whole room behind her. It seemed to go on forever. A year ago it had seemed to be a prison, and now it was a castle.

She sat down on the bed and hid her face in her hands. Her shoulders shook with sobs and tears drained past her fingers. All her 'learned words' drained away, and it seemed her body only remembered how to cry.

Mamie Conway wailed with anguish. Rushing to the bed, she circled the sobbing girl with both arms. "Oh, honey! Darling girl, I'm so sorry. We didn't mean to do the wrong thing. We can put everything back the way it was. Don't you worry, honey. We'll have it back in no time. I saved everything."

Rebecca raised up and looked at the man... then the woman. All her newly-learned words came flooding back with a shout.

"NO! DON'T CHANGE A THING. That old house was evil but this one is beautiful. I love everything you did for the house and for me."

In a subdued, but relieved voice, Mamie commented, "We thought th' blue on the walls'd be the same as your eyes. And look, Zeke. It is! The perfect shade'a blue!"

Phil quietly stepped back and whispered to Zeke, "Let me know if I can do anything." And he slipped out the door. Rebecca was going to be all right. That girl was made out of tempered steel on the inside. Only the outside looked like an angel!

But the old man had whispered back, "Might check back in a couple'a days. Girl could be wantin' a buggy ride...? Or somethin'." Phil gave a nod and a quick smile.

As Sarge braced his legs to hold back the buggy from a runaway down the steep lane, Phil noted, "Somethin's gotta be done about this drive. The wrong horse in the shafts'll get somebody killed." Looking from side to side, he noted there was plenty of room for a pair of 'hairpin' curves that would make the drive three times as long, but ten times safer.

He'd need to tend to that between assignments. Somehow it just seemed natural that it would be himself that did it. Get Rebecca's two mules over here with the dirt slip, and a couple of days would have it done.

Then a sly smile of remembering crossed his face at the memory of the three gold pieces. Apparently God had wanted him to be kept available for a while, and not take on work from someone else.

The sly grin also remembered Gabriel's five well-chosen words about the 'wrong pocket.' Had that been a wink in his right eye, or just the reflection off his silver arm shields?

Phil preferred the wink.

ONE YEAR AFTER DEAD HORSE SPRINGS

It was actually two days before Christmas and Phil hitched the two donkeys to the dirt slip on the wagon, and started out for Wolfpath. He'd fix that straight-up-and-down driveway before someone got hurt.

It was amazing that it had gone so long. Well, he'd fix it now.

It would take a couple of hours to get the equipment over to Rebecca's drive way, and that gave Phil a good chance for a little thinking. Slightly over a year ago he had been sent to Dead Horse Springs for the winter. It was an experience he would never forget.

Since then, he had spent nights in the tent at eight different locations, the equipment being carried by the mules and Little Bit going along for protection. (She also made a hit with the children, especially when Phil told them she was his 'watch dog').

He had performed three weddings. It seemed almost like magic that, though the state expected to furnish a license to marrying couples, it took only his word to actually set the moment. One of his favorite weddings was when he joined deputy Burley Collins from Burnt Tree Junction to his lady who operated the roadside stand. Lovely lady was Miss Annie Jo.

Little Bit had worked out up to promise. Her reputation was enhanced by being a light sleeper. That might be from breeding, but likely more so because she knew that somewhere there was a solid and quiet house where she could have been, but here she was with a canvas roof over her head and all sorts of creeping things around about. Face it… why wouldn't any sensible eight-pound dog be a nervous, jittery sleeper?

And there was that unwelcome visit to the young lady down the road who could perform surgery on four month puppies that essentially changed their entire lives. That she didn't understand the reason for the change was certain. She'd had nothing to do with it. But it had happened, anyway.

Didn't make sense. If a master who seems to loves her… would do that to her… what could she possibly expect from fur-bearing four-footers, feathered two-footers and the scaly belly-crawlers? It was something to think about, and worth the loss of a little sleep that could easily be made up the next day.

Ma loved weddings. That Phil, her first born, was legally qualified to perform a marriage was phenomena of the highest element. Weddings were, fortunately, something Phil could describe to her entirely. Other parts of his life were not so much.

She would dearly love to hear how he (with Gabriel's help) escaped the gangs and the wolves and how he still got through a funeral. The problem with Ma was that she loved everyone, and she loved to talk. Phil, without being told, was certain that it would not be pleasing to his heavenly Boss if the whole of Ridge Road knew every problem of his life and how he handled it.

The weddings made him give more and more thought to his own situation. How could he possibly ask a girl to put up with what his life was turning out to be? His sisters would certainly not stand for it, and weren't they ordinary girls?

Here he was, getting older by the day, and something needed to be done about it. More than once he spoke to his heavenly teacher, "Gabriel… this would be a good job for you." Gabriel, however, showed no interest in playing Cupid.

Oh, well, right now there was a road to fix. Better get at it.

First, man up with the ax and bring down about four trees that were in the way of the new road. The trees would need to be cut up for firewood, and that took time. And sometimes he saw Rebecca.

She told him that Mamie wondered if she should be bothering Phil before the road was fixed. Zeke had chided Mamie, telling her the girl had to have friends. Important… for certain.

Rebecca took him from the chopping ax to the bluff where the huge rock held up so much of the earth. The massive boulder was as big as ten houses, and maybe bigger, but there was the cleft where she had tried to hide.

Tiny! It was only a wide crack on one side of the rock, and hardly big enough for a young coyote, or maybe a pair of raccoons. Rebecca shook her head in amazement… it had seemed so much bigger. She must have been very tiny when she was stolen.

She made a trip to the place where she had buried Lucy. How had she managed to get here there? Not easily. She had found a piece of canvas and had dragged the body down the steps and pulled it onto the canvas. Inch by inch she had pulled it to a spot where flowers grew, and then had brought the shovel to dig.

She had never dug a hole before, and it took a long time. Then she had pulled the canvas into the hole with the wrapped body on it, and had covered Lucy over with the edge of the canvas.

She had shoveled the dirt back over her, hardly able to see for the tears coursing down her face. Several times she'd had the urge to crawl into the grave with her. She very well understood why Lucy chose to stop breathing. Life was a daily struggle, seemed hardly worth the effort. It might eventually have been her own self just giving up, if she had not escaped the way she did.

She would spend Christmas with the old couple, and the next day he would bring her to Darkhorse Farm for a visit. His sisters would be her neighbors when she left the school.

One good thing about roads in Arkansas. So often they had a rock bottom that did not go to mud every time it rained. This one did fairly well. He might have to bolster it up later but there were stones aplenty.

On Christmas Eve it began to cloud up, and moisture began to fall. It was a phenomenon that happened twice or three times every year. When the temperature was just right, and moisture fell, everything it touched became coated with a sheet or sheath of ice. Even the smallest twig on a bush seemed to pull moisture from the air and form a tube of ice around itself.

The leafless trees whispered as the ice sheaths crackled and rubbed together. Remaining leaves of bushes glistened with crystal and the air was so clear it seemed one could see forever.

Christmas morning was a wonderland and Rebecca walked about trying to take in the fact that what she saw was hers... forever.

Mamie stewed one of the older hens and created an unbelievable dinner. With pies. And candy made from peanuts and honey. And a lot of talk about whether she should go back to the school, or was it time to come and live in her house? Finally, the old couple told her she must ask Phil what he thought. He was out and about in the world enough to know what would be better.

By the end of Christmas day, the weather had changed and a south wind had sprung up. Within hours the woodland was dripping with melted ice and the flat stones were no longer slick. The freeze-up was short lived, just the way it always was, and the next morning Phil was there with the buggy, trying out the new road.

Yes, well, it needed a little more work, but it had a good start. Not nearly so dangerous.

It was on that day that the weekly mail came, and there was a letter from Dead Horse Springs.

A pleasant flood of memories passed over him.

NEW YEAR'S EVE CAPER

Phil read the letter twice. Heart pounding and head whirling as he saw possibilities, though likely remote, to further his own agenda.

Dear Brother Phil,

Our church is planning a Watch Night get-together at the church to welcome in 1912. It would likely last until 2:00 and have talks, singing and whatever else we can arrange.

It would be our extreme pleasure if you were free at that time and could come. We would expect you to be part of the schedule, and you would be put up at the Parnells.

Also, we were thinking that you might be courting a lady by this time, and if she is willing to join us, we would welcome her, and she would be put up with the Argosys.

We realize this is sudden notice, and there is no time for you to respond, so just come ahead if you can. Everyone wants to see you.

Brother John Cummings, Pastor, Dead Horse Springs

What immediately jumped into his mind was a three-way delicious dilemma. There was the wonderful addition Rebecca would add to the activities, second was his desire to see everyone at Dead Horse Springs again, and third… his terrible dread of asking Rebecca to join in such an involved trip (that was going to look seriously like a courtship) and that he be turned down. A turn-down would be a setback from which he would be unlikely to recover. At least, for a long time.

All right… just face it. If he intended to have a garden, he must put his plow point into the ground at some time and make a furrow. Or else, he could resign himself to being alone forever because he predetermined that no girl would put up with his life.

Or, thirdly, he could begin a courtship by asking the girl to go to an event with him. He could find out quickly if she was open to an invitation. But that was the problem. Perhaps he should start with something other than an over-night with her being put with strangers.

But worst of all, the decision must be made within an hour or two. *Gabriel, where are you…? Did you do this…?*

So when he was taking Rebecca home after the day-after-Christmas visit with his family, he merely handed the letter to her. The buggy traveled down Ridge Road and turned off at Wolfpath. Glancing sideways he saw her read the letter twice. At least she was thinking.

She held the letter, looked out the windshield of the buggy and sighed. She firmed her chin and moistened her lips. She drew in a big breath and asked him, "I think you might be asking me to go with you. Right?"

"Yes, I am. Absolutely."

"Do you know the Argosys?"

He nodded. "They're the family that gave me Little Bit. I thought I might take her along so they can see her. Young Troy quite hated to see her go."

The buggy reached the new hairpin-curve road and turned in. It was really a lot better than the old straight-up road, but really needed more work. Soon. Rebecca still held the letter. That had to be a good sign.

"Phil, I still don't have enough words to say what I want to say, but would it be all right if I showed the letter to Aunt Mamie?"

"Absolutely. I would want you to."

The pink tongue circled her lips once more and she tried to smile. She needed more practice hiding nervousness. So did Phil.

'Aunt' Mamie Conway read the letter twice and handed it to Zeke. Zeke read it once and handed it back to her. "Rebecca, do you like this fellow?"

Startled, she nodded, and stuttered, "Yes-s-s-s."

"Then go. I'd figger you to be in good hands. You got a lifetime to make up, and this'd be a good startin' trip for you."

Then Aunt Mamie to Phil. "What would she need to take?"

"Uh, well… clothes for two days and night clothes. Heavy coat and scarf. Buggy gets a bit drafty even with the flaps down. I have quilts for her feet, and Ma'll make a lunch."

Mamie nodded. "I'll help 'er. It'd be early, wouldn't it?"

"Really early. Still dark. It's quite a long way."

Then to Rebecca, "You sure you want to go?"

A deep breath and a nod. Then to Phil, "You'll want me to sing, won't you?"

"Absolutely! You'll be perfect for this meeting."

"Then I'll go."

Dark was falling as Sarge pulled the buggy up to Ridge Road. Phil didn't notice. He could have lit the lanterns for Sarge, but he hadn't thought of it. Fact was, by now Sarge knew Ridge Road like his own feed box.

Phil's heart was pounding out of his chest, seemed like. *Gabriel, where are you? You're here to help me, so where are you?* No way he expected the angel to appear, but it seemed a good thing to ask.

But there he was, only for a moment. "The girl isn't as dangerous as the wolves, so you should be able to handle it." Phil glanced around, but the angel was gone almost before he came.

As Sarge pulled into the yard, Phil had calmed down. If he didn't want to spend life alone, he would have to make sure he didn't. One way or the other, this would be a start.

An early start.

He hitched Scout with Sarge in the two-seater family buggy as there would be boxes and lunch, and whatever Rebecca took along.

In the reflected light from the kitchen lamp, they loaded on an old suitcase and a couple of boxes. Aunt Mamie looked for, and found, the inside hooks of the buggy for hanging clothing that must not be allowed to wrinkle.

Rebecca, outfitted in the new black, white and red cape, climbed aboard. She settled herself against the basket containing Little Bit, who lifted her nose, sniffed and settled again into the snug basket.

With a click of encouragement to the team, they were on the way. Not a word until the buggy pulled up onto Ridge Road and headed west.

The buggy flaps were still up, because there seemed to be no wind, however it was only polite to check on his passenger's comfort.

"Warm enough?"

"Sure am. I have a brand new traveling suit. Mamie said I'd need one sooner or later, and she found just the thing to make it from."

"Make it? She sewed a suit?"

"Sure did, but she let me help. When she was cleaning, she found two overcoats made from all wool. She took them apart at the seams and washed and pressed 'em, and wasn't sure what to make out of them. Quick as she learned about my trip, she knew. It wasn't an hour till she had the skirt cut out and it had straight seams that I could do. Then she made the top."

Hmmmm, a suit out of old overcoats... what could it possibly look like? But Rebecca wasn't through.

"The coats had satin lining so she put it in the skirt so the wool wouldn't scratch my legs." A pause for thought, then, "'Course she didn't need to line the jacket 'cause I have a warm blouse under it."

"So that makes you warm enough... ?" Silly question. She already said she was warm enough. But it seemed like words were required.

They were three miles down the road when the sun popped over the tops of Echo Mountain and flooded the valleys and ridges with light. Just the presence of the sun made the weather seem warmer. Scout and Sarge were perfectly matched, and knew each other well. They trotted along like a couple of proud carriage horses.

Ma had put a pair of heated stones at the places where their feet would be, and warmth had radiated up under the quilts over their knees.

"Phil, tell me about your friend, John Cummings. I get nervous when I meet a lot of strangers." Phil could identify with that statement.

"They won't be strangers long. Actually, I don't know John at all. He wasn't ready to come last year so I filled in for four months. You'll love the people, though, and they'll love you. No problem there."

Little Bit stood and stretched, stepped daintily out of her basket and into Rebecca's lap. Rebecca reached her mittened hand and gathered the small canine into a wad and stuffed it under the quilt with only her nose showing.

Little Bit heaved a sigh, audible above the clipping of the hooves, and settled herself comfortably on Rebecca's lap. Phil groaned inwardly, wondering what the dog's loose hairs would do with the overcoat 'traveling suit'. Well, he guessed he'd see when they got to the diner in Wishbone.

Ma would have packed a complete dinner, but Phil would only take a half a dozen applesauce cookies. Then Aunt Mamie insisted on a pair of fresh, hot jelly biscuits to eat before they started. One thing about Arkansas farms, there was food if nothing else.

"Phil, you could tell me a story, couldn't you? Maybe one you know by heart."

"A story? You mean a Bible story?"

"Any kind of story you want to tell. I just want to hear your words. I need to learn how to put words in sentences like you do."

"Like I do…?"

"Mmm, huh. I learned the way the girls at school talked, and the way the teachers talked. And now I know how Aunt Mamie and Uncle Zeke talk. You know something, Phil? Those two talk with each other like they were two sides of an apple, or that they maybe had only one mind between the two, and knew what the other one was sayin'. Purely amazin'." She paused for several dozen clicks of horse hooves on the flint graveled road.

Then, "I hope I can do that someday with someone I like. They really like each other. But now I need to know words from other people, and I like the way you say words. You're different from your sisters."

Another painful silence.

Phil had been scraping his brain for something maybe a bit different, something that would intrigue her. Oh, yes, of course! There was the time that the prophet Elisha and the ax head that swam. (II Kings 6: 5-7)

He told Rebecca about Elisha when he was training the sons of the prophets because the prophets were busy and Elisha was a good teacher. He had the young men down by the river chopping wood, and the iron ax head flew off into the water. The river was likely the Jordan, and it had a very muddy bottom. The man couldn't find the ax head for the mud, and what was worse, the ax had been borrowed.

The young man rushed to Elisha and told him what happened. Elisha asked the young man where it happened, and the man took him there. He pointed to the place where the ax head splashed into the water.

Elisha cut a stick of wood and tossed it into the river, and the stick, instead of floating like it should, sunk, and the ax head that had sunk, came to the top of the water. And here was the good part! The ax head did not just come to the top of the water… the Bible says it swam.

Phil concluded with his own opinion. "I picture that old ax head scooting along in the water until it came to the river bank, where Elisha told the young man to pick it up, and he did."

And running alongside that story as he told it was a series of pictures in his mind. A hackberry tree has limbs that are welded to the tree like they are made of iron, but when the limber persimmon tree blew against the limb where Phil sat, it broke. The slender tree that wasn't strong broke the limb of the tree made of iron.

In view of that, what was so different from that and the swimming ax head? Miracles still happen. Phil had felt from the start that Gabriel was there, only had chosen not to be seen.

Phil glanced toward his passenger, and the blue eyes sparkling in the morning sun were the exact color of Blue Lake, down south of the ridge.

"Phil, I love your stories. You tell them like you love them even if you've told them a dozen times. I need to hear more words. I think about that a lot. I just didn't get a chance when I was little. Poor Lucy didn't have many words to give me. She did good to teach me the abc's and the words she knew." And Rebecca turned toward the windshield and lapsed into thought.

Of the many things Phil had experienced, the need to search for more words had not been one of them. What would that be like…? Starvation in the mind for the want of words? Hmmmmm.

It was afternoon when he reached the cut-off that led down into Wishbone Hollow. Such a unique little town. It had everything, but just not very much of it.

He could have stayed on the ridge and gone on to Dead Horse Springs, but he chose not to. He'd go down into Wishbone, let the animals rest a while, and they'd find a place to eat. The Hotel had a clever little diner that served excellent hot chocolate, and that sounded like a good starter.

He tied the horses at the hitching post and helped Rebecca down from the buggy. Now he'd get to see the overcoat-turned-traveling suit (whatever that was!). Little Bit was put back in her basket and told to "STAY" in a firm, I'm-not-playing-with-you voice. She wasn't happy, but she sunk her head down in obedience. Phil covered her over with an edge of the quilt.

This was December 31st, 1911, and a few people were still moving about. Christmas was over and some of the visitor shops were already closed. There were folks buying food, and children running and jumping in their new clothing.

The diner was cozy. It had tiny round tables with legs made of heavy wire. The chairs had twisted wire legs, and looked like they wouldn't hold anyone over six years old, but they seemed to.

Rebecca looked in every direction, attempting to take it all in. They chose a table, and he helped her remove the bulky cape. She had to be a mass of wrinkles, but she couldn't eat in the cape. He hung it on the rack with his own coat and hat and returned.

Rebecca had adjusted her chair and just turned to be seated, and Phil got his first look at the overcoats in their new shape. Skirt... black and not a wrinkle anywhere. It fitted like it was made for her... which it had been... and flared just slightly. Around the hem was a four inch band of black and brown wool, with just a thread of tan running through it. It moved gently with her movements, and settled easily in the chair when she sat.

Made from an overcoat? Couldn't be!

And the... what did she say? Jacket? It was made from the black and brown plaid and more like a vest with two huge buttons in the front where the fabric lapped over. The simple sleeves stopped at the elbow and were trimmed with a border of solid black. The blouse under the jacket was tan fabric and trimmed with buttons and lace. Also, no wrinkles. Now, how did Aunt Mamie manage that?

He wasn't much into women's clothing, but that outfit looked really good and after hours of riding there were still NO WRINKLES! Aunt Mamie had something there! Sure enough, Rebecca was going to be wearing that outfit for years, if he had his way.

Hot chocolate with marshmallows to start with. Peppermint tea with a half a dozen red-hot candies tossed in. What next? There was fried chicken, fish or beef stew. Rebecca thought she'd have the fish. She was too fascinated with her surroundings to be as interested in food as she would otherwise have been.

People around her, talking. Smells of every kind. Cinnamon left over from Christmas, and the bell decorations still tinkled with every opening of the door. So this was what the outside world looked like while she had spent years seeing only her house. And Miss Lucy.

Then he took her for a short walk down the street, just to limber up. Dead Horse Springs was still four up-hill miles away.

Phil, of course, knew exactly where the church was, but John Cummings he had never met, but he would have known him anywhere. There he was! Wide, friendly smile, fairly pulling them into the church building.

From one of the classrooms came Annette. Rosy red hair and violet eyes, smile to match John's. John introduced her. "This lady has promised to marry me, and we decided to have the ceremony just after midnight."

"Tonight...?" Incredulous actually. Weddings didn't just happen in the middle of the night, but it looked like this one... "Wait! Who is going to do the ceremony?"

"You, of course. Why else did you think you were invited?" Then a hearty laugh.

"But what if I hadn't come?"

"I was certain you would, but if you hadn't, I'd have gone down in Wishbone. They got a preacher down there that'd do it."

While this conversation was going on, Annette and Rebecca were eyeing each other like an eagle eyes a jackrabbit. Annette... bursting with words of excitement for the coming event, and Rebecca... grasping for words from another person. Words she could listen to.

They turned and walked away from the men, chattering and listening as though they'd known each other forever. Just before disappearing behind a door, Annette stopped Rebecca and turned her around, exclaiming over the suit. "Oh, it's perfect! Just perfect and such a wonderful fit. Such darling hanky pockets!"

Phil, while listening to John, knew he would have handed over a shiny quarter to have heard Rebecca proudly tell her new friend that the suit was constructed of two men's overcoats. But if Annette was amazed at the suit, just wait until she heard Rebecca sing.

The ladies entertained each other until supper was served at the Parnell's, and people began gathering in. Troy Argosy bee-lined straight to Phil. "Did you bring Little Bit? Where is she?"

"Classroom," he was told, and the boy disappeared like ice cream on a hot day.

WHAT GOD HATH JOINED

Neither Phil or Rebecca had ever attended a New Year's Watch Party, of course, nor had they heard of such an event. Must be a city thing. So it was all new and fascinating.

The gathering started in the early evening, with families bringing their specialty of food. They laid aside their bundlesome winter clothing and prepared to have fun. After all, it only comes once a year!

Annette and Rebecca were inseparable… with one of them bursting with the need to talk, and the other a sponge reaching out to absorb the words. As neither were acquainted with the locals, it was easy.

Annette had excitedly waited for this day, intending to be married on the first day of the New Year, just to get things started right. She had her dress hanging in John's office… and would Rebecca like to see it?

Rebecca would… and the two never left the office until the meeting was called to order. Introduction, then group singing. Rebecca stared from one person to the other. Such a LOT of songs and everyone seemed to know the words. Purely amazing.

Phil's storytimes were interspersed among the other things, as that was a way to keep the children attuned. Also Rebecca… hanging on every word and following the motions as Samson went about his life, ignoring God's commands. There was the time the enemy surrounded him, expecting to take him down, and he picked up a jaw bone of a donkey and used it as a weapon.

With it he fought and later bragged "…with the jawbone of an ass I have slain a thousand men," with no mention of the super strength given to him by God. (Judges 15: 15-17)

While Phil told it, he reached to the floor for the imaginary jaw bone, and swung it in every direction amid the goggle eyes of the children. He sound so believable, Rebecca sighed with appreciation of his skill.

The story went on. Samson allowed himself to be attracted by a girl belonging to the enemy, and she just about did him in. Then he met his own end. (Judges 16: 28-29)

When God finally allowed him to be captured, the enemy poked out his eyes. He was harnessed to the grinding mill (and here Preacher Phil walked in circles, head bowed and arms in position for pushing the imaginary handle.) Some of the children wiped their eyes with sorrow for the poor, disobedient man.

When he was brought out to be made fun of, he was placed by the pillars of the temple, and then he remembered God. "…Oh, God, remember me… that I may get even with these people for poking out my eyes." (Verse 28)

God heard his final prayer and gave him strength to pull down the house where everyone was. Samson was killed, but all the dead that were killed with him were more than he had killed in his life.

Then Preacher Phil sighed loudly, looked at the children, and told them. "Yes, God heard his prayer, but just think how much good he could have done with all that strength if he had obeyed God from the first."

And the children nodded and began to clap their hands in appreciation. Rebecca clapped with them. Oh, if she only had words like that! But where could she get them? Not from the school or from Annette, though their words were appreciated. She needed words that came from the inside, from the heart, lungs, mind and voice. She needed Phil's words.

And she sang. While she sang, a pin could have been heard to drop in the audience. Stunningly beautiful. Even the children clapped.

As had happened at the funeral, she was requested to furnish an encore.

And food was served. Every kind and taste that was imaginable. After that, Preacher John spoke and sort of told stories from the Bible, but they were nothing like Phil's. With Preacher John, they sounded like something he read… with Phil it sounded like he was there and saw everything, or maybe it was even about him while he was acting out the story.

When Phil told of David 'lopping off the head' of the Giant, one little boy quickly looked down to the floor as though he thought that was where the huge head would fall.

Small children were put to bed on floor pallets and more songs were sung. Preacher John had set his alarm clock on the pulpit and when the hands reached straight up and down, whistles were blown, horns were tooted and tin can drums were banged. Then the noisemakers were put away and everyone joined hands while Preacher John prayed for a blessing on the New Year.

Annette slipped away and motioned Rebecca to follow. In the office hung the dress of white satin and lace. She lifted it from the hanger and it slid down over her shoulders. Annette looked like a shining candle. Rebecca helped with her hair, then lifted the gauzy veil over her head.

She stepped out of the classroom to a gasp of *ohs* and *ahs*, which she returned with a smile.

Phil stood with his Bible, and John stood before him, and was joined by Annette. Phil arranged them facing each other. He told them, "John, reach out your right hand and hold to Annette's right hand. Now with your left hand take her left hand." They obeyed.

"Now both of you look down at your hands. You are holding to each other, and have no hands left to hold to anything else. Look at the design your arms make. There are two triangles no matter how you stand or how high you lift your arms.

"We are told that the triangle is the world's only totally ridged figure whose sides cannot be pushed apart. You are, in effect, welded together forever as long as you keep your clasp tight.

"Now, friends of this church, you are gathered to witness the joining of this man and this woman in marriage. So do you, John Cummings, take this person whose hands you hold to be your mate forever?"

"I DO,"

"Do you, Annette Cravens, take this person whose hands you hold to be your mate forever?"

"I DO."

"Then, for now and forever you are one, sharing the good and the bad, in good times or bad times, in sickness and health, and especially in sadness and in joy. I now pronounce you married life partners for as long as you both shall live."

The small building roared with the applause, and rushed around the couple to share in the joy and shake their hands. And the cake was brought out by Mrs. Parnell. White with fluffy white frosting, and no one was hungry, but everyone wanted a taste.

Then small children, who were asleep on the floor pallets, were aroused, coat-ed and hat-ed and taken to the buggies and wagons. Last to leave were the Argosys who practically clasped Rebecca to their bosoms. Troy carried the basket containing Little Bit, and they were off.

Phil left with the Parnells, and the empty church was left with the newlyweds. What a way to start the New Year of 1912!

It was a short night. Phil appeared at the Argosy's barely after sunrise to collect Rebecca. "No thank you" for breakfast, they had food from last night's party and wanted to be on their way.

Actually, Phil wanted to go back to Wishbone. Most of the stores would be closed but the diner's doors were always open, and there were store windows to look into. Most valuable of all, there was time. Time to let Rebecca see everything she wanted to see, along with the promise that they would come back and spend a whole day looking around.

It was near noon when Scout and Sarge were headed up out of Wishbone to Ridge Road and home. Little Bit stood and stepped out of her box and into Rebecca's lap, curling comfortably against the traveling suit made of old overcoats. The wind was pleasantly sharp and the sun shone into the front the buggy.

Rebecca settled comfortably against the corner of the seat, eyes half-closed. There was so much to think about for a girl who had spent years having nothing of interest in her thoughts.

"Tired?" Phil asked her.

She smiled and shook her head. But she had very little to say. The day wore on with a few comments about this and that. When the animals in the traces began to climb the last hill that would take them to Burnt Tree Junction, the sun had set and a moon hung on the eastern horizon.

The moonlight shone palely on the whiteness of the flint stone gravel. Phil was determined to learn about her silence. "Did you see anything in Wishbone that you liked?"

A nod. "A lot of things. I'll like looking inside the stores sometime."

"For something special?"

"Maybe. But not from the town."

"Did you like the church?"

"Really nice... for them."

"But not for you, huh? What would you really like, if you could have anything in the world?"

"I can't say right now."

Hmmm, now what did that mean? "The people really seemed to like your singing."

"They were very nice."

"But that is not what you are thinking of that you like."

A sad and silent shake of the head. "What I want is something I cannot have."

"Are you sure you cannot have it? Do you mind telling me what it is?"

The question was followed by a long silence. "I'll be fine. I just didn't know about a lot of things and how they fit together."

"Did someone say something to..?" He had, in fact, ignored her miserably. It had seemed that she and Annette had so much to say, he'd not bother her while she had a friend.

"Oh, no. Everyone was nice." Little Bit wormed her way from the quilt, stretched and reached up with a warm tongue on Rebecca's chin, then resettled on her other side. The road before them had leveled off and there would be less than an hour to go. He'd told Zeke they'd likely not be back tonight, and Ma was ready with a bed for her. So, if he had only a short time to find out what the problem was, he needed to get at it.

Also, he didn't want to seem demanding. He had no right to be. She had come with him like he asked. Maybe he did something he didn't realize. "Sweet Rebecca, has this trip been a disappointment to you? I'm so sorry if it has."

"Oh, no. I liked everything."

"But you saw something you liked that you couldn't have."

"No, I only saw it in my mind. It was when I sang 'Rock of Ages' that it came to me. I want to have a Rock to crawl into… one that's big enough for me. I know where I want it to be, but I can't have it."

Puzzled, Phil sought to make sense of the strange words before they reached home. He sensed a presence but when he looked around, the back seat of the buggy was empty, as he had known it would be. "You saw a Rock that is big enough for you?"

"Yes, and I want words. Their church was very nice, and people came from everywhere because they wanted to talk and be together. But their church was made of wood and painted. I hadn't really figured out what was wrong until I saw the church down at Wishbone."

"The Wishbone church? How was it different?"

"It was like one great big rock, and there was room inside for a lot of people besides me. And it wasn't mine. It wasn't for me."

"Uh… you want your own church…?"

"No, just my rock. It could be for everyone."

She was talking. If he just kept it going, maybe he'd get a clue as to what was on her mind.

(Gabriel, this time not visible, was doing what he could, but Phil could be SO dense sometimes. This girl was an important part of God's plan for Phil, but she was limited in her ability to explain, and she was shy. It was necessary for Phil to learn how to handle this. And he WAS trying, Gabriel had to admit.)

"Rebecca, if you had a rock church, where would you put it?"

She sat up so suddenly she startled Little Bit into a tiny 'yip.' "Oh, I know exactly where! I'd have it out on the bluff where the other rock is, the one with the tiny cleft. I've looked around my land and I have enough rocks to make the walls. I just can't move them and I don't know how to stack them to make them stay.

"It'd be like the song that asks the rock to 'cleft for me.' That'd be to make room for everyone who wanted to hide from problems and puzzles, and from things they hate and things that hate them. Maybe rest a while. You see…? I said I knew it was something I couldn't have, but that doesn't keep me from wanting it."

Scout and Sarge turned, without direction, into the lane for Darkhorse Farm. Through the trees they could see a lighted lamp in the window. Thoughtful Ma.

Gabriel might have released a sigh, if angels actually sigh. It was touch and go for a minute there, but possibly the girl had managed to plant enough seeds to make the idea grow. Phil needed a girl like Rebecca to challenge him. Give him a focus.

If Rebecca had not been stolen as a baby, she would not have been here. If there had not been Lucy, Rebecca would not have been here. If the man had not chained her to the stove... same thing. If Phil had not gone to Wolfpath, he would not have heard her. If the gang had not played a trick, using the Hollanders' name, he would not have been here.

The ways of the Boss were indeed great and mighty, and he could fit pieces of his humans together in the most unique ways. A lot of things had to happen, but the fact, now, was that Rebecca WAS here, and what was Phil going to do about it. For a human as clever and filled with dogged determination as was ever born, Phil lacked the spark to see through and understand what he had.

That valuable gift within himself. And he couldn't see it.

Rebecca saw, and her explanation was very good, except for one thing, and perhaps she'd add that later. At this point in time, what she really wanted was access to the words as Phil used them... words that drew such clear and exciting pictures. She wanted to hear words that Phil used... so unlike the school, Aunt Mamie and Annette. Only Phil's words painted pictures in her head that she could look at later and remember the words he used to describe how people felt.

The buggy stopped at the porch and he helped Rebecca to the ground, and up to the porch. He opened the door, and she disappeared for the night. He took the animals to the barn and fed them, leaving them in their stalls until morning. They could use the rest.

The buggy was pulled into the shed, and Gabriel was no longer there. It had been a good day, and the seed had been planted without the help of the Roman soldier. That was good. It was about time the soldier left the human to go on his own.

Phil closed the corral gate without thought, as his attentions were elsewhere. This had been an unusual two days, and it was going to require a lot of thought... though he hadn't known it until about an hour ago.

Rebecca didn't want pretty things. She didn't even ask for a machine that would make music for her, though he knew she would like that. What she wanted was a solid rock place of solace where she would feel no more pain from her earlier life. She wanted to be surrounded by strength and security that would last through storms and emotional fires. A place to flee when frightened. She wanted to take others with her.

Now, how in the world could he get that for her? But the seed had been planted, and Phil was fertile soil. Gabriel was not certain he would not be needed again. But now while the thought was strong within Phil... he would wait. Maybe the human would let it grow.

Phil opened the door of his cabin and entered, expecting a feeling of peace... as usually happened when he came home tired. Peace. Soft bed. Sleep.

But that was not to be.

The moon that had shone on the flintstone road now made a pattern on the pattern on the faded quilt of his bed. A pattern of squares, like a house, maybe. Or maybe a church...? Now what made him think of that?

True, Rebecca's land had many stones. Farmers in Arkansas usually gathered stones every year and carried them to the edges of the fields. Result: stone fences. But no farmer had actually put Rebecca's land into crops. Stones were everywhere, and reason told him that just inches beneath the grass roots were hundreds more stones.

Enough, and more. Why not a stone church? Here he was, going on 24, young and strong, and he learned easily. If he had to, he'd go ask the preacher at Wishbone how to start. Brother Hopkins... wasn't that his name?

But anyway, anything he ever wanted to know, he was confident that he knew how to find out. With a weary sigh, he turned to his side, adjusted the pillow and shut his eyes.

Gabriel had left the building… the planted seed had sprouted. The human was allowed to sleep.

With the coming morning sunshine, surely the seed would grow.

SO BUILT WE THE WALL

Phil woke up with the winter sunlight shining through his window, needling him to get out of bed. He sat up and looked around. Strange.

There seemed to be some sort of incompleteness nagging at him as though he had forgotten to close the hen house against the possums, but it was years since that had been his job.

Something. Something about the party. OH! And it came flowing back into his head like Ma filling the milk glasses in the table. Full pitcher, and the milk foaming in the tall glasses.

Rebecca's wish for something she couldn't have, and his distress at not being able to give it to her. What was it? He rubbed his foggy eyes hoping to massage some sort of memory behind his eyes so he could see how it would work.

Rocks. It involved rocks.

Somehow she needed a lot of rocks… or, no, she did not need them. It was he that needed the rocks… but what for…? Oh, there it was. A shelter.

She wished for a rock shelter big enough for her and others where they could be safe and be comforted. Comforted with songs and stories that meant something important.

And she said she had found a lot of rocks on HER land. Sixty acres, was it, and rocks were everywhere in Arkansas. Well, he'd have to go look it over. She was depressed after she saw the nice church in Dead Horse Springs, but she did not want wood. Wood was not good enough or strong enough for the shelter she felt she needed.

He rubbed his eyes, put on his clothing and walked to the house. He was met with chatter, giggles and laughter. The aroma of popped corn and boiled syrup.

Popcorn balls, it would be. Interesting thought, that though they called it popcorn balls, when it turned out to be small clumps of popcorn held together with cinnamony syrup that hardened to a delectable mouthful of crunches.

Squeals and giggles. His best memory of his sisters was their eternal ability to find something to giggle about, and Rebecca was right in there with them. Where was that silent, thoughtful girl of yesterday?

After lunch he took her home. This would be a good time to walk out onto the bluff with the idea of a building. Maybe it was solid enough for a foundation and maybe not, but it turned out to be a flat-ish rock appearing to be twenty feet thick at the exposure, and maybe much thicker back in the hillside under the grass and bushes.

It stood out from the ground like a shelf, just a flat, thick sheet of volcanic leftover from when the mountains had been formed. Well, there was plenty of foundation. That would hold any building of any weight that a person could put on it. Even stone.

All right, about the building stone. Rebecca led him here and there, and there were sheets, piles and scattered stones. Big, small and in between. Plenty of that. He nodded to himself. He'd seen enough for now.

He paid his respects with Mamie and Zeke, and Rebecca followed him to the buggy. She lowered her eyes and spoke seriously.

"I need to say to you, pay no mind to what I said yesterday. You got enough to do without my wants hangin' on you. I'm fine, and I did have a lot of fun on the trip, and I really like Annette. It would be fun to see her again sometime."

Without waiting for a reply, she smiled, waved, turned and walked rapidly back to her house. To safety. Away from the man full of doubts that she knew wouldn't understand her halting words. Couldn't possibly understand. Her fault, of course. Maybe some day she would have the right words to be understood.

She showed the popcorn crumbles to Aunt Mamie who threw back her head and laughed. "Oh, that brings back such good memories! About the funnest thing a couple of girls can have is making popcorn candy or fudge. Popcorn was the cheapest, and I always thought it was the best."

Rebecca couldn't help being happy with the old woman and her memories. So she'd add a bit more. "Aunt Mamie, I met a girl my age and she just loved my traveling suit. Wondered where I got it. I loved telling her we made it from an inside-out man's overcoat!"

And Phil turned Sarge toward Ridge Road and knew he had blown it. He had done all the wrong things. What was the matter with him? She now knew for certain that he was just too dense and stupid to understand. Why would she spend time with him again?

Gabriel wondered the same thing. He was needed again. The angel was bound tighter than a bowstring at the dumb-headedness of some humans. Yes, Gabriel was wound up and had a wonderful lot of ammo.

"Phil, you'd pour water on your own head and complain about the rain. Step back and think. What is a stone building except four stone walls hooked together? How did you find a job when you went to work 10 years ago?"

"The poster tree at the Junction," Phil answered the thought in his head.

"How could you find someone who knows how to make a stone wall?"

"Same place. But I never made a wall that big."

"Neither did Nehemiah until he returned to Jerusalem to build the WHOLE wall around the city. Remember how you tell the story about the enemy who had taken over the city, and he had to drive it out?

"About the sorting out and counting those who could do one little part? About assigning them a place to work?

"Remember how you'd frown and squint up your face when you were the enemy picking a fight with Nehemiah's builders, and the how children would squint and frown with you...? And then when the enemy fires arrows at your workers? Remember how the children duck?

"And then how you divided your workers (Neh 4: 16) and had half of them working while the other half stood guard to fire back the arrows. Remember how you drew back your 'bow string' and let fly your 'arrows' at the enemy? Picture the little boys as they sat in their seats and mimicked you. They understood exactly what you were saying.

"So after a time, the enemy leader shouts up at Nehemiah on the wall, telling him to come down and talk about it, and how you put your hands around your mouth and 'shout,' 'I am doing a good work and I cannot come down.' And then the enemy made fun of Nehemiah and said, 'If a fox bumped against the wall, he could knock it over,' but you kept picking up 'stones' and piling them on each other.

"Phil, I hate to say it, but you need to be hit over the head. That girl you think you love told you exactly what to do… so why are you not picking up stones and laying them on top of each other? Open your ears and listen to your own stories!

"And then you can sum it all up by saying, like verse 16, 'So build we the wall… for the people had a mind to work.'

"Now, Nehemiah had no idea how the people would work until he gave them the job. Likely the people didn't know either. So state your intention, post your sign and see what happens. Then go see Preacher Hopkins and ask for a lesson if you think you have to. Does God have to tell you everything?" Seemed so.

By now, Sarge had reached Ridge Road and was heading toward the farmhouse. Phil hunched over in the buggy seat, the reins limp in his hand while Sarge took him home. There was no way he could build a whole stone building. And what about Rebecca? Gabriel had been right that she had finally told him what she wanted. So what next?

He remembered reading about when God told Abraham to leave his home and family and 'go to a place where I will show you.' The former owner of his Bible had penned in ink, 'Every journey starts with one step.' Phil had been impressed when he had first read the note, and now he was impressed again.

Maybe he could find a flat board for the sign. It would last longer than cardboard. He would write, "Wanted: Stone mason for day work for a week."

He found the board and it took only minutes. Then he saddled Sarge, went to the road and hammered the sign to the tree. He turned Sarge toward the Wolfpath. He'd go back and look at that bluff. Alone. Apparently Gabriel was going to make a nuisance of himself until he went.

Gabriel, on his white horse, rode unseen beside Phil as thoughts whirled in the human's head. This thing of 'being chosen' was getting to be a bit of a trial. Then, with a grin, the human told himself, *But I wouldn't have it any other way.*

Gabriel nodded and grinned. The human was coming around. Hardheaded, he was, and blind. Couldn't see his fingers in front of his face without being helped. Send him a beautiful girl with the message, and he hides his face. But now he's headed right again.

And Gabriel didn't leave. He stayed by his charge with unseen strength until Phil had convinced himself he was serious. Next, Phil stepped off the flat stone of the bluff measuring a space for a thirty by sixty foot space. Lots of room. He began to whistle to himself, "Rock of Ages, cleft for me…."

Sarge raised his head from the dry, winter grass he was chewing on and looked toward the path. Then uttered a conversational whinny that was answered from below. Phil heard hoof steps on the path below him, then saw a horse coming up the new road. Around the brush came a bay mare and a familiar face. Leon Hollander.

"Friend, I think that must be your sign back on the tree. Thought I'd catch you and see what you had in mind, and here you were. Saved me the trouble. What ya got in mind?"

Gabriel waited. Would Phil be strong?

Phil took in a brave breath and told Leon, "Thought I'd scout out a place to put up a stone church house. This look like a good place to you?"

"None better. I'll tell Pa, but I know he'll say, 'you get together a heap'a rocks to start with, and dig a foundation, and he'll bring us over for a day to get it started.' After that, anybody can carry on until it gets up to the winders."

"You know how to build with stone…?"

"Sure, man. Cheaper'n boards and lasts longer. But I know one thing. On somethin' good like a permanent church house, he'd say to put up a board buildin' first, and then we'd lay the stone on afterward."

"Build the wooden building first, huh…?"

"That's what Pa'd say. I reckon he'd have us help on that, too. We'd be wantin' to come here on a Sunday. Be a lot closer'n Echo Mountain."

"Thanks. You helped a lot. Now I got some thinkin' to do on gettin' started."

"Sure, man. I gotta go but I'm sure glad you was here. Saved me chasin' you down." A click and a yell, and the bay mare was headed down the hill to the path.

Phil turned around toward the north and looked out over the valley. "All right, Gabriel. I know you're out there somewhere. I see your fingerprints all over this project." Then Phil grinned at his own action, swung aboard the saddle, and Sarge headed for home.

One thing about Phil, he knew when he got lost… but not always how to get back in line. Sometimes he even needed help to get started again, and 'every journey begins with one step.'

THE BLUFF OVER WOLFPATH

All right. The Hollanders were aboard with his massive scheme, but he needed others. Here he was, not yet 24 years old, and stirring up the whole of Carroll County, all the way from Berryville to Eureka Springs.

What if he was wrong? What if he told everyone what needing to be done, and he was not able to do it? Just who was he to be giving orders? He could imagine the whole of Carroll County laughing at him and the stupidity of his youth.

Stop it! Get out of the way… you other angels. The 'discouragement' angels were there before he even got started.

Nevertheless, he made his way out onto the rock with the cleft. He stepped off a rectangle 30 feet by 60 feet, a generous size for a country church… store… auction building… gathering place or anything you could name. According to the population of the Ridge, the stepped-off space would accommodate them all.

All right, Leon Hollander told him there first needed to be a lumber shell. That would be the upright studs and roof rafters, and eventually the paneling of the interior. Phil had no idea how this was figured. Quantity or price.

So, get help.

Turner's sawmill was located down in the valley by Blue Lake where the Turner family owned a lot of timber. Simon Turner had been in school when Phil was, so he should be the first contact. He'd be the one to say who could do the figuring, and who could help get it started.

"Come on, Sarge. We gotta make a little trip. Wouldn't want you hangin' around the stall gettin' too fat for your saddle." Sarge turned his large handsome head toward the human putting on the saddle. He hadn't a clue about the words humans made, just the sounds. This time it was a soft, relaxed sound that usually matched a trot down Ridge Road or to somewhere close.

The stallion playfully nipped at Phil's coat sleeve, and the human circled the stallion's jaws in a loose clasp… then patted his neck. Sarge replied with a ripple of his lips and a soft whicker down in his throat.

The human swung aboard, and his comforting weight settled the saddle onto the saddle blanket, and they were off.

Turner's sawmill was a busy place. Logs being hauled in every direction, it seemed, while young men he knew and some he didn't know busied themselves with this and that. And there was Simon.

"Hey, Phil! What goes…?"

Well, Phil was about to tell him. Simon nodded his head encouragingly and knowledgeably.

"Yes, we can help you figger. Fact is, that'd be my job anyway. I'm thinkin' you just want to figger the skeleton for now. That'd be a whole load'a boards anyway bein' it'd go down Wolfpath and up."

Relieved, Phil advised, "I've done some work on the 'goin' up,' addin' in some hair-pin curves. Ain't as bad as it was."

"Good. Now, knowin' my pa like I do, he'll be givin' you a day'a labor, maybe two, of my time to help. Gettin' started ain't bad, it's just gotta be right."

Phil wanted to be sure. "Givin' your time? Not chargin'?"

"Yeah, 'cause he'll be wantin' to get the church started. Be too far for us to come fer regular meetin's, but there'd be a chance that a church on the ridge could get some youngens headed the right way. Gangs been formin' that's causin' folks to get nervous."

Phil nodded. For him, nervous wasn't really the word. Perched in a hackberry tree in a storm in a pen of hungry wolves… that was nervous. Fact is, that was a tad more than 'nervous' but he let it go.

When would he be ready for the load? Well, let's say in about two weeks. That'd give him time to dig the foundation. And manage somehow to get Rebecca's millions of rocks out of the hillside and down to the bluff.

Phil's pa didn't usually have much to say, and this time was no different. He was ready to pitch in, though. This being the midwinter, work was light for farmers so he bundled his sons, 17, 15, and 12, into the wagon, along with their heavy sled. Taking both mules, he followed his strange, firstborn son to a piece of land that didn't even belong to him to build something that he had no clue as to how to begin.

Leon was there. Someone needed to point out the type and size of rock needed, and he took one of the sleds and the three boys off into a pasture with the two cows staring at the strange humans.

Pa and Phil took the other sled, and having an idea of what to get, began to select and load the stones on the sled that was in the barn. (Where was that sled when he had to make a travois to transport Rebecca?)

No matter. It was here now. Phil had begun to quit wondering how things became the way they were. He was now living a life with no rules… swimming with no arms… giving orders when he had no idea where he was going. Or what he would say next.

Pa was a big help. He worked with silent determination and fierce singleness of purpose. He wasn't sure what he was doing all this for, but he was determined to show support to his strange firstborn while the young man fought his demons. Even when he was little Otoe, he was different and seemed to follow his own internal instructions.

Phil, in fact, WAS facing his demons. Having no teenage gang to harass him, the demons did their work within his mind. Their boss didn't care what they did or how, just as long as they were successful in the end. The best method of achieving success was creating doubt, along with depression.

They circled in Phil's head, searching for new ways to attack. They found a lot of them. Even with the encouragement of Leon and Simon, there was the feeling that he was plunging into the unknown, and he really didn't know why. Jumping off a cliff with no valley below him.

Ma was silent but concerned. Pa was working as hard as if he was expecting wages. Like he always did. But Rebecca was nowhere to be seen. Back to school, no doubt, and Phil was glad. He didn't think he could take her look of disappointment when he didn't understand what she wanted. While he was out here on her rock making mistakes.

The thing was, Phil didn't know much about girls except his sisters. If they had been asked what they really wanted most in the world, they would have immediately rattled off a half a dozen easily obtainable items. Personal items... not something for 'everybody.' Or a 'rock' big enough to hide in.

Phil had been loved and protected all his life and could barely understand a girl who had been stolen, enslaved, almost killed and never loved just because she existed. Not surprising, actually, that she should be very different, but how was he supposed to know what to do...?

And here he was without an invitation, planning a venture that would affect the whole county, or... it would make him the laughing stock of the century.

And Gabriel was there. Not visible... just observing.

This was not the first time a battle was waged within the human mind. The angel could have cited hundreds down through the ages, but his assignment at this point was taking charge of this one person whom the Boss had chosen.

Phil selected rocks and loaded them onto the sled. Pa took them to the jobsite and unloaded while Phil selected the next load. He could hear his brothers laughing and playing at their work, having a one-sided contest to see if their pile of rocks would be bigger than that of the 'old guys.'

The demons fought on. What would Phil say if all these rocks were piled up, and left for the rabbits and the meadow grass? What would the neighbors say?

Burt Hollander showed up with eight (count 'em, eight!) sets of strong arms. He divided them into four pairs and set them to work. They levered the biggest stones into Zeke's ditch, and pounded them into solidarity.

And after three days, Pa and the brothers had other work to do, the Hollanders had to leave and Phil struggled on alone. The first load of boards came from the mill, and Simon measured, drove stakes, strung out cords to mark the shape, and began to place the joists for the floor.

Handing Phil a hammer, he instructed the nailing, and moved on to the risers. When he came tomorrow with the next load, he'd bring Thomas along as all three of them would be needed to raise the side panels.

The demons continued. Phil was almost dizzy from the whirling thoughts. Doubts. Discouragements. Frustrations. They had such a lot of weapons!

Aunt Mamie was no help. And Uncle Zeke was even less help. He was out there with the shovel digging a long ditch beside a string tied to stake in the ground. And he wasn't talkin'. The Hollanders came back for a work day.

Aunt Mamie had penned up three fat hens that had quit laying eggs, and had wrung their necks… plucked their feathers, cut them up and tossed them in the kettle. When the weak winter sun was high and the fellows showed signs of quitting for lunch, she tossed in the dumplings. At the exact moment of fluffy lightness, she gathered every plate and bowl she had in the kitchen and put them, with the kettle, on a tiny sled.

Nearing the job site, the aroma of the chicken dumplings, golden with melted fat, turned all heads. The stunned workmen lined up for bowls of the delectable winter dish, and came back for seconds.

Then stones of every size tumbled into the ditch, arose to ground level, and continued upward. Burt Hollander assigned his sons and grandsons into four pairs, with one selecting the next stone, and the other pounding, chipping and fitting it with no gap between. Each one was positioned to slant outward at the bottom as there would be no mortar used. It was an ancient skill that dated back to the stone dwellings in Ireland… the ones that even had stone roofs.

Phil, nailing boards to the floor, was amazed. Glancing their way between nailing boards, fascinated at their skill and speed, his heart pounding. Maybe there wouldn't be just a rock pile for the rabbits. Maybe there would at least be an arbor with a floor. That would be a plus.

NO! the good angels yelled. Phil yelled… HE WOULD NOT be permitted to settle for less than what Rebecca saw in her mind, even if he had to set every stone himself, and if it took him all his life. What was that verse about resisting the devil to make him go away? (James 4: 7) It went, "Resist the devil and he will flee from you," and it was written by Jesus' own half-brother, so he should know.

Resist. RESIST! That means fight back and argue with conviction. *Get out of the way, devil. You're just messing things up.*

If angels can smile at the progress of humans, Gabriel might have been grinning from ear to ear. "Atta boy, Phil! Hit 'im again."

Phil did. "Old devil, just think about where you're goin'. You're gonna be tossed into the lake of fire with the rest of the liars." (Rev. 21:8)

Days passed. Rain and storms came, but the work waited patiently. It was there when the sun again shone.

There were many days that Phil did work alone, but he was faithfully served a hot lunch by Aunt Mamie. When the stones reached the height of the windows, Burt Hollander brought back his crew for three days, and that took them to the top of the windows and the placing of the long stone for the crown above each window.

Aunt Mamie sliced up a whole cured ham and served it hot within biscuits. The next day, all the scraps, fat and marrow were cooked with white beans and served in bowls.

In March, Simon came with the interior paneling and stayed to get him started. Zeke cut cedar trees into fourteen inch lengths and began to skillfully create roof shingles with his hatchet. Pa came back to hammer shingles. Light work… with Phil to carry them up the ladder to him.

And Simon came with the windows. The mill did not make windows but Simon had to go to Berryville anyway and offered to bring them in. Phil nodded. He needed all the help he could get, but he dreaded to get the bill from the Turners. Simon kept saying to wait until the job was finished, and they'd settle up.

Phil tried to push it from his mind. Another trial of faith. *God, I sure hope you got somethin' in mind to use for money.*

It took Simon two more days to help set the windows and doors in place. It was a touchy job, and not to be trusted to amateurs. Simon also supervised setting the locks.

Phil had a bit of what might be called an ear for music, like he knew for sure that Rebecca's singing was extraordinary. Between other duties, he pondered, but did not know what for. There was some way. There had to be some way for Rebecca to learn what she wanted to learn. More songs, for certain.

It was the second week in April that Pa climbed down the ladder for the last time. He rubbed his weary knees, but smiled with satisfaction that the last shingle had been hammered in place. He stood and watched as Simon drove the last screw into the door hinge.

He and his son held their breath as Simon tested the swing of it. Not even a squeak. With the toe of his worn boot, he nudged the door toward the lock, and a satisfying click sounded as the tumblers of the lock engaged.

And Phil, hearing the reassuring click that enclosed the huge 'cleft within the Rock' knew it promised 'safety and love.' He knew the sound of that lock was music sweeter to him than anything in the world, short of Rebecca's voice.

Reaching in his pocket, Simon pulled out a slip of paper. "Pa made up a bill. No hurry. Pay it when you can." Phil unfolded it as Simon gathered his tools. The amount at the bottom was exactly the same value as one of the gold pieces from the funeral of Preston Davis, Jr. Totally unbelievable! A 'wrong pocket' miracle. Gabriel knew all along.

With a wide smile of friendship and satisfaction of a job completed, Simon clicked his team into action and headed down the hair-pin curves of the new road, now packed solid by the increased traffic.

Phil was alone. He opened the door and walked to the back of the church, closest to the bluff. He looked out, and saw none of the bluff's grass or trees, only space… open and eternal. Rounded hills, tinged with blue, meeting the blue of the winter sky.

It was mid-April and he had not seen Rebecca since Christmas holidays. Her assigned birthday was just ahead, and she would see the stone building for the first time. What if Phil had done the totally wrong thing?

To the empty building he shouted, "Go away, devil. Too late for you!" The sound echoed from one wall to the next. No benches. Would people bring quilts to sit on the floor until something could be arranged?

A tap of the door, and it swung open. Zeke walked in, looked around and nodded. "Right spiffy, huh!" was his remark, but he came to Phil with a serious expression.

"You're knowin', I reckon, that we'll be goin' after that girl, right soon. There was words that me and Mamie thought to pass on to you."

Phil nodded, and lowered himself to the floor beside Zeke. "Speak on."

"Well, Mamie and me, we had a lotta talk. We're knowin' you know the shape that girl was in even better'n anyone else, but you're young and might'a not noted other things. She's a right pretty girl, and got a lotta things goin' fer 'er. What's important now is what she ain't got.

"Where she was, she's never seen another girl bein' courted. She don't have a idea how a fellow acts when he likes a girl, or what is right to say to 'im when he pleases her. She's never seen nothin' about girls and fellows spendin' time… just like friends… to get to know each other. She ain't knowin' she needs to talk about what she thinks and feels and wants. She's scared to be happy, 'cause it might not last. She might be actin' in a way a fellow don't understand."

Phil nodded. That, at least, had been plain to him.

Zeke continued, "Now, we ain't tellin' you nothin' 'cause we don't know nothin', but we been in position to see things, havin' 'er here, and such. The thing is, you're young too, and she could be a puzzle to you. Most fellows find themselves puzzled at girls, but you'll be the worst, if you try to be her friend and maybe nothin' more. 'Course, we don't know what you have in mind, bein' a preacher and all."

The old man stared out the window and nodded to his own thoughts. "Times we looked at 'er and saw a girl maybe eighteen, but we found that in some ways she was forty years old, and others she was about six. Parts'a her got older faster, on account'a what she'd been through. Other parts didn't have no chance to grow, proper-like. We was wantin', Mamie and me, for you to know that.

"If you was to get to thinkin', and decide with what all else you do, she'd be too much for you to deal with, we hoped that maybe you'd let her alone. She can't hardly stand no more disappointments, and it scares her, makin' her hide inside herself.

"Knowin' her like we do, we know she'd be open to turnin' over this bluff to the church, and lettin' you do what you need to do. The thing is, she's sorta, well, attuned to you and your stories, and you'd need to help her understand if all you want is a pretty girl for a friend. She might think that'd be enough, but it wouldn't. Not for long.

"We're hopin', Mamie and me, that you won't take no offense at me a'talkin' to you like this, but we got to knowin' you, and we thought you'd understand."

Phil nodded. "I understand completely. Do you have any suggestions of what I should do if I think we might be more than friends?"

Zeke stood and studied something outside the window. Phil stood up beside him. Zeke finally found his words. "We was thinkin' that, on a Sunday or when you could, you'd come over for dinner, or just for this and that. Maybe you'd take her to your house so she sees your sisters. She sets a great store by them when she sees 'em. And your ma.

"Maybe be with her enough that she isn't so shy. She's been hurt, and I might say damaged, in a way that can't be fixed, so it just has to be lived with. Are you understandin' what I'm tryin' to say?"

Phil reached out a hand, and Zeke took it. "I think I understand. I thank you for this talk, it couldn't have been easy."

"No. Mamie and me, we talked a lot and thought we owed it to you, us bein' older and seein' a lotta things." He looked around, "Gonna have to make some benches, huh? Wish I had the skill to do it."

Together, the two men left the beautiful new building, and closed the door with the musical click. Gabriel was left alone.

He nodded, and told the walls, "Like Nehemiah and the walls of Jerusalem, I can say like he did it: 'so built they the walls… for the people had a mind to work.'" And he disappeared, leaving only an echo in the empty room.

REBECCA TURNS NINETEEN

According to the made-up records of Carroll County, Arkansas, Rebecca reached the assigned birthday on 1 May. Zeke and Mamie hitched up their buggy and went after her.

Phil began to seriously make plans for new church benches, but did not know where to start. He really needed to have benches before he could advertise for a minister. He was acutely aware that it might take a while to find someone willing to come… even a beginner. Time to get started.

It wasn't like an established community like Dead Horse Springs; that was close to a small town with all its benefits. This stone church was a quarter of a mile off Ridge Road, and there were very few farms within a mile of the building. Circling out for two miles, there was a satisfying number, and five miles enclosed a lot more.

Another thing. The 'path' called Wolfpath really was not much more than a path. It had, however, a good rock base that did not go to mud with every rain shower, but it was heavily overgrown. Phil knew what to do about that, for hadn't he done jobs like that since he was twelve?

He'd just set himself to the clearing, and maybe somewhere in the aching muscles and sweat he would have a glorious idea of what to do about the benches. Surely God didn't want the congregation to sit on the floor and have their legs 'go to sleep.'

While he was getting his tools together, his next younger brother rode in, and tossed an envelope his way. "Picked up your mail for you, bud."

Mail, huh. Well, might it be an invitation to come speak. Good timing. Except for the brush-clearing, he was essentially between jobs.

Greetings, Brother Darkhorse.

We thought of you concerning a furniture change in our church here in Berryville. Due to an expansion, we have added a number of benches to our auditorium, and the church voted to purchase all new ones as our present ones could not be matched in design.

So we find ourselves with 20 benches 10 feet long, and 3 deacon's benches four feet long. We also have a pulpit that has become excess to our needs. Knowing of your wonderful work there on Ridge Road, we thought you might not have

267

decided on your interior furniture, and could find use for these benches until you make your decision.

We have them here in the church, and are eager to get them where they might do some good. They are in excellent shape, with only a few places that need new paint, and we have a small supply of the paint we used for them. Please let us know if you have a use for the benches, as they are crowding out one of our classrooms.

Yours in Christ,
Pastor Owen Wallingford.
Berryville, Arkansas

Hesitantly, reverently, Phil returned the letter to its envelope and bowed his head. Flowing into his mind came the words, "O thou of little faith, wherefore didst thou doubt?" (Matthew 14: 31)

Into his mind's eyes, there flowed the picture of Peter in a fishing boat, who, on seeing Jesus walking on the water, begged Jesus to let him come to him.

Jesus said, "Come" and Peter did... but then he turned his eyes from Jesus and looked at the water all around him. Beginning to sink, he cried out, "Lord, save me."

Jesus did, but chided Peter by saying he had too little faith. Phil had always been impressed that Peter had actually had had enough faith to ask to walk on water and had taken a few steps. The others in the boat did not do that. His faith had taken him a few steps toward his master, but then he looked away to other things.

The handsome stone church was now finished, resplendent with its shell of stones from a cow pasture in Arkansas. Some stones were pale and sharp-cornered, striped with tan. Some stones were black from volcanic material, some hardened with embedded quarts, some polished smooth by rain and snow. So many kinds... and all made by God and hidden in the cow pasture for when they would be needed.

They now surrounded a comfortable building like a cleft in a rock, and were standing proudly on another underground rock, certainly put there by God for that purpose. It had been built by work, faith and the grace of God. So where did the faith go that he, Phil, had used to accomplish his part of the work? He shook his head in bewildered dismay. He had been acting as though he was in charge and carrying the load on his back, when all along, he had been carried.

Never happened!

It was still early in the day. Striding to the pasture for Sarge, he soon had him saddled and was on his way. If the Berryville pastor had gone home, he'd just stay overnight and see him in the morning. The great gift of benches, just at the moment of his discouragement, was too precious to risk a minute.

Sarge sensed the excitement in Phil's greeting, and was ready to gallop, hooves beating a staccato on the flint gravel. The sun was sinking too fast. The church was empty and locked. Disappointed, Phil found a stable he could hire for the night, and was permitted to spend the night in the stable feed room.

Brushing off his clothing, feeding Sarge, and accepting a cup of coffee from the stable manager, he was off. The pastor found Phil seated on the doorstep, with Sarge standing by… brushing flies with his tail.

After a brief greeting, Phil said, "We'll take the benches. I figger maybe about six loads, but my pa'll work on it right away. You can't imagine how I appreciate this."

"Yes, I can. I started a similar work, and we already have another plan for getting the benches to you. There are four of our members with wagons and trailers, and they think they can deliver them in one trip. Can we reach the church from the road, and can you accept them today?"

"No road yet, and yes. We'd need work on the road for the trailers, but they can come to my house, and Pa'll take 'em on to the church. I live right off Ridge Road."

Pastor Wallingford nodded. "Then why don't you go have breakfast somewhere, and I'll contact our drivers. They can load up and follow you."

Thus dismissed, Phil left, but who could eat? However, he needed a place to wait, and seated himself in the diner. Pancakes. Perfect. And coffee. His heart pounded almost painfully, and he had trouble believing what had happened. He kept forgetting to swallow… imagine that!

Gabriel was there but Phil did not need to see him. He did, however, pound into Phil's stubborn head… "Wherefore didst thou doubt? WHEREFORE DIDST THOU DOUBT?" Phil cringed from the internal drumbeat.

The trip back to Burnt Tree Junction was a lot slower than yesterday's ride. Phil rode from the front to the end of the caravan, back and forth, ready to be of help if needed. Benches. Beautiful. Worn in just the right places. A light touch of paint… maybe. Maybe not. He really liked the slightly worn places… showed they had been used.

The sun was low as the empty wagons with trailers circled in the yard and headed back to Berryville. They would be far into the night getting home but they didn't seem to mind.

Pa had helped with the unloading, silent and working with purpose. Looked like about 12 trips, maybe 15, taking two and three at a time on his wagon.

Zeke Conway came out onto the bluff to help unload the benches. All help appreciated… these were good, sturdy seats made of heavy lumber. Last forever, certainly.

Then at the last, he took the opportunity to bring up the mention of Rebecca.

"That girl, you know, she's about to come home. That birthday they gave her comes up in a week, and we, Mamie and me, thought we'd go over really early to get 'er, in case she needed somethin' from town that we'd need to get.

"That way would put us comin' by your place about the middle of tha afternoon. That bein' her birthday, and we thought, Mamie and me, that she'd ought to have some kind of a remembrance of it. Bein' she never had a birthday before that she could remember.

"We could have a special cake for her there at her house but there's just the two'a us, and what fun would there be in that? If we was to have it at yur place, we could stop by for a few minutes and cut the cake, then we, Mamie and me, could come on home, and maybe one'a you folks could bring her on home after she had some fun. She's set quite a store by your girls… them havin' fun and laughin' and playin' games that it takes more than one to play."

While the old man talked, Phil's mind was turning summersaults. Birthday! Presents! What would be correct to give her under these interesting circumstances? Maybe something from the family… or maybe just from him, personally. Needed a bit of thought, that question did.

Zeke nodded at his own speech. "Seems like she's never had a party 'afore, bein' she had no birthday. Or no name, for that matter. It's gonna be our aim, mine and Mamie's, to let her be a real girl of whatever age she really is. Your girl's'd be a real help there."

Pa, who would never have thought of it, agreed in an instant. "We'd be honored to do that, Zeke. You're right, that girl… she's got a lotta catchin' up to do."

Phil jumped in, "And don't be concerned about her gettin' home. I'll bring 'er on but it might be gettin' on dark by that time." Then he set his mind to the gift, one that would be just from him.

Not jewelry, or perfume, or fancy hankies that were usual gifts. They just didn't seem to fit the situation. Maybe a picture…? Or, say, why not a book? There was that store in Berryville that sold books. He'd never been in there but surely they'd have something.

But after he had searched the shelves, the lady clerk thought he might be needing a little assistance. "Could I help you find something, sir?"

"Could be, if I knew what I was lookin' for. I need a present for a young lady that I haven't known very long. Don't really know what she likes. Sorta had me puzzled."

The lady nodded, knowledgeably and walked down the aisle. Pulling a slender book from the shelf she handed it to him. Shiny cover, bright-colored flowers, and the words, GARDEN RHYMES, printed in fancy letters on the front. "Think about this for a 'first time' present. Not too big, not too little and makes a nice keepsake for a girl."

He opened it. Decorations on every page. Rhyme about a butterfly and a toad that lived under a rock. There were poems about birds and bees, and even about a spring rain. Hmmm, why not? Had to decide on something, didn't he?

And it was very pretty. The store would wrap it for him. He paid for it and looked at other books. Look ahead. If she liked this one, what others would she like? He saw titles he recognized from his sisters' gifts. Anne of Green Gables. The good ship Albatros. Books for girls about 13 to 15. Would that seem too young? He'd had puzzles enough in his mind to scare him, before his talk from Zeke. Now he was terrified. With a discouraged sigh, he tucked the wrapped gift into a saddle bag and turned Sarge toward home.

His sisters excitedly decorated the house with birthday signs. A cake appeared from the Conways, and in due time they arrived with the birthday girl. The fun and giggling began, and Phil looked on as his sisters took over. Why couldn't he understand her and know how to give her fun? Would it be possible to learn?

Thinking back on his own life, he doubted it. He took things too seriously. Always had. Thought too much. Read too much. Well, he'd take one minute at a time and see how it went.

In late spring, the days were longer, and the party moved to the porch while they played games in the last light of the day. Junebugs zoomed clumsily around the light, landing with clawed feet in the girls' hair. Screams and squeals as they were pulled out and tossed away.

Then in the cool dusk, he helped her aboard the small buggy, and Sarge knew where to go. When they reached the Ridge Road, he handed her the wrapped package. She looked at him with a question in her eyes.

"Birthday present," he told her. "Thought you needed something to remember the day."

A smile. "I'll never, ever forget it." And slowly and delicately she untied the bow and set aside the fancy ribbon. Opening the paper, she lifted the book and looked at it as it lay on her hand. "Pretty picture," she commented.

Phil's heart sunk. She didn't like it. It was the wrong thing to give her. So what now? "Open it up…" he suggested.

She did, and thumbed through a few pages. Then she silently closed it and put it on the seat between them. Folding her hands in her lap she watched the road ahead.

"Rebecca, the book was for you."

She looked up brightly. "I know."

But when he helped her from the buggy and turned to the house, she left the book on the seat. He started to pick it up, but she shook her head. "For you to read."

He stopped, stunned. "But… ?"

She turned to him, her face crumbling into sobs and tears, and she turned and ran to the house, leaving Phil stunned and silent. It was as though his feet were nailed to the soil of the yard. In a couple of minutes, Zeke strode out of the house like a man on a mission.

"NOW WHAT DID YOU DO? I THOUGHT YOU…" And the old man was too mad to speak.

Phil shook his head quickly. "I don't know that happened. She had fun and then I gave her a present, and she didn't want it. And then she began to cry and ran away." As proof, he picked up the book from the seat and presented it to Zeke.

The old man quieted, took the book, and saw the problem. "The poor girl. She don't know what to do with a gift. She don't know how to say what she don't know, and is afraid of doin' the wrong thing. If you want to, let me have the book and the wrappin', and Mamie'll try to find out the problem."

Slumped and wilted with discouragement, he handed the book to Zeke, and could only say, "I'm sorry. I had no idea…?"

"Don't worry, Son. The answer'll be somewhere in 'tween you and her, and Mamie'll find it. Why don't you find a reason to come over tomorrow about noon?"

Phil nodded. "The road needs a little shapin' up. I'll come. Zeke, I wouldn't done nothin'… I just…."

"I know. Don't be worryin'. This here's what I was sayin' and likely there'll be a lot more things like it. You gotta decide if you got patience…?"

"I will. Goodnight, Zeke."

He stepped aboard, and Sarge turned to the road. Phil let the reins lay limply in his lap. What now? He put Sarge in the corral and returned to his cabin. His sanctuary. With a firm push, he closed the door, securely locking out the world and the things he didn't understand.

Rebecca seemed so normal like other girls, then suddenly she was from another country. Like here, the first thing he tried to do to show her she was special, she'd handed it back.

So what was the use of trying? Zeke was right.

The wrong angels circled the room laughing with glee! One little setback and he had folded. This was going to be easy! Storms and guns and wolves and hackberry trees didn't do it, but one little thing that he did to himself…? Imagine…! Their boss was certain to enjoy this.

Gabriel spent the night in Phil's cabin to make sure the devil's angels did not go too far. Zeke would pull him through this one, and Phil was a fast learner. But he was also human. Somehow, God thought this human was worth the trouble.

As Gabriel had stated, Phil had a stubborn-headed streak. He had been determined to fix that hairpin-curved lane, and, by crackies, girl or no girl, he'd get fixed, and that would be tomorrow. By sheer force of his will he pushed Rebecca from his mind. He'd tend to that later.

He'd fix the road. Then he'd go to Berryville, that being closer than Eureka, and he would ask about that talking machine that played music. Called a Victorola, presumably after the fellow that made it. It was advertised by some company back east, and it sounded like something he could use in the church.

Seemed that by winding a crank, it would turn a plate that talked or sang whatever sound had been pressed into the plate. Phil couldn't visualize how it could happen, and at this point, didn't really care. Important was that it actually did what it was said to do.

It was pictured in magazine he saw when he was buying the ill-fated book. Looked easy to move… not much bigger'n a bushel basket. Likely cost a bundle, but that would be God's problem, if it was something the church needed. The thing was, Dead Horse Springs had folks that actually knew the words and tune to the songs and didn't have trouble singing them. But not the Church on the Rock.

If he had something that played music and sang words, then the church attendees could sing with it until he could do better. A preacher that might be interested would expect that some music could be sung. The magazine didn't say how many songs the machine knew how to sing. Maybe the nice lady at the book store knew something.

While he shoved dirt into place and shored up a low spot with flat stones, he managed to ease his mind. If it happened that the thing with Rebecca couldn't be fixed, he still had a life to tend to. *So get a hold on yourself, Phil,* he demanded.

"Atta boy, Phil," was Gabriel's silent comment.

He was just finishing up when Zeke showed up. "Son, like I said, there was things 'tween you and her. She didn't know what a birthday present was. Mamie sorta straightened it out, and if you'll go on up to church 'afore you go home, Mamie'll bring 'er on over."

With a wave of his work-worn hand, he left Phil to either follow up… or not.

Setting his head to the decision, Phil decided he'd leave the mules here… they belonged to Rebecca, anyway. He'd brush himself off and walk on out to the Rock.

Mamie had been watching, and she and Rebecca turned that way. Phil had sat himself down and waited. Mamie sat the girl on the bench a few feet from Phil, and she bowed her head to her lap, where she held the book in both hands.

Mamie began. "I'm here to be like a spider and spin a web 'tween you two. It don't bother me how it goes, but you two ain't understandin' each other. Rebecca, she ain't never had a birthday, but she was given one, not knowin' what some folks make of one. Phil, he wanted to honor the birthday, not knowin' Rebecca didn't know what one was. Rebecca, she sees a book she likes, but she knows it isn't for her to take with her. Phil, he thinks she don't like the book. Rebecca, she thinks the book is somethin' he'll read to her, 'cause he knows she needs words and she needs to hear words. She knows how to read, but not how somethin' like poems should sound. Phil, he don't know that, not knowin' she wants to hear him say words, not leave her to read 'em.

"Rebecca, she sees she done somethin' wrong, and don't know what. Phil, he knows somethin' happened that he don't know the meanin' of, and there's no one to tell 'im. Rebecca, she knows he's disappointed in her 'cause she ain't like other girls so she wants to give up and run away. Phil, he don't know what to do when a girl runs away. It seems to him she don't like him or his gift, so he's ready to leave her alone… not bother her. Rebecca, she don't want to be left alone, and she don't know the words to say what she thinks, and Phil, he can't read her mind."

275

Mamie had looked from one to the other. "Now, was that about what happened?"

Phil, first. "Aunt Mamie, are you saying that she thought the book was for me to read to her, so she could hear the words of the poems?"

Both the old woman and Rebecca nodded deeply.

Then Rebecca, "You sayin' he ain't what you say 'disappointed' in me, so he don't mind readin' to me? I never, ever heard a word like 'disappoint' that means that somethin' wasn't like I expected it. I didn't know it was a real way of feelin', that other people felt just like I do."

Aunt Mamie stood up and straightened her apron. "Anything else either one'a you want to say?"

Phil, next. "Rebecca, I would be very pleased and excited to get to read to you from any book you want. Readin' is a thing I do best. Especially rhymes."

Then Rebecca nodded, eagerly. "I hear so many sounds I never heard. But I can learn if I just hear 'em said."

Mamie pursed her lips together with an act of pure satisfaction. "All right. I got things to do, so I'll go. Now, if you to have another problem, bring it to me 'afore one'a you runs off cryin', and the 'tother one gets mad." With that, she marched down the aisle and out of the church.

Rebecca handed the book to Phil. "Words sound different with different folks. The girls at school sounded like squirrel chatter. Fun and happy. Some folks words sound like feet marchin'. Some are like an eagle, echoin' and fierce. Aunt Mamie and Uncle Zeke sound like a bubblin' kettle. Tasty and comfortin'. Preacher Cummings sounded like wind blowin' around the corner. Same sound, over and over. Annette was like a bubblin' spring. I like them all, but I like words like you say."

Phil was silent, trying to wrap some sensible reference around what she said. Truly, she had only heard Miss Lucy for years. Hmmm, such a colorful description of human voices..

Rebecca continued. "Miss Lucy was like... well, like slow footsteps on gravel. Easy to know what words she'd say next. You, Phil, you have words that are music. Some up, some down, all connected together like beads on a string. I think maybe that is hard to do, and I should not ask you for stories and words just so I can know how to say them. I think you have things to do and don't have time to read from the book with the flowers and bees. Do I say sense to you?"

Phil had been nodding, and drew in a surprised breath at the description that his words were like music notes on a string. "I think you make very good sense. I like you very much, and I thought I'd disappointed you with the book. I would like very much to read to you."

He opened the book to a picture trimmed in scenery of dragonflies hovering over a pond with cattail stalks around the edge.

He began, "This one is called PIECES OF GAUZE. Gauze is the thin cloth like the wedding veil Annette wore." Rebecca nodded.

> *The sunshine is warm on the small meadow pond.*
> *Spring cattails are new-grown and green.*
> *Pollen is golden on fresh lily stalks*
> *Where the promise of summer is seen,*
>
> *She hovers. A deep figure eight is described*
> *With her wings… sparkling layers of light.*
> *She pauses, her feet clasp last year's lily stalk.*
> *For a moment, she rests from her flight.*
>
> *She had climbed to the top of the old lily stalk,*
> *Her drab, muddy skin sloughed away.*
> *She had paused in the sun for her lace wings to dry*
> *It was only a moment's delay.*
>
> *Then she lifted away like the breath of a sigh.*
> *The meadow flowers waved their goodbye.*
> *This was the dragonfly's day in the sun,*
> *With her mate… spiraling high in the sky.*
>
> *With her eggs she returned to the pond of her birth*
> *Gliding in on her dual wings of gauze.*
> *Twisting and whirling lace wings in the air*
> *… Those wings… made of slices of gauze.*
> *Wings of lace… made of slices of gauze.*

At the end, Phil drew in a cautious breath. Did he do right?

Rebecca nodded. "See...? It's music. The words sing like a song, but when some people say the words, they don't sing. Preacher Cumming's words did not sing." She paused. "But some of the words... I don't know what they are."

"Which words?"

Rebecca pointed to cattails, golden, clasp, and meadow. "Those, and some others I have never heard."

"Rebecca, I am not disappointed with you. I have time to explain. There are about forty poems in this book, and we can go through each one. Or, if you would rather hear a story, we can do that. When I say a word you don't understand, you may stop me if you want to, so I can explain. I would love to help you."

As he thought about it when he crawled into bed, he forgot to mention that some days he might not be available... such as tomorrow. He had made up his mind, firmly, that he would make a trip into Berryville to the book store and find out about the Talking Machine. Reason told him that a machine that talked should also be able to sing. The curiosity itch had begun to drive him crazy, now that it seemed that the breach between himself and Rebecca had patched itself. Thanks to Aunt Mamie.

And another thing. If all she wanted was the sound of spoken words, the books belonging to his sisters should work nicely. The one they had seemed to like best was *Anne of Green Gables*. He'd try that next. Right after the poems.

But there was the trip to Berryville... though no one was expecting him, and he didn't have to go. But then, yes, he did. He'd absolutely have no rest until he did. It was rather like when the good angels... hey! Could it be... them...?

Of course not. It was just that he wanted to help Rebecca. However, that was not exactly true. What he really wanted, at this time, was to be with her and see if they... well, he really didn't know. Anyway, he'd go to Berryville tomorrow, and then...

Gabriel shrugged his shoulder and drooped in momentary disgust at the denseness of humans on matters of the most importance to them.

Just as Phil would have dropped off to sleep, Little Bit left her basket, hopped up to the stool, and on into the bed, landing in face of the other occupant of the bed. "Ahh! Ouch! Little Bit, your toenails are too sharp."

Positioning the dog at his back, near the window, he sighed and closed his eyes. Then he sat up so quickly, the coverlet sent the dog flying to the foot of the bed. Little Bit took the hint and jumped down to her basket.

Phil reached into the basket and lifted her back on the bed… by way of apology. Then he lay back, eyes wide open. WHAT was he thinking…? That trip to Berryville and back in the small buggy would provide hours of opportunity to help her with her punctuation and word usage. Literally hours!

In addition, that was what Zeke and Mamie had hinted at. Take some time to get acquainted and learn to converse from their widely divergent understandings. He'd go to Wolfpath early before she became involved in some other activity, and if she didn't want to go, he'd still have time to leap in the saddle and make a quicker trip.

As he pulled up the buggy up the hairpins of the lane, another thought emerged. That girl, who had missed vast chunks of her life, might well enjoy looking at new gadgets. *Phil*, he scolded himself, *Where are your brains?*

Gabriel shrugged. "Yeah, that's what I'd like to know."

At the Reading Room book store, Phil and Rebecca stood looking at the picture of the little machine with a bell-shaped gadget attached. Little hollow pipes about three inches thick were standing around the machine.

A voice behind them questioned, "Are you needing a Victrola Talking Machine?"

Phil turned, looking into the face of a young man about his height. "Don't know yet," he admitted. "Sure are curious, though. Gettin' a Talkin' Machine, what does it say that a fellow'd want to hear?"

"I'd have to say the name's a bit misleading. Mostly it sings songs off those cylinders you see settin' by it."

"It sings? You don't say! What songs does it sing?"

"Which ever one that's on the cylinder that comes extra. It has lots of songs, and more can be ordered."

"How'd a body get to listen to it sing without already buyin' one?"

"Easy. Just step back into the music room."

Rebecca and Phil looked at each other, but followed the man. He fed the machine one of the cylinders, and wound the crank. Flipping a lever, he stepped back and watched Phil's face.

The cylinder and the needle connected and the strains of "Amazing Grace" floated out into the small room. Phil jerked his gaze toward Rebecca, whose eyes were round as saucers as she scrunched shoulders and backed against the wall. The salesman turned the machine off.

"Sorry, Miss. Didn't mean to scare you. Should have known, though, because most folks are surprised at the sound."

Rebecca relaxed her shoulders… almost… and demanded. "Where did those words come from?"

With a smile, the salesman picked up a cylinder. "See those wavy lines? Those words are right here on this little pipe called a cylinder and this needle knows how to read them. Each cylinder has a different song."

Phil examined the cylinder while Rebecca looked on. The salesman watched them both. He knew, for a fact, that the fellow was going to manage to buy a machine, and he wondered, with a smile, if the serious-faced man realized it.

He did. "How much for one of the machines and about a dozen songs?"

He was quoted a figure about half the size of the remaining gold piece.

Phil nodded, "And I'm guessin' a body could just sing along with that machine, if they had a mind to?"

Salesman. "They surely could. Not only that, a hundred people could sing with it and it wouldn't care a wit."

Phil realized the humor in the salesman's voice. No matter. "To my way'a thinkin', that'd be a way for a body to learn the words and sounds so they could sing without the machine. That's what I've been lookin' for. Gonna need it soon. How do I get one?"

"I'd have to order it, but the company ships quickly. Maybe two weeks. Could be sooner. I like to have an extra one here, anyway, so I'll go ahead and order. You can come by in a couple'a weeks and pick it up. What songs would you like?"

"You got a list?" He did.

Phil did a fair amount of lip biting. All he had to go on, other than Rebecca's three songs, was whether the title sounded interesting.

Back in the buggy and heading home, it was just too hard to keep their minds on the poem book. "Phil... could you just tell me a story? Anyone you like. I just want to listen to the music of the words."

Music of the words. What a description. He chose the story of Ruth who left her home to journey with her mother-in-law, Naomi. The story was actually about Naomi. The job God gave her cost her a lot more than anything God had asked Phil to do. Even being in a storm over a wolf pen, sitting on a hackberry limb was not so bad as losing a husband and two sons.

It seemed that she left her country to escape a famine, and went with her husband and two sons. While she was in that country, the sons married and then her husband and sons, all three, died but we don't know how. Didn't matter. The fact was that Naomi had been sent to that other country to bring Ruth, a daughter-in-law, back with her.

There was that interesting matter of inherited property that provided Ruth another husband, and a baby. And the really fun thing was, that little baby boy named Boaz was the grandfather of David, that killed the giant.

As Sarge's hooves sounded a tattoo on the roadbed, Phil began to 'live' inside the beautiful story of how God worked the pieces of his human puzzle together.

They always fitted perfectly with himself. There he had been, momentarily on Sarge at the bottom of a lane, and heard a moan from somewhere. A slight shiver passed over him. Was Rebecca part of the puzzle of his own life?

Her eyes never left his face while he told the story. "See? Can't you tell how your words fit together like all sizes of beads on a string?"

They brought the Victrola to the Church on the Rock, wound it up and slipped on a song with an interesting title. After a few music notes, it began:

Some glad morning, when this life is 'ore... I'll fly away.
Like a bird from prison bars has flown... I'll fly away.

281

I'll … fly… away, oh glory, I'll… fly… away.
Some glad morening, when this life is 'ore
I'll… fly… away!

Rebecca gazed at the machine, eyes glazed with pleasure. Phil watched, and decided that never was a gold piece so well spent.

A SHEPHERD FOR THE CHURCH ON THE ROCK

It was time. The church was completed, and the benches in their place. The music was taken care of until something better could be found, and the relationship with Rebecca seemed to glide more smoothly. Along with a few bumps of misunderstanding.

The residents of the Ridge… the flock… needed a shepherd. An earthly shepherd… and the beautiful building deserved the best. He set a time and posted the date of the first gathering. It would be to see where the minds of the people were, and collect ideas.

The building would be the 'gatherer,' as it was, to bring the people to the place where they would knit themselves into… well, he wasn't really sure, but he'd take it one thing at a time.

First, he sent a note to John Commings at Dead Horse Springs. How did the church go about finding him…? And what should Phil do to interest someone in coming to Burnt Tree Junction…?

He posted it in the Darkhorse mailbox, and moved on to other duties. There were a number of families who would not normally see his notice on the posting tree and must be visited personally. That took up several days.

Then it was time. As buggies and wagons arrived the Church on the Rock began to be filled. Phil watched, being unable to get enough of the sight.

At the set time, he called the group to order. Would everyone form a continuous line around the edges of the church, and join hands? Children were invited if they wished. It was necessary to present a united front when he asked them to follow him in prayer as he sought God's choice for a shepherd to lead this flock.

"Dear Lord…" he began, and poured out his heart in petition for the right choice for these wonderful people, many of whom had given sweat labor on the church.

Then he asked them to sit down, and would those who had usomething to say please lift their hand. Mr. Burt Hollander, from on past Wolfpath Creek, was first.

Solemnly, he stood and strode toward the pulpit. Standing behind it, he placed his hands on the Bible, the Book that was once the pride and joy of another of God's servants.

Gabriel was there. His sculptured, but invisible, Roman soldier head waved back and forth in denial. Oh, the denseness of some humans, and what effort God went to with them, just because they were chosen. They were chosen, because they allowed themselves to be chosen… and those humans who did that were rare.

Yes, Gabriel knew this, and also knew his duty. Another trip to Dead Horse Springs to save the day for this blithering knothead of a human who used humility like a garment, rolling himself up in it. Hiding himself within it. Preacher Commings was the one to bring him out of it. Gabriel must officiate, as no one knew Philemon Darkhorse as well as he.

The note reached its destination and found its way into the hands of John Commings. The young man read the note in abject disbelief. He read it again and flicked it high in the air, where it kited across the room on a breeze. Snatching up his writing paper, he began.…

Phil Darkhorse,

I have your note here in my trashcan.

I cannot believe the stupid, pig-headed blindness of one of my best friends! What a ridiculous and insane question to ask me!

For someone who has bought the field, removed the stones, planted the seed, pulled the weeds and harvested the grain, who would believe that the fruit of his labor would be given over to someone who has merely acquired a book education as part of his calling?

For someone who has traveled through the Holy Scriptures at least six times, if I don't miss my guess, and who has ferreted out every grain of meaning and interest in his community, I would expect a better opinion of his own abilities.

For someone with a golden tongue who can crawl into a story and pitch out portions of meaning and interest for adults and very small children alike, I would expect more pride in the gift given to him by his Heavenly Father.

For someone who has harvested his crop from the hills and hollows in sunshine and snow, on foot, horseback and wheels, and who has slept on the ground and in buggy seats, I would expect him to recognize that he has earned a place at the table, and may now occasionally rest at the feet of his Lord.

You have been the recipient of special gifts, and you refuse to open them. You are the blindest, deafest person I know, and I can't say enough things about you, but this I will add.

You have fully paid your dues in study, in shoe leather, and of time in the saddle, along with coins, not of silver or gold.

You, with your own calloused hands, created the meeting place for Burnt Tree Junction, much the same as the people of Dead Horse Springs created the place for me. I am proud, but you have reason to be twice as proud.

In answer to your request, if I told you how I was attracted here, I would be remiss in my obedience to my God. You have twice what I have, and more. So get yourself a new suit to build your confidence and stand behind your pulpit with pride, until God calls you on to a bigger place.

By the way, when you marry the beautiful young lady you brought to sing for us, let me know, and Annette and I will come to give you courage!

Yours in Christ,
John Commings

Gabriel was rather proud of the result and the fruits of his trip and the choice of his words, and didn't mind letting Preacher Commings feel some pride. The note was quite better that he could have managed on his own, but it was necessary to get Phil's attention.

Of course, before he got the letter from Rev. Commings, he would have heard Burt Hollander as he stood behind the pulpit of Church on the Rock and made the desires of the community absolutely clear.

The neighbor down the road on Wolfpath stood silently before the people of his community and surveyed the gathering of about seventy persons. He waited until every eye was focused intently on him.

"Friends, and the rest of you who will become friends, I stand before you because I cannot remain seated and allow a travesty to be committed. I did not know that our Brother Phil was going to say what he said, but now I'm glad he said it. Those of you who do not know him now know how humble he is.

"But here is the truth. We need not and we must not look for a shepherd… a pastor of this beautiful stone building he has brought up from a dream and from the stones of the meadow. Yes, a lot of us have helped, but this building did not get started until our brother started it.

"Many of you have heard him explain the examples from the Bible he has read so many times. Much larger churches would adore to have a chance to get him, but we have him already.

"Now I ask you to stand with me while we thank our Blessed Lord for the gift he has handed our community."

They stood, and Burt Hollander began, "Our dear Lord, we thank…."

But Phil heard none of it because the tears in his eyes, and the beating of his heart. He finally gained control, and could thank the assemblage, and he was yet to receive the verbal thrashing from a fellow preacher… at this moment riding in the mail bag of the postman.

Gabriel, from the rear of the church, watched for a minute. If angels can sigh, he must have sighed a great relief. A job well done and completed, just as it had been assigned to him. From now on, this loyal friend and servant of the Boss might be able to proceed, following the guidance of the voices from within.

If not… well, he'd be there when needed.

"THE FATHER'S GOOD PLEASURE..."

It came about on a late summer afternoon.

Brother Philemon Darkhorse sat on the 'deacon's bench' of the Church on the Rock, jiggling his knees to pacify his two-month-old son. The door pushed open and three-year-old Emmaline crowded her way in.

Phil was performing papa duty, so Aunt Mamie and Rebecca could can tomatoes without concern for a fussing boy and a girl underfoot.

The tiny girl, hardly able to transport herself, now firmly clutched the miniature replica of a piano, containing a total of eight keys that pinged different tones when pushed. It has been a recent gift from her doting grandparents who were sure they detected musical talent. Surely a voice like Rebecca's would have been passed onto her daughter.

Phil grinned with pride. She would soon be plinking on the keys, but Young Johnny was used to it.

Three months after he took the pulpit, he had sent for John to perform the ceremony for himself and Rebecca. Zeke and Mamie were persuaded to stay on at the farm, and an additional room was added for the new couple.

It hadn't been particularly easy... but who expected it to be? Lovely Rebecca could now speak as well as anyone, but still loved the musical words. The Church on the Rock now had a piano, and someday the Lord would send someone to play it.

There were times of discouragement, and that was when Phil once more read John's letter. It now occupied a place of honor... in a frame... behind a pane of glass... and in a favored place on the bedroom wall. Demons were still around but they now seemed easier to recognize.

He lifted his son to his shoulder and strolled to the back window. From it, he could see no trees or rocks... the view seeming to be from a position standing on a cloud. The range of mountains moved from green to blue... and even more blue until it faded into the red of a sunset.

The precious warmth and small weight of his son against his shoulders was a joy… as was the *plink, plink* of the toy piano and the tuneless songs of the player.

Zeke and Mamie remained healthy, and the timber grew plenty of firewood.

The way things seemed to be going, there would be a need for a couple more classrooms, but the pastures provided rocks aplenty. When he might have felt guilty because of his 'good luck,' he remembered the words of Jesus as recorded by Luke, the doctor.

"Fear not, little flock, for it is your Father's good pleasure to give you the Kingdom." (Luke 12.32)

Phil wanted, more than anything, to give the Father pleasure. Still, there were times when he really missed the giant Roman soldier appearing on his milk-white stallion. At times it seemed that the sight of the angel was just the memory of a small boy's imagination.

But if that was true, why was HIS imagination seen by Will, the young man of the Wolfcreek episode (who was now a regular attendee on the third bench, east end) or seen by the good people of Dead Horse Springs?

And if angels can smile, would not a smile pass over the face of Gabriel, and possibly a twinkle in the eye?

Imagination? Hey! Whatever it takes to further the Boss' agenda! Even if it requires causing an old reprobate of a mountaineer to reach into the wrong pocket and part with misered gold!

Even better than the fish with money in its mouth to pay taxes.

ADDITIONAL BOOK SERIES BY JOANN KLUSMEYER

The Great I Am Bible Story Series for Kids
6 books

The Young Pioneers Adventure Series for Kids
5 books

The Wentworth Triplets Mystery Series for Young Teens
3 books

Footsteps in the Canyon Adventure Series for Young Teens
4 books

Burnt Tree Junction: Historical Fiction for Adults
6 books

Ozark Mountain Historical Fiction Series for Adults
7 books

Taming the Wilderness Historical Fiction Series for Adults
7 books

The Sheltering Stones Historical Fiction Series for Adults
5 books

The Trilogy of Wishbone Hollow Historicial Fiction Series for Adults
3 books